Alaskan Refuge
Series
(Books 1-3)
by Alana Terry

Identity Theft

by Alana Terry

"For now we see only a reflection as in a mirror; then we shall see face to face. Now I know in part; then I shall know fully, even as I am fully known." 1 Corinthians 13:12

CHAPTER 1

"Dinner was fabulous." Kurtis flashed that same boyish smile Lacy had grown so used to. "Just like you."

Lacy's lip trembled. She hoped he didn't notice. She tried to meet his eyes. He deserved that much, at least.

"It was awful sweet of you to cook so much." What Kurtis didn't know was how long she had agonized over her recipe books. What kind of meal was appropriate for a night like this?

"Don't mention it." In fact, she hoped he wouldn't.

Kurtis leaned back in his chair. So content. Could she really end things like this? No warning, no explanation ...

"So, I've wanted to talk to you about something." Lacy tested her voice. She should have warned him. Should have given him some hint of what was coming. She studied his face, the laugh crinkles around his eyes, the little bit of scruff on his chin, the soft jawline that made him look more like a first-grade teacher instead of a state trooper.

Her gut squeezed up, as if someone had clenched a fist around her stomach. She could get through this. She had to. It was for Kurtis. It was for the best.

"Daddy! Daddy!" The small, squeaky voice shot a searing pain through Lacy's chest as Madeline rounded the corner and skidded to a stop by the table. "It's skipping again."

Kurtis scooped his daughter up in his lap and nuzzled his nose behind her ear. "My munchkin needs help with the DVD, huh?"

She stuck out her lower lip and pouted. "It skipped."

"Well you know what that means, don't you, Munchkin?" Kurtis winked mischievously at Lacy, who smiled through the gnawing emptiness in her heart. "That means you get to start over from the very beginning."

Once realization set in, Madeline's eyes widened in delight. "Really?"

"You heard me."

She almost jumped off his lap, but then she eyed his plate. "Can I try a bite of fish first?"

He shook his head. "Miss Jo made a special adult dinner tonight. This is just for us."

She pouted and wrinkled her nose. "Does it have peanuts? Is that why I don't get any?"

"No." Kurtis gave Madeline a pat on the bottom and set her down. "But now go eat your chicken nuggets like a big girl, ok?"

Madeline scurried back down the hall. Kurtis had already changed her into her footed pajamas in case she fell asleep on Lacy's bed. It was the middle of summer, but the mosquitoes were so bad nobody in this part of Alaska dared to wear shorts even indoors.

Lacy watched as Madeline disappeared around the corner. Kurtis stared at the empty hall with a contented expression on his face. Lacy had never known a more attentive father. In fact, until she met Kurtis at the daycare, she had imagined they were mostly figments of overactive imaginations or literary archetypes.

He turned his eyes back on her. Kind eyes. Eyes that would in a moment or two betray sadness, shock, grief. How could she endure the next five minutes? Would he try to change her mind? She had never seen him angry before, not even after her co-worker Kim accidentally gave Madeline a granola bar with peanuts in it at the daycare. Kurtis was away on a domestic violence call when it happened, but when he got back, he assured Kim it was only a mistake. Then, to thank Lacy for her quick use of the EpiPen, he asked her out on their first date.

"This salmon was fabulous," Kurtis declared. "A perfect dinner." He leaned forward, stroking Lacy's cheek with his finger. "Everything you do is perfect."

If only he knew. If only he realized why Lacy had spent so much time on tonight's meal. In the past four years since she moved to Glennallen, she had learned cooking could be therapeutic to numb her mind from painful memories. It could be utilitarian to provide meals for two dozen daycare kids as cheaply and healthily as possible. Now, she realized cooking could also be a way to say good-bye.

"So, what's the big news?" he asked after taking a sip of sparkling cider. She had thrown it into her cart at Puck's grocery store at the last minute. Now, she regretted it. She regretted inviting Kurtis and Madeline over for dinner. Maybe she should wait. She could call him and tell him by phone.

That way she wouldn't have to see his face, didn't have to watch the way his laughing eyes brimmed over with hurt. Betrayal. It would be easier that way, at least for her. Easier if she didn't have to watch him react.

No. She was a grown woman. She couldn't wimp out. She had stalled too long. She had to get it over with. Get on with her life.

"I'm moving." The words fell flat. If she were still involved in theater, any decent director would make her redo that line. But she couldn't do theater anymore. No drama, no voice lessons, nothing from her former life.

Kurtis set his cider goblet down slowly. Tenderly. He no longer smiled, but his eyes were still so soft. So compassionate. From their first date on, she had known he was the kind of man who would understand. If she had told him everything, he would have found the right words to say. Would have helped carry the loneliness that had been thrust on her four years ago.

"Moving?" He licked his lip. "Wow, that's ... Well, I mean, that sounds like an adventure. When?"

"The end of summer," she answered.

His smile was forced, but it didn't waver. "What are you going to be doing?"

There was a reason she didn't know her plans yet. It was so she couldn't give him any clues. She couldn't have him following after her. Some people used the word *uprooted* to talk about moving. With Lacy, it was more like splattering paints onto a canvas until there was no way to tell what hid beneath all the layers.

She squeezed her eyes shut for a moment. Why had she thought she could get through this? He was right there, with just a foot between them. She could reach out, sob the entire story into his shoulder. He was strong enough to take that burden from her. But she couldn't ask him to. It was impossible.

As impossible as good-bye.

"I might go back to school." It wasn't a lie. She had thought of giving college another try. Had thought about it for the past four years.

He swallowed. "That's ... that's amazing. Good for you. I always told you that you could be anything. Do you know what ..."

"I can't see you anymore." She blurted out the words as fervently as she would have clutched at a life saver if she were drowning in the Copper

River. She let the words topple out of her, gaining momentum as they spilled out. She watched her message snowball and take force, gaining speed until full realization punched him in the face.

Kurtis scrunched up his nose. His expression revealed shock, everything except for his eyes. There was no surprise there. No anger. Just the sadness. The incurable hurt of Lacy's betrayal.

"Is it him?" he asked. "Is it Raphael?"

Lacy regretted ever telling Kurtis about him. She should have known better. "No. It has nothing to do with him."

In a way, that was true. But in on the other hand ...

Kurtis took a slow sip of cider. She wanted to jump up from the table and refill his glass. Anything so she wouldn't have to see his reaction. From down the hall, chipper music from Madeline's movie waltzed uninvited into the dining room.

"I'm sorry," Lacy whispered. If only she could tell him the truth. He would understand. The temptation to reveal everything clung to her limbs, like dead weight in a marshy bog.

He stood up.

"What are you doing?"

He punched buttons on his phone without responding. She wanted to stand, too. Wanted the memory of being with him one last time. Feeling his strong arms surround her. He was a trooper. A protector at heart. She shut her eyes, remembering the feel of their first embrace. Stinging hot memories mingled in her gut, and she wanted to run to him. Forget life had existed before they met.

But she couldn't. Instead, she sat motionless while Kurtis scowled into his phone.

"What are you doing?" she repeated.

He held out his cell. "I want you to see something." His voice was still soft, but there was a restrained tremor behind it. "Do you know what this is?"

Lacy averted her eyes as soon as she saw the picture. This wasn't really happening. This couldn't be happening.

"Do you remember when I went to Anchorage a few weekends ago?"

"I remember."

No. No, this couldn't be. This wasn't real.

"I didn't tell you what I was shopping for." He brought the phone closer to her face. "This is for you. The jeweler is resizing it. I just have to go pick it up."

She shook her head. No. If she could have disappeared by sheer force of will, she would have.

"I love you, Jo." He dropped to his knee in front of her chair, still holding out the screen to show the glistening white gold band in its black velvet case. "I was waiting for the Fourth of July, for the salmon feed. Now hear me out. I know that your mind is set to move, and you know I'd rather die than try to stand in the way of your goals. I'm not going to beg or anything. But listen. I've only got six more months until my placement in Glennallen is up. That's not very long. Then wherever you are, I want you to let me join you. Start a new life together."

A single hot tear slipped down her cheek like melted crayon wax, searing her skin. She didn't wipe it away. How many times could her heart break before it shattered into a pile of shards, never able to heal again?

"I don't need an answer now." He put his hand on her knee. She wanted to grab it, wanted to beg him to whisk her away to an imaginary place where pain from the past could never reach her.

She remained immobile.

"Promise me you'll think about it." He tilted up her chin and gave her a small kiss as he stood. He cleared his throat. "Munchkin!" he shouted down the hall.

Madeline scurried toward them, looking adorably plump and squishable in her pink pajamas. "Time for dessert?" she piped.

Kurtis didn't meet Lacy's gaze, didn't acknowledge her silent pleading. *Forgive me.*

"Give Miss Jo a hug good-night."

Lacy knew the sound of Kurtis's tight voice would haunt her dreams.

"But my movie isn't over," Madeline whined.

"You can watch another one at home," he mumbled. It was enough to mollify his daughter. Madeline spread out her arms so Lacy could pick her up for a hug.

Please forgive me. The words stuck in Lacy's throat. She caught Kurtis's eyes for a fleeting second, recognized the piercing pain that stabbed searing hot into her heart as well.

"Thank you for dinner." He was either braver than she was or a better actor, because he managed a faint smile.

"Wait," Madeline protested. "You haven't kissed her yet."

Kurtis glanced awkwardly at Lacy. Slowly reached his hands out. Lacy's feet steadily closed the distance between them. He wiped her cheek with his thumb and brought his lips close. "Good-bye," he whispered.

She didn't have the breath to answer back.

"That wasn't a very good one," Madeline announced with a pout.

"Come on, Munchkin." Kurtis caught his daughter and swung her into his arms. "Let's go home."

CHAPTER 2

It took half an hour for Lacy to clear the dishes off the table. If she were younger, she would have been surprised she wasn't crying. But she had learned four years ago tears were a luxury that rarely came in the midst of a crisis. They tarried, refusing to let you lose yourself in the bittersweet rush of grief, forcing you to walk through fire with your dry eyes wide open.

Her foster parents would tell her to forgive. She could almost hear Sandy's voice in her mind. *You can hold on to anger, or you can let it go and let God make the best of your situation.* It was a simple premise, really, and it probably worked for good Christian folks like the Lindgrens, folks who took in foster kids and raised them up and helped them graduate high school and saw them through community college. But Sandy would never live through what Lacy had.

It wasn't fair.

She couldn't think of Carl and Sandy, or grief and homesickness would charge at her like an angry moose, knocking her breath out. A tsunami wave far too strong to withstand. Besides, what was the point of dwelling on the Lindgrens? It wasn't as though she would ever see them again.

She hosed herself down with mosquito spray and threw on her shoes. It was almost nine o'clock, but that didn't matter. It never grew fully dark this time of year. She stepped outside, where it was as bright as it had been at noon when she stood out and watched the preschoolers climbing on the daycare jungle gym. At the beginning of summer, she and her co-worker Kim had complained until their boss finally broke down and purchased a propane-operated mosquito trapper. The gizmo was awkward to lug around and cost the daycare five hundred dollars plus gas, but it kept the bugs manageable. Madeline had helped Lacy count the bites on her arm earlier that afternoon.

Only seventeen.

If ever there was a night for ice cream, this was it. Puck's grocery store was only a five-minute walk away. Lacy hardly drove anywhere in the summer except for her monthly four-hour trip to Costco in Anchorage. Lately, she had been tagging along with Kurtis, who was used to driving long distances since he was one of five troopers covering an area the size of Ohio.

Kurtis. Lacy sighed. She hadn't meant to hurt him. She knew it had been a mistake to go on that first date. But it had been winter. She had been lonely. And bored. And if any man could manage to get Lacy to stop aching for Raphael, it was him.

Now she realized she had expected the impossible. What else could she do but cut him loose? He was still young. Good-looking. Rustic enough to appeal to tough Alaska girls, civilized enough to speak to their romantic whimsies. And Madeline ... Over the past few days as Lacy had been preparing tonight's dinner, she had wondered who she would miss more, Kurtis or his daughter who smothered her with kisses and asked Lacy almost every day to become her new mommy.

Lacy hurried through Puck's parking lot, eager to get inside and away from the bugs. Eager for her ice cream. She stopped short when she saw Kurtis through the window. He was pushing Madeline in a cart. She didn't study his expression, didn't try to guess how well he was handling tonight's news. She scurried around the corner without going into the store. One good thing about summer in Glennallen was all the small shops stayed open to cater to the numerous tourists who drove through. She would grab herself an ice cream at the Brain Freeze. She deserved that much, at least. She just hoped she'd make it there before Kurtis came out of the store and spotted her.

She sprinted across the street. She hated running away like that. Of course, there was no way she could avoid him indefinitely. Glennallen was just too small a town. She was still an East Coast girl at heart, really, fond of the fast pace, the crowded streets, the bright lights, the dazzling skylines. But that life was closed to her now.

She had lost track of how many times she and Raphael had daydreamed about their future. She was finishing up a few classes for her associates and wanted to pursue an undergrad degree in theater. He would set up an art studio in Boston or Cambridge. New York was always their end goal, but for now she wanted to stay near Carl and Sandy, the closest thing she had to family after a childhood spent in and out of foster care. Raphael often told her how proud he was of her, how she had risen above all the negativity in her past to forge a better future for herself. She loved the way he talked to her, the way he encouraged her. She would have never made it to where she was if it weren't for him.

Not that it mattered now, anyway. She couldn't even transfer her credits from the community college. Two years of grueling work had been a total waste. *No use dwelling on the past*, Sandy would tell her. Simple adages, like *Don't cry over spilt milk* that did nothing to address the horror, the loneliness Lacy had lived through. Why was she thinking about Sandy so much lately? If she could just pick up the phone, talk to her. Tell her about Kurtis. But that was impossible, too.

She stepped into the Brain Freeze and glanced around, thankful she didn't see any of the daycare families. She was tired. All she wanted was to forget. Go back in time, never get in the car with Raphael that night.

She ordered a small sundae. It would be about half the size of what she could buy in Anchorage and cost her twice as much, but that was Glennallen for you. People had to pay the heating bills some way. At least the Brain Freeze was bug-free.

Mostly.

She chose a seat by the window and stared outside. Would she see Kurtis's red truck drive by after he left Puck's? Had she really done the right thing? It wasn't fair to him. But did she have any other choice?

A bicyclist spun down the sidewalk. Funny how Alaskans could ride or jog or hike all night long if they wanted and only have to worry about mosquitoes and an occasional grumpy moose. She thought about the weekends when she and Raphael would ride the Boston trails for miles. She let her eyes follow the cyclist. There was something familiar about the way he held himself. Something about his posture ...

He glanced up. Their eyes met as he whizzed past her window.

Raphael?

She whipped her head to follow him. He didn't slow down, didn't look back. It had been her imagination, that's all. A silly mind trick. Even if Raphael were alive, what were the chances ...

She couldn't see him anymore. Had he circled around the back parking lot? Had he recognized her, too? How many times had she fantasized about this very moment, bumping into him again after so many years?

Too many years.

Their last night together was supposed to be a celebration. Lacy had just finished her spring semester of community college. Raphael told her it was a big surprise. She didn't admit it to anybody, not even Sandy, but she wondered if this was it. The night he'd propose. They'd talked about it enough, hadn't they?

She didn't know why he brought her so deep into the North End, but she never questioned him. It was a surprise, he told her. The dock he drove toward looked mostly abandoned. It was dark. Nobody was around. It sounded like Raphael's idea of something romantic. Creative Raphael, never content to do anything the traditional way.

"Are you sure you're not lost?" she asked, and he smiled that sideways grin he only got when he was nervous. That's when she knew. This really was it. The Night. She tried to remember every image. Every detail. Then one day when they had a family of her own, she could tell her daughters about the night Daddy asked her to marry him.

Only that's not what happened.

Raphael's whole body tensed behind the wheel the minute the two men appeared. Lacy had been holding his hand, and his fear rushed through his body into hers. "What's going on?" she asked.

"Nothing." He turned off his headlights and reversed the car. "Nothing. I just made a wrong turn."

That's when she saw the body, tied up, struggling. Afterward, she could have sworn she heard the man yelling, but the victim had been gagged and Raphael's car was too far away, so the detective said that was impossible. Still, she heard the sound of muffled pleas even in her dreams, just like she could hear the splash when his murderers dumped his body into the water below.

"Go, go, go," Raphael whispered, coaxing his car. At the time, Lacy still hadn't processed what she had seen. It couldn't be real. Her eyes were playing tricks on her.

"Go, go, go."

Raphael's last words were interrupted by the squeal of tires. He maneuvered the car around and pushed down on the gas. He made it back to the main road before their pursuers caught up. Lacy didn't remember screaming when the gunshot shattered the back window. She sometimes had a vague memory of the airbag exploding into a burst of dust, but she couldn't be certain. Maybe her brain was just trying to fill in the pieces.

She woke up in a dim room, surrounded by three somber police men shooting questions at her as soon as she opened her eyes, pausing only for a moment when a nurse came in to check her vitals.

"Where's Raphael?" Lacy croaked.

The men exchanged awkward looks before one of them declared what she already knew.

"He's dead. I'm terribly sorry, miss."

CHAPTER 3

Lacy thanked the Brain Freeze waitress who brought her the sundae. The ice-cream was ho-hum, definitely not worth the six and a half dollars it cost her. She hated worrying so much about money. She wished Drisklay had given her a different witness protection identity. The daycare couldn't afford to pay her more than minimum wage. The problem was year-round jobs were hard to find in a tourist trap like Glennallen, where weeks straight of negative-thirty temperatures kept all but the hardiest of long-term residents away.

It was the perfect place to hide, really, at least according to the witness protection folks. Four hundred residents, most of whom kept to themselves in typical Alaskan style. She had come in the spring. At least, it was spring in the rest of the world, but here there were still two or more feet of snow on the ground and several weeks of gray mud and gush before it thawed.

It wasn't just the climate she had to get used to. They gave her a whole new name, a new identity. Jo. So brusque, so unfeminine. Sure, she had sometimes wished her birth mom had come up with something unique, something more memorable than plain old Lacy, but Jo? That took longer to get used to than the continual daylight in the summertime or the depressing bleakness of the drawn-out Glennallen winters.

She stared out the window at the place where the bicyclist had disappeared. She knew in her heart it couldn't really be Raphael. The police, the detectives, the press, everyone said he died in the crash. She was left alone. Alone to mourn him in silence. Alone to hide until the two murderers who had chased them went to trial. Alone to testify against the people who wanted her dead.

She thought the witness protection program would be temporary. Drisklay said he'd keep her safe until the trial, and after that she'd be as free as a bird. Then it came out that the murderers boasted a web of Mafia connections. Things got increasingly complicated from there.

Still, she had held on to naïve dreams. Maybe the police knew the Mafia would come after Raphael and helped him fake his death for his own protection. She couldn't get over the impossibly thin thread of hope that he was alive, suffering a trapped, anonymous life in witness protection in some secluded area. She hadn't gathered up the funds or the courage to travel yet, but if she did, maybe she would run into him one day. Reunite at an airport. Catch his eyes on a crowded subway. She couldn't count how many nights she had fallen asleep picturing his face when his eyes met hers. She rehearsed the hug, the kiss, the tears that would mingle on both their cheeks. Crying together over the lost years, vowing to never spend life apart again.

But deep in her heart, she knew her hopes were nothing more than foolishness. Wishful thinking. Impossible dreams she clung to because the pain of reality was too hard to accept.

She stared at her miniature sundae and realized it was melting in front of her while she daydreamed of the past. A perfect metaphor for her life these past four years, really. She picked up her spoon just as the bell on the Brain Freeze door jingled and a new customer stepped in.

She sucked in her breath. Her pulse skyrocketed.

The man walked in, caught Lacy's eye, and gave a shy smile. "Hey, Jo."

She swallowed her disappointment. "Hi, Kurtis."

CHAPTER 4

Madeline ran up to Lacy. "Daddy says I get to have an ice cream because we didn't stay late enough at your house and you didn't even give me any dessert."

Lacy forced a smile. "That was awful nice of him." She avoided Kurtis's gaze.

"Daddy says now I have to be good and promise to sleep in until eight o'clock tomorrow."

"Really? Well I bet a big girl like you can do something like that, can't you?"

She puffed out her chest. "I slept until eight-thirty last Sunday. Daddy was mad because we were late for church, because he promised he would help me make pancakes, but I spilled ..."

"All right, Munchkin," Kurtis interrupted. "You take this ten dollars here and go tell Miss Cathy up at the counter what you want, ok? And be sure to bring back my change."

Madeline's eyes widened. "Can I get a big one this time?"

Kurtis frowned, but his eyes stayed soft. "You know the rules."

Madeline sighed dramatically as she turned around and marched to the counter.

"Mind if I sit down?" Kurtis gestured to the seat. "Or if you'd rather be alone, I can ..."

"No, go ahead."

He slipped in the seat across from her.

"I was just ..." She took a bite of sundae and didn't bother finishing her thought.

"I'm sorry I left so abruptly." His tone was so kind it plunged icy pangs of guilt into her heart. She should be the one apologizing to him. She regretted so many things. Stringing him on for a year and a half, making him believe she was available. Making him believe her heart still didn't belong to a man who may or may not have been killed in a car crash. The past year and a half with Kurtis had been nothing but lies. She had told him the information Drisklay had spoon-fed her about her past life. That was

16

all. He didn't even know her real name.

"Don't apologize." She resisted the temptation to take hold of his hand which rested between them on the table. *Old habits* ...

He took a deep breath. "I've been thinking about it, and I'm sorry if I came across as too forceful. I was just ... I was afraid of losing you."

She watched his Adam's apple while he swallowed.

"It's just that after Renee died, I thought I'd never get over it. I thought I'd have to carry that pain around with me my entire life. And I was ok with that, because I had the munchkin. But then I met you, and I was laughing again, and smiling. Madeline told me a few weeks after we started dating that she liked you because you made me act like a good daddy."

Lacy wanted to interrupt, but Kurtis held up his hand.

"You know I love you, Jo. I've already told you how I was going to propose to you at the salmon feed on the Fourth. But I know you've been through a lot, too. You were in a serious relationship, and you lost Raphael just like I lost Renee."

Drisklay hadn't concocted that part of Lacy's backstory. After a few dates, she told Kurtis about a past boyfriend who was killed in a car accident. Looking back, she probably should have changed Raphael's name, but it didn't really matter. Not with someone like Kurtis. The most honest Lacy had ever been with him was when she was talking about Raphael. In a way, the two of them had mourned their lost loves together. The difference was Kurtis had healed.

Lacy hadn't.

Madeline proudly carried her dessert to the table and glanced at her father, who didn't react when she set down a large sundae. She gave Lacy a conspiratorial grin and dug in with her spoon.

"What I'm trying to say," Kurtis continued, "is I'm willing be patient. Whatever it takes, however long you need, I'm willing to wait for you. I want to be with you. But I've been selfish, pushing things when you're not ready. And I want to ask you to forgive me for that. Can we just rewind a few months, start off a little slower? I don't want to scare you away. You're the best thing that's happened to me since ..."

He glanced at his daughter and sighed, letting his words trail off.

Lacy stared at her melting sundae. What had she done to deserve kindness like this? And why couldn't she reciprocate? Was it because of that remotest of possibilities Raphael was still alive? Even if he was, how could she possibly find him? How could she hope to randomly bump into one person out of hundreds of millions?

She knew what she should do. She should accept Kurtis's proposal, or at least keep dating him until she felt ready to take that next step. But her entire identity was a lie. Until she truly learned to embrace her identity as Jo, until she let Lacy die, how could she take such a drastic plunge? It had been a mistake to ever date him in the first place. What if Raphael came back and ...

"I'll do it," she blurted.

Kurtis furrowed his brows and looked at her as if she had a fever. "What do you mean?"

"I mean yes. The picture on your phone. Fourth of July. I'm saying yes." She spoke cryptically because she knew Madeline was listening in on every word while she pretended to be absorbed in her ice cream treat.

Madeline's eyes shot up and she looked from Lacy to her dad. "So you're doing it? You're really getting married?"

Lacy figured that with as crowded as the Brain Freeze was combined with how loudly Madeline shouted out the news, every local in Glennallen would hear by the end of the weekend.

Kurtis wrapped his arm around his daughter. "We're having an adult conversation here, Munchkin. I'll tell you all about it when I tuck you in tonight, ok?"

She pouted.

"If you're really good, I'll let you pick out a candy bar before we go, but you can't eat it until tomorrow."

Her eyes brightened, and she took another noisy slurp of sundae.

Lacy's legs were trembling. Why did they keep it so cold in here?

Kurtis reached out and took her hand in his. "I appreciate that. I really do. And I hope one day you'll let me put that ring on your finger and make things official. But right now, I think you just need time. And I've already promised you as much time as you need." He leaned forward. "I want your whole heart. You know that. I'm not settling for half."

Lacy's lip quivered. "I don't deserve you."

Kurtis didn't seem to hear. "I love you so much. You know that, don't you?"

She nodded.

He glanced at the clock on the wall. "It's getting late, Munchkin. We better go."

"What about my candy bar?"

"On the way out." He sighed and turned to Lacy. "Can I drive you home?"

She had lost her appetite. "Sure." She forced a shaky smile. "Thanks."

They didn't speak on the drive back to Lacy's apartment. It was an awkward two minutes, and Lacy kept trying to think of a way to break the silence. She replayed their conversation in her mind. Were they engaged? Had they broken up? Why were things so confusing? If she really was Jo, she would marry Kurtis in a heartbeat. He was an attentive boyfriend, a caring father, and he had raised a terrific kid. He was the perfect match for someone like Jo, a small-town daycare worker living a simple life in rural Alaska. No debt, no student loans, no real ambitions. That's the life Jo was made for.

But as hard as she had tried to seize her new identity, Lacy still wasn't Jo. Tonight of all nights, it seemed she never would be. She was an East Coast girl. A theater aficionado. All but engaged to an up-and-coming contemporary artist who loved her wildly. Passionately. With Raphael, she had felt exhilarated. Terrified. Excited. Overwhelmed, all at the same time by his zeal and ardor. Life with him was like sky-diving. One thrill after another, peaks of adrenaline, new adventures — spontaneous adventures — every day. She couldn't even guess how many miles they had put on Raphael's air-brushed Saab, driving from one art show to another. Life with Raphael was like the East Coast itself. Fast-paced. Vibrant. Colorful.

And Kurtis? With Kurtis, Lacy felt safe. Safer than she had ever felt in her entire life, actually. With Kurtis, she felt cherished and protected and adored. But there wasn't much difference between feeling adored and feeling smothered.

Still, she should try. She should try to patch things up with Kurtis. There were worse fates than ending up with someone safe. Besides, if the Mafia ever did catch wind of where Drisklay had stashed her away out here in the middle of nowhere, it wouldn't hurt to be married to a state trooper with a whole arsenal of guns in his personal collection.

Kurtis pulled up in front of Lacy's apartment. "I'd walk you in, but it looks like the munchkin is about to fall asleep."

"I'm not asleep," Madeline protested through a yawn.

Kurtis passed his phone to the backseat. "Here, find the pictures of you and Grandma at Disneyland last year. Look through those while I say good-night to Miss Jo."

Madeline didn't protest, and Kurtis leaned toward Lacy. "You know I'll always care for you, right?"

Why did he say it that way? Why didn't he say he loved her like normal? She imagined responding that she loved him too, but the words caught in her throat.

"I'm gonna let you go now." His voice was so quiet. What was he saying? Was he saying he was dropping her off for the night? Or was there more to it? More than Lacy was ready to admit right now?

He cupped her cheek with his hand and pulled her face closer. Slowly. Tenderly. As if they both had all the time in the world. His lips met hers a centimeter at a time. Warm. Soft. Just like his embrace. Strong. She sucked in her breath. She wanted to keep him here with her forever. What was wrong with feeling safe? Why had she ever complained about that? She pressed her hand against the back of his head right as he pulled away. His eyes bored into hers. An expression that spoke such tenderness, such bittersweet longing.

"Good-bye, Jo," he whispered.

She opened the truck door, forbidding herself from crying. There would be time for that later. A hot bath, a long cry, and a full night's sleep. She didn't look behind when she heard Kurtis's truck pull away. She knew when she went into the witness protection program her entire life would change, but she had no idea how heart-wrenching the process would be. Four years later, she was still a mess, still grieving Raphael, mourning her lost life. Still wishing she could be Lacy again.

She sighed as she entered her apartment. She never bothered locking her door. That was one Glennallen habit she had picked up right away. Drisklay would probably force her to sit through an hour-long rant if he knew, but this one small act of defiance encouraged her. A small trace of the carefree, rebellious Lacy still remained.

She didn't see him sitting at the dining room table until she was only three feet away. She screamed.

"Lacy? It's me."

Blood drained from her face. She reached out for something to hold onto for balance.

"Raphael?"

CHAPTER 5

Her body couldn't do anything but stare. She had rehearsed this very second so many times since Drisklay and his team relocated her up here. She had imagined how it would feel, the initial surprise, then the shock giving way to euphoria. She had pictured herself running to him, envisioned that first embrace spanning so many tumultuous years. The pain would wash away like marker lines on a dry-erase board.

Instead, she froze in the middle of her own apartment.

He stood. He looked different. Older. Had she aged that much, too? How could she tell? Drisklay hadn't allowed her to take any photographs with her. Too dangerous.

"What are you doing here?" Her breath came in shallow spurts. "How did you find me?"

He ran his fingers through his hair. Glanced around nervously. Let out a chuckle. "Ever since the accident, I've been dreaming of this day. Praying I would find you." He laughed again. The sound was out of place. "I think the only word to call it is a miracle."

She squinted. Was it some sort of hallucination? His face was older, with lines across his brow she had never seen before. His chin was puffier, as if he had put on excess weight, but his voice was the same. Her eyes might deceive her, but her ears couldn't. "It's really you?" She hardly dared to breathe, as if a hard exhale might blow him away into vapor. She still hadn't taken a step closer.

"I was wondering the same thing." His eyes lit up with dancing joy. "I was riding along the Glenn, and I was thinking about something nice and cold to drink, wondering what that ice cream place had, and I looked in the window, and it was you. I tried to blow it off. My mind's played that trick on me dozens of times. But I came back around, and it really was you. I was sure of it."

She heard his words but was unable to string them together coherently in her mind. "How did you get here?"

"Well, I watched for a minute and knew I was either going to make a huge fool of myself or else I was going to always wonder if God really had answered my prayers after all these years. I had already told him if you were with someone else, if you had found someone nice to settle down with, then I didn't want to stand in the way. You know, *Thou shalt not covet thy neighbor's wife* and all that stuff. But then this girl was walking down the road, and I asked her if she lived here, and when she said she did, I pointed through the window and asked if she knew you. And she said, 'Oh, yeah, that's Jo. We work together at the daycare.' So I told her I was your brother and that I was here to surprise you for your birthday but I forgot my phone where I had written your address. So she pointed me to your apartment. And I took a chance sounding stupid, but I asked her if you had a roommate or anything, and she said no, you lived there alone. And well, I'm telling you it took me forever to make up my mind. I could have just left you a letter or something, and I nearly did, but then I started to worry that maybe it wasn't really you. Or maybe you had moved on and I'd spend the rest of my life wondering if you got my note or if there had somehow been some mistake. And I prayed, and I really felt God speaking to me, like he was saying, *Son, you've been asking for me to bring her back into your life for these four years, so what's the problem? Don't you trust me to take care of the details?*"

He was winded from his speech. His eyes sparkled, but Lacy knew him well enough to detect the nervousness behind all that excitement. Even now, she longed to run to him, to forget the trauma of the past four years. Instead, she could only manage saying, "You're in Alaska?"

"Just visiting," he answered. His eyes darted around her room.

She felt naked. Exposed.

"I decided to take the summer off to bike around the country, and I thought to myself, *I've never been to Alaska. I should get on that.* I'm coming back from two weeks up and down the Richardson. Biked from Tok all the way to Fairbanks. I'm on my last stretch now. Heading back to Anchorage tomorrow."

"You're leaving?" She heard her own voice quiver.

He stepped forward. She waited. Expectant. He came up slowly. Took her clammy hand in his.

"I thought you were dead," she whispered.

"It's a long story. Right now, I just want to look at you. I can't tell you how long I've dreamed of this day. I never really thought ..." He swallowed. "I'm not sure I ever believed in miracles until now."

"You're religious," was all she could think to say.

"So much has changed these past four years. So much." He brought her hand close to his face as if he might kiss it. He leveled his eyes. "But one thing is the same. I have never stopped loving you."

She pried her hand away, wondering how different this meeting would be if she were wearing Kurtis's engagement ring.

Raphael gave a little chuckle. "I know it's insane. Really, I do. If I hadn't given my life to Christ and had faith that he can do the impossible, I wouldn't have believed it myself. Look, I know you're a little freaked out. And we have a lot of ground to cover. I just ... I've been waiting for you for the past four years. And now that I've found you, it's like I want to sweep you up in my arms and transport us back to four years ago and never drive down that ..." He cut himself off short and started over. "Transport us back to when we were happy. Happy and young and madly in love and dreaming those crazy dreams for our future. Remember? We were going to backpack Europe and visit all the art museums and come home to our studio and spend our weekends watching shows on Broadway. Just me and my Lacy."

It wasn't until he said her name that she started to tremble. Nobody had called her Lacy in four years. Even when Drisklay telephoned to check up on her, he insisted on using her alias.

Raphael put both arms on her shoulders, as if that could stop her shaking. She was crying, his voice, his touch releasing a tidal wave of pent-up emotions and forgotten longings.

"I need to sit down."

He held her elbow and led her to the dining room table, where Kurtis had proposed to her less than two hours earlier.

"Do you need a drink?"

She nodded faintly, hardly able to focus on his eyes anymore. He opened her fridge, pulled out the goblet of leftover cider. "Is this still good?" Without waiting for an answer, he poured it into a clean cup from the dishwasher and handed it to her. The drink stung her sinuses, but at least it cleared her dizziness.

"I guess I gave you quite a shock." He smiled, that same mischievous grin she had fallen in love with another lifetime ago.

Finally she found her voice. "I just can't believe it's really you. I thought ..."

"You thought I was dead, right? Thought they killed me and dragged off my body to the wharf?"

She nodded. "But I still hoped ..." She didn't have the strength to finish her sentence. Why couldn't Raphael have visited Glennallen sooner? Why couldn't she had bumped into him her first summer in this rat hole? If there really was a God, and if he really had led Raphael to her after all these years, why couldn't he have done it way back then?

He sat down across from her. "There's so much we have to catch up on. I don't even know where to start."

Neither did she. Part of her was afraid she would wake up and realize this was all a dream, her mind's way of running away from Kurtis after he proposed to her earlier.

"So you're working at a daycare?"

She nodded, the motion inviting another wave of dizziness.

"Do you like it?"

"It's ok." She didn't want to talk about her job, the dirty diapers, dirty dishes, dirty noses that always needed wiping. She should tell him about Kurtis. She should mention it before ...

"Alaska, huh? It's pretty up here, isn't it?"

"Yeah." She took another sip of cider, wincing as the fizz burned her throat.

"Your hair's longer."

"Uh-huh." As soon as she moved up here with her short pixie cut, she started growing it out to protect herself from the cold in the winter and the bugs in the summer.

"Jo, they call you, right?"

She stared at her half-empty cup.

He frowned. "You don't look like a Jo to me."

She should say something. Do something. How many times had she dreamed of sitting across from Raphael, pouring out her heart, telling him everything about the past four years of loneliness and isolation?

"Are you happy?" He asked the question so casually, but it punched her straight in the gut.

"Not really." It felt strange to not have to make up lies, not have to spew out rehearsed lines handed to her by the folks at witness protection.

He put his hand on the table but stopped before touching hers. "I've missed you."

"I've missed you, too." It was probably the most honest statement she had made in the past four years.

"Do you want to talk about it?"

Her eyes threatened to brim over again. "Not really." She forced a laugh. She hardly knew how to act like herself anymore. One day, she hoped she could look back on tonight and enjoy a full, long belly laugh.

Raphael sat back in his seat. "How about I do the talking then?"

She nodded, the heaviness already lifting from her shoulders a small bit at a time.

He ran his fingers through his hair. "Wow, this is harder than I thought. I don't even know where to start. At the beginning, I guess. You want me to tell you about the accident?"

"No." She hadn't realized her voice would sound that forceful.

He fidgeted with his hands. Artist's hands. Hands that were always painting or sculpting or photographing. She had missed them so much.

"Well, after everything that went down, they put me in witness protection. Same sort of thing as you, I'm assuming. New home, new name. It sucked. They had me working as a courier. Driving around some hunky-dunk Midwest town running deliveries for divorce lawyers and grumpy realtors. I hated it. Couldn't meet anybody, couldn't go anywhere. They even told me to stop my art."

"Really?"

He nodded. "Of course, I didn't listen. I sold a few photographs under a made-up name, but it was terrible. I'd spent the past eight years of my life building my portfolio, expanding my network. And now they wanted me to start over from the beginning peddling photographs at craft bazaars? I got low. Really low. It was like I was an actor and the producer just threw me into a different play, different setting, different lines, different cast, and no direction."

Lacy wondered how many times she had used a similar analogy.

"Figured my only outlet was gonna be my art. So I went back to it for real. At first, I tried to disguise it. Make sure someone with a trained eye couldn't link it to me. The old me. Do you know how hard it is trying to paint like someone else? It didn't work. So finally, I decided if I couldn't be a professional anymore, I'd at least paint for myself. Who knew? Maybe one day they'd tell me I didn't have to be in witness protection anymore, and I'd have enough works to sell to set me up for a lifetime. You could always hope, right?"

Hope. It had been one of Lacy's worst enemies during her first few months here in Alaska. Hope that it had all been some sort of nightmare. Hope that Drisklay would call and tell her it was safe to go home. Hope that Raphael would show up magically. Unexpectedly.

"Anyway, I got so depressed I actually ended up ... well, they put me in a hospital. Made me talk to a shrink and everything. But what can you tell a shrink, you know? When you're supposed to be someone else, I mean. But one thing I talked about was being homesick. And the hospital psychologist, she had no idea who I was or where I was really from, but she made me write a list of why I should or shouldn't move back home. And I realized the only thing keeping me away from Massachusetts was fear. I mean, can you believe it? You knew me, Lace. I wasn't scared of anything.

"So I started to think. It made sense to keep my new name and whatnot, maybe not hang out in the exact same circles as before. But how bad could it really be, you know? The guys who'd given me the hardest time were both in jail. I suppose they might have had buddies or something ready to teach me a lesson, but what was I gonna do? Spend the rest of my life shuttling divorce papers around town? I moved back about a year ago. I'm living in Waltham now. Best choice I ever made."

"And nobody's bothered you?" Lacy asked. Was it really that simple? Could she really move back home, resume her old life just like that? After all of Drisklay's dire warnings and morbid projections about what would happen if she ever returned? Was it really as easy as Raphael said?

He glanced around. "I started going to church. I guess that's the one good thing that came out of everything. And I figured if God wants me to live, well, I'm going to live. And if not, at least I know where I'm headed, right?"

Lacy hadn't thought about God much in the past four years, unless it was to blame him for letting her life take the unfortunate twists and turns it had. This was a new side of Raphael she wasn't sure if she was comfortable with or not.

"Oh!" He smiled and leaned forward, eyes twinkling. "You'll get a kick out of this. I've been going to Carl and Sandy's church."

"My foster parents?"

"Yeah." He sighed. "I wish you could connect with them again. I know they miss you."

Her throat constricted. She had lost hours of sleep since moving to Glennallen trying to recall the exact sound of Sandy's voice. With Carl it was easier, because if she wanted to she could download his sermons and listen to his confident, booming preaching at any time. But Sandy ...

"That's neat you get to see them still."

It wasn't fair. If Massachusetts was safe enough for him, wasn't it safe enough for her? She could have moved back years ago, forgotten the blasted mosquitoes, the unbearable winters that dragged out over half the year.

"You could come with me." He stared so intently into her eyes she didn't know whether to laugh or cry or run away. "We could be safe together."

No. No, this was happening too fast. It reminded her of swimming in the ocean once as a little girl when the undercurrent caught her in its black, deathly grasp. It tumbled her over so many times she didn't know which way to turn to get to shore. For a few paralyzing seconds, she didn't even know which way would lead her to the surface. To air.

Her cup of cider trembled in her hand, and Raphael picked it up and set it on the table for her. "I'm sorry. I wasn't trying to upset you."

"I'm seeing someone." The words rushed out automatically.

He didn't speak right away, and she did what she could to fill the silence.

"He's a trooper. We've been dating for over a year now. He has a little girl. She's four." Why was she saying all of this? Was it because she was afraid she might tell him about the ring, about the proposal, so instead she cluttered the empty space with trivia?

Raphael licked his lower lip. He picked up Lacy's cider cup, examined it mindlessly, and set it down again. "I'm glad you told me." He forced a little smile. "I guess I shouldn't have barged in here like this, and ..." He tousled his hair in both hands. "You must think I've been totally insensitive. I'm sorry, Lace."

She couldn't meet his eyes.

Raphael made a move as if to stand up and stopped. "Is it serious?"

She shrugged. "I don't really know right now. It's confusing."

He glanced at the door. "Do you want me to leave?"

It wasn't fair. After all the waiting, all the loneliness, the fruitless fantasizing, now here he was, and she didn't know what to say. "I'm pretty overwhelmed, that's all."

He sighed. "I should have been more thoughtful. Geeze, Lace, you've been through so much already. I don't want to make this harder for you. I listen to my Bible when I ride, you know. I've got it on audio, and just today I was reading about John the Baptist and how he says about Jesus, *He must become greater, and I must become less.* Maybe that was a message for me. I don't want to stand in the way of a good thing. If God's brought you someone who's honest and solid and who'll take care of you ..."

She never knew why she did it. She just couldn't stand listening to him talking like that anymore. She had to make him stop. Either that, or he would do the noble thing and leave her to enjoy some sort of peaceful, lulling happily ever after with Kurtis. She bent forward and kissed him. He sucked in his breath while his lips met hers, and then he wrapped his arms around her, entwined his fingers in her hair. He tasted just like she remembered. If she had a thousand words, she could never express how much she had missed this.

They fell apart, both panting. "Wow." He rubbed his head and repeated, "Wow."

She scooted her chair back, afraid of the feelings his kiss had awakened. "I shouldn't have done that."

"Maybe not." He grinned. "But I'm sure glad you did."

"I can't ..." She held up her hands. "I shouldn't be ..."

He stood. "I understand. It's, well, I can guess it's pretty complicated."

She lowered her eyes. "Yeah." Heat rushed across her face.

"But it was nice, wasn't it?"

She wiped her mouth self-consciously. "Yeah."

"Really nice." Why was he looking at her like that? Didn't he know how irresistible he was? He took a few steps toward the door. "I should go, shouldn't I?"

She should stop him. Keep him here forever. Once she explained everything to Kurtis, he'd understand ...

"Do you mean *go* go?" Her voice squeaked a little.

He paused with his hand on the doorknob. "Is that what you want me to do?"

"No, I ..." She took in a deep breath, trying to clear her mind, which was still racing after the feel of his lips pressed hungrily against hers. "I ... I need time to think. It's nothing personal."

"No problem. I'll give you my number."

She fumbled for her phone in her purse, thankful for something to occupy her hands. She kept her eyes on the screen and typed in his name. "All right, I'm ready."

He rattled off the number. Her fingers trembled a little when she punched them into her cell. What if she got it wrong? What if he went to Anchorage tomorrow and she never saw him again? Maybe she should leave with him. Maybe she should just ...

"I don't fly out until Monday. There's time."

She nodded, eager to get him out of her apartment, searching for an excuse to make him stay.

"It's going to be all right. You know that, right?" He touched her gently on the shoulder, and she tried not to jerk her arm away. This was Raphael. Not the phantom she had dreamed about, pined after for so many years. He was really here, the warm sweetness of his kiss no longer just a bittersweet memory but fresh on her lips.

He bent his head down and kissed the top of her head. "I'll be waiting for your call. If you're happy here, I wish you both all the best. You know that, right? And if you decide you want to come back, well, like I said, I'm driving to Anchorage tomorrow." He glanced at her, his eyes hopeful.

She couldn't speak. She could scarcely breathe. It felt as if someone had stabbed her in the heart and her blood was spilling out in a puddle on the floor.

He held up his phone. "Just call me either way, ok? Even if it's just to say no thanks. I really ..." He cleared his throat. "I really don't want to go another four years wondering, you know?"

She bit her lip.

"Hey, you've still got a Bible, right?"

"Yeah." Drisklay hadn't let her take the one Carl and Sandy signed for her high school graduation, but she found a freebie at the Glennallen thrift store and brought it home, even though she had only opened it once or twice since then.

"Look up Jeremiah 29:11, all right? It's one of my favorites."

She nodded, hardly able to lift her hand to wave good-bye as he walked out of her apartment.

CHAPTER 6

She stared at the door for several minutes after he left. She didn't want to go digging for her thrift store Bible, so she opened up a Scripture website on her phone. What verse had he said? Jeremiah 29:11. It had been so long since she and Sandy had read the Bible together over milk and cookies at the Lindgrens' dining room table. She couldn't even remember which testament she should look in. Thankfully, the webpage made that part easy enough for her. Her phone took some time to load, and she glanced around her apartment. Other than the cup of cider on the table, was there any proof Raphael had been there? She glanced at her cell, wondering if his name and number would be there in her contacts list if she were to look it up.

Jeremiah 29:11. The verse finished loading. She read it slowly. *"For I know the plans I have for you," declares the Lord, "plans to prosper you and not to harm you, plans to give you hope and a future."*

A future? What kind of a future was there for her as long as she stayed in witness protection? A future away from Carl and Sandy, the only parental figures who had ever really loved her. A future in Glennallen, a town with absolutely nothing going for it except for the fact that it was remote and catered to tourists in the summer. A future working at the daycare until she lost every ounce of patience with the children and was forced to quit. And then what? Getting a job at Puck's grocery store? Bagging canned goods and stocking shelves the rest of her life?

Hope and a future. Until tonight, Lacy hadn't really allowed herself to hope for anything besides a mild winter. There was Kurtis, of course, and his proposal. Just a little bit ago, she had all but thrown herself at him, begging him to ignore her initial rejection. But he knew she hadn't meant it. Not really. And now, if he found out about Raphael ...

The sting of that last kiss burned her lips. Shame congealed in her veins. What had she been thinking? How would Kurtis feel if he found out?

She glanced at the verse on her screen once more. *"For I know the plans I have for you."* Well, at least somebody did. She was embarrassed to think about how thoroughly she had turned her back on God since she moved here. When she first got to Glennallen, she had gone to the chapel because she missed Carl and Sandy and thought being in a church on Sunday might assuage a little bit of her homesickness. But she got bored. She was tired after working long hours at the daycare. She went back to the chapel when she started dating Kurtis because it was important to him, but other than that hour and a half on Sunday mornings, she rarely thought about the Lord.

How many times had she gone over that evening with Raphael? They could have gone to any pier in North End. They could have dined at any restaurant across the entire Boston-Cambridge area. Why there? Why then? And if God really had a plan for her life, couldn't he have stopped them?

Well, what if that verse was right? What if witnessing the murder on the pier really was part of God's plan? That meant he wanted her in Glennallen. He wanted her to suffer the loneliness, the heartache. Why? So she could meet Kurtis? Then why had he thrown Raphael back into her path?

And if God wanted her to marry Raphael, why had they been separated for these past four years? Even if the Lord wanted to grant them a dramatic reunion after all they had been through, why didn't he stop Kurtis from coming into the picture, complicating everything with his patient understanding?

The phone was heavy in her hand. It was too much to think about tonight. Yet again, she felt that God must be punishing her for some horrible thing she had done in the past. And if he was God, that was probably his right. But why were there people worse than she, people who beat their children or were strung out on drugs, whose lives weren't thrown into chaos? She never doubted God's existence, not really. But it made so much more sense to think of him as a benign being in some far-away universe, too busy to care about the day-to-day affairs of an East Coast foster girl.

Too busy to intervene when Lacy needed him the most.

Well, the answers weren't going to magically appear on her phone. She closed the Bible website and stared at the screen. Should she call someone? Who? Raphael had just left. She could call him now, ask him to take her away with him to Anchorage. Go back with him to Massachusetts. In a day or two, she could be home with Carl and Sandy.

But where would that leave Kurtis? At least his wife was really dead. Renee had died in the hospital. He had seen her buried. He hadn't lived the past several years wondering, dealing with the nagging suspicion, the spark of hope that was almost too painful to acknowledge. But what if she was magically found to be alive? Wouldn't it be his right to dump Jo and spend the rest of his life with his first love?

She should call Kurtis. He was so level-headed. So thoughtful. Even just talking through things with him would help. But to do that would mean revealing her past. What would he say when he learned her entire identity was a fabrication? Somewhere in his vast reserves of compassion, there must be an end to his patience and forgiveness. If he found out the truth, if he found out she wasn't a foster kid from Michigan who moved out to Alaska to fulfill a lifelong dream, what would he say? What would he say if he discovered she hated the cold, hated mosquitoes, hated the claustrophobic, isolated feeling that came from living in a town of four hundred?

What would he say if she told him that she was in love with Raphael? That she had never stopped loving him? That she had known deep in her heart he was still alive even while she was dating someone else? Kurtis was a saint. But she couldn't expect him to sympathize with that. And if he did, if he looked at her with those tender eyes and told her he understood and forgave her anyway, she would feel even more wretched.

Why had Raphael come? Why had they ever gone to that pier in the first place?

"For I know the plans I have for you."

Well, that was all fine and good and poetic, and Lacy figured that people like her foster mom Sandy would read a verse like that and derive a great deal of comfort from it. But it only made Lacy feel worse. If God had a plan for her, that meant he wanted her in witness protection. He wanted to ruin her life. And then, just because he was all-powerful and just because he could, he was going to throw Raphael at her right after Kurtis proposed.

Some plan.

She shut off her phone. It was late. The sky was still bright enough you could drive without headlights even though midnight was less than an hour away. She plodded to her room without bothering to brush her teeth or change into her pajamas. She closed her curtains, but the light still spilled in through the sides. She plopped onto her bed and threw the pillow over her face. Two mosquitoes buzzed in her ear.

Alaska sucks.

She rolled onto her side and tried to sleep.

CHAPTER 7

She woke up the next morning with at least four new bites. One was on her ankle, the most annoying spot of all. It was a little after eight, and she wondered if she'd be lucky enough to go back to sleep. She was still exhausted. She had lain awake half the night listening to the bugs and trying to organize her thoughts. God might have plans for her future like Raphael's verse suggested, but it had taken her until two in the morning to come up with any plans for herself.

She just hoped she wouldn't regret them.

She flipped on her phone. There was already a text message from Raphael. *Breakfast this morning?*

She wasn't going to think about the shock of seeing him again. She wasn't going to think about the fire that burned in her gut when they had kissed after so many years. *Gotta do something first*, she replied. *Lunch instead?*

Today might be the hardest day of her life.

As she dressed, she thought about calling Kurtis beforehand. Warn him she was coming. But she couldn't bring herself to do it. If she got him on the phone, the temptation would be too strong to tell him everything she needed to say without looking at him. She couldn't do that to him. She had made up her mind and had the bags under her eyes to prove it. She would never forgive herself if she took the easy way out now.

It took fifteen minutes to walk to Kurtis's house, which helped clear her mind. Her heart pounded faster than normal by the time she arrived, but her limbs weren't as jittery as when she first started out. A slight breeze had kept most of the mosquitoes at bay. When she had made up her mind last night, she pictured walking to Kurtis's in a rainstorm or getting swarmed by a hundred bugs at once, but the trip itself had been surprisingly calming.

She knocked on the door, feeling more like Lacy and less like Jo than she had in years. Lacy wasn't afraid of change. Lacy wasn't afraid to tackle life head-on no matter what the cost. The only thing Lacy feared was a cage, a cage that after today would no longer confine her.

Madeline answered the door, still in her footy pajamas. "Miss Jo!" Her excited squeal sent a pang of regret through Lacy's heart. What had she expected? She knew how hard this would be. It didn't matter, though, she reminded herself. It had to be done.

"Hi, sweetie." Lacy pried Madeline off her leg. "Can you tell your daddy I'm here?"

Madeline scurried away yelling, and Lacy stepped in and shut the door to keep the bugs out. Kurtis came out a moment later in flannel lounge pants and a white undershirt, drying his hair with a towel. "Hi, Jo."

She couldn't tell from his voice if he was happy to see her or not, but she couldn't focus on that. She would say what she came here to say, and that would be all. She was about to apologize for stopping by unannounced, but that was Jo talking, Jo the demure daycare worker who had never really existed. She glanced around the house, at the moose antlers on the wall, the plastic pink princess toys strewn across the floor. She hadn't admitted until now how much she would miss all this.

"I came here to talk to you. Do you have a minute?"

He looked at her quizzically before leaning down to Madeline. "Why don't you grab a Pop Tart and run downstairs to watch some cartoons? I'll make us pancakes in a little bit."

"Is Miss Jo eating with us, too?" she asked.

"I don't know."

Kurtis avoided meeting Lacy's eyes as Madeline skipped downstairs. He pointed to the couch. "Have a seat." He took the lounge chair opposite her.

Lacy had already decided not to waste time on chitchat. What was the point? "I'm heading to Anchorage. I came to say good-bye."

His expression didn't change. Where was the kindness, the compassion she had grown to expect from him?

She rushed to fill the silence. "It doesn't have anything to do with you. I want you to know that. You're a ... well, you're an amazing guy, and I'm really thankful I got to know you." She couldn't read him. Was he angry? "I just, well, I'm leaving, and I didn't want it to come across like I was running away or anything ..."

Who was she fooling? That's exactly what she was doing. No, that wasn't it either. She was embracing her own life for a change. Making her own plans.

Kurtis continued to stare.

"Why don't you say something?" she finally asked.

"When are you leaving?"

"Today. As soon as I get packed."

"It was Raphael, wasn't it?" His voice was so soft, she leaned forward to make sure she heard him. "At your apartment last night."

"Ra ..." The word caught in her throat. "My apartment?"

"I went back, you know. Went back to tell you I didn't mean it. Went back to tell you that even though the nice-guy thing to do is wait until you're good and ready, the truth is I'm dying inside. I want to be with you. I know last night I said I would wait because I want your whole heart, but it was a lie. I said that for you, because I thought you needed space to sort your life out. But I want you now. I want you here with me, wearing my ring, using my name, raising my daughter with me. I came last night to tell you I couldn't stand the thought of waiting anymore. It was killing me. That's when I saw him leave your place."

Her stomach dropped. "It wasn't what you're thinking. It wasn't ..." She stopped short at the memory of Raphael's kiss. She couldn't lie anymore. "It was Raphael. You're right about that. But it's not like I was seeing you both at the same time. Until yesterday I thought he was dead."

"In witness protection, you mean." The words came out flat.

Nervous energy raced up Lacy's spine. "What are you talking about?"

Kurtis let out his breath. "I'm a simple guy, Jo, but I'm not stupid. I know what happened to you."

"What?" She felt like a parrot with a one-word vocabulary.

"Listen, you told me about Raphael. You told me he was killed in a car accident. You gave me the name of your foster parents. You think I couldn't figure it out?"

"But I never told you where I lived."

"No. You did the smart thing and kept that a secret from me. But how many Carls do you think there are who take in foster kids and pastor a church and are married to a woman named Sandy?"

She didn't know what to say. She had never heard him speak like this. "Are you angry?"

"Angry?" He raised his voice. "Geeze. Do you think that little of me?

Of course you had to lie to me. Of course you had to keep the past tucked away. If I were mad about something like that ..."

"Then why are you yelling?"

He paused to take a breath. "I didn't mean to. But you can't understand that I'm on your team here. I've known about this for weeks. Want to know when I put it all together? When I tried to find Carl so I could ask him for your hand in marriage. And I didn't find a Pastor Carl and Sandy in Michigan where I was looking, but I found them in Massachusetts. So I called. Asked if he had a foster daughter named Jo. He said he and his wife had a lot of foster kids over the years, but nobody by that name. I said she moved to Alaska four years ago. He turned evasive and finally hung up. You think after a decade as a trooper I can't smell suspicious? So I started searching more. Looking up Raphael, trying to figure out how he died. And guess what? He wasn't alone in the car. There was a girl there. A girl your age who testified in court and then disappeared. You think I can't put things together? So then I start to think, the girl got put in witness protection. What about the boy? What if his death's just a cover-up, too? And then I realize why you're having a harder time moving on than I did when Renee passed. You're holding onto hope that he's still out there, that maybe one day you'll find each other, live out your happily ever ..."

"I'm not going to Anchorage with him," Lacy interrupted. "With Raphael. I'm not ..." She paused so she wouldn't fumble over her words. "I'm not choosing Raphael over you. It's been four years. Do you know how weird that is? He's been going to my dad's church. He's all religious now. Do you think I'm just going to throw away this life to be with someone I hardly know anymore?"

"Then why Anchorage? Why so fast?"

"I need to get out of here. I need time to think. Decide if I even want to keep living as Jo anymore." Her voice caught. "And I can't make a decision like that while you're here being so nice and caring and understanding, and I can't do it with him spouting off Bible verses and talking about how it's some big miracle we found each other."

Kurtis frowned. "But don't you find it just a tad suspicious that after four years you just randomly bump into him, in Glennallen of all places?"

Lacy sat up in her seat. "I told you I'm not leaving with him. I need time to think, and I can't do that if both of you are ..."

Her phone beeped. Probably another text from Raphael. She ignored it.

"I can't do that if both of you are trying to pressure me."

Kurtis relaxed in his chair. "So you're going to Anchorage to take a little time to figure things out. Is that it?"

"That's what I've been trying to tell you."

"And where does that leave me? What about this Raphael guy?"

"I already said I don't know. I can't be expected to make any decisions like this until I know more what I want. At this point, I'm thinking of just flying back to Boston and living my old life again."

"You can't do that. It wouldn't be safe."

"That's what you're telling me. But how am I supposed to know until I get a little breathing room and figure things out for myself?"

He sighed. "All right. I'm not going to try to stop you."

She eyed him quizzically. "You angry?"

He shook his head but remained quiet.

"You understand why I couldn't tell you the truth?"

"Of course. I'm a trooper, remember?"

She stood up. "You'll say good-bye to Madeline for me, right?"

"If that's what you want." He sighed. "Do you need a ride to town, or is he taking you?"

"I'm driving myself."

He raised an eyebrow. "Is your check oil light still blinking?"

"Only sometimes," she lied. She had forgotten all about that.

"Why don't you let me at least change it before you go?"

She stared at the door. "I'm sure I'll make it just fine."

"It's a four-hour trip, Jo."

"I know. I'll be ok."

Why couldn't he understand? Didn't he realize she couldn't keep accepting his help whenever a problem came up? Didn't he realize this move was something she had to do on her own?

She took a few steps toward the entryway but stopped and turned around. "I'm sorry. About everything."

He avoided her eyes. "Me, too."

She couldn't leave him like this. She inhaled deeply. "If I was Jo, you know I would have said yes yesterday and meant it."

"Yeah, I know."

He didn't stand up to see her out. As she passed the stairs to the basement, she heard the soundtrack to Madeline's princess movie playing softly. She paused for just a moment to listen and then opened the door and let herself out.

CHAPTER 8

The walk back to her apartment seemed to take hours. Was she really doing the right thing? Was she ready to pack and go? She felt bad leaving the daycare on short-notice, but Kim and one other part-time worker could pull together to make up her extra hours. Attendance was low this time of year anyway, with so many families going fishing or camping or vacationing in the Lower 48. She was probably doing the daycare's budget a big favor.

She thought about Carl and Sandy, about how easy it would be to hop on a plane and fly back to Massachusetts. If she had the money, that is. She could sell her car in town, maybe get one or two grand for it. That was a start. Enough to get her back home. Or put down a payment on an apartment in Anchorage. A very small apartment. What should she do?

"For I know the plans I have for you," declares the Lord. Yeah, well, so far his plans for her life hadn't worked out all that swimmingly. It was time for her to make her own decisions. Make her own plans.

Whatever that meant.

She got home and pulled the small suitcase out from under her bed. Drisklay had told her to keep a small bag packed and ready so she could take off at a moment's notice if her cover was ever blown. She had packed it four years ago and never opened it since. She couldn't remember what was in it anymore. She took the contents out one at a time and laid them on her mattress. Two blouses. A pair of jeans. Hair brush, tooth brush, tooth paste. Socks, underclothes, and a coat. That was all. You could study the whole thing without learning anything about her except her bra size. How was it that her whole life had been stripped away from her until all that was left was this little carry-on full of belongings that meant nothing to her? It was because they weren't hers. They weren't Lacy's. They belonged to an imaginary woman named Jo who worked at a daycare, had never gone to college, and lived in a remote town in Alaska where the temperatures could drop to negative fifty over Thanksgiving.

She had been living Jo's life for too long.

She put the nondescript items back in the bag and pulled out a few more things from her closet. If she was staying in Alaska, she should take the heavy winter stuff she had accumulated. But if she went back to the East Coast ...

No, she couldn't think like that. She hadn't made a single decision herself in four years, at least not an important one. Even dating Kurtis had felt like part of her cover story, not something she would have done if she were still living her own life, if she were still Lacy. She tried to ignore the memory of his expression when she left his house earlier. She had expected him to be hurt. Of course he would be. It would have been easier if he had tried to talk her out of moving or even lost his temper. Instead, he was so stoic, which wounded her even more deeply.

She sniffed, reminding herself that nothing was finalized. She might spend two days in Anchorage. She might spend two years. All that mattered was that this was a decision she was making for herself. Nobody was making it for her, no witness protection marshal, no larger-than-life boyfriend, no former love who had materialized out of nowhere after four years of torturous waiting.

Where she went after Anchorage was her choice as well. If she came back to Glennallen, that would be her decision and no one else's. Same thing if she returned to Massachusetts to be with Carl and Sandy. If she accepted Kurtis's proposal, or if she and Raphael resumed their romance after a four-year hiatus, or if she found someone else entirely down the road or chose to stay single for the rest of her life, those were decisions only she could make. She wouldn't let anybody dictate her life anymore.

Her phone beeped, and she realized she had missed several texts from Raphael. She was avoiding him. It was all so strange, his coming back from the dead. And all his talk now about God and the Bible and Carl's church? His family had been Catholic, if she remembered right. He came to church with her on holidays or if Carl and Sandy invited him over for lunch after the service, but it wasn't a big part of his life. Hers, either. They were too busy living to really settle down and dwell on the metaphysical for long. She knew there was a God, she knew the Bible was basically true, and she figured that one day she might actually study it on her own instead of just at the dining room table with her foster mom. How many Bible verses had Raphael mentioned last night when he came over? What had gotten a hold of him? She needed time to absorb it all. She sent him a text back. She had already decided she'd meet him for lunch and explain to him what she had just told Kurtis. She was going to Anchorage until she figured out her next move, and if Raphael was the same man he'd been four years ago, he'd be ok with that.

Her packing was interrupted by a knock on the door. Kurtis? In all honesty, she would have felt hurt if he let her leave without trying to change her mind, but she wasn't ready. Not yet. She bustled into the kitchen, where a pile of dirty dishes overflowed from the sink onto the counter and stacked themselves into precarious three-dimensional shapes. Great. Her landlord would love her for this.

The knocking again. It wasn't like Kurtis to be impatient. Raphael, maybe? But she had just texted him and made plans to meet in an hour.

The door burst open. She slammed her rag onto the counter and stormed into the dining room. "What are you ..."

She froze when she saw who it was.

"You didn't lock yourself in." Detective Drisklay stood in the middle of her living room, frowning. He pointed his paper coffee cup at her door. "How many times did we tell you to lock yourself in?"

Lacy couldn't move. Couldn't speak. Couldn't explain to him that this was Glennallen, Alaska, where people went on month-long vacations without locking up. While they were thawing out in Hawaii or whatever warm coast they escaped to, their neighbors brought in the mail and placed it on their dining room tables.

Drisklay pulled out the chair where Kurtis and Raphael had both sat the night before. He was a detestable sight. Lacy didn't trust him enough to take her eyes off him. "What are you doing here?" she asked.

"You need to get your things together." He spoke so casually, as if they were discussing a piece of math homework.

Lacy had always despised math.

"You said we were done meeting face to face."

He shrugged and took a big swig of coffee. "Things change." Drisklay scanned her apartment. She knew he was taking everything in. He wouldn't miss a single detail. "So, how much time do you need to pack?"

The room was spinning. Her head was as light as the helium balloons Raphael had won for her at the Salem fair so many years ago. She steadied herself on the table. "Do I have to?"

He shrugged. "You're a free citizen, but obviously I can't guarantee your safety if you fail to comply."

"Why?" she demanded, ignoring the nagging suspicion growing in her gut.

"Your cover's blown. Someone in the trooper's office's getting a little too nosy."

"That was just Kurtis. He wouldn't ..."

"We've never lost a placement yet," Drisklay interrupted. "You think I want the first time to be on my watch?"

"Where do you want me to go?"

"You know the drill. You'll get all the details once you're safe. It's a total reboot. New papers, new name, the works. I'll use the bathroom while you get your bag. I assume you've kept one packed and ready like I told you."

Lacy forced herself to look at him in the eye even though her insides were quivering like one of the many minor tremors she had experienced since moving here. "No."

"No, you don't have a bag, or no you don't want me using the toilet? It's a long drive to Anchorage, you know."

She took a deep breath. "No, I'm not going with you. I'm not going through it all again."

He set his cup on the table and looked at her as if she had just told him she wanted to visit the moon because she was in the mood for some cheese. "So I guess you'll just sit tight here, wait for the Mafia to come into your unlocked house and finish what they set out to do four years ago?"

"The trial's over. Nobody has any reason to hurt me."

He frowned. "Revenge can be quite a strong motivation. Sometimes I think you fail to appreciate just how powerful these men are."

"I'm leaving Glennallen anyway. I don't need you to relocate me."

He shrugged. "It's a free country, but I beg you to remember that these men know your identity."

Good, she thought to herself, *that means I can go back to being Lacy since the Jo cover's already blown.* "All you know for sure is that the trooper knows who I am, right? Good, because I just told him today when I broke off our engagement." She didn't know why she mentioned that part. What would

Drisklay care?

He shrugged. "You think about it while I use your toilet."

After Lacy moved in with the Lindgrens, her foster mother told her, "Hatred is a force as strong as death itself." If that was true, Drisklay would have suffered a fatal catastrophe as he sauntered uninvited down her hall. Lacy stared at his half-empty coffee cup and wanted to spit in it. It was a childish gesture that wouldn't have solved anything except relieve her tension for a few seconds.

She ignored the sweaty, clammy feeling around the collar of her blouse. She had already resolved to get out of Glennallen, but there was no way she was going through an entire relocation with Drisklay and his cronies. She'd drive into Anchorage, slip in anonymously amongst the hundreds of thousands of people there, and stay put until she made up her mind. This was her life, her future, after all. Not his.

He came out of the bathroom and picked up his paper cup. "You ready? Where's your bag?"

"I said I'm not going."

"You were serious?" There was something in his dead-pan expression that might have been humorous under different circumstances.

She nodded.

He sighed. "I'll stick around through the end of the day. Call me when you come to your senses."

CHAPTER 9

Her whole body was shaking by the time Drisklay left, but she ignored the trembling and went back to her room to finish packing. Nothing could change her mind. Not now. She had regained control of her life for the first time since it started spinning rampant four years ago. She flipped through her wallet to see how much cash she had. Just enough to fill her tank and maybe buy a few groceries to start off in Anchorage. She didn't know anyone out there, but that didn't matter. Lacy was never afraid of meeting new people, seeing new places. This would be an adventure, an adventure she could determine for once.

Carl and Sandy would worry about her if they knew. They were always so safety conscious, which was probably why they were never thrilled with Raphael in the first place. But she didn't answer to them anymore, even though she hadn't stopped thinking of them since Raphael told her he went to their church. And if he was right, if Massachusetts was safe for her now, she could go home.

At last.

Of course, that was getting ahead of herself. First Anchorage. Give herself a few days to settle in. Decide from there what to do. It was too early to meet Raphael for lunch, but she was anxious to get on the road. There was nothing left for her here. Nothing but old memories, old identities.

And Kurtis.

Of course, there was still Kurtis.

But she'd have time to think about that in Anchorage. Her co-worker Kim had a sister in town. Maybe she needed a roommate. It was summer. Wouldn't there be a plethora of kids in need of nannies? Or she could go to the University of Alaska, fill out their application for student aid, get a dorm on campus. There were enough options she didn't need to worry. Everything was going to work itself out.

Finally.

She grabbed her suitcase and a backpack and threw them in her trunk, and then she came back to fill a Costco box with a few random items. The rest could go to whatever tenant took over after her. She wouldn't get her security deposit back after leaving the apartment such a mess, but once she sold her car, she wouldn't need the extra cash.

She took a deep breath.

Everything was going to be just fine.

She left her apartment keys on the dining room table, started up her car, and drove to the Elk Hotel. That was one nice thing about a town as small as Glennallen. There was only one place that lodged out-of-town guests. She hurried in and stopped at the front desk. "Hi, I have a friend staying here. I was wondering if you could call his room for me."

"What's his name?"

Lacy stopped. She didn't even know what alias Raphael was using. "Umm, can you try ..."

"Well, look who showed up!" His voice boomed from the top-level balcony as he leaned over with a grin. "I was just getting ready to text you. Give me a sec, and I'll be right down."

Lacy smiled sheepishly and waited near the stairs. She felt as anxious as she had at her junior prom. She kept fidgeting with her hands, wondering what he would do when he came down. She didn't feel ready for another kiss, even though that one last night had felt so good, if not long overdue.

Raphael was all smiles as he hustled down the stairs to his own syncopated rhythm. "How's my girl?" He placed his hand on the small of her back and noisily pecked the air about an inch away from her cheek in classic New England style. He still wore the same cologne, that inviting masculine scent. How had she lived the past four years without him? "What have you been up to? I thought you weren't free until later."

"Plans changed. I, um ..." She glanced at the desk clerk. "Well, you want to head outside? Go on a walk or something?"

His eyes darted to the window. "Sure. My bike's locked up and secure. I'm all yours."

They stepped outside, and Lacy swatted away the mosquitoes that swarmed her face. She took her hair out of her ponytail to give her ears and neck more protection. "I've been thinking," she began tentatively, "and I've got to tell you some things. Part of it's good, and part of it's not." There, was that enough of a warning?

He walked beside her with his familiar, easy step. She had forgotten the simple joy of being beside him, being together, enjoying the outdoors. The Wrangell Mountains stretched out before them, tiny dollops of snow from last winter still capping the peaks. He slipped his arm around her waist, unassuming. Natural. "Start with the good stuff."

"Well, I've made up my mind about a few things. I went over to see ..." She faltered before saying his name. It sounded so strange talking about him. "I went to see my trooper friend. And, well, I said I was going to Anchorage to give myself time to put everything together."

Raphael nodded thoughtfully. "Sounds reasonable. He took it ok?"

"Yeah." She wasn't willing to get into details of their conversation and was glad he didn't press it any further.

"What's the bad news, then?"

She slowed her pace. "Well, I feel like in some ways I need to have the same conversation with you. I mean, I'm thrilled you're here, but before I go anywhere, before I make any big decisions about our relationship, I need time to think through it all."

He let out a little laugh. "You have no idea how glad I am to hear you say that."

"Really?"

"Well, it's weird for me too, you know. I mean, don't get me wrong. I was so excited last night I only slept for two hours, but on the other hand, it's like we've been living totally separate lives these past four years. We're different people, whether we want to admit it or not. And well, as stoked as I am to imagine what God might have in store for us, I think it's good to slow down a little. Give ourselves time to think things through. Pray about it. Make sure we're doing the right things for the right reasons, you know?"

She nodded, taken slightly aback. She had expected this conversation to be harder.

"So Anchorage, huh?" he said after a minute. "What will you be doing once you're there?"

"I don't even know what I want to do anymore."

"You ever think of going back to school?"

"Maybe, but I'd have to start over at the beginning. All of my credits are under my old name ..." Her voice trailed off, and neither of them said anything. She wondered if he was thinking the same thing she was. She could go back to Lacy. There was always that option. Transfer her old credits to UAA, enroll in ...

No, she was moving to Anchorage so she had time to think. She couldn't get ahead of herself.

They reached the end of the sidewalk and turned around automatically. Raphael glanced at the time on his phone. "It's a little past eleven. Is that too early for lunch?"

"Actually, I'm leaving today. I guess that's the rest of the bad news." Had she told him that part yet? "It's not because of you or anything, I just ..."

"I know. You're itching to be alone and make sense of everything. And when I'm around that just confuses the matter."

"That's not what I ..."

"I'm just teasing." He nudged her playfully. "Well, I got to get to Anchorage, too. Care to drive with me?"

"Nah, I'm taking my car. I'm selling it for my seed money."

"Not a bad idea." He sighed. "Does that mean no lunch?"

She could hear the disappointment in his tone. "Well, what if we make a date in Anchorage?" she asked. "Dinner tonight?"

A grin spread across his face. "Deal. I'm buying."

She grinned, too. "Good, because I'm officially broke."

"Hey, do you want me to ..." He stopped on the sidewalk and fidgeted in his pocket. "We could find an ATM and I could let you have ..."

She shook her head. "No. This move, getting away from here, everything, I've got to do this on my own." How could she explain it to him? How could she explain how she could never really find out if she was Jo or Lacy or some other stranger she hadn't even met yet until she went through this alone? "But thanks." She let her hand rest on his shoulder for a moment. Their eyes locked.

He gave her a smile. "You got this, Lace."

Deep in her heart, she knew he was right.

CHAPTER 10

She said good-bye to Raphael when they reached the hotel again. It was easier knowing she would see him in Anchorage at the end of the day. Maybe the drive would give her time to think through things a little more. Maybe by dinner, she'd have formed some kind of plan for the next few weeks. Tonight they would meet in Anchorage as free adults. The thought made her almost giddy as she crossed the street to Puck's grocery store. She had about a hundred dollars left in her bank account. In a week, she'd get her last paycheck from the daycare. Money might be tight in Anchorage, but it wasn't as though she had made it big wiping snotty noses on the playground, either.

She was on the road fifteen minutes later, speeding out of Glennallen, heading for a new life. Her enthusiasm was short-lived, however. She had just passed the native church in Mendeltna when her change oil light flickered. Her car sputtered and lost speed. She pushed down again on the accelerator, but the engine ground in protest.

Flipping on her emergency lights, she eased over onto the side of the road. Thankfully, nobody was behind her. She tried to pick up speed, but the engine shuddered once more and then died. So much for that idea. For the faintest moment, she wondered if Drisklay had sabotaged her car. He was so convinced she needed to stay in the program. Maybe he got kickbacks based on how many protectees he kept corralled in their rightful places.

She flipped on her cell phone. Coverage was spotty from here most of the way to Anchorage. She got a faint signal and spent another two or three minutes deciding who to call. She gave one final attempt to turn the engine over. It coughed faintly before grinding again.

Nothing.

She had to go back. For a minute, she thought about walking all the way to Glennallen, but that was ridiculous. It would take her half the day, and the bugs were atrocious. She needed to call for a ride.

Call who? Kurtis? Raphael?

She looked at both men's names in her cell phone, testing each one out in her mind. Kurtis would drop everything, bring Madeline with him, and probably find a way to tow her car back to Glennallen. He'd spend the rest of his day off fixing it in his garage. Could she expect him to do that after the way she'd treated him?

She could ask Raphael to pick her up. It would give them more time to talk, but the most he could do would be to drive her back to Glennallen, where she'd probably end up needing Kurtis to help get her car anyway.

She sighed. Was this fate? God's way of keeping her humble right when she thought she was figuring out how to live once more? She thought again of Drisklay and pictured how smug he would look if he saw her here stranded on the side of the road.

She had hesitated long enough. She pulled Kurtis's number up on her cell phone and bit her lip, fighting to keep from hanging up before he answered.

"Hello?"

"It's me. I hate to do this to you, but I had some car trouble outside of Mendeltna. Can you come get me?"

Silence. What was he thinking?

"The oil?"

"Yeah." Why hadn't she listened to him? He had been harping about that change oil light since spring.

A sigh. "All right. The munchkin's in the bath right now. It'll be a few minutes."

"Take your time. I'm not going anywhere." A week ago, they probably would have both laughed.

More silence. For a minute, she wondered if he would ask her why she hadn't called Raphael.

"I'm sorry," she added.

"It's not a problem. Give me half an hour to dry her off and get to you."

"Thanks," she added, but he had already hung up.

CHAPTER 11

Getting stranded on a stretch of the Glenn Highway as scenic as Mendeltna might not have been quite so terrible if she had thought to bring bug spray with her. She locked herself in the car and killed three mosquitoes before the buzzing finally stopped. At least it wasn't too hot. Half an hour. It wasn't a big deal. It's not like she had anywhere to rush to in Anchorage. She didn't even know where she'd be spending the night. She should take advantage of the time to finish off some business. Like telling the daycare she was leaving. And asking Kim if her sister knew of anybody in town who needed a nanny or house-sitter or roommate. But she was too mentally exhausted. She thought about her conversation with Raphael, how he said he had hardly slept more than a few hours last night. He was so excited. Sometimes she wondered why she wasn't more so. Was it the religion thing? Raphael had always been a decent person, but it was strange to hear all those churchy things coming out of his mouth. He sounded like her foster dad.

She had been thinking of Carl and Sandy more and more since Raphael showed up. She wouldn't be surprised if that was where her future would eventually take her. She had never really considered Anchorage the final destination, more like a time-out of sorts, a chance to rest and revive and take inventory on what she wanted out of life.

What she really wanted was her identity back, but even if that was safe, she wasn't sure how it would work. Would she just go to Drisklay and demand her old birth certificate and photo ID? What kind of paperwork would be involved in something like that? Would it be as formal as when she joined the witness protection program and became Jo in the first place? What if Drisklay wouldn't cooperate? What if he was so offended she didn't stick it out in his program that he refused to give her the right papers back, refused to let her resume her old identity?

As long as she was living the life she wanted, did it really matter? Why couldn't she do what Raphael had done, go back home but keep living under her new name? Well, she would have time to figure all that out in Anchorage. Right now, she just needed to wait, needed to sit tight until

Kurtis got here.

Why did it have to be him? Maybe because he was the only person she knew very well in Glennallen, her only real friend. If he was even that anymore. There was so much she had to think about, so much to mull over.

A car pulled up behind her, and she turned the emergency lights off. That was one nice thing about this part of the country. Roadside assistance didn't come from insurance companies. It came from good Samaritans. She rolled down her window to wave the stranger past but stopped when she saw who it was.

"What are you doing here?" She stepped out of the car.

Raphael was smiling his mischievous grin. "What are *you* doing here?"

"Car trouble," she admitted.

"Can I help?"

"Not unless you've gotten handier with mechanics than you were four years ago."

They both chuckled. It felt good to laugh.

"But really," she said, "what are you doing here?"

He shrugged. "I figured I'd hit the road. There wasn't much to do in Glennallen but sit around and watch the maids clean the rooms. I left not long after you did. Good thing, too, I guess." He glanced at her car. "Do you know what's wrong?"

"I have someone coming over to take a look." She didn't want to admit the whole thing had been her fault. Why hadn't she let Kurtis take a look at the oil when he offered?

Raphael just nodded. She was glad he didn't pry.

"Want to hop in?" he asked. "We're going the same way."

She didn't turn him down automatically. She needed her car for the money, but then again, how could she sell a vehicle that didn't work? She still felt bad about pulling Kurtis away from his day off, too, and would be happy to tell him he didn't have to come out after all. More than anything, she would be glad for an excuse to not see him again, at least not right away.

"You know what," she said, surprising herself by how readily she made up her mind, "I think I'll do that, if you're sure it's ok with you."

He gave a half-grin. "Just don't spill your Coke on my seat like you did driving to that show in Baltimore. You remember that?"

She laughed and popped open her trunk. "That's not fair. I would have never spilled it if you hadn't sped around that corner."

"How was I supposed to know there were speed bumps all up and down that road?" he asked, grabbing her two bags.

"I don't know," she countered playfully. "Maybe you could have read one of the *signs* on the road, or is that too easy of an answer?" She took the Costco box and carried it to his backseat. "Is there room for all this?"

He took down his bike from its rack and hefted her things into his trunk. "Oh, yeah. You know me, still traveling light after all these years, except now I travel with the Holy Spirit."

Her smile dropped. Her neck and shoulders ached with heaviness.

"What's wrong?" he asked.

"Two minutes. We almost made it two whole minutes before you started talking church."

He hooked his bike back onto the rack. "Does it offend you?"

She shook her head. "No, it's not that. It's just, I feel like I hardly know you anymore. You sound like my dad when he preaches, and I just ..."

He tucked a strand of her hair behind her ear. "Hey, it's cool. I don't want to shove anything down your throat. But you know me. When I get a good thing going for me, I get excited."

"I know. And I didn't mean to sound critical, it's just ..." She didn't know how to finish.

"A lot has happened these past four years. It's gonna take us some time."

"Yeah."

They both got into their seats.

"So, what are you gonna do about your car?" he asked.

She wished she could just leave it there and let someone else deal with it. "I guess I'll see if my friend can tow it back to Glennallen for me."

"You can say his name, you know."

Lacy avoided his eyes.

"The trooper you were seeing. He has a name, I assume."

"Yeah." She bit her lip. "Hey, do you mind if I hop out and make a phone call real quick? I'll be right back."

"Sure." He still had that same jocular smile. He glanced around once. "Just don't take too long. These bugs are terrible."

CHAPTER 12

A minute later, Lacy was back in Raphael's car, on the highway speeding toward Anchorage. She hadn't been able to get hold of Kurtis, but she left a message to tell him she had a ride and to ask him if he'd mind towing the car to Glennallen until she figured out what to do with it. She offered to pay him for his time once she got settled in, even though she knew he'd never take her money. She still wasn't sure she had made the right decision, but if the car was busted, it could be days or weeks before she got out of Glennallen. By then, she might lose her fortitude. She had to do this now. It was the only way.

She tried not to think about Kurtis. She should have never asked him for help with the car in the first place. Oh well, it was too late now. He was probably already on the road, already in a no-coverage zone. Should she have left him a note on her dashboard to explain what was happening?

The longer they drove, the more she realized she wouldn't be coming back to Glennallen. She was tired of the daycare, sick of the bratty attitudes, the whiny voices, the kids complaining when they had no idea how good their lives really were. She was tired of everything, really, tired of the long winters, the bug-infested summers. There was no fall to speak of here, and spring just meant everything was gray and mushy while the piles of snow melted.

"You tired?" Raphael asked, stealing a quick glance at her.

"Yeah." She was surprised again at how uncomfortable it was with him. Ironic, really, that she had dreamed for so long of meeting him again, and now that they were in the same car, she could hardly put two words together.

Raphael put on his sunglasses. "I've got some snacks in the back. You hungry?"

"No. Thanks."

"So, you got everything you'll need? Passport, all that stuff from witness protection?"

She nodded, tired of the awkward chitchat, and stared at the scenery. Even in summer, the evergreens along this stretch the highway looked dried out and dead, more brown on top than green. Why did everyone always talk about how beautiful Alaska was? Was there anything she would miss about life out here?

There was Kurtis, of course, but he had never really known her. Sure, he put enough details together to figure out her true identity, but that didn't mean he knew her. He didn't know her favorite Boston restaurants, the kind of paintings she was drawn to, which conductors of which East Coast symphonies she liked best. He didn't know she was on first-name basis with a handful of art critics, or that she had once studied theater under a Tony Award nominee.

She thought she would be relieved to leave Glennallen. Where was the sense of freedom she had expected?

Change is always hard, she reminded herself, but at least this was one change she could control, not like her placement in Glennallen four years ago. So why did she feel like a little girl again getting driven from one foster home to another?

"I hope your car's all right." Raphael and she had never struggled in the past to find things to talk about. What was the problem?

He took a deep breath as if he was about to speak but remained silent. She grabbed her purse and fumbled through the contents, unsure what in particular she was searching for.

"What do you need?" he asked.

"Just looking for my Dramamine."

He smiled. "You and your motion sickness. I guess some things don't change, do they?"

"Not on these windy roads," she murmured, and remembered she had used the last pill on her most recent trip to town with Kurtis.

Raphael ducked down and craned his neck. "Whoa, look at that! Is that a bald eagle?" He pointed at a shadow out his window.

Lacy couldn't remember how many eagles she had spotted before she stopped seeing them as beautiful, majestic creatures and started viewing them as the disgusting rot-eaters they really were.

"Careful." She resisted the urge to reach over and steer for him.

"I'm paying attention." He put both hands back on the wheel.

"Sorry. It's just this part of the highway makes me nervous." They were speeding along the edge of a mountain, a single lane away from a five-hundred-foot cliff.

"I'll be careful," Raphael promised.

"You might want to slow down a little." She eyed his speedometer. He wasn't used to this kind of driving. The East Coast didn't have mountain stretches like this. Not with such terrifying drop-offs.

They also believed in something called guard rails.

"As you wish." The familiar hint of mischief was back in his voice, and Lacy realized he hadn't spoken about his new zeal for the Bible or Christianity since they got on the road. Had she offended him in Mendeltna?

"So," he went on, "have you thought about calling Carl and Sandy? I know they'd love to hear from you."

There was so much she wanted to tell him, about her conversation with Drisklay, about how Kurtis had gotten in touch with her foster parents. "That would be nice," was all she replied. She stared out the window and wondered for the second time if she should ask him to turn around. How rude could she be, expecting Kurtis to tow her car all the way to Glennallen for her when she doubted she'd ever return? She had just dumped it in his lap on his day off, expecting him to drag Madeline out of the bath, get her dressed, drive twenty minutes, hook his truck up ... Could she get any more selfish?

She pulled out her phone. "Hey, would it be weird for you if I called just to check in about the car? I feel pretty bad just dropping it on him like that."

"Of course not."

Lacy turned on her phone and then flipped it back off. Stupid cell phone reception.

"Not there?" Raphael asked.

"Bad coverage." Stupid state.

"Want to turn around? Meet him back there?"

The last thing Lacy needed was to be around both Raphael and Kurtis at once. Her life was confusing enough already. She wasn't technically dating either of them, but on the other hand, she hadn't broken up with them either. Of course, you can't break up with somebody who's been murdered. She'd been right about the detectives faking Raphael's death. A trick from the folks at witness protection so everyone would think he was murdered until he appeared at the trial. She had waited. Hoped ...

"Why weren't you there?" she asked quietly.

"What?"

"At the trial," she explained. "I kept expecting them to call you to testify. I kept hoping you'd show up. But you never did."

"That's a good question." His voice was strained. A little more uncertain. Not like Raphael at all. He glanced over at her and sighed. "Listen, I need to make a confession. You're not gonna like it."

CHAPTER 13

"About that trial ..." Raphael's fingers tensed on the steering wheel. He scratched the back of his neck. "This isn't easy to talk about, you know. But I guess you deserve an explanation. So, the short version ... wait, is that my phone beeping or yours?"

Lacy opened her purse. She had missed two calls from Kurtis and one from a blocked number. "Hold on," she said, unsure if she was ready for whatever Raphael was going to say. "Let me see if I can get any coverage here."

She called Kurtis back, but it went right to his voicemail. Fine with her. She was already experiencing about as much awkwardness as one person could handle. "What were you saying?"

Raphael adjusted his sunglasses. "So anyway, about the trial. I think for everything to make sense, we need to rewind. Go all the way back to the accident."

Lacy's whole body tensed. She didn't realize she was gripping her seatbelt until her fingers started to hurt.

"There's a lot about that night you don't know. And it's been eating me up since it happened. And, well, it's not gonna be easy for you to hear."

The car was rushing. Too fast. She checked the speedometer. Only fifty? It felt like twice that.

"So those men on the dock, everything that happened ..." He swallowed once and reached for her hand which fell limp in his. "It wasn't an accident. Not really. And I've never forgiven myself for it because it was my fault. In a way."

She wanted him to turn around. Wanted to go home.

"I'd gotten myself into a mess." The words tumbled out of his mouth. She couldn't stop them. Like a deadly avalanche. "You know me. You know how I was back then. I wasn't the smartest kid, made some dumb choices, but I never got into the really bad stuff."

Lacy felt just like she did on rollercoasters. Everything whizzed by, gaining momentum. There was no way to get off once you were strapped in. The exit came after the ride was over, after your stomach was lodged up in the top of your chest and your throat was sore from screaming and your fingers were numb from gripping your restraint. The only difference was this particular ride wasn't fun or exciting or adventurous. And there was no way to gauge how long it would last before it ended.

"I had some guys mad at me. I was out of my league. Way out of my league. You know I wasn't the type to go digging for trouble. I just wanted to live simply. Me, you, my art. I would have been happy with just that. I should have been happy with that. But, well, things happened. I made some bad choices, got mixed up with the wrong people."

Lacy didn't care. She wanted him to stop talking. Erase time. Make it so the past four years never happened. People always talked about how struggles make you wiser. More mature. Not the accident. It had robbed her. Stolen her identity, torn her from her boyfriend, and botched her entire future.

Her entire future.

Where would she be now if it hadn't been for that night in the North End? She'd have finished her bachelor's degree. She and Raphael would have gotten married, wouldn't they? Of course, they would. How many art galas had she missed in the past four years? How many concerts? How many Broadway shows? Would she have continued to pursue her acting career? Would anything have come of it?

She'd never know. The accident stripped all that away from her. She had blamed God. Blamed the car. Blamed Drisklay. Blamed the criminals who waltzed into her field of vision to dump a living person into the wharf. In all this time, she had always thought of Raphael as a victim as well.

Had she been mistaken?

"I was going to propose to you that night."

It was the last thing she wanted to hear. She gripped the handle of the car door, her mind begging for an escape.

"I had the ring in my coat pocket and everything," he continued. "But I was in this mess I told you about. I had to get away. Lie low for a while. I was gonna tell you all this that night at the pier. I swear ..." His voice caught, and Lacy wanted to clear her throat on his behalf. "I spent so many nights awake, wondering what to do. I couldn't sleep. Couldn't eat. Couldn't paint. I knew I had to skip town. I couldn't stand the thought of leaving you, but how could I ask you to go with me? Leave your foster family, your classes, everything you'd known."

Her throat muscles clenched. She would have given up all her plans to be with him, would have given them up in an instant. Instead, every single dream was shattered like broken glass, and she went four years without even knowing if he was alive.

"I took you to the pier to tell you everything. Come clean. Geeze, Lace, you have no idea how messed up I was. I had this show I was supposed to be getting ready for, the one at the Menagerie ..."

"I remember," she whispered as flooding memories came crashing over her. Suffocating her.

"And I hadn't been able to paint in two weeks. I was so torn. Finally, I realized all I could do was come clean. Tell you everything. And then, if you'd still have me, I was gonna ask you to leave with me. I had a plan. There was a guy. He was gonna meet me at the pier. He was gonna help us get ..."

"Is that who they killed?" she whispered.

Raphael's throat worked loudly. "I never meant to get you involved in any of this." He squeaked out the last words. "I'm so sorry."

He sniffed. She couldn't look at him. Couldn't handle the torrent of emotions that would drown her if she saw his tears.

"You hate me, don't you?" he asked.

She took in a choppy breath. "I don't know what you did to make those guys so mad at you." She thought back over her relationship with Raphael. The romance. Passion. Adventures. Friendship. "All I know is I was in love with you. I would have gone with you anywhere." She swallowed away a painful lump.

"Anywhere," she repeated, the word searing hot in her throat.

CHAPTER 14

Lacy's phone rang, freeing her from the weight of Raphael's confession. She hesitated and then held up her finger to Raphael before answering. "Hello?"

"Jo? It's me. Where are you?"

Raphael shot her a nervous glance. Was he worried she would change her mind? Why shouldn't she after what he had just told her?

"We just passed Eureka. Did you find where I left the car?"

"Yeah, and ..."

She strained her ears. "You're breaking up. Can you say that again?"

More static.

"Hello?" She waited another few seconds and then hung up. Stupid cell reception.

"Everything ok?" Raphael asked.

"Yeah, just a bad signal." She was so sick of this state, so sick of its backwards technology, its ridiculous bugs. A mosquito the size of a New England housefly landed on her. She slapped it, splattering blood all over herself. "Gross." She flipped open the glove compartment. "Do you have any napkins or anything?"

The compartment was empty except for a piece of paper from a car rental place with a strange name filled out at the top.

Maxwell Turner? It didn't sound like Raphael at all. Another imperfect fit. Just like Jo.

She glanced at the form again and saw yesterday's date stamped in the top corner.

Yesterday's? Didn't he say he'd been in Alaska for weeks?

"No, I don't have anything in there." Raphael reached to shut the glove compartment.

"Rats." She forced a laugh. "I hate it when I squash a bloody one."

Snippets from her conversation with Drisklay ran through her mind. *Cover's blown. Someone getting a little too nosy* ... Raphael himself had just admitted to having connections with the murderers on the pier.

"I'm not feeling good." She tried to make her voice sound natural.

"Need to roll your window down?"

"No, I really think I'm about to be sick. Can you pull over?"

"Sure. Let me just get us to a shoulder."

She grabbed the door handle. "No, pull over now. I'm gonna throw up." At the rate things were going, she wouldn't need to pretend.

"Ok." He eased to the side of the road. Think. She had to think.

Her cover was blown. Drisklay had flown out here to tell her that. She thought it was Kurtis putting pieces together, calling her foster parents. But what if it was something else? What if she was wrong?

Why would Raphael make up a story about being in Alaska for weeks if he just got here yesterday? He had already acknowledged his connection to the North End criminals. Could he be part of ...

No, this was Raphael. They had spent two and a half years almost inseparable before the accident. They knew everything about each other.

Everything.

He had found her so easily at the Brain Freeze. Like he had known right where to look ...

She was outside of the car, bent over. They couldn't stay here for long. The road wound so much that cars behind them wouldn't see them in time to stop. But what could she do? Flag down the next motorist? Take her chances and try to run?

A green car whizzed around a bend, speeding toward them from the opposite side of the road. It slowed down for a second as if the driver knew Lacy was in trouble.

"Oh, no."

Something about Raphael's tone sent goose bumps springing up on Lacy's neck.

"Get in the car." He reached across and tugged the back of her blouse. "Get in now." He checked his side mirror nervously. "Buckle up." He pulled her into the car and slammed on the gas before she could even shut the door.

"What are you doing?"

"We've got to go. Now." His voice was scared. Tense.

That's when she realized what a horrible mistake she had made. "I changed my mind," she blurted. "I want to go back."

"What?"

"Please. My whole life has been in Glennallen. I'm not ready to give all that up yet."

He took in a deep breath. "I don't think now's the best time for ..."

"I was confused. Please. Just take me home." Her heart was racing. He was going to refuse. He wouldn't let her go. This had been ...

"Listen." His voice was strained. His knuckles were white against the steering wheel. "I need you to stay calm and do exactly what I say."

Her phone beeped, and she pulled it out of her purse, relieved to finally be in an area with reception. She had to tell Kurtis what was happening. She glanced down at the screen. He had left her over a dozen texts over the past twenty-five minutes.

Car's tampered with. Get back here.

Pick up your phone. Where are you?

Get him to turn around.

Sit tight. We're on our way.

CHAPTER 15

"Please take me back." She heard the anxious edge in her own voice. She had to tone it down. Calm her nerves.

She angled the screen so Raphael couldn't read the texts. Could she really have misjudged him so drastically? The more she fought against the inevitable conclusion, the more sense it all made. Why he missed the trial. Why he was able to find her so easily in Glennallen. Why Drisklay had come to warn her.

She took in shallow breaths, afraid Raphael could hear how nervous she was. Good thing she had taken so many acting classes. Good thing she had spent four whole years living as another human being. If anyone could keep up a charade to survive, she could. She looked around. Was there anything she could use as a weapon? What if he tried to throw her out the car? On one side of them jutting straight up was the mountain, cruel and unyielding. On the other side a two-hundred-yard drop. She glanced at him without turning her head. Couldn't arouse his suspicion.

Kurtis, where are you?

"It could have been perfect between us, Lace," Raphael mused. She wasn't sure if she was supposed to play along or not. "It's like some gut-wrenching tragedy, where life just gets in the way."

"Please, I want to go home." What did she have in her purse? A cell phone. A wallet with her fake ID. What could she do, shove it down his throat?

"You have no idea how much I loved you."

Either he was just a good an actor as she, or he was planning something desperate. Her lungs worked in fractions. Labored jerks. So much for that deep diaphragm breathing her acting teachers always advocated.

"I just want you to turn around." Maybe she was wrong. Maybe Drisklay's visit had hurled her over the edge. Made her paranoid. Tonight she and Raphael would sit across from each other at an Anchorage restaurant and laugh.

Please, God?

Facts didn't lie. Dates didn't lie. She had to refocus her energy. Stop trying to deny the truth and find a way to get herself out of this mess alive.

"Turn around." She spoke each word succinctly. Strongly.

He glanced in the rear-view mirror. "Why?"

"Take me home, or I swear I'm calling the cops."

"What's going on, Lace?" he asked. The way he spoke her name made her stomach churn.

She couldn't do this. Couldn't pretend anymore. Couldn't pretend she was calm and collected. Couldn't pretend she wasn't scared. So scared she was either going to pee or throw up. Maybe both.

"The date's wrong." The accusation tumbled out of her mouth. "The one on your car rental papers. It says you got here yesterday."

Raphael let out his breath in a loud *huff*. "That's because I got tired and decided to drive to Anchorage instead of riding my bike back like I first planned. Geeze, Lace, is this an interrogation?"

She didn't speak.

He let out a sigh. "After everything we've been through together, the least you could do is trust me."

Could she?

Shame heated her cheeks. She stared at her lap.

He cleared his throat. Threw his glance in the rear-view mirror once more. "It happens to me, too. All the time. Like I think I see someone following me. Or I hear someone trying to break in at night." His chuckle was discordant. Unconvincing. He patted her knee. "This whole ordeal turned me into a nervous wreck." He let out his breath.

Her hand still clenched the door handle.

"If you want the whole truth, I'm not up here just to cross Alaska off my bucket list. I was running away."

Her whole body was tense. The road twisted ahead of them and disappeared around the mountain bend.

"I went to a public art show at the Commons last month and thought I saw someone there. One of the men I'd gotten involved with before the accident."

She shut her eyes. Could you disappear by sheer force of will?

"A few days later, I thought someone was following me. So I headed out here until I could figure out what to do."

She didn't know if she believed him or not. All she knew was she wanted to go home.

"That green Dodge that we passed earlier," he went on. "I didn't get a good look, but for a second I thought it was the same guy." He let out a sad-sounding chuckle. "I told you, this whole way of living will make anybody paranoid."

A horn blared behind them. Lacy's eyes shot to her side mirror. It was the same Dodge they had seen. It must have turned around, because now it was directly behind them. Speeding straight toward them.

Raphael swerved into the left lane. They were so close to the drop-off Lacy could feel the front wheel tilt before the car corrected itself.

The Dodge whizzed by and slammed on its brakes in the middle of the road. Raphael tried to pass on the right, but there wasn't enough room to clear the mountain. The passenger mirror flew off. The whole side of the car scraped against the rocks, the screeching sound grating in her ears even louder than her scream.

The Dodge pressed against them. Was it trying to squeeze them into the mountainside? Raphael slammed on his brakes. Lacy's body flew forward. The seatbelt jolted against her collarbone. "Who is that?" she demanded.

"It must be someone who knows about us."

"Us?"

"I'm sorry, Lace. I never wanted you to get caught up in any of this."

The Dodge had switched to reverse and was about to ram its bumper into them. "Move!" Lacy reached for the steering wheel, but Raphael had already jerked it to the side. The Dodge plowed into the back seat instead of straight on, but the momentum was almost enough to push them off the road. Lacy's head was light, a helium balloon ready to float off into the clouds.

The Dodge pulled ahead.

"Hold on," Raphael told her. "He's coming at us again." The green car jerked to a stop, shooting a small pebble onto the windshield of the rental, creating a small chink in the glass. Lacy winced. Raphael had time to angle the car and pull up a few feet before the Dodge rammed them again in reverse.

"Are you ok?" Lacy could only take in the choppiest of breaths.

"I'm gonna turn us around." Raphael maneuvered the car on the narrow pass while the Dodge pulled ahead. Lacy gripped the door handle, holding her breath and praying he wouldn't misjudge and send them flying off the road. As soon as Raphael straightened his car, the Dodge flipped itself around in a three-point turn. The sound of her own pulse flooded Lacy's ears.

"Careful," she begged, her heart fluttering all the way up by her throat.

Raphael sped ahead. They were back on their way to Glennallen, but the Dodge was right behind them. And now they were driving on the other side of the road, the cliff's edge about a foot and a half away from Lacy's shoulder. She sucked in her breath, dizzy with fear, terrified that an extra ounce of weight might tilt the car off balance and send them careening to their deaths.

"I'm sorry," Raphael panted.

She didn't care. It didn't matter what he was apologizing for. It didn't matter what alias he used, or whether he rented his car yesterday or three weeks ago. All that mattered was they were speeding back in the direction of home. Toward Kurtis. Toward safety.

Her phone beeped. New voicemail. Did that mean there was coverage here? She pulled it out and dialed 911.

"Hold on!" Raphael shot his arm out across her chest right as the Dodge hit them from behind. Their car lurched forward to the sound of metal crumpling. Lacy's head whipped forward and then snapped back with so much force she couldn't see anything but black for a second. She wanted to ask Raphael what was happening, but she didn't have the breath to make herself heard.

"Can't this thing go any faster?" Raphael grumbled.

Her phone beeped again and flashed its ominous message. *Call failed.* Why had she ever moved to Alaska? She hated living here. She certainly didn't want to die here.

Raphael maneuvered around a hairpin curve without slowing down. She sucked in her breath, certain they were about to free-fall off the cliff. The speedometer raced past seventy. She clutched the door handle. *Let me out*, she wanted to beg, but she couldn't find her voice.

The car made it around the bend, and Lacy had a clear view of a straight stretch of road ahead with a red truck coming their way. "Is that ..." she started to ask but stopped, afraid to hold onto hope until she knew for sure. She waited for Raphael to get closer, begging God for deliverance. The Dodge had slowed down around the curve but was gaining momentum behind them.

The truck sped toward them. "That's Kurtis!" Lacy shouted. She recognized Drisklay in the passenger seat but didn't even wonder what he was doing there. It didn't matter. Kurtis was here. He would find a way to help. He was a trooper. He was trained. He'd know what to do.

Everything was going to be just ... Hope froze in Lacy's veins. What if Kurtis had Madeline in the truck with him? What if something happened to her?

Kurtis slowed down to let Raphael pass and gave what Lacy thought was a brief nod. She turned around to watch what would happen next. Kurtis's truck was in the middle of the road now. Was he trying to keep the Dodge from passing? What if he got hit? She scrunched down in her seat, trying to brace for the sound of the two vehicles crashing, praying Madeline was somewhere far away from all this.

The Dodge swerved, barely squeezing between Kurtis's truck and the rocky mountainside.

"Let me out. Let me get in with Kurtis."

"I can't do that," Raphael answered in a monotone.

No amount of Dramamine would cure this kind of sickness. Kurtis had turned his truck around and was coming up behind them.

"Let me out," she repeated.

"You have to trust me."

She stared over her shoulder. Was it possible the Dodge was falling back? Kurtis's truck came roaring up around the bend behind them. She squinted to avoid seeing the crash that never came.

"I know I've done some horrible things in my life," Raphael said. "But I'm telling the truth when I say I never wanted you to get messed up in all this. Just like I'm telling the truth when I say I've always ..."

He sped around another curve, and Lacy gripped her seatbelt as the car wavered, struggling to keep its center of balance. She let out her breath when it straightened out, relieved for a short second.

"Look out!" Her warning was accompanied by a blaring horn from an RV camper directly in front of them. Raphael had swerved into the oncoming lane. There was no way they could avoid it. Lacy shot out her hands to brace for the impact.

But instead of crashing, they gained speed. She peeked at Raphael, who was frantically trying to gain control of the steering wheel. A shadow whizzed past her window. Tree branches scraped at the sides of the car.

They were rushing down the cliff.

She was deafened by the sound of her own scream. She grabbed the bottom of her seat and shut her eyes. Faster. A bump, and they were airborne. They landed again, and the bottom of the car scraped the rocky edge, but they hadn't reached the valley yet. They weren't slowing down, either. She opened her eyes. The view from the window turned and spiraled. They were spinning. She stopped screaming long enough to catch her breath and then began again. She had no idea how much longer they'd plunge until they hit the bottom, but she doubted she'd still be alive when they did.

CHAPTER 16

"It's ok. You're going to be just fine." She heard the voice but couldn't see anything. She tried to open her eyes. Only blackness. She blinked again. Nothing.

"I'm here." A hand reaching out to her. She was pinned down, trapped. The voice was soothing. "Can you move?"

I think I'm dead. She said the words but couldn't hear them.

"Drisklay's calling the ambulance. They'll get you to Anchorage. You're going to make it. Just hang in there."

She recognized that voice.

"Kurtis." This time her mouth managed to form the sounds.

"It's me." He squeezed her hand. "Save your energy. I'm right here. You're safe. I'm not leaving you."

She blinked again. Bright light from above pierced through the veil of darkness. She saw shadows but not distinct forms. Her head felt disconnected from the rest of her body.

"Where's the munchkin?" Her mouth was so dry she couldn't form any more words.

"Shh." He patted her hand. Brushed some of her hair out of her eyes. "I dropped her off with another trooper's family. You remember Taylor, right? Don't talk. Just hang tight."

I'm gonna take a nap now. She only had enough energy to form the thought before she blacked out.

***

A horrific, grating noise, louder than any chainsaw.

Men yelling over the racket.

A presence by her side. Constant reassurance.

"She's going to be ok, isn't she?" Pleading in his voice.

She strained to hear the answer before everything fell once more to inky, black silence.

***

"You are one lucky girl."

Her eyes were so dry it took several attempts to blink them open. Drisklay sat next to her, sipping from a Styrofoam coffee cup.

She tried to speak, but her tongue was like dry cotton. She was on a bed. White linens. Lights all around. Too bright.

"You're in Anchorage. Sacred Heart Hospital." Drisklay cleared his throat.

She tried turning her head. Couldn't understand why she felt so confined.

"They got you on some pretty strong pain meds," he explained. "You'll be disoriented for a while, but at least you shouldn't hurt."

She tried to wiggle her fingers. Toes. Anything.

"Don't worry. Doctors expect a full recovery." He stood. "Your friend is a lot worse off. Frankly, I didn't expect either of you to survive that kind of crash." He cleared his throat. "Well, it's time for me to sleep off this coffee. I'll check on you again in the morning."

A nurse bustled in and played with the IV lines hooked up to Lacy's arm. Heaviness surrounded her like fog. She shut her eyes and drifted off once more.

***

"So she's ... You say she's going to be ok, though, right?"

Lacy kept her eyes closed. Let the words float around her like a summer breeze.

"Yeah. Once she heals up from the surgery, she should be as good as new."

"How long will that take?"

"Hard to say. As long as she comes off the anesthesia without any problems, she'll move out of intensive care tonight."

"And then where will she go?"

"To the regular floor. Get her strength back. Are you her husband?"

"No, just a friend."

"Well, when she wakes up, I'll tell her you stopped by."

***

Dreams. So many dreams. Kurtis smiling over her, about to nuzzle his nose against hers when his face morphs into Raphael's.

Screaming. Pummeling down in the darkness. Branches scratching at her face. Clawing at her skin. Trying to catch her.

Raphael's unconscious body beside her, staring blankly ahead.

***

The nurse poked her head through Lacy's door. "Someone's here to see you. Are you up for a visitor?"

Lacy winced as she raised the back of her bed to sit up a little. She wiped sweat off her brow. She had been having a bad dream, a nightmare of some sort. She couldn't remember the details.

"Yeah, I'm awake." Her voice sounded groggy. This was her third day post-surgery. Or was it her fourth? She had a hard time keeping track of time. She knew Kurtis wasn't coming back until the weekend, though, and Drisklay had flown home to the East Coast. Was it Raphael, then? Nobody had told her anything about him, where he was, how he was recovering.

If he was recovering.

"Oh, my little baby, it's been so long since I've seen you."

Lacy bit her lip as Sandy bustled into the room, rushed to her bedside, and clasped her hand. "Oh, my little sweetheart, so much has happened to you." And right then and there, before Lacy could ask a single question, her foster mom started to pray.

"Oh, precious heavenly Father, I love you so much. I love you for saving my sweet Lacy's life. I love you for protecting her from the men who were trying to hurt her. I love you so much, Lord, and I pray you would fill my sweet little girl with so much joy and peace and healing that she would be wrapped up in your arms from this moment on until she leaves this hospital, even stronger than she was before."

Sandy went on longer, but Lacy was too disoriented to pay much attention.

"How did you know I was here?" she asked when Sandy was done.

"Your friend called. The nice policemen. Kurtis, I think his name was. He called me and Carl, filled us in on what happened. I'm sorry I wasn't here sooner, sweetie. It took us a couple days to get everything figured out, you know, get the tickets, make all the arrangements." She shook her head and clucked her tongue. "Just look at you. I hope you'll forgive me. I wanted to be here sooner, really I did."

Lacy was about to respond, but Sandy was still talking. "It's just eating your father up inside that he couldn't come, too, so he made me promise to give him updates night and day on how you're improving. You look so beautiful, sweetie. All grown up. You've let your hair grow out. It's so much nicer that way."

Lacy wanted to laugh, which was just as painful for her incision site as crying. "I can't believe you're here," was all she could say.

"And I'll be here as long as you need, sweetie. Well, at least a week, and after that we'll just have to see how things are going, because you know Carl. He's just a mess when there's nobody there to cook and clean and make sure he gets on a matching tie before he preaches. But you know I'm gonna be here for you, precious. That's why I came as fast as I could."

She took Lacy's hand and kissed it. "I'm just so happy. It's such a relief to see you. It could have been a lot worse. Raphael, he's not doing well from what I can gather. I asked them, you know, while they were showing me to your room, but of course it's hard to get any real information. But that could have been you, darling. Your policeman friend said they caught the man, the one chasing you. He won't be troubling you anymore. Now, I don't think Drisklay would agree to it, but you know you can always come home and live with us if you ever need." A spry smile stretched across her face. "But from the sound of it, I wonder if that policeman friend of yours has other plans. Maybe?"

"He's a trooper," Lacy corrected.

Sandy took a deep breath. "Well, now, you just sit tight and get your rest, and I'm going to find me a bathroom, because I got off the plane and took a cab right here I was so anxious to see you. But now that I know you're ok, I've really got some business to tend to. I won't be long, darling. Don't worry about a thing."

She swept out of the room, but even after she left, a warm, loving presence remained wrapped around Lacy's body, filling her with a peace she hadn't experienced in four lonely years.

CHAPTER 17

The nurse handed Lacy a slip of paper. "Here's the prescription for your pain meds. You can stop by any pharmacy and get them filled."

"I'll take care of that for you, hon." Sandy reached out and took the form. "She probably shouldn't take them on an empty stomach, either. Right?"

The nurse shrugged. "I guess not."

Lacy was ready to go outside, to enjoy the fresh air once more.

"Doctor Jacobson wants you to check up with your general provider in a week. Do you need us to help make you an appointment?"

"Do you have a doctor in Anchorage, sweetie?" Sandy asked, as if Lacy needed a translator. She lowered her voice. "Do you have insurance? Because Carl and I can help with the medical bills, you know."

"It's all right," Lacy insisted. Money had been tight working at the daycare, but at least her pitiful pay qualified her for state health insurance, so her entire hospitalization would be covered. That was one perk of getting transplanted into an oil-rich state.

The nurse made a little mark on her clipboard. "Well, if you don't have any other questions for me, you're free to head home."

Lacy forced a smile, even though the word *home* stabbed at her heart like a giant icicle. "Thank you."

"Oh, one more thing," Sandy inserted. "Is she supposed to be taking baths or showers or just leaving the area dry or what?"

"I'd stick with sponge baths until you see your doctor in a week," the nurse replied.

Lacy felt like apologizing for her mom. "Thank you," she repeated, hoping Sandy didn't have any other questions.

The nurse nodded. "Just let the charge nurse at the front desk know when you leave."

"Are you sure she should walk? Don't you have a wheelchair she can use or something?"

The nurse raised an eyebrow. "Do you want a wheelchair?"

"I'm all right," Lacy answered.

"Are you sure?" Sandy pressed. "You just had a major surgery, and, well, I hate to say it, but you look like you've been in a fight or something. Wait, Raphael never hit you, did he? I didn't want to say it when you two were so close, but I always had a bad feeling about him."

Lacy shook her head. She had been so happy to see Sandy she forgot how smothered her foster mom could make her feel.

Sandy held onto her arm while they made their way to the exit. "Carl said it would be all right for me to rent a car for the day while we settle in. I've checked us into a little missionary house that belongs to an old seminary friend of his. They're not charging us, which is awful sweet of them."

Once outside, Sandy handed her ticket to the parking valet. "Could you be careful, sir?" she asked. "It's a rental."

They sat down on a bench to wait. Lacy's mind was still reeling, replaying all the details of the past few days so her doped-up mind wouldn't mix them up. The man in the Dodge, the one who followed Raphael to Alaska, was behind bars. By all appearances, he was the last link to the murder on the North End pier. It should be good news. Great news. Except it was clouded by the fact that Raphael was still in critical condition. Nobody could guess if he'd pull through. Lacy had wanted to see him once she was well enough to walk, but the nurses said he was refusing visitors. Was that it, then? Was that how their whole tragic story was going to end?

The valet arrived with the rental, and Sandy insisted on holding Lacy's arm to the car and buckling her once she got in. "The mission house should only be ten minutes away. If I don't lose our way before then," she added with a grin.

Lacy adjusted the seat belt strap so it wasn't pressed against her incision site. Sandy got lost within two turns of the hospital but filled the extra driving time prattling on about grandchildren and foster kids Lacy hadn't thought of in years, some she had never met. Her mind zoomed in and out of the conversation, either from the exhaustion or the pain meds or a combination of both.

Half an hour after they left the hospital, Sandy's phone rang. "I'm a block or two away," she answered, "if I got my directions right. Sorry for making you wait ... Yup, I'll see you soon." She hung up the phone and turned down a cul-de-sac in a small neighborhood full of duplex-style houses.

"Who was that?" Lacy asked and then saw her old car parked in one of the driveways. She also recognized the man getting out of the front seat.

"Did I forget to mention it?" Sandy replied with a massive grin. "We're having company."

CHAPTER 18

Lacy couldn't read Kurtis's expression when he opened the door to help her out of Sandy's rental.

"You ok?" he asked quietly.

She was still trying absorb the fact that these two people from her very distinct and very disconnected lives were both staring at her, studying her reaction.

"How do you feel?"

She didn't know how to answer him. Part of her wanted to feign illness and hide in bed for the rest of the day.

Kurtis took one arm and Sandy another, and they led her up the porch steps to the mission home. Sandy reached into a hanging basket and grabbed a key. Once inside, she put down her bag and yawned. "You two get comfortable. I've got to rest for a minute."

Kurtis shut the front door. "Should we head to the couch?"

Lacy felt even more awkward than she had the first time Madeline caught them snuggling together at Kurtis's house. "Where's the munchkin?" she asked.

"She's at the daycare now. Kim will take her back to her place at the end of the day. I'm not staying long. I just came to drop off your car." He cleared his throat. "And see how you're doing, of course."

"So Sandy called you?"

"I called her, actually. I figured you'd want her to know about the accident. And then she just stayed in touch whether I wanted her to or not." He let out a little laugh.

"I hope she didn't bug you too much or anything."

"No." His good-humored smile was back. She had missed that. Kurtis adjusted in the couch so his leg was close to hers without actually touching it. "She said you were leaving the hospital, and I had the day off, and well, I figured you'd want your car back."

"You didn't have to, you know." Lacy tried to read any hidden meaning behind this visit. He could have held onto the car. Could have kept it in Glennallen so she'd have a reason to go back once she recovered.

"No problem. My buddy Taylor is heading back from town today, so it worked out perfect. I'll just catch a ride home with him. Your car's fine, by the way. Whoever was after you, looks like he unhooked the alternator, that's all. Sucked your battery dry, but we got it up and going just fine. Made it all the way to town today with no problems." He flashed a grin. "And I changed your oil, too."

"Thank you for everything." She had a hard time meeting his eyes.

"Don't mention it."

She didn't know what else to say. Soon, they would have to talk. A lot. About the past. About Raphael. And then about the future.

It was a conversation she dreaded more than just about anything.

"Listen," she said, "I'm really sorry about ..."

"Shh." He put his arm around the back of the couch, careful not to touch her. "You don't need to worry about that right now."

"But if I hadn't ..."

"Let's just save all that for later, ok?" There was that compassionate look in his eyes again. How could she have taken him for granted for so long?

Something in Kurtis's pocket beeped, and he took out his phone.

"It's Taylor," he said. "He's outside waiting for me."

"That was fast."

The same warm expression. The same soft glance.

She realized then she didn't want him to go. "When are you coming back to town?"

The hint of a smile. "I have next Thursday off."

"Good," Sandy shouted from down the hall. "She'll need a ride to the doctor's office. Want to volunteer?"

Lacy looked for a place to hide her face, but Kurtis only chuckled. "I can take you to your appointment." He leveled his eyes. "If that's all right with you."

She didn't know what to say. Her life, her relationships were all in limbo while she waited to hear about Raphael. Was he recovering? Would he even survive? He wasn't answering his phone calls or text messages, and the doctors refused give her any real information.

Stupid patient privacy laws.

Now, here was Kurtis, the same sweet, steadfast Kurtis who had been so good to her. Watching her attentively. Waiting for her response.

"That would be fine," she answered.

He let out a sigh. Was there more to be said?

Not here. Not now.

But when?

He walked to the door. "Coffee afterwards?" he asked. Gentle. Hopeful.

"Good idea," Sandy called out.

Lacy let out a choppy breath. "Maybe if I'm feeling well enough by then." She couldn't take her eyes off Kurtis. What had happened to them?

"I guess I'll see you Thursday then." He turned the knob and was gone.

CHAPTER 19

"So, you heard from that nice policeman lately?" Sandy asked as she folded laundry at the Anchorage mission house.

"He's a trooper." Lacy had forgotten how many times she'd corrected her mother in the past few days.

"I still don't see what the difference is." Sandy put one of the pans away. "Well, have you heard from this *trooper* friend of yours lately?"

Lacy rolled her eyes. She was so glad to see Sandy, to be in the same house, to talk about the past without having to remember all the lies of her cover story. But still, there was only so much smothering a New England girl could take.

Sandy folded one of her floral skirts. "Well, if you don't want me prying around in your love life, I can respect that."

"It's not that." She didn't want to shut Sandy out. God knew she needed someone she could turn to for advice right about now.

Sandy put down the blouse she'd been folding and sat down on the couch. "Then what is it, sweetheart?"

Lacy let out her breath. She knew her mom liked Kurtis. Of course she would. Kurtis was polite, attentive, respectful. He had been thoughtful enough to call Sandy to let her know about the accident. But there were some things her foster mom didn't understand.

"I don't know." Lacy stared over the top of Sandy's shoulder to avoid making eye contact. "There's so much going on right now."

Sandy grinned. "Like the fact that an Alaska state *trooper* bought you an engagement ring? Remind me again, was that before or after he saved your life in the car crash?"

"He's not the one making things confusing. It's ..." She let her voice trail off.

"It's Raphael," Sandy finished for her.

Lacy studied her fingernail and nodded.

"You still have feelings for him?"

Lacy's spine tingled at the hint of incredulity she detected in Sandy's tone. Why shouldn't she still have feelings for him? He was her first love.

The first man she ever imagined spending the rest of her life with. The first man besides her foster dad she had ever trusted.

Sandy leaned forward on the couch. "You know I'm only looking out for you, honey, don't you?"

Lacy stared at the pile of clothes.

"Come on," Sandy pressed. "What's going on? You can talk to me. We could always talk things through."

But that was before, Lacy wanted to point out. Before Raphael made his boneheaded mistake and got them mixed up in some Mafia drama that stripped Lacy of her identity, her entire life. Four years lost. Completely wasted.

So why was she mad at Sandy and not at Raphael?

Lacy shook her head. "Everything is so confusing."

"That's perfectly understandable, dear. You've been through so much. And now there are two men in the picture, and you don't know what you're going to do, but any choice is bound to hurt at least one of them. Is that it?"

Lacy swallowed past the lump in her throat. "Yeah," she croaked.

Sandy nodded and tucked a strand of hair into her braid. "I understand entirely."

Lacy knew her mom was just being polite. What would Sandy know about it? What would she know about mourning a lost love for four years only to find he was really alive? What would she know about being close to a strong, protective man who'd never met the real you? When had Sandy ever been split, torn between two lives, two loves, two identities?

"You know I adore Carl," Sandy said. "He and I are every bit as much in love today as we were on our wedding day. Even more so, actually."

Lacy nodded. Living with Carl and Sandy was the first proof she'd had that happy marriages weren't simply lies Hollywood rom-coms tried to sell.

Sandy leaned back on the couch and crossed her arms, so Lacy knew this would be a long story.

"Before I met Carl, I was going steady with a young man from my father's church. He had just finished medical school and wanted me to move with him to Alabama. He was kind. Considerate. Polite. From a well-off family, nice folks in their Southern mansion, the package deal."

Sandy adjusted her French braid over her shoulder. "My parents adored him. Our families adored each other, really, which is part of the reason why both David and I felt so comfortable in our relationship. He was a few years older than me, but what did that matter? When he asked me to move to Alabama with him, my parents couldn't understand why I didn't start packing that same day. There was just this gut feeling, though, this premonition that if I moved with David away from home, away from both our families, we'd lose ninety percent of the things that made our relationship so perfect. Does that make sense?"

Lacy nodded.

"But my mom really wanted me to go, and I didn't want to be alone. So I transferred from UVA to Alabama to be with him while he was doing his residency. Do you have any idea how hard hospitals make those residents work?"

Lacy didn't want to break the flow of Sandy's story by answering.

"He was so busy, I'd sneak to the hospital once or twice a week, drop off a snack or little note or something, try to keep him well fed and encouraged. Other than that, we went a whole semester hardly seeing each other. It was a lonely time for me."

Lacy bit her lip. Unless Sandy went four years living the life of a perfect stranger, forbidden from speaking to anyone from her past, Lacy doubted she knew the real meaning of loneliness. But maybe that wasn't fair, either. It couldn't have been easy for her mom back then, away from home, away from her family ...

"And that's when I met Carl." A slow smile spread across Sandy's face, and Lacy instinctively grinned back.

"Carl was basically everything David wasn't. He came from a broken home, no family name, no money. And of course, you had the race issue." She chuckled to herself. "I tried for three months to work up the nerve to tell my parents."

"What did they say?" Lacy asked.

"Nothing. I always chickened out. I let little bits leak out. Told them how busy David was, how I wasn't so sure anymore I wanted to marry a doctor if he was going to be so tied up with his patients I'd only get five minutes of his time. And finally, my mom read enough between the lines to realize there was another man involved. I'm sure she was disappointed, but she was reasonable. She said she wanted me happy. Said if David wasn't the one for me, she just wanted to know I was loved and taken care of whoever I ended up with." Another laugh. "That's before she knew Carl was black."

"How'd they find out?" Lacy asked.

"Well, I had to make things official with David first. He knew we were drifting apart, but before I could really give my heart to Carl, I had to tell David everything."

"How'd he take it?"

Sandy let out a sigh. "That wasn't so easy. He understood the part about me breaking up with him because of his schedule. Honestly, I think he was relieved. He'd been feeling guilty that he couldn't give me more time and attention. I mean, he was the one who uprooted me from my home, dragged me to a brand-new state, and then basically forgot I existed. At least, it felt that way sometimes. So in that sense, he understood completely.

"What he couldn't figure out was why I would leave him for Carl. I mean, a black, penniless campus minister who had to go around to churches three months out of every year to beg for his salary — that was a real blow to David's ego, you know? How could I prefer someone like Carl when I could have been with him? But he got over it. Eventually."

"Do you ever talk to him anymore?" Lacy tried to keep her expression neutral, hoping Sandy couldn't perceive the reason for the question.

"Not really. He was an important part of my life for a season. We had fun memories, enjoyed each other's company. In fact, I'm still friends with his mother and sister. Send them Christmas cards every year. But David? Well, we both moved on. He found another girl, they got married, Carl and I eventually moved out of the South, and that was that."

Lacy chose her next words carefully, hoping she wasn't giving too much away. "But do you miss him? I mean, *did* you miss him? Or were things just so good with Carl that ..."

Sandy interrupted with an unlady-like snort. "So good with Carl?" She leaned forward. "Good? Try sitting in a diner for an hour while waitresses walk right by and ignore you and tell me how good that is. Or what about having half your extended family refuse to call you by your married name? You call that good? Or getting your windshield egged. And those are the things I can laugh about now. It got worse. Lots worse. Even the police didn't do much to help. They had this attitude like, *If you didn't want to get regular death threats, lady, why'd you go and marry a colored man?* There was one night I got a call from the hospital. Carl'd been beat up. Attacked by five or six men. Teens, actually. Boys. Do you know what it does to a man's ego to get beat up by thugs nearly half his age? The hospital wanted my permission to donate his organs if he didn't make it, that's how bad it was.

"So if you're asking me if I ever wondered what life would have been like if I'd chosen David instead of Carl, the answer's yes. A hundred times. And I'm not saying a hundred times total. It was more like a hundred times a day, at least during the ugliest spells. Did I wish things were easier like they would have been if I'd married David? Absolutely. But did I regret my decision to choose Carl?"

Lacy leaned forward to hear the answer.

Sandy leveled her eyes. "Never." The word echoed through Lacy's chest, its reverberations falling in sync with her pulse. "Never."

Sandy took up another blouse. Lacy was just going to hang it up in the closet, but Sandy still folded it with perfect creases that could put a clothing store worker to shame. "You thinking about Raphael?" she asked quietly.

Lacy nodded.

Sandy offered a reassuring smile. "Well, I know better than to give you my opinion. If I had listened to my mother, I would have never chosen Carl. Never had the amazing ride we've had. Never met you, our other kids ... That's what would have happened if I'd gone for the safe and easy route."

Safe? Why did it always come back to that? It seemed pretty clear that of the two men, Kurtis was the safe one. Is that what Sandy was talking about? Was she telling her not to settle for safe?

"So you're saying I should be with Raphael?" Lacy asked, wondering if that was even an option anymore. She still hadn't heard from him since the accident. Even once he recovered, Lacy didn't know if she'd learn to trust him again after everything they went through.

"I'm not saying anything of the sort. I don't need to tell you again how I get all nervous and unsettled every time I think of you two together. Now, maybe that's not fair of me. Maybe that's just because you were involved in that incident together so long ago."

Lacy fidgeted with a button on her blouse. She still hadn't told her mom about Raphael's role in the accident at the pier.

Sandy crossed her arms. "Now, I know my mom had her reservations about Carl. Said she didn't understand how I could throw away every chance God had given me for a good life to take such a crazy leap of faith as marry a colored man. I don't think it was flat-out racism on her part. Not totally. A lot of it was her just knowing how hard it would be if we did marry and wanting to protect me from that. I was naïve, see? I thought with all the progress we'd made in the civil rights movement that people would be more accepting. My mom knew better than that and was trying her hardest to look out for me." Sandy adjusted the rose-patterned skirt she was wearing. "Just like I'm trying to do with you. But whatever you choose, if you marry the policeman or give Raphael a chance once he's pulled through his injuries or turn them both down and go have wild adventures somewhere else, I'm giving you my full support. That's something my mom never said to me, and I'm not about to repeat that same mistake."

Lacy offered a weak smile. "Thanks." She was so tired. The pain pills still made her groggy, but she could hardly sleep two or three hours at night before waking up in a clammy, itchy sweat. Maybe it was a side-effect of the medicine. Or maybe it was just her body's way of reacting to her trauma. Either way, she knew she couldn't hold her eyelids open for much longer before she had to lie down for a nap.

Sandy stood and gave Lacy a kiss on the forehead. "You just think about what I said, all right? And don't forget to pray. God will always answer his children when they ask him for wisdom." Sandy paused. "Is that your phone beeping, dear? Do you want me to bring it to you?"

She handed Lacy her cell.

"What is it, sweetheart?" she asked. "Is something wrong?"

Lacy stared at the screen, hardly trusting her eyes. "It's Raphael. He wants me to come see him at the hospital."

CHAPTER 20

Lacy couldn't remember feeling so nervous before. Not during any of her theater auditions or college exams. Not on her first date with Kurtis or the night on the pier when she thought Raphael was going to propose to her.

Sandy pulled Lacy's car into the parking lot of Sacred Heart Hospital. "Take all the time you need, sweetie. I'll just take a walk and give my legs a good stretch."

Lacy nodded. At least Anchorage was smart enough to spray for mosquitoes, so the bugs weren't that unbearable.

Her legs were weak as she took one tentative step after another into the main entrance of Sacred Heart. Her stomach quivered as if her body was afraid she'd be admitted again, operated on, and sent home with meds that turned her brain to fuzz but only took a slight edge off her pain. She knew Raphael's room number but had to ask the volunteer receptionist how to get there.

"That's in C Tower. Third floor. You can take the stairs or the elevator," the elderly man told her.

She would definitely take the elevator.

When she got to his hallway, her gait slowed even more. The incision site from her surgery throbbed. She took in a deep breath. She could do this.

Whatever you choose, I'm giving you my full support. That was easy for Sandy to say — Sandy, who had made her decision decades earlier. Lacy thought about her mom, torn between a safe man her family loved and a boyfriend who promised adventure. Passion. Danger. She had never imagined Sandy with anyone but Carl. She had turned down the safe man.

Should Lacy? Kurtis was so compassionate. He would understand. She had known Raphael for so many years. Had waited for him for so long. She had never gotten over the pain of losing him, and now that he was back in her life, how could she turn away from him? Especially now, when he faced such a long road to recovery? How could she desert him when he needed her to nurse him? Encourage him?

They had been so great together, she and Raphael. They could look at the same painting and come away with entirely different impressions, but their differences gave them an hour's worth of engaging conversation. They loved the same things — art, theater, Broadway, road trips. The only drives she and Kurtis took were to Anchorage to fill up on staples at Costco. The most danger she had ever experienced while dating him was traveling over the mountain pass at a conservative forty miles an hour.

But what was wrong with safe? That's the question she had asked herself time and time again. She knew she was still functioning in crisis mode, her brain still reeling from the accident. At some point, she'd have to address what Raphael told her before they crashed. He had made some bad choices. Really bad choices. Choices that cost Lacy four years of her life. How could she be sure he wouldn't repeat the same mistakes again? What if they got married and he did something similar? What if they had a child?

She pictured Kurtis's daughter, so cuddly and headstrong. Lacy would do anything to guard Madeline and only imagined the protective instinct would be stronger once she had a child of her own. How could she forgive herself if she and Raphael had a kid they weren't able to keep safe?

Safe. That same word again. Offering so much comfort, especially after all that Lacy had been through. But so smothering at the same time. The bugs won't bite you if you live in a plastic bubble, but does that count as really living?

She stopped outside Raphael's door and checked the number three times. Was she ready for this? No. But she was here. Raphael was injured. He needed her. Every other decision could be put on hold until he recovered.

It was the only plan she had as she stepped into the room, but it would have to be enough.

CHAPTER 21

He looked so weak lying on the bed. His arm was in a cast. His face was bruised and covered with cuts, a massive bandage taped over one eye. A nurse adjusted his IV bag and nodded at Lacy.

Raphael glanced over. "What are you doing?" he demanded.

She stopped short of the bed.

"What are you doing?" he repeated. His voice was gravelly, as if each word hurt his throat.

"I came to see you."

"I don't want visitors."

Lacy held her cell in her palm. "You sent me a text." Could she have misread it?

The nurse came around the side of the bed. She put her arm around Lacy's shoulder, walking her a few steps to the door. "His memory's not so good right now," she whispered. "Head trauma."

"Maybe I should come back later."

The nurse shrugged. "It's up to you. He's not the best of company, but maybe seeing someone he knows will do him good. Are you a friend?"

"Yeah. I thought I might cheer him up." How could she have been so wrong?

"You're welcome to try." The nurse pat her arm and slipped out of the room.

Lacy went to Raphael's bed. Her steps were slow. Uncertain.

He didn't look up. "I never texted anyone."

Her throat constricted. "I just wanted to see how you were doing."

"Well, get a good look and tell me what you think."

Lacy knew head injuries could alter personalities. She knew there were tons of medications that could make Raphael so agitated. If there was one thing she had learned from her foster parents, it was that love was unconditional. She tucked the corner of her blouse back into her pants. "I'm glad you're out of the ICU." The cheer in her voice was forced and artificial.

"Makes one of us."

She took a deep breath, trying to remember all the good qualities that had made her fall in love with Raphael in the first place. "I've been waiting to hear how you've been doing."

He didn't look at her. "Just peachy. Can't you tell?"

"I'm sorry this happened," she whispered, wondering if saying so would only make him angrier. For some reason, it all felt like her fault. The car chase. The crash. His injuries.

"No worse than what I deserve," he mumbled.

She took a step closer. "Don't think that way. You're not the one running people off the road ..."

"I led them right to you." His voice was suddenly stronger. "Don't you realize that, Lace? Can't you put the pieces together? I led them right to you."

"You had no way to know you'd find me in Alaska."

He let out a mirthless laugh. "I always knew you were trusting. I didn't think you were stupid, too."

Why was he saying this? Why was he acting this way?

"I came to Alaska because the Mafia put me up to it." For the first time, he looked right at her. His eyes were dark, like angry storm clouds. "Are you getting the full picture now?"

She hoped he didn't notice the way her lips trembled.

"They told me they'd kill me if I didn't help them get to you. Threatened my parents and brother. They said if I didn't help find you, they'd go after Carl and Sandy, too. I had to try something. Carl had told me about the phone call from the trooper in Glennallen. That's how I knew where you were. The biking tour, the life-long dream of coming to Alaska, it was all a lie."

Her world was spinning. She needed a cup of water. Where was that nurse?

He shook his head. "I may as well have killed you myself and saved the Mafia the effort."

She was weak. Hardly able to stand. She was so dizzy she couldn't focus on him. He was talking like a lunatic. Was it the medicine? Why had the nurse left her alone with him? Somebody would come check on them soon. Explain again how this was all the side-effects of the drugs. That had to be the reason, right?

"It wasn't your fault." She wasn't sure which of them she was trying to convince.

He let out his breath in a frustrated huff. "Have you been listening to anything I said? Geeze, Lace, get it through your skull. I brought these men to you. I practically held the gun to your head for them."

"Why?" Her voice trembled. She glanced at the door. Suddenly, safe was a word that sounded a whole lot more inviting.

"I didn't have the heart to tell you everything at first, couldn't scare you away. So I tampered with your car, made sure you couldn't make it to Anchorage without me. I was gonna tell you everything on the road. We had to get out of Alaska, start over somewhere else. I thought we had enough of a head start on them. I thought I could drive us to Canada, get lost with you there. But I just dragged you into even more danger. I should have finished everything off in Massachusetts. I should have known they'd follow me here."

It wasn't true. It couldn't be. "But it wasn't your fault," she insisted again as a gunshot ripped through the air, shattering her eardrums.

CHAPTER 22

She was frozen. Paralyzed. Somewhere in the back of her head, she felt her vocal cords screaming but wasn't sure if the sound came out or not. Her ears buzzed. Swarms of angry, high-pitched mosquitoes.

"Get down." Raphael's voice was garbled, as if he were talking under water. Her vision was blurry. Like watching a scratched DVD where everything appears in freeze frames.

Raphael's hand on her shoulder. Stronger than she would have guessed. Pushing her to the ground. She hit her hip on the floor. Banged her head on the hospital bed. Shouldn't she feel the pain?

Another gun shot. Why did they have to be so loud? A scream. Raphael's scream. She had never heard a person make that noise.

Drops of blood splattered on her blouse. Was she injured? She couldn't feel anything. Had her entire nervous system shut down?

She crouched low, certain the attacker would keep shooting. She wondered how small she could make her body, envisioned turning herself into nothing but a speck. A dot.

Shouting. Curses coming from the doorway. Was there more than one of them, then? Another shot. This time, Lacy heard herself scream. Ear-grating. Soul-piercing scream.

Terrified voices in the hallway. Her mind projecting the image of the shooter into her brain even though her eyes were squeezed tight.

"Get him out of here." An authoritative voice. Strong. In control. Someone she could trust.

"Check on the patient." Scared. She never knew so much fear could be packed into a single phrase.

"He's been shot."

A nervous bustle all around her. Lacy stayed crouched in place.

"Got his artery."

More uneasy exchanges. Shouted orders.

Raphael's hand stretching out for her. Reaching down from the hospital bed. "I'm so sorry, Lace."

A worried nurse. "Shh. We're gonna try to get you through this."

"Where is she?" That strong voice again. Stable. Safe. "Jo?"

She couldn't answer. Couldn't open her eyes. But it didn't matter. He found her. Dropped by her side and wrapped her up in his arms.

"Are you ok?" Kurtis. Why was he here? How had he known where she was? "Are you hurt?"

"I don't know."

He ran his hands over her. It wasn't until she felt his sturdiness that she realized she was shaking.

"You're ok," he finally breathed and hugged her once more, resting his cheek on the top of her head. "You're safe now."

CHAPTER 23

Hours after the shooting, Lacy was still trembling. Two officers had driven her to the Anchorage police department. They didn't tell her what she was waiting for, but she had a pretty good idea.

They settled her in a room they assured her was completely secure. It was cold and drafty, with a dank, almost mildewy smell. A female officer asked her a few questions about the shooting, quickly realized Lacy was too stunned to offer any helpful information, and then left her alone with a cup of orange juice and half a jumbo Costco muffin.

She didn't realize someone was watching her from another room until she took out her cell to call Sandy and a loud, projected voice shattered the silence. "No phone calls, miss. It's for your own safety."

She put the phone on the table in front of her.

Secure. The officers told her she was secure, but that was a far cry from feeling safe.

She was cold. Could she ask for a blanket? Why had that woman just left her with tepid juice and an old snack? Lacy had so many questions. Was Raphael ok? How had Kurtis shown up? And why? Who was the shooter and what happened to him? Had anybody thought to explain to Sandy what was going on, or was she still waiting at the hospital, wondering what was taking so long?

She hated being cooped up in here. Cooped up with nothing but questions. She tried to squeeze her eyes shut, but all she could see was Raphael's blood staining her blouse. Why hadn't the police offered her a change of clothes? Couldn't they see how filthy she was?

A knock on the door. Lacy stood up from her metal folding chair.

"You in here, Jo? It's me."

Relief rushed over her like an avalanche at the sound of Kurtis's voice. She flung the door open. "What's going on? Where's Sandy? Is Raphael hurt? Why are they keeping me locked up in here?" She rattled off each question without pausing for breath.

He frowned. "Are you sure you want to hear everything right now?"

She bit her lip and nodded. It was like waiting for an injection you knew would hurt, but the anticipation was worse than the shot itself.

"Ok." Kurtis sat in another fold-up chair beside her. "So, to start off, yes, Raphael was hurt. It's ..." He lowered his voice. "It's pretty bad. They're doing what they can, but nobody seems too hopeful."

She wanted to tell him. Tell him how Raphael pushed her down out of the way of the bullet, but she couldn't find her voice.

"And they brought you here because we got the one shooter, he's in custody, but nobody knows if there were others, too. So they're gonna keep you here until Drisklay ..." His voice caught. He cleared his throat. "Drisklay's on his way right now."

She had expected that much. Expected it and feared it, too. Lacy couldn't meet his eyes. "Does Sandy know?"

He swallowed and nodded. "Yeah. I told her everything. She's grabbing a few things for you, and then she'll be over. It'll be her turn next."

"Her turn?" The pronouncement sounded ominous. "Her turn for what?"

He stared at his knees. "To say good-bye."

The words hung in the air between them, filling the heavy spaces. It was so dense, Lacy wondered how either of them were still breathing.

So this was it. Lacy had been so ready to be rid of Jo, ready to slip out of her old identity just like she was ready to change out of her bloody blouse. But not like this.

Drisklay was coming. That could only mean one thing. A new placement. Except this time, Lacy couldn't argue with him about whether or not it was necessary.

She sighed and shut her eyes. She knew there would be no tears. Not today. Not tomorrow. They probably wouldn't fall for a month. Maybe two. She'd be driving somewhere with her new driver's license, listening to the radio station in a new town on her way to her new job, and a song would come on. Something that would remind her of Kurtis. Raphael. Sandy. Everything that had happened to her. That's when she would cry.

Then and not before. Betrayed by her own body, which felt some primitive need to conserve energy in this time of crisis instead of offering her the immediate release she craved.

"How did you find me?" she asked. "How did you know I was in trouble?"

"Something had been bugging me since the accident," Kurtis explained. "Your car, somebody tampered with it. Somebody in Glennallen. But the Dodge that was chasing you was coming from the other way. So I got to thinking, and all I could figure was Raphael had done it. Maybe he wasn't who you thought he was. Then Drisklay got in touch, said he was worried because you weren't returning his calls."

"I thought he was just trying to get me to go back to Glennallen."

"He was trying to keep you alive," Kurtis corrected her. "And then I told him what I'd figured about the car, and he said it was suspicious enough that we should look into it. So he made plans to fly back here, and I dropped Madeline off at the daycare with Kim and drove down myself. I called Sandy when I got to town and asked where you were. She said you went to the hospital to visit Raphael, and ..."

"It wasn't his fault, you know." Lacy wasn't sure why she said it. She just couldn't stand the way Kurtis spoke his name. "I mean, he was involved, but he wasn't trying to hurt me or anything." Was that true? Or was she just making excuses?

"He should have thought of that before getting you mixed up in any of this." Kurtis let out his breath. "I mean, I understand you two have a past together, but seriously ..."

Couldn't they talk about something else? Anything else?

He frowned. "If he wanted what was best for you, he should have thought enough to stay away. He should have ..." He waved his hand in the air. "Never mind."

She was glad when he dropped the matter. "So did Drisklay say anything about where I'll be going from here?" she asked.

Kurtis's hard-set expression softened. "You know he can't tell me that sort of thing."

She nodded. "Yeah. I know. I just thought, with you being a cop and all ..."

"I'm a trooper, remember?" He forced a smile.

Lacy couldn't return it.

"I need to go soon. Got a long drive home." He stood up. "I'm just glad you're going to be safe. Finally."

He took a step toward the door, and Lacy realized in that moment what a fool she'd been. A fool to let her memories of Raphael tarnish her relationship with Kurtis in the first place. A fool to turn down Kurtis when all he'd ever wanted to do was keep her happy. Safe. A fool to have spent so much energy wondering if she could really settle down with someone like him.

Now, it was too late. This was good-bye. This wasn't a boyfriend and girlfriend taking time off to step back and evaluate their relationship. This wasn't getting dumped, hoping one day your ex might regret it and realize what a horrible mistake he'd made.

This was good-bye. Just as final as if one of them had died.

They could have been so good together …

"I'll miss you." She stood and took a step toward him.

"Me, too." His voice was tight as he opened his arms.

What else was there to say? It wasn't as if Lacy were moving to go to college or study abroad where she could write or call whenever she missed him. She couldn't promise to let him know when she arrived safely at her destination. Neither of them knew where she was going.

That's the way it had to be.

Their hug was awkward at first, like two partners at a junior high dance. Then he rested his cheek on the top of her head, and she felt the rise of his chest as he inhaled. He ran his thumb across her cheek. She looked up at him. His lips were so close. So kissable. She shut her eyes as one of his tears dripped onto her face.

"Good-bye." He stepped back. Lacy watched him leave, listened to the hollow sound of the door as it clicked and locked in place behind him.

CHAPTER 24

The silence was haunting. Heavy. Relentless. Icicles of loneliness weighing down on her heart. Why had she let any of this happen? She should have never gotten in the car with Raphael last week. Never left Glennallen.

But then what? Wait to get killed by the man who followed him to Alaska?

Raphael. She would never see him again. She knew it just as plainly as if he had died from his injuries. Maybe he would die. Lacy saw the next few weeks stretch lifelessly before her. Checking the Alaska Daily News website, constantly reloading to see if there was any information of his passing. Would the media find it newsworthy enough to report? Would anybody else in the entire blasted state care? Would she ever know what happened to him?

She had been mad at God, angry at him for forcing her to choose between two men. She had grumbled. Complained. Now, he was taking both Kurtis and Raphael away from her. That should teach her for whining so much. Why couldn't she have been content? Content working at the daycare, staying in Glennallen. The Fourth of July salmon feed was only a week away. She could have been engaged. Married Kurtis. Adopted Madeline. Added a few more kids to their family. Two weeks ago, that sort of a future seemed so confining. Restricting.

Lacy would do just about anything now to reverse the clock and change what had happened. Stop Raphael from coming to Alaska in the first place. She didn't hate him for what he'd done. It was his fault, but she couldn't hate him. She didn't love him either, though, not like she had in the past. She loved his memory, wished it weren't tainted by all the horrible mistakes he'd made. But she was no longer in love with him.

Maybe she had grown up in the past week.

Maybe she had become more like Jo than she originally realized.

She was hungry. Weak from the trauma of the day. The trauma of the past four years, really. How much could one person endure? *"For I know the plans I have for you."* Was this some cosmic version of a practical joke or something?

Raphael had found peace in religion. Solace. He threw himself into his new zeal for Christianity the same way he pursued his art. The same way he pursued Lacy. He wore his faith on his sleeve but still kept on making one dumb choice after another. No overdose of spiritual fervor could offset his immaturity.

She thought about Kurtis, how she felt comfortable if he mentioned God and just as comfortable if he didn't. He lived out his faith instead of parroting fancy church phrases, instead of thrusting his religion on anyone with a strong enough stomach to listen.

For I know the plans I have for you. Lacy wondered if God really did have a plan for each person's life, or if it was more like a Choose Your Own Adventure story, where he knew all the possible outcomes but let everyone flounder around on their own to figure everything out.

Oh well. There was no use dwelling on any of this. What would it help?

The door burst open, and Lacy didn't experience the repugnance she usually felt at Drisklay's appearance. This wasn't his fault, either. After Lacy had made such a big fuss about no longer needing his protection, he was here again, ready to whisk her away to someplace safe. She should feel grateful. Instead, she felt nothing.

Empty.

Like a black winter sky when clouds cover all the stars.

He took a sip from his Styrofoam cup. "Jo."

She had spent so many years hating that name, that identity. She had been a fool.

He set his cup down, splashing a few drops of cold coffee on the table between them. "I didn't expect to be back in Alaska so soon."

She waited. Waited for his lecture about how dumb she had been to resume a relationship with someone from her past. Complain about how her and Raphael's stupidity cost the program so many thousands of dollars for their new relocations. Remind her how crucially important it was to stick to the directives. Obey the rules. Never trust anybody. Never let anybody come close to learning about her past. Instead, he sat down with a groan. "You've had an eventful day." He folded his hands on the table. "So, let me tell you what's gonna happen from here."

Lacy refused to think back to the night four years ago when she first met Drisklay and had a very similar conversation. She was a different person now. Older. Hopefully wiser. Whatever was going to happen to her, she would accept it like a mature adult. Drisklay was trying to help her, and she was going to jump through whatever hoops he laid out for her without complaining. Her life and future depended on it.

She nodded. "I'm ready."

CHAPTER 25

Drisklay's briefing was just as long and involved as his first one had been back in Massachusetts. Apparently, he had an entire twenty-minute speech memorized where he talked about all the dangers that might befall a protectee who leaves the program. Scare tactics, really. Except Lacy didn't need those anymore. She had already been terrified into compliance.

Her next stop would be to a safe house out of state. Drisklay didn't tell her where it was, just told her she'd fly out with him in a few hours. She'd wait there for a week or two, however long it took the department to put together her new cover identity. She listened to it all as if she were a distant observer. A member of the audience watching a crime drama in a theater. Maybe a new minimalist musical.

Definitely not a comedy.

"Do you have any questions for me?" Drisklay asked, tipping his cup back to take in the last few drops of coffee.

She licked her lips. "How's ..." Drisklay had been talking for so long, she couldn't trust her voice. "How's Raphael?

He frowned. "He took a lot of chances. You know there's no way we can guarantee safety for someone like that."

That wasn't good enough. She'd spent four years wondering what had really happened to him that night at the North End. Even though she knew there was never going to be a future where she and Raphael ended up together, she refused to step into the next act of her life without knowing the full truth.

"What did the doctors say?" She tried to make her voice sound forceful but wasn't sure she pulled it off.

Drisklay stared at his empty cup. "He didn't make it. Too much blood loss."

Lacy let his answer float in the air around her. Took in the truth a small breath at a time. *He didn't make it.*

Drisklay made a move as if he were going to drink again but changed his mind. "I'm sorry."

Didn't make it.

Lacy knew at some point the realization would hit her full in the gut. Maybe on the plane with Drisklay, or maybe once she got settled in her new home in the Lower 48. All the sorrow, the grieving, the regrets — that would all come.

Later.

Now, she had a plane to catch. A safe house to reach. She hoped wherever they took her at least had some good movies. Her brain could use some mindless numbing.

"Well." Drisklay stood. "I have a few details to oversee before we head to the airport. In the meantime, I think there was somebody who ..."

The moment he cracked the door open, Sandy shouldered her way in. She was carrying a backpack, a small duffel, and several shopping bags. "I'm here, sweetie."

Drisklay squeezed past all the luggage and shut the door behind him. Sandy set the bags on the floor and hurried toward Lacy. They hugged. Lacy did what she could to mentally record the feeling of her mom's hands around her back, wondering how long until the memory faded and dissolved.

"I'm sorry," Sandy sniffed, laughing at herself. "I promised myself I'd be the strong one here." She tilted her head and pouted at Lacy. Mascara dribbled down her cheeks. "I brought your stuff." She gestured toward the bags. "That's the backpack and duffel you had at the mission home. And I went to the store to grab some other things." She pulled various items out of the shopping bags. New socks. A few cute hair accessories. Tampons and deodorant. "I got a couple books, too. I don't know what you like to read these days, so I just picked out some that looked interesting. I didn't know how long you'd be on your flight or ..." She let her voice trail off.

"Thanks," Lacy mumbled.

Her mom sniffed loudly. "I'm so sorry all this happened, dear."

"I know."

"Some people would say something like *Everything happens for a reason*, or *God won't give you more than you can handle*. But the truth is, God gives his people things they can't handle every single day. It's not fair. It's not pleasant. It's just life." She sat in the folding chair, and Lacy caught a whiff of fabric softener wafting from the folds of her skirt. Could she remember that smell always?

"God is good," Sandy continued. "We can't ever doubt that. And his Word tells us he'll work things out for our good if we love him. But that doesn't keep bad things from happening. All these horrible events that have happened to you, those are bad. Still, we got to hold faith that God knows what he's doing. He can make good come from all these tragedies. He *will* if you trust him." She sighed. "I wish I could tell you more, sweetie. Wish I could give you all the answers. But here I am, hardly a crumb of wisdom to my name, and you're probably starving for a whole loaf right about now."

"It would be nice," Lacy admitted. They talked a little more. Lacy explained about how Kurtis grew suspicious about the car and drove down to Anchorage to check on her. How Raphael had been involved with everything from the start. How surprised Lacy was to feel so little at the news of his death.

"That's because it hasn't sunk in, sweetheart," Sandy explained. "You see, God knows that some things are easier to take in little by little. Bite-sized chunks, if you will. Now, I know Raphael did you wrong, and I bet you feel like you should be angry with him. The fact is, you probably will be. That's just a part of grieving, darling. And don't you think that just because he's the one who put you in all that danger that you shouldn't mourn for him. I'd be worried over you if you didn't. That boy was important to you. I remember you two together back in Boston. You had a chemistry. A bond. Might not have been the wisest or most godly of bonds, but that don't matter right now. What matters is he's gone, and eventually you're going to have to process all that. Cry as much as you need. Nothing cleanses the soul like prayer and a good sob. And don't feel pressured to get over him too soon either, hon. That's the other mistake some folks make. Don't rush the grieving period. I always like to picture my tears are the rain that's gonna water the flowers God's sending my way. He does that, you know, makes beauty out of our sorrow. Sometimes it takes longer than others. That's why we need to ask him for patience."

She reached out and stroked Lacy's cheek as Drisklay's voice carried into their room from the intercom. "Five more minutes, then we got a plane to catch."

Sandy wrapped her arms around Lacy. "I pray for you every single day."

Lacy wished she knew how to respond.

"Is there anything you want me to tell your dad?"

Lacy took in a deep breath. "Just tell him not to worry about me. Tell him ..." She faltered once before finding her voice again. "Just tell him I'm safe, and I love him a lot."

"We both love you." Sandy held her even tighter. She wiped her eyes. "I know this has to happen, sweetie. It's for your own safety, but it's just so hard."

Lacy nodded.

"Now one more thing," Sandy went on. "Let's say down the road you meet some nice young man. Someone like that trooper friend of yours who wants to marry you. As long as he loves you and he's a believer, you both have our blessing. Ok? He doesn't need to dig around and investigate and call Carl out of the blue this time. Got it?"

Lacy tried to laugh along with her mom but couldn't.

Sandy's whole body sighed as they held each other for the last time. "I know I can't ask you anything about where you're going, and maybe you don't know yet either. But wherever the good Lord takes you, honey, my prayer for you is that you'll realize how much he loves you. Wherever you are. Whatever heartaches you've had to suffer. His love for you is greater than all of that. So you draw close to God, sweetie, and when you're praying to him, feeling his big, powerful arms wrapping around you and holding you tight and keeping you safe, you remember your daddy and me are praying for you awful fierce. Those times you feel the Holy Spirit right there with you, comforting you, that's gonna be God answering our prayers and showing you how much you're loved."

Lacy bit her lip. Maybe she could find those tears today after all.

Sandy took in a deep breath. "Now, I'm not gonna say good-bye, because good-byes are for people who don't know Jesus and don't have the hope we do that one day we'll all be together again. You just hang on 'til then, sweet thing. Brighter times are coming your way. I just know it."

She kissed Lacy's cheek and with a flourish of her long French braid and rustling floral skirt, she was gone.

CHAPTER 26
– one week later

Tired. Lacy was so tired. Tired of the Texas heat. The safe house had air conditioning, but it hardly made any difference. The whole town had gathered for their little Fourth of July parade two blocks over. She had listened all morning to bagpipers warming up across the street.

She had forgotten how many movies she'd watched since Drisklay dumped her out here. She'd breezed through all the historical and romance novels Sandy bought, even though none of them had really interested her. Sometimes she wondered if this was what certain believers imagined purgatory would be like. A lot of waiting. Some sorrow. Disappointment. Occasional anger. Fear. Loneliness.

And not a whole lot else.

Lacy sat on the safe house couch with her legs tucked beneath her. Drisklay had taken her phone so she couldn't access her Bible app, but Lacy had found a worn New King James Bible on a bookshelf at the safe house, right next to a nine-year-old Cosmo magazine and a Jehovah's Witness publication. She hadn't been reading Scripture systematically like Carl did, starting at the beginning and working his way through to Revelation. She usually just flipped around until something caught her eye. She'd spent a lot of time in Jeremiah lately.

"For I know the plans I have for you."

She was glad someone did. Drisklay would be here in an hour or two with more information, but right now all she knew was she was going to South Dakota. She'd spent a lot of time praying her new home wouldn't have as many mosquitoes as Glennallen. She also would prefer to work somewhere where she didn't have to change a dozen diapers a day.

"For I know the plans I have for you."

Lacy had already decided that once she got to her new home, she would find a church there. Maybe even work up the courage to join a Bible study or prayer group. She didn't want South Dakota to turn out like Alaska, where she only knew one or two casual acquaintances. No wonder she had felt so lonely there. Things had got a little easier once she met Kurtis, but ...

She spent most of her waking hours trying not to think about him. She couldn't let her past life poison her future like she had before. She had come to Alaska still pining for Raphael, still mourning his loss, grieving to the point where she could never move on with her life. In South Dakota, she couldn't live another four years wishing for things that would never be. She remembered what her mom told her about breaking up with her doctor boyfriend. *He was an important part of my life for a season. We had fun memories.*

That's what Lacy wanted to hold onto when it came to her relationship with Kurtis. The memories. Memories of cuddling together on the couch while Madeline put on impromptu ballet shows. Of driving to Anchorage together, holding hands and enjoying the quietness of each other's company. Of helping Madeline build her very first snowman or take her first step on ice skates.

Those were good memories, and she was trying desperately not to sully them with the sorrow of this move. Sometimes things just didn't work out. It didn't mean Kurtis was a bad fit. It didn't mean the two of them weren't compatible. It just meant life had gotten in the way of what could have been.

In some ways, Lacy was glad to be starting over. Glad she didn't need the constant reminder of how foolish she'd been to waste four whole years agonizing over someone like Raphael. With him, it was easier to confine his memory to a distant point in the past. They had been good together back in Massachusetts, but everything after that had been a waste of energy at best. A nearly fatal mistake at worst. If only she had realized that sooner.

Sometimes she would look back and dissect those two and a half years she'd spent with Raphael. Were there signs? Could she have known what sort of jeopardy he'd drag her into, how much pain a few years of carefree spontaneity with him would cost? Lacy had finally begun to experience something new when it came to Raphael, something she had longed for during those four agonizing years in Glennallen.

Closure.

She couldn't change the past, couldn't take back those years they'd spent together travelling the East Coast in his Saab. She wasn't even sure she'd want to. Of course, she'd happily reverse time and never drive with him to the pier, but if Raphael was making such bad choices, they were bound to catch up to him eventually. It could have been worse. She could have been killed. Even if Raphael's contact hadn't gotten murdered that night in the North End, what would that mean? A life on the run with someone who offered fun and excitement but absolutely nothing by way of security.

He was an important part of my life for a season, Sandy had said. Her mom was so wise. Lacy hoped that she'd eventually learn to do the same thing with Kurtis. Move on. Accept the good times they'd had without wishing they could continue. With him, though, it was harder. Kurtis had never jeopardized her life, never cost her four years of pain and isolation. Still, she would have to go forward. She considered her placement in South Dakota God's way of giving her a new start. How many people would kill for a chance like that? Forget all the mistakes of the past, forget all the doomed relationships, the wasted time. A chance to start over with a clean record.

Lacy was trying to be grateful for that.

It was a start.

CHAPTER 27

"So here we have your identification."

Lacy took the card Drisklay handed her and stared at the picture, a close representation of herself on a South Dakota driver's license. *Marissa Hummel.* Well, it was better than Jo. Her birthday had changed. She was a year and a half older now. Fifteen pounds heavier. She hoped that wouldn't prove prophetic. She flipped the card around as if there would be more to discover about herself there.

"Birth certificate." Drisklay passed her the crisp page, and Lacy stared at the names of parents, dates, and cities she had never heard of. She'd have to get used to it. This was her life now.

"My folks made you a resume. I think you'll find you have a little more to work with than what we gave you last time."

Lacy's hands shook just a little as she held up the paper. Right there on top was an associate's degree dated three years ago. She doubted if whoever put it there would realize how vindicated it made her feel. Those community college credits she took in Massachusetts hadn't been completely wasted after all.

She scanned her employment history. Marissa Hummel had volunteered at an animal shelter since high school and then worked various retail jobs before moving to nowhere, South Dakota. "This would be great if I ever want to work at Petco."

Drisklay took a sip of coffee. "Good. You've got an interview there next week."

"Where? At Petco?"

He strummed his finger on his disposable cup. "I figured you could use a break from kids."

Lacy took a deep breath. It was a lot to take in. Of course, it was going to feel a little overwhelming. But she could get used to it. She was older now, more mature. There were worse jobs than working at a pet store, right? She had been reading in Philippians a few nights ago and came across a verse about complaining. *Do all things without complaining and disputing.* For the first time, Lacy experienced what Carl and Sandy and other Christians talked about, how reading the Bible could reveal your own sinfulness. It wasn't as pleasant or exciting as they all made it sound.

She thought back over the years she spent in Glennallen, how she'd always found something to complain about. The weather, the mosquitoes, the daycare kids. She had grumbled incessantly about Drisklay and the witness protection program even though they were the ones who kept her alive.

She wasn't going to live like that until she withered up and died a bitter old woman. So what if Petco wasn't the future she'd pictured for herself? She couldn't change it. It wouldn't be easy starting over, but she could do it.

She hoped.

Drisklay handed her the rest of the small file. High school diploma. Childhood shots record. Last, he held up an unmarked envelope.

"What's this?" she asked.

He cleared his throat. "This is something my team and I have decided to leave up to you."

She wasn't sure she liked the way he was looking at her.

"Your assailants will be looking for a single woman, so we agreed we had to come up with a different cover."

He opened the envelope and handed her a slip of paper.

"Certificate of divorce?" Lacy read.

Drisklay nodded. "This guy, this Frank Bulgari, you married him right out of high school, divorced him a year and a half later. No contest. No kids. No baggage. Just a blip on the radar."

Lacy didn't want to touch the page. There was something else Drisklay wasn't telling her.

"That's option one." His fingers hesitated before he pulled out another form. "Here's option two." He passed her the document.

"A marriage license?" Lacy stared at it. "What, you're giving me an imaginary husband? I think people will eventually figure out that I'm not living with anybody."

"That's why we have a gentleman pre-screened and chosen for the job."

Lacy was sure she misheard him. Was this his way of making a joke? *Pre-screened?* He couldn't really think he could take two perfect strangers, bind them together with his forged marriage license and actually expect them to live together, could he?

She reached for the divorce paper. "Give me that one."

Drisklay chewed on his red coffee stirrer. "Before you make up your mind, maybe you want to meet your potential husband." He glanced at the document. "A certain Mr. Hank Murphy."

The name sounded like a sixty-year-old plumber. Not Lacy's idea of a romantic conquest.

"Mr. Murphy is a gym teacher at a private Christian school. Baseball, football ... You name it, he can coach it."

Lacy stared at the forged wedding certificate. "So you found this guy who's willing to marry a girl he's never met and ..."

"It's not quite that simple," Drisklay interrupted. "He's got experience that would allow him to offer certain protective services. And he's on the run too, you see. So in a way, hiding you two together would be a two-for-the-price-of-one deal from our end of things."

That's what this was all about? Lightening his paperwork load?

"I really don't think ..."

Drisklay pulled out one more envelope. "Before you make up your mind, take a look at the file we have on him."

She rolled her eyes but did as he requested. Hank Murphy's portfolio was about like hers. Birth certificate, college diploma, driver's license ... She pulled out his identification and squinted at the grainy photo. "Wait. Is that ...?"

One corner of Drisklay's lips curled up in an unsettling grin that looked completely out of place and unpracticed on his otherwise expressionless face. "I'd like to introduce you to your potential husband, Mr. Hank Murphy."

He turned his head and mumbled something into his hand-held radio.

The front door opened, followed by the pitter patter of excited, tiny feet rushing down the hall. "Daddy says you might be my new mommy!"

Lacy had already gotten down from her chair and knelt on the ground to catch Madeline, who ran with arms outstretched for a hug. Lacy nuzzled her face in Madeline's hair, surprised by the tear that was sneaking down her cheek.

"Daddy says the bad men who tried to shoot you are angry with him because he arrested one of their friends. He says we get to move to a whole new state, and if you say so, we can all move together and you and Daddy will be married, and I'll be your daughter, and I'm never allowed to say anything about Alaska because it's a really big secret and we don't want the bad guys finding out where we are, so it's kind of like hide and seek, and won't you please marry Daddy so we can all be a family?"

Lacy didn't know what to say. Was this some sort of trick? Drisklay's attempt at humor? She looked up at him, saw him hiding a wide smile behind his coffee cup.

Lacy rose to her feet. Kurtis stood behind his daughter, looking both shy and hopeful. "For the record," he said, "I voted against the big surprise entrance."

Lacy stared at him. Blinked her eyes to make sure all this was really happening. It had to be a dream.

He took a step forward. "Munchkin and I have to lay low one way or another." He brought his face closer to Lacy's and whispered, "We've already gotten two death threats, and I caught an intruder lurking around the daycare."

The acid in Lacy's stomach curdled. Someone had gone after Madeline?

"I called Drisklay, told him what was going on. Said I had to leave anyway, so why couldn't I leave with you? Help keep you safe and get the munchkin away from all the drama. I guess he thought it was a good idea." Kurtis took her hands in his. "I don't want to rush anything. If you're not ready, if you need more time to think about it ..."

Outside, a marching band played a slightly off-key rendition of *The Stars and Stripes Forever.*

Kurtis shifted his weight and took a small box out of his pocket. "But, well, I've already got this ring, and it *is* the Fourth of July ..."

He dropped to one knee and opened the case. Madeline was hanging on his arm, beaming as bright as Alaska's midnight sun.

"Marissa Hummel, will you be my wife?"

Madeline let go of her dad to wrap her arms around Lacy's leg. "Please?" she begged.

Lacy didn't know if she was doing more laughing or crying. "Yes," she answered. "Yes, I will."

Kurtis slipped on the ring. It was a perfect fit.

Madeline bounced up and down, clapping her hands. "Goody, goody, goody!"

Drisklay cleared his throat. "We better get down to business if we want to have you three in South Dakota by tonight."

More music from the parade floated by. Kurtis and Lacy sat down in front of the pile of documents. Drisklay stirred his empty coffee cup. "So now that we've settled on that, let's talk about your new life."

Termination Dust
a novel by Alana Terry

"All your children will be taught by the LORD, and great will be their peace."
Isaiah 54:13

Note: **The views of the characters in this novel do not necessarily reflect the views of the author**, nor is their behavior necessarily condoned.
The characters in this book are fictional. Any resemblance to real persons is coincidental.
No part of this book may be reproduced in any form (electronic, audio, print, film, etc.) without the author's written consent.
Termination Dust
Copyright © 2018 Alana Terry
2018
Cover design by xx.
Scriptures quoted from THE HOLY BIBLE, NEW INTERNATIONAL VERSION®, NIV® Copyright © 1973, 1978, 1984, 2011 by Biblica, Inc.® Used by permission. All rights reserved worldwide.
www.alanaterry.com[1]

1. http://www.alanaterry.com

CHAPTER 1

Kimmie should have never mentioned the funeral home to her stepfather. What had she been thinking?

Maybe it was defiance. Or maybe the grief was keeping her from acting rationally.

"You think I'm made out of money?" Chuck bellowed. "You're just like your mother. That woman was always nagging me, every day of my life. *More, more, more.* It's all she could say."

His voice rose in a mocking falsetto. Kimmie's mother was lying in the morgue, but Chuck continued to mock her heartlessly. "*Honey, we need more grocery money. Honey, we're late on the car payment.* Do you know how much I hated her whining?" He blew his nose then dropped the used paper towel onto the floor.

He and Kimmie both stared at it, a familiar battle of wills as he silently demanded she clean up after him.

She glowered at him.

Things were going to be different now. They had to be. Her mother — God rest her soul — had wanted to escape. For years, Mom fed Kimmie dreams of freedom in hushed whispers. "We can go move to your sister's in Anchorage. Meg will take us in."

But Kimmie had learned years earlier not to get her hopes up. Mom wasn't going anywhere. And in her darkest moments, she hated her weakness. Maybe it was Kimmie's fault. If she'd only been more supportive or more courageous, she could have forced Mom to leave. Her sister only lived a four-hour drive away. Mom could have gotten help. She could have been safe.

But Mom refused to run away. She decided to remain trapped here in this trailer, stuck in a life with no other purpose than picking up Chuck's snot-ridden paper towels, heating up his canned chili, opening his bottles of beer. Mom and Kimmie had both stayed, a silent agreement, a vow they never spoke but both understood. Kimmie would never leave her mother. Not here, not with Chuck.

So Mom had taken the only escape she could.

Now Kimmie was free to go. She could walk out that door, show the spunk and self-respect and courage Mom could never manage to conjure up.

That's what she should do. That's what any outside observer would expect her to do, like that kind trooper who responded to Kimmie's call the day Mom died. Even now, Taylor's soft eyes and soothing voice gave her confidence.

Courage.

You didn't deserve any of this. She could almost hear the trooper whispering the words to her. He was new to the force, not one of the regulars who used to come and do well-child checks when Kimmie was still a minor, back when she was expected to lie away every single bruise and cut on her body.

When Taylor came to her trailer, Kimmie was struck by how young he looked. She was a confused mess after finding her Mom's body in the garage, but he listened to her patiently, even offering to make her tea to help her calm down. The suggestion made her feel like an entirely different person, the kind of person who kept her kitchen stocked with nice things like tea bags and sugar cubes and pretty, matching mugs.

Instead, they settled on lukewarm Cokes.

Kimmie and Taylor had sat at the folding table in the kitchen and talked. Even though the questions were all pointed toward explaining her mother's suicide, she felt like he understood her. Only at one point, Kimmie got flustered when Taylor asked why she stayed at home when nearly everyone else in Glennallen left rural Alaska after high school.

"My mom's not very healthy," she stammered, fumbling over her words. It was difficult to know which tense she was supposed to use as the EMTs were at that same moment preparing to transport her mom's body after cutting her down from the garage rafters. "I've been watching over her."

The real answer, as Kimmie knew, was far more complicated. She thought she recognized in Taylor's eyes an expression of compassion. Understanding.

Did he know what her life was really like? Could he guess?

Maybe it was because he was the only man even close to her age who had spoken to her kindly in years. Or maybe because as a trooper he signified everything Kimmie had been longing for — bravery, confidence, the ability to protect others — that she hadn't stopped thinking about him since that first meeting three days ago.

And now it was Taylor's voice she heard in her head, the same man who sat with her the day her mom died, drinking Coke because as far as Kimmie knew Chuck had never owned a single tea bag in his life. *You didn't deserve any of this.*

Taylor didn't understand. Even if Kimmie wanted a happier life, freeing herself from Chuck wasn't nearly as simple or straight-forward as opening that door and walking down the driveway toward the Glenn Highway, hitching a ride to Anchorage where her older sister would be ready to take her.

Her stepfather cleared his throat — a wet, phlegmy noise that made Kimmie feel nauseated. Or maybe that was the hunger. When was the last time she'd eaten? Chuck had skipped breakfast and lunch, perhaps dealing with the loss of his wife in his own way. But when Chuck didn't eat, that meant the family didn't eat. Kimmie was older. She was used to hunger pains.

It was harder for Pip.

She'd put her half brother down for his afternoon nap about an hour earlier, sitting on their bed with his head in her lap. Like most days they spent at home instead of at the daycare where she worked, she smoothed Pip's forehead and sang him to sleep. The ditties were the ones her mother taught her, the ones she and Pip both loved, Bible verses set to music. Chuck would throw a fit if he heard them, but some football game was blaring on the TV, drowning out Kimmie's clandestine melody.

And we know that in all things ... all things ... all things ... And we know that in all things God does what's best for those who love him.

It had been one of Kimmie's favorites when she was Pip's age, a time before Chuck, before this drafty trailer, this squalor. A time when Mom looked young and happy, always waiting with open arms for cuddles and hugs, always ready to make up a new song.

And we know that in all things ... all things ... all things ...

With drooping eyelids and cheeks stained with tears, Pip had looked up at her and in his own invented sign language made a flame. The fire song was his favorite, and Kimmie felt her own soul encouraged as she sang him the words.

When you walk through the river, you know I'm with you.
When you pass through the water, I'm right there by your side.
When you walk through the fire, you'll never be burned.
Those flames, they won't set you ablaze.

Maybe Mom's little tune is what gave Kimmie the courage to confront Chuck after Pip was finally asleep. Then again, *confront* was far too strong a word to describe the way she tip-toed into the living room, her heart thudding in her chest, her hands clammy with sweat.

"I think we should have a funeral." She'd been shocked that her voice didn't squeak.

Chuck crushed his beer can and tossed it onto the carpet, hocking a wad of spit in the direction where it fell. "Don't got the money."

Kimmie knew that was a lie. Mom had died the day before her deposit from welfare cleared the bank. Factoring in Chuck's disability payments, Kimmie knew there was money to be had. It usually took Chuck at least ten days into each month to drink through their funds. Besides, her sister could cover any actual expense, but now wasn't the time to rub her stepfather's nose in Meg's success.

"I'm not asking for anything fancy," she persisted, "but you were married for ten years. The least you could do is give her a proper burial."

This time, the loogie Chuck spat landed on the carpet near Kimmie's bare feet. "The witch killed herself. No Christian pastor's gonna bury her, and funeral homes aren't nothing but a rip-off."

"I already called Glennallen Bible." Kimmie had anticipated and was ready for her stepfather's arguments. "The pastor there said he'd be willing to ..."

Chuck pointed the remote at the TV screen and turned up the game until the sound of wildly cheering fans made Kimmie feel as though her teeth were rattling in place. She folded her hands across her chest. "I think it's at least worth considering."

Chuck glowered at her. "You telling me how to take care of my own business?"

She shook her head, but it was too late. Chuck was out of his seat.

Kimmie only had time to flinch before he swung out his arm and slapped her hard across the face.

"You talking back to me?"

She set her jaw so he couldn't see her pained expression.

"You're no better than that witch of a mom of yours." He spat in her face, and Kimmie was relieved at the smell of stale beer. When Chuck was drunk, he never bothered to waste too much energy beating her.

He pushed her aside, and she stayed down, praying and hoping he'd be too tired to persist in his fight. Praying and hoping Pip would sleep through his father's rage or at least have the good sense to stay in his room.

Chuck gave Kimmie's back a half-hearted kick then stomped back over to his recliner, flinging several dirty napkins and half a bag of spilled sunflower seeds onto the floor by his feet.

Kimmie didn't mention the idea of a funeral again.

CHAPTER 2

Later that night, Kimmie stared out the window in the bedroom she shared with Pip and listened to her brother's gentle snoring. A full harvest moon rose through her window, providing enough light that she could still see the white tips of the mountains behind the trailer. As a child, Kimmie always loved that first sprinkling of snow on the mountain peaks — the termination dust that signaled the end of summer, the start of a new school year.

She'd been a good student. Even after her widowed mother moved them from Anchorage and into Chuck's trailer when Kimmie was a teen, she had managed to keep up her grades. The Glennallen high school was small, just a little more than two dozen in her class, but Kimmie had been popular enough and respected. She learned how to pretend well enough that, as far as she knew, she never gave anyone reason to suspect what kind of hell she was living through at home.

In a way, those high-school years — riddled though they were with petty fights, catty gossips, acne breakouts, and nearly paralyzing self-consciousness — were easier than the life she was leading now. School gave her a place to escape, a sanctuary where for seven and a half hours out of every single weekday Kimmie was free from her stepfather's incessant demands, yelling fits, and occasional beatings. That's why seeing the termination dust on the mountains at the end of each August always left Kimmie feeling hopeful.

Free.

But all that was in the past now. Her friends from high school left Glennallen years ago, some to college, others to jobs in Anchorage or the Lower 48. In fact, Kimmie hadn't even graduated with her class. Pip was born over Christmas break during her senior year, and since the delivery left Mom weak and anemic, Chuck decided Kimmie would stay home to help watch over the house and the baby. She earned her GED the same month her friends from high school started moving away from home, mostly for good. Kimmie didn't blame them. How many times had she fantasized about leaving herself?

She and Mom had dreamed about it in scared, hushed whispers in the bedroom while Chuck dozed on his littered reclining chair.

"Meg will take us in," Mom always declared. Kimmie's older sister was seventeen when Chuck came into the picture, and she had successfully convinced Mom to let her live with her best friend so she could finish her senior year with her class in Anchorage.

Chuck was glad there was one fewer mouth to feed.

As Kimmie quickly learned what kind of man her stepfather was, she dreamed of a home with Meg. A life in Anchorage — and more importantly a life free from Chuck — would make putting up with her sister's infuriating superiority complex worthwhile.

The unfortunate — maybe even pathetic — truth was that Mom was too scared to leave Chuck, and Kimmie was too loyal to leave Mom alone with a monster like him. And so they suffered together, drawing hope from their plans of escape whispered in dark bedrooms while the man who held them captive snored loudly from his easy chair.

And the years passed.

Mom grew gray, then got pregnant. Kimmie dropped out of school, and the baby brother she expected to despise snuggled up against her chest, with little dribbles of milk leaking from the corners of his mouth and gas bubbles that made him look like he was smiling directly at her.

Kimmie was so protective of her little brother, she swore she'd kill Chuck before letting him harm such a helpless, innocent creature. But as far as she knew, Pip's father had never raised a hand to him, a mystery Kimmie didn't know whether to attribute to their shared genetics or shared gender or maybe even the miraculous answer to all those prayers she'd prayed over Pip when he was a soft newborn who smelled like milk and baby powder.

It took almost a year for Mom to recover from the trauma of her home birth, where she'd been attended only by Kimmie and Chuck, who refused to let any member of the family set foot in a hospital or doctor's office. Even once her body repaired itself, Mom never regained her energy, and the bulk of the parenting fell on Kimmie. Apparently, this was Chuck's plan from the beginning. He wanted Mom free to wait on him, to dump his tin cans of beans and chili into the stove pot every few hours, to keep him in constant supply of sunflower seeds, cold coffee, and freshly opened beer. By the time the condensation no longer glistened on the can, the booze was declared too stale, and Mom was sent to the kitchen to fetch another.

Kimmie strained her ears to listen for Chuck's snoring. Even before Mom's death, he'd stopped sleeping regularly in their room. Apparently, it was much easier to remain in the reclining chair twenty-four hours a day. She was surprised he still made the effort to walk himself to the toilet, an act which comprised the entirety of Chuck's physical activity if you disregarded the exercise he got hitting the members of his family.

All except Pip. God continued to answer Kimmie's prayers for his safety. For her brother's sake, she was grateful. But that also complicated any plans Kimmie might make about her future. Mom was no longer Chuck's hostage. As tragic as her suicide was, Mom was now free. Which meant Kimmie could leave.

But what would happen to Pip?

She turned to look at him, sucking his thumb in his sleep. She should probably discourage the habit, but tonight she didn't have the energy or the will. Pip was so young. Too young to lose a mom. Younger even than Kimmie had been when her father died. She didn't have any memories of her dad. One of her biggest fears was that Pip would forget their mom entirely.

How do you keep someone's memory alive? How do you keep a child from growing up and forgetting entirely? Kimmie had lost track of how many times as a kid she said or thought something like, *my Dad died when I was four, but it's not that big of a deal because I didn't really know him.*

How could she have been so wrong? About her father, about everything? If Mom were here, Kimmie might ask. Not about her father. That subject was clearly off-limits for as long as they lived under Chuck's roof. But what was Kimmie supposed to do now, especially without Mom's guidance?

She stared out the window. Wispy clouds had drifted in and found their way just below the full moon, which lent them an eerie glow. Kimmie didn't believe in ghosts. The only afterlife she trusted in was the picture of heaven Mom had taught her from her earliest years. She was supposed to feel happy for Mom, now free from her suffering, free from her life held prisoner to Chuck.

A siren wailed from the Glenn Highway. Kimmie thought about Taylor, the kind trooper who'd shared Cokes with her in the kitchen just a few days earlier.

What was he doing now? Did he think of her? What would he say if he knew what Kimmie's life was really like? What would he do?

Pip made a little whimper in his sleep. Kimmie pulled back his tattered blanket, crawled onto the mattress next to him, and stared at the wall where the harvest moon cast dancing shadows from the drifting clouds outside.

CHAPTER 3

Kimmie woke up to a crisp autumn morning. She and Pip had been clutching each other in their sleep, whether from the cold or the sheer loneliness of their existence and the grief they both shared.

She slid out of bed, careful not to wake him, and peeked out the bedroom door. Chuck was still asleep in his recliner, but the quiet and peace of the morning wouldn't last long. If she was lucky, she'd have time for a shower without hearing her stepfather yell about all the money she wasted running the hot water.

Maybe if he fixed all the stupid leaks in this cheap trailer, she wouldn't be so cold all the time and need to thaw herself out under the scalding flow.

Kimmie had taken these past few days off from work, but they needed her back at the daycare soon. One of her coworkers had recently moved away — no one knew where — and Kimmie and her friend Jade were now the only reliable staff.

Kimmie had mixed feelings about returning to work. On the one hand, since Chuck had refused to offer her mother even the simplest of funerals, there wasn't a whole lot for her to do at home. No relatives coming to visit. Her sister Meg would take care of the body in Anchorage, and since Meg was married to a real estate agent with enough money to pay for a five-bedroom home on the hillside and two or three tropical vacations a year, Kimmie figured Meg would find a way to give their mom a nice burial even if Chuck wouldn't let them plan a formal service.

It wasn't right. Mom had been the most faithful, God-fearing woman Kimmie ever knew. And now she was gone, without a single pastor to pray over her gravesite or a gathering of friends to share memories from her life. Kimmie wondered if Mom still had any friends in Anchorage, if Meg would find anyone to attend a service in her honor.

Everything about the past week felt wrong. Surreal. Like a badly written script where none of the characters acted like themselves. A knock-off of real life, poorly written and unnecessarily tragic. Kimmie kept waiting for the director to stop the cameras and rant about the terrible quality of the plot, the cheap acting, and the senseless scenes.

Kimmie tiptoed into the bathroom, careful not to wake Chuck up. While she waited for the water to heat up, she stretched in front of the smudged mirror. Mom had been a prisoner, leaving the trailer to go to the grocery store and back and that was all. So she'd developed an entire morning calisthenics routine, and when Kimmie was younger, she'd watch her mother exercise in unmasked adoration. Sometimes Mom would sing her Bible songs while she stretched and worked her muscles.

Whatever you do, work at it with all your heart, since you're working for God and not for men.

Above all else, love each other deeply, deeply, deeply, for love covers over a multitude of sins.

Kimmie took off her pajamas and stepped into the shower, wincing as the hot water scalded her skin. She'd only have two or three minutes before Chuck would be pounding on the door, snarling at her to turn that cursed shower off, but for right now she could enjoy the quiet and solitude.

She could stand under the steaming spray as the heat melted away her icy chill.

She could pretend, if only for a moment, that Mom was in the kitchen, brewing Chuck's coffee, preparing the family's breakfast. She could hear her mom's faint humming in the echoes of her memories.

Above all else, love each other deeply, deeply, deeply, for love covers over a multitude of sins.

If only Mom had realized sooner that sometimes not even love itself is enough to save you.

CHAPTER 4

Kimmie hoped the rest of the morning would pass smoothly. Some days her stepfather was tired enough that he left Kimmie and Pip alone. Chuck had never said so, but it was tacitly understood that all the chores now fell on Kimmie since Mom wasn't here to do them. After her shower, she wrapped her hair up in a towel and headed to the kitchen to start on Chuck's coffee.

"What you all dressed up for?" He was already at the folding table in the dining room, sitting before a dirty, empty mug. A painted picture of the Grand Canyon chipped away from its enamel.

Kimmie glanced down at her jeans and sweater. "I'm going back to the daycare today." He must have remembered. Since Chuck's trailer didn't have a landline or any cell reception, Kimmie's coworker Jade had stopped by the house yesterday to beg her to return to work. Chuck had been in the middle of a half-drunk, half-naked outburst even though it wasn't even dinnertime yet. Kimmie had been embarrassed, more on Jade's behalf than anything else.

"When you gonna be home?" Even when he wasn't drunk, Chuck had the tendency to slur all his syllables together, making the noises that took the least amount of muscle control or mental effort.

"Three," Kimmie answered, "like normal."

Chuck's biggest stipulation when it came to Kimmie's work at the daycare was that she clocked out before the school-aged kids got dropped off. Pip always went with her, and Chuck didn't want his son picking up bad habits or germs from the elementary-aged students. Every once in a while, his demands left the center with an uncomfortable staffing predicament, but Chuck was resolute. The day Kimmie and Pip came home at 3:08 instead of 3:07 would be the day her stepfather marched to the daycare himself and told her coworkers she quit. He'd made that threat multiple times, and Kimmie knew he'd follow through. Since the daycare got her out of the house, and more importantly gave Pip the chance to play with kids his age and toys besides crushed beer cans and spilled sunflower seeds, Kimmie would do anything in her power to keep her job.

Even placate her stepfather, whose bare stomach bulged over his flannel pants as he sat half-dressed at the table, waiting for his food.

She grabbed two slices of white bread and threw them into the toaster. While she reached for the coffee, Chuck mumbled something.

"What'd you say?" she asked.

He glowered at her, as if her inability to understand his pronouncement was a reflection of her own mental incompetence instead of his embarrassingly poor diction. "I said I'm gonna need you home now. No more daycare for you."

Kimmie had been prepared for this conversation and was actually surprised it took four whole days until he brought it up. Thankfully the extra time gave her plenty of time to fine-tune her argument. She wouldn't go into details about how the daycare was such a better environment for Pip and might even help him to start talking in full sentences soon. There was no reason to appeal to Chuck's fatherly nature since he didn't possess any at all, so she answered Chuck in the language he understood best.

"We won't be getting Mom's welfare anymore. I was thinking if I kept working at the daycare, I could help with the budget." Kimmie was treading dangerous waters. There was no way Chuck could concede to being dependent on an uneducated girl in her twenties, but she also knew that the fool was capable of doing simple math and had to realize he couldn't afford all that booze on his disability payments alone.

She held her breath, waiting for a response, not knowing if her stepfather would reluctantly give in or begin a loud and obnoxious tirade that was certain to wake up Pip. For years, she'd tried to stash away little bits of pocket change from her paycheck, storing up a small but treasured cache of one- and five-dollar bills. She'd imagined it might eventually turn into enough to convince her mom to take Pip and leave. It wasn't living expenses they needed. As snobby as her sister and her rich Anchorage husband might be, they wouldn't turn away their own flesh and blood. Mom's biggest fear had been that Chuck would demand to keep Pip. Even though there was no court in the nation that should award someone like Chuck sole custody, Mom wouldn't leave without enough money to hire the best lawyer in Alaska just to be sure.

Kimmie never mentioned her plans, but Mom found out about the extra money lying around. Toward the end of each month, when Pip hadn't eaten a hot meal at home in weeks and Chuck was bellowing for more beer, her mom would sneak into her room and whisper, "Don't you have a little something? Just to hold us over a few more days?"

And so Kimmie would relinquish the ones and the fives she'd managed to stash away. Eventually, Chuck realized what she was doing. From that point on, he made her sign her paychecks over to him.

At present, Kimmie had $2.23, all in change, to her name, which she kept hidden beneath the torn lining of one of her winter snow boots.

From his spot at the table, her stepfather glowered at her. He was probably straining to do the calculations, figuring out if having a fulltime slave to wait upon his every need was worth giving up so he wouldn't have to live off his disability alone.

"Home by three," he grumbled. He slammed his empty mug on the table and then slid it toward Kimmie to fill with the black sludge he called his morning coffee. "And no school holidays."

Kimmie turned her back to him, figuring that now was not the time to let her stepfather see her smile.

As long as she and Pip had that job at the daycare, that job away from Chuck, she could plan. She could scheme. She could call her sister from Jade's cell phone and beg her to come and pick her up.

Pick her and Pip up, actually.

How a girl Kimmie's age with no real job experience, no education, and no future prospects could assume guardianship of her half-brother against the wishes of his biological parent still remained what seemed like an insurmountable impossibility, but as long as she got those few hours alone with Pip each day without Chuck's constantly surveying every move she made, she was going to figure something out.

She had to.

CHAPTER 5

After Kimmie fixed her stepdad's breakfast, she added his dirty dishes to the ever-growing pile in the sink and then went back to her room to wake up Pip. Working the morning shift meant that she and her brother could count on both a hot breakfast and lunch in a single day. There probably weren't all that many nutrients in the microwave croissant sandwiches or canned SpaghettiOs they served at the daycare, but calories were calories. At least Kimmie's job gave her brother more to live off of than the sunflower seed shells his father spat onto the floor.

She knelt on the mattress, leaned over her brother, and nuzzled Pip's ticklish neck with her nose. "Wake up, Buster. We get to play today."

Pip rolled over and blinked at her, his expression momentarily vacant until his face broke out in a cautious smile.

"You ready to go back to work with me?" she asked.

Pip grunted, and Kimmie spent a few minutes she didn't really have snuggling with him in bed, breathing in his fresh morning smell that still managed to feel clean even though she could never wash him without his throwing a fit.

She pulled out some of Pip's clothes and watched him struggle for his independence before helping him take off his pajamas and get dressed. A few minutes later, they were on their own, making the walk to work. An icy wind stole its way through their thin jackets. She took hers off and wrapped it around Pip to provide an extra layer of warmth.

Hiding her hands in her sweater sleeves to better protect them from the cold, Kimmie gestured toward the mountains. "See that, Buster? See the snow on the mountain tops?"

Pip's eyes widened slightly, Kimmie's only indication he had heard her. At home, Chuck hated any loud noise that didn't come from his own body or his television set. In addition, he was convinced that Pip's speech delays meant he was stupid, and he berated Kimmie anytime he caught her talking to her brother, certain that his mute son was incapable of comprehension.

After being cooped up in the house with Chuck for the past four days, Kimmie realized how freeing it was now to be able to speak clearly.

131

"Did I ever tell you what the first snow on the mountains is called?" she asked. Pip had been distracted by a car speeding down the Glenn and was no longer staring at the Wrangell Mountains in the distance, but Kimmie was grateful to have found her voice again and continued on with her explanation.

"We call it termination dust because it looks like someone sprinkled white dust on the tips of the mountains. *Termination* means ending, and the first snow tells us that summer has ended and winter will be coming soon."

She glanced down at her brother, trying to gauge how much of her explanation he might have understood. He was focused on the way her jacket sleeves hung down by his side, nearly dragging on the ground behind him. She bent down, tied the sleeves loosely together, and kissed his cheek. One of the hardest parts about Pip's speech delay meant that Kimmie was always wondering if her brother understood just how much she loved him. How she'd do anything within her power to protect him.

Even die.

Even kill.

CHAPTER 6

Kimmie stepped into the Glennallen daycare and held the door open for her brother. Before Pip was past the threshold, Kimmie was wrapped up in Jade's arms as her friend attempted to squeeze all the breath out of her lungs.

"I'm so sorry about what happened."

Kimmie didn't know why the reaction surprised her. Knowing what she did about Jade, she shouldn't have expected anything different. Jade was effervescent, extroverted, and probably twice as strong as Kimmie would ever be. Her hug of condolence was as smothering as it was compassionate.

Once freed, Kimmie took a step back. "Thanks. It's good to be back." She helped her brother escape from his layers of coats, pulled out his favorite tub of matchbox cars, then followed Jade into the kitchen.

"What are we making for breakfast this morning?"

Jade held up the Pillsbury can. "Cinnamon rolls."

Kimmie's stomach gurgled. She hoped Jade didn't hear. Kimmie kept the door to the play area propped open so she could supervise the few kids in attendance and suddenly felt sheepish. She'd been so focused on her and Pip's grief over the past few days she'd hardly thought about Jade's visit yesterday. What kind of impression did Jade have of her and her family now? With a stepdad who lazed around the house all day belching out his beer and stripped half naked, a half-brother who refused to speak, and a mom who killed herself...

She caught Jade staring at her and felt herself blush. Oh, well. Jade never seemed to have a problem speaking her mind or interacting with other people who did. Kimmie took in a deep breath. "I'm really sorry if my stepdad made you uncomfortable when you came over. He's ..."

She struggled for the right words. *He's always like that, sometimes even worse? He's a monster of a man, and I wish he was the one who died instead of my mom?*

She calmed her quivering voice and explained, "He's got a lot to deal with right now." Why was she making excuses for him? Because otherwise she'd have to find a way to explain why she was still living with the beast when she was free to walk away.

Theoretically free, at least.

Kimmie was already starting to feel just as trapped as her mom had been. There had to be a way to distance herself from her stepfather without abandoning Pip. Maybe she could ask for more hours at the daycare. Then at least she and Pip would be here instead of at home. It would mean more money for Chuck's drinking, and he'd have the trailer to himself ...

But that was the problem. He didn't want the trailer to himself. He wanted someone to pick up all his stained napkins and snot-covered paper towels, someone to fetch his coffee and make sure his beers stayed icy-cold. The man at the funeral home told Kimmie by phone it was natural for people who'd lost a loved one to suicide to feel angry at the deceased, but initially she'd balked at the suggestion. How could she be mad at her mom? For all of Kimmie's begging and pleading, it had become apparent that only dying would free Mom from her servitude. In Kimmie's most honest musings, she'd feared that one day Chuck's anger could lead to murder, and she was relieved that Mom had met death on her own terms.

Mom's suicide was a small act of defiance against a man who'd held her in terror for years. But now Kimmie wished she could take her mom by the shoulders, force her to observe exactly what her death had done. Kimmie was even more trapped than she'd been a week ago. All of Mom's responsibilities now fell on her, and even though Kimmie hated to admit it, Chuck wasn't the only one worrying about how they'd keep the family afloat without those regular welfare payouts.

Worst of all were her worries over Pip. How could a three-year-old understand the finality of death? And since he didn't speak, Kimmie had no idea what he was thinking. Did he figure Mom had abandoned him? That she stopped loving him and ran away? Pip hadn't cried any more than normal these past few days, and even though it seemed like he clutched Kimmie more closely at night, it could also be that she was the one clinging to him.

"He doing all right?" Jade's voice came from right behind Kimmie's shoulder, making her jump. She realized she'd spent the past several minutes staring at her brother. While Jade's little girl and the other early arrivers grouped in the main area coloring or playing in the massive dollhouse that once belonged to Jade's daughter, Pip was in the corner by the cubbies, right where Kimmie had left him. Instead of racing his cars up and down the carpet like most kids would, he focused all his attention on lining them up in concentric circles. Kimmie knew that if she got closer she'd see he'd organized them by color or size or model or whatever other system caught his fancy today.

She forced herself to smile. "Yeah, it's hard on him, but he's handling things really well."

"Does he understand what happened?"

Kimmie didn't know if Jade was asking about their mom's death in general or her suicide specifically. She shrugged and offered a noncommittal, "It's hard to say."

"How did he do at the funeral? Was that pretty rough on him?"

Kimmie's face grew hot. How could she explain that her stepdad was so heartless he wouldn't even allow them to plan a service?

The oven timer dinged, distracting Jade and freeing Kimmie from the conversation that was destined to grow more awkward the longer it dragged on.

"Cinnamon rolls are ready!" Jade called out. Jade's daughter and the other children cheered and clamored and caused a minor stampede in an effort to be the first seated at the kitchen table. Pip, on the other hand, frowned at the box of cars, studying them as if they were Einstein's theory of relativity, then made a careful selection. He held the truck up, squinting as he turned it around to examine it from all angles before adding it to his circle of cars, perfectly placed and impeccably lined up.

CHAPTER 7

The daycare was quieter than normal, with the Cole twins out with strep throat and another child whose family was on vacation in the Lower 48. The comparable calm was a mixed blessing. With the grief of losing her mom sitting at the base of her neck like a thirty-pound backpack, Kimmie was grateful that today's crowd seemed fairly content to play with only minimal need for supervision. On the other hand, the minutes seemed to drag by as slowly as the Alaskan sunset on the summer solstice.

After breakfast, Pip beelined right back to his toy cars, working himself into an angry panic when he discovered one of his trucks kicked out of place. Kimmie finally managed to calm him, but she had a few new scratches on her arm for her efforts.

As far as fits went, this one was relatively calm. Once Pip was contentedly absorbed in his sorting work again, Kimmie made her way back to the kitchen where Jade was scrubbing down the table with disinfectant.

"Have you made any coffee yet?"

Jade glanced up from her work. "No, you go ahead. I could use a cup myself."

Kimmie hated coffee until she started working at the daycare. Jade showed her the difference between a nice fresh roast and the generic stuff Chuck always bought. Kimmie was also pleasantly surprised to discover that her coffee didn't have to be so strong it poured out like sludge and that a little bit of flavored creamer made a big difference in cutting back on the bitter taste.

Keeping partial attention on the kids playing in the common room, Kimmie pulled down the bag of Alaskan coffee and changed out the old filter.

"What time is it?" Jade asked.

Kimmie glanced at the clock above the sink. "9:45."

"Is it me, or is this day dragging on?"

Kimmie was glad she wasn't the only one who felt that way. A few minutes later, the two women were sitting in rocking chairs on the far side of the playroom with steaming mugs of freshly brewed Kaladi Brothers coffee in their chipped mugs.

"Here's to you." Jade held her cup high. "With prayers for peace and comfort for you and your family after all you've gone through."

Kimmie had never seen anyone make a toast with a mug of coffee before, but she appreciated Jade's thoughtfulness. Taking a small sip, she scanned the room to make a quick mental count of the kids. Jade's daughter Dez was playing by the dollhouse, Noah was coloring at the kiddie table. The Abbot brothers and their cousin Chinook were climbing up and down the small indoor kiddie gym, pretending to be pirates.

"We'll have to get ready for story time pretty soon. You want me to do it today?" Jade asked.

In the past, Kimmie took on reading duty. The kids loved to hear her do her voices, and Kimmie appreciated their enthusiasm and rapture. "I don't mind," she said. "I'll do it."

Jade glanced at her with what looked like the start of a question in her expression, but instead of saying anything she just took another sip of coffee. "That works for me," she said. "I've got to go disinfect that bathroom at some point anyway."

Kimmie would never complain about working with someone who would rather scrub toilets than read a few books out loud. They both finished their coffee, and while Jade helped the kids who needed assistance in the bathroom, Kimmie picked out a few books.

Everyone loved Dr. Seuss, and reading his books had become so second nature Kimmie could do it with only investing a small chunk of her mental energy. Another one of her personal favorites was *There's a Monster at the End of this Book*, but she wasn't sure she had the energy today. She had to get the voice just right to make it sound scary enough to keep everyone amused without actually frightening any of the littler kids. Kimmie had no guidebook on grief, but she suspected that the sooner she could get back to doing all the things she did before, the sooner she could say she had finally moved on.

With the monster book in her hand and a few other especially funny ones thrown in for good measure, she pulled the rocking chair to the center of the playroom.

"All right, guys," she called out, wondering if her voice sounded natural. "Grab your magic carpet square and let's read some stories."

Noah came running first, eager to grab his favorite spot right in front of Kimmie. Chinook sat next to Dez, and the two girls giggled when one of the Abbot boys tripped over an untied shoe.

Everyone was here except for Pip. Kimmie glanced at the bathroom. Had Jade taken him to the toilet?

She leaned forward and laid the books out on the floor in a colorful spread. "All right, guys, if you promise not to touch these or fight about them, I want you to think about which story you want to read first. When I get back you can each tell me your choice and we'll take a vote."

Even before she got out of her chair, she realized she'd set the kids up for failure by making them promise not to fight. She hurried toward the bathroom. Jade was leaning over the toilet, yellow rubber gloves on her hands and hot pink earbuds on her ears. She glanced up. "Need anything?"

Kimmie peeked behind the bathroom door as if her brother might be hiding there. "Have you seen Pip?"

Jade took off her gloves and paused whatever she was listening to on her phone.

"What?"

Kimmie repeated her question, then glanced back at the circle of kids, half expecting him to have joined the group.

"I'm sure he's around here somewhere." Jade's statement of the obvious only made Kimmie's hands clammier.

"I'll check the kitchen," Kimmie said. "Can you see if he went to the nap room for some reason?"

Jade tossed her rubber gloves onto the sink, and Kimmie glanced at her brother's box of cars by the front door. Where had he gone?

She poked her head into the kitchen. "Pip?" After glancing under the table and sink, she checked the broom closet and even the lower cupboards.

"I didn't see him in the nap room." Jade licked her lips. Kimmie knew she wasn't in a strong enough emotional state to determine the exact time to freak out, so she took her cues from her friend.

Jade fingered her chin, glancing sideways. "Think he could have gone outside?"

"I'll go check." Kimmie hurried toward the exit. He knew he wasn't allowed to play outside by himself, and most of the time he was terrified to be away from Kimmie even for a few minutes.

She glanced at his cubby. If he had gone outside, he'd forgotten his coat. Where could he be?

Her heart started pumping wildly, and she didn't know if the surge of terror she felt was a rational reaction or not. How could she? She'd never lost her brother before. In fact, until last summer when he discovered his love of matchbox cars, he'd hardly ever let Kimmie out of a five-foot radius from wherever he was.

"Pip?" A cold blast of air confronted her when she stepped outside. It didn't make sense. Pip was the kind of kid who threw fits when anything in the daily routine changed in even the slightest detail, a kid who had until recently refused to be away from his sister's side while she was at work. Why would he have gone onto the playground by himself?

"Pip!"

She leaned down, peeking in all the tube slides, checking and double-checking anywhere a three-year-old Pip's size could conceivably hide. The choices were fairly limited. Two minutes later she was back in the daycare building, and Jade's nervous shaking of the head revealed that her search had been just as fruitless.

Kimmie's breath grew short. The daycare began to spin in her periphery.

Her brother was lost.

CHAPTER 8

Kimmie stood paralyzed in the entrance to the daycare.

Pip ... lost?

It didn't make sense. The concept was too complicated for her brain to register or compute.

He couldn't be lost. He was playing a game. That's what this was. Of course, he was the only kid in preschool who never caught on to hide-and-seek, but maybe he'd finally figured it out and wanted to prove how well he could do it.

"Pip!" Kimmie called out, her voice infused with false cheer.

The children stared at her from their seats in the reading circle.

"Maybe we should do the books later," Jade suggested, and Kimmie couldn't figure out why her co-worker was worried about story time when her brother was missing.

"Pip!" Kimmie hurried to the nap room, retracing the steps Jade must have made just a few minutes earlier. "Pip?"

Her voice was shaky. Uncertain. So were her tentative steps. Was she worried that she'd trip over her brother if she weren't careful? He wasn't that tiny. He couldn't have turned invisible.

"Pip!" She tried not to sound irritated. Wasn't that some sort of dog-training rule? She couldn't remember where she'd heard it. If your dog takes off, don't sound angry or he'll be scared to come back to you. She forced herself to smile. Made her voice higher than natural. "Pip?"

Nothing.

Back to the bathrooms, running now. What if Jade left out the cleaning supplies, and her brother got into them? She flung open the door. No Pip.

She ran back outside, onto the playground then past the daycare fence. Searching everywhere, racing through the parking lots, haphazardly running up the side street. He wouldn't have come all the way out here, would he? And why hadn't she seen him? Was she so busy drinking her coffee she stopped paying attention? Or had she gotten complacent, convinced he would never voluntarily move away from his box of cars? Was she just as guilty as Chuck, who thought that since Pip didn't talk he was incapable of making decisions for himself? Of having an opinion?

Where could he have gone?

She was sprinting now but halted at a stop sign on top of the hill. There was no way Pip was all the way out here. Not without his coat. Not without her. He was scared of just about everything.

Including being alone.

She spun around. She had to find him.

Racing downhill was harder than running up, when the rush of adrenaline helped her defy gravity. Her early sprint had been fueled by the hope that she might find her brother and catch up to him. But she couldn't dawdle now. She had to keep looking. Couldn't slow down.

She pictured him lost and alone, wandering alongside the Glenn Highway. Maybe he'd gotten hurt and freaked out. Maybe he ran into the woods behind the daycare, scared and bleeding. Or worse, what if someone grabbed him? She would have heard if someone came into the daycare, but what if Pip wandered off and was at this moment in the back seat with some predator ...

She wanted to throw up. Emptying her stomach would at least make more room for her stinging lungs and racing heart. She hurried back toward the daycare, praying Jade had found him. Something was wrong. Something in the parking lot.

A trooper's car? What did that mean? Had Jade called the dispatcher to report a missing child? Or what if it was even worse? What if Pip had tried to cross the Glenn? What if he'd been hit by a car? What if ...

"Don't you work here?" asked a tall man in his crisp, blue trooper uniform.

She knew that voice, but she was so distraught she had a hard time placing it.

He stretched out his hand. "Taylor Tanner. Nice to see you again."

Warmth rushed through her as his palm touched hers, loosening her voice. "I'm so glad you came. I don't know what happened. He was with the cars all morning ..."

He stared at her quizzically, and she realized she was about to start crying. It was too much. Couldn't God see that? Too much. First her mom's death, then Pip getting lost, now this trooper looking at her with so much compassion and empathy.

"Kimmie! Is that you?" Jade called from the open doorway. "Come on in. We found him."

Breath rushed back into her lungs, and she was too relieved to acknowledge the trooper's questioning expression. She ran past him and into the daycare. Falling onto her knees at the sight of Pip, she wrapped her arms around her brother, burying her face into his dinosaur T-shirt.

"He crawled into the dollhouse," Jade explained. "Poor thing must be exhausted. I found him in there taking a nap."

Pip looked at Kimmie. It was rare that she could be entirely sure what he was thinking or feeling, but if she had to guess, right now she'd say he looked scared. "It's okay," she told him. "I'm just glad you're safe."

She studied his face. What was he looking at? She glanced over her shoulder.

"Oh, right." She stood and faced the trooper. "Thanks for stopping by. I guess we've got everything under control. I'm so sorry we bothered you."

His gentle smile spoke of both bemusement and curiosity.

"Trooper Taylor's come here to talk to the kids about stranger safety. Remember?" Jade was staring at Kimmie as if those words should make an ounce of sense. "We talked about it at our last ..." She stopped herself. "Oh, right. You weren't there. You mean I didn't mention it to you this morning?"

Kimmie shook her head.

"Well, that's what's on the schedule for today. Kids," Jade called out, "I want you to grab your magic squares one last time, and we're all going to listen to Trooper Taylor. He's come all the way over here today to talk to us about staying safe, so I know you're all going to put on your listening ears and give him your full attention, right?"

Kimmie was glad for the commotion to get Taylor's focus off of her. She was glad that Jade was here to take charge and tell the children what to do. More than anything, she was glad to have her brother here, safe and sound. He'd never played near that big dollhouse before. Maybe it was a good sign. Maybe it was a positive step forward in his development if he was starting to show interest in something other than his cars.

The kids were staring at Taylor with rapt attention, and Kimmie realized they were quieter and more disciplined than she'd ever seen them. Even Pip had grabbed his carpet square and was sitting down quietly with the others.

Kimmie pulled one of the rocking chairs behind the semi-circle of kids and sank down into it. With the trooper maintaining the children's entire focus, maybe Kimmie could take the next few minutes to decompress.

Maybe she could finally relax.

CHAPTER 9

Jade stood in front of the circle of carpet squares, clapping her hands together to hold everyone's attention. "All right, students, what do we tell Officer Taylor for coming to speak to us today?"

A melancholy chorus of *thank yous* sounded around the room. The children were dismissed for playtime. Jade stepped up to Kimmie. "I'll get lunch ready if you're all right handling things out here."

Kimmie's eyes were on the trooper. Taylor had stopped to help Jade's daughter tie her light-up shoes. "Hmm?"

"I said I'll get lunch ready," Jade repeated. "That okay with you?"

Kimmie pried her eyes away from the touching scene. "Yeah. Sounds good. You need help?"

Jade shook her head. She looked as if she were about to say something, then just shrugged and walked off. Kimmie scanned the room to make sure she kept better track of her brother. Pip was by the dollhouse again, watching two girls playing make-believe. Maybe he really was starting to move past those cars. It would be a huge step forward for him. She just hoped that Chuck would never find out if his son liked to play with dolls.

"It's Kimberly, right?"

She let out a surprised, "Oh," when she realized Taylor was standing right next to her.

"Kimberly?" he repeated.

She nodded, flustered. Hadn't he already left? "Kimmie," she told him. "Or Kimberly. Whichever you prefer."

She cleared her throat and pulled her eyes away from his, focusing again on Pip. Her heart was starting to swell. He'd never shown an interest in imaginative play before, and with what limited knowledge she'd gleaned from the daycare's scarce resources on child development, she knew make-believe was a huge milestone in cognitive development. What if he actually picked up one of those dolls and started to play with it? For the first time, she realized why all those daycare moms and dads were obsessed with carrying their smartphones around to get pictures commemorating all their children's proud achievements.

Jade's daughter noticed Pip staring at her. Kimmie was afraid she'd say something mean and braced herself to jump in and intervene. Instead, Dez held out the doll. Pip stared, and Kimmie held her breath, waiting to see if he'd reach out for it.

"He's a cutie." The trooper's words yanked Kimmie back to reality. He smiled down at her, and she flushed.

Taylor held her gaze. "I just wanted to tell you again how sorry I am about your mom. How's the little one taking it?"

Kimmie glanced at her brother again. He'd taken the doll but just stared at it as if he weren't certain what exactly it was doing in his grasp.

"He's all right," Kimmie answered, and then fearing that her answer sounded too dismissive added, "all things considered."

Taylor nodded as if he understood exactly what she meant, which would be a small miracle seeing how Kimmie didn't even know what she was saying. *How is he? All things considered?* How was a three-year-old supposed to act and feel and think after his mom commits suicide to free herself from an abusive husband? Kimmie felt her hands balling into fists. At least anger gave her a sense of power, however false. It was far more comfortable to feel fury than grief. She couldn't pinpoint who or what she was mad at — her mother for killing herself, her stepfather for being a monster of a human being who couldn't even make his own coffee sludge, God for allowing so many misfortunes to steal away any chance Kimmie had for hope or joy. Maybe even the earth itself for continuing to exist and spin and function normally even though Kimmie's entire world had been shattered.

Taylor cleared his throat, and Kimmie braced herself for some kind of senseless remark — *all things happen for a reason,* or some other unhelpful platitude like that. Instead, he held her gaze and said, "You know, if I'd have known you'd be working here today, I would have planned things differently. I was going to stop by your house a little later this afternoon. I need to talk to you. It's important."

Something flopped inside her gut, and she was pretty sure it had nothing to do with Taylor's kind features, his intense stare, and his perfectly pressed navy-blue uniform.

Pretty sure, but not positive.

Danger signals zinged through her brain, and she braced herself for some terrible blow. The state had decided Pip wasn't being cared for well enough and was going to take him away to be raised by strangers. That had to be it. Why else would he look at her with that apologetic stare?

"I have to head back to the office before long, but do you have a few minutes? I'd love to find a quiet place to talk."

CHAPTER 10

If Taylor expected to find anything resembling privacy here, he'd obviously never spent much time in a daycare. Fortunately, Jade announced that lunch was ready a few minutes later. Kimmie and Taylor could talk in the playroom while Jade served up the kids in the kitchen. Kimmie pulled out the rocking chair, and Taylor sat on top of the coloring table. Kimmie didn't have the heart to ask him to move, and she hoped none of the kids would come out and see the trooper in uniform breaking one of the daycare rules.

Taylor strummed his fingers on his thigh and looked perfectly at ease. Kimmie just wished he could lend her a fraction of his calm and self-possession.

"I wanted to talk to you about your mom."

Kimmie felt her breath whooshing out her lungs. It was hard to tell if his words left her more surprised or relieved, but at least it didn't have to do with Pip.

She had a hard time knowing where to look and found her eyes flitting between Taylor's black shiny boots, the glistening gold badge on his chest, and the tiny hint of stubble accenting a strongly defined jawline.

"This is a little awkward." Taylor's words belied his demeanor, which remained perfectly casual. "We've had a few discussions at the station that have caused us to look a little bit deeper into your mother's case."

Kimmie stared from his boots to his badge and back down again. What was he saying? Was her family in trouble because her mother killed herself?

Taylor looked over his shoulder. The door to the kitchen was closed, and the empty playroom suddenly felt very large and very quiet.

He lowered his voice. "I hate to be the one to bring this up, but I thought given the circumstances it might be best to talk to you first instead of going to your dad."

Kimmie wanted to correct his mistake, but the word *stepfather* died on her lips before she could speak it.

"I can't go into details, and I know this is obviously a sensitive topic. I just wanted to give you a little warning so you aren't surprised."

She had no idea what he was saying. She had no idea how she was expected to respond. When had people stopped speaking in plain English? She pried her eyes away from his badge and stared at her hands which fidgeted in her lap. "I'm afraid I don't really understand."

He smiled at her and apologized. "I guess I was being kind of vague. I don't want to sound like an alarmist or anything, but there's something I think you should know."

Time, breath, even her pulse stood still while she waited. Taylor leveled his gaze and didn't say a word until she managed to raise her eyes to meet his.

"There's a chance they're going to open up an investigation looking into your mother's death."

Kimmie understood the individual words but not their coherent meaning when strung together. What was he saying?

Taylor must have sensed her confusion. He let out a sigh, leaned forward, and explained, "We're starting to think this might not have been a suicide after all."

CHAPTER 11

A moment later, Taylor returned from the kitchen and held out a Dixie cup full of tepid water, which Kimmie sipped in miniature installments.

"I'm sorry," he said. "I should have waited to find a better time to talk."

She stared at him, trying once more to piece together the meaning of his words. A dozen different questions jumbled in her brain, but she couldn't focus on a single one long enough to ask it. She replayed everything she remembered about that horrible day. Stepping into the garage, the surreal grisliness of it all. Shouting for her stepdad, tackling Pip to keep him from coming in, waiting for what felt like hours for the troopers and ambulance crew to arrive.

Not a suicide ...

"Other members of the family have raised a few questions."

This time his words' meaning came to Kimmie clearly. "You mean my sister?" Who else would voluntarily get in touch with the troopers like this? Kimmie had only talked to Meg that first day. Since Chuck refused to keep a landline and the tiny subdivision where they lived was notorious for its spotty cell coverage, she'd had to walk to the neighbor's and beg to borrow her phone for such a private conversation.

Taylor didn't deny that Meg had gotten involved. "At the scene ..." He stopped himself. "At your house, I mean, there were a few questions we had. And talking with your sister has raised even more."

Kimmie's brain was spinning but instead of an efficient machine taking her to the conclusions she needed to arrive at, the mental chaos was more like a hamster in a wheel, spinning helplessly but always remaining in the exact same spot.

"What kind of questions?" she found herself asking.

"Well, your sister says your mother wrote notes. Notes about how she felt at home." He leveled his gaze. "A few of the notes are at your sister's in Anchorage, but she thinks there's more. Can you think of any special place your mother may have kept them? A favorite hiding place? Somewhere private?"

Kimmie shook her head. The idea of privacy in a family like Chuck's

149

was almost humorous.

Taylor sighed. "Well, if you think of something, will you let me know?"

"Sure." Kimmie stared at the wall.

Taylor waited until she looked straight at him. "Do you feel safe at home?"

Kimmie bristled. What happened in the privacy of Chuck's trailer was her business and no one else's. Nobody, not even an Alaska state trooper in his impeccably pressed uniform, had the right to pry into her life, unlocking all those secrets she vowed to keep buried and hidden.

She tilted up her chin. "Of course I do."

His eyes were full of empathy, and at that moment she wished she could escape his intense scrutiny.

"If you're sure. Some of the things your sister told us ..."

"Meg's Meg," Kimmie announced, as if that were all the explanation necessary. "She's dealing with her grief the only way she knows how. I'm just sorry it's causing more trouble and hassle for you at the station."

Taylor didn't look away as he reached into his breast pocket. "I want you to have my card," he said. "I'm writing my cell number on the back. You can call me any time. Call me at the station or at home if it's an emergency."

She had no idea just what kind of emergency she was expected to find herself in and certainly didn't feel like asking. She took the card, shoved it into her pocket, and vowed to forget about it. Forget Taylor and forget this nonsense about her mother's death. Meg was Meg, which might not mean anything to the trooper, but it meant a lot to her. Her sister was only out to raise trouble. That was all. Who knew what kind of lies she'd concocted about Kimmie and Pip and their life with Chuck? How would Meg even know? She hadn't been up to visit in years.

Taylor continued to stare at her intently, and she wished her mother hadn't raised her to be the kind of girl who was perfectly polite, perfectly unable to cut a conversation short because she didn't want to appear rude. She had no idea what this trooper was suspecting or insinuating, but she didn't have to sit here and take it. She could tell him to leave. It wasn't as if he owned the daycare.

But she continued to sit and stare, hoping he'd end the meeting on his own.

"I want you to think about what's best for your brother." What was he suggesting? Think about what was best for Pip? What else did Kimmie have to think about since their mother died? If she weren't thinking about what was best for Pip, she'd be in Anchorage by now, maybe even on her way to the Lower 48 if she found a way to get down there. A way to escape this chaos that had consumed her life.

Taylor had no idea what he was talking about.

"I really should get back to work now." Kimmie glanced up at an imaginary clock on the wall. "Thank you for your concern." Even now, she was unable to drop her upbringing, unable to be anything but polite and cordial.

Taylor reached out and touched her wrist. He didn't grab it, or she would have jerked away. The touch was shocking. Kimmie sat frozen for just a second.

"I just want to make sure you're safe, you and your brother both."

If Taylor was concerned for her safety like he claimed, he should have thought about that before talking about investigations prying into her private family affairs. If he wanted what was best for Pip, he'd stay far away from her home, from her stepfather.

Chuck hadn't been named as a suspect, but Kimmie was certain that if her sister were involved, Meg would have blamed Chuck. For years, Meg had begged Mom to leave Glennallen or at the very least to let Kimmie come live with her and her new husband in Anchorage. Finally, the fighting grew ugly enough that Chuck refused to let Mom have anything to do with her oldest daughter. It was just like Meg — spiteful, selfish Meg — to go around making accusations.

Not that they were entirely baseless. How many times had Chuck threatened to murder Kimmie's mom? How many times in a drunken rage had he beaten her so badly she passed out?

Kimmie's core was shaking when she walked the trooper to the door of the daycare, but it wasn't because she was mad at his suggestion Mom's death might not have been a suicide.

It was because he'd confirmed Kimmie's most secret fear, the one she'd been trying desperately to hide even from herself — that her stepfather could actually have committed the murder.

CHAPTER 12

Kimmie had a terrible headache and was grateful for Jade's help in getting the kids ready for their afternoon nap. Only a few of them fell asleep, but the rest managed to remain relatively quiet, looking at books or playing with a toy or two in their cots. Jade was getting ready to organize the bookshelves when Kimmie came behind her.

"Hey." She tried to keep her voice sounding as natural as possible.

Jade glanced up, and Kimmie rubbed her sweaty palms against her jeans. "Umm, do you still have free long distance on your cell?"

Jade pulled out her earbuds and yanked her phone out of her pocket. "Yeah. You need to call someone?"

All her co-workers at the daycare knew about Kimmie's phone situation, and whether or not they thought it was weird that a young woman living in the present day could survive without a cell phone or even a landline at her house, they always let her borrow their phones to make quick calls here and there.

Kimmie reached out for the cell, shuffling her feet and not quite able to meet Jade's gaze. "It might be a little longer than normal. I haven't really talked with any of the relatives since Mom died, and ..."

Jade waved her hand in the air. "Take it. Go. You can even head outside or something if you want privacy. We're fine here for a while."

Kimmie wasn't sure if she should be hurt by the way Jade was acting so dismissively or if she should simply be grateful for the chance to connect with someone outside Glennallen.

"I'll try not to be too long," she promised. Grabbing her coat, she made sure that Pip was comfortable in his cot. He was one of the only kids who regularly managed to drift off to sleep, and he was already drooling slightly when Kimmie made her way out to the playground. Sitting down on one of the swings, Kimmie dialed the number from memory, begging it to go through.

Please pick up. Please pick up.

Kimmie let out a simultaneous sigh of relief and a shiver from the cold. Swinging her legs softly back and forth, she found her voice.

"Hey, Meg. It's me, Kimmie. Got a minute? We need to talk about Mom."

CHAPTER 13

Kimmie waited so long for her sister's response she started to worry she'd called the wrong person. She pulled the phone away from her ear to check the number again.

"Meg?" she finally asked.

"I'm here." Her sister let out a sigh, and Kimmie braced herself for some sort of big-sister lecture or maybe a guilt trip. *Why didn't you know Mom was suicidal? Why didn't you do anything to stop her?*

Instead, Meg asked, "Are you okay? Where are you calling from? Is anyone else there?"

Kimmie knew she was talking about Chuck and shook her head even though her sister couldn't see the gesture. "No, it's just me. I'm at the daycare, but the kids are resting, so I'm on the playground. I'm by myself."

"Okay." Meg sounded relieved. "Listen, I'm really sorry I haven't gotten out there yet. I wanted to be with you. I really did."

It's not too late, Kimmie wanted to say, but her voice betrayed her, and she let out the expected, "It's okay. I know you're busy."

"It's not that." Meg sounded flustered, the same vibe she gave off to anyone and everyone. The vibe that yelled *I'm a busy woman with five hundred important things on my to-do list.* "I'm just worried for you. I don't want you staying with him, Kimmie."

Her heart sank. Why had she expected anything different? This wasn't a conversation between an older sister comforting her little sister, the same little sister who found their mother hanging from the garage rafters. This was a conversation where Meg simply continued the argument she'd started with Mom years ago, except now she was fighting with Kimmie: *Leave Chuck. Move in with me in Anchorage.*

"I can't leave Pip." If Meg had invested any time in getting to know her half-brother, she'd understand, but by the time Pip was born, she and Mom were in the ugliest stage of their *leave Chuck and let me save you* feud.

"Right now, it's you I'm worried about." Even while she spoke, Meg sounded like she had twenty other things on her mind, a hundred other errands she'd rather be doing than having this conversation with her disappointment of a sister.

That's easy for you to say from your privileged high tower, Kimmie wanted to shout. If her sister had stuck with the family instead of insisting on spending her senior year in Anchorage with that boyfriend who dumped her the week before prom and the best friend who gossiped about it behind her back, Meg would understand what things were really like under Chuck's roof.

Why Kimmie couldn't just walk away.

Why Mom couldn't either.

She tried to steady her voice. She wasn't Mom. This wasn't her fight to have with her sister. She just wanted information. "A trooper stopped by," she said, hoping that Meg would pick up the cue and fill her in on whatever details she'd given Taylor's station.

Silence.

"He said they're maybe going to look a little deeper into everything that happened." Kimmie waited. *Jump in at any time, Meg. Don't wait for me.*

Her sister let out an impatient huff. "Well, I'm worried about you, all right? There's some things you don't know. About Mom."

Kimmie rolled her eyes. So all of a sudden her sister was an expert on the dead mother she hardly visited? "Like what?" *This should be good,* Kimmie thought and waited for her sister's response.

"She called me last week."

That was news. "She did?" For the entirety of their relationship, at least as far as Kimmie knew, whenever Mom wanted to talk to her daughter she had to beg Chuck to let her go over to Mrs. Spencer's, the neighbor, to borrow the phone. Over the past few years he'd gotten so belligerent whenever Mom showed even a spark of independent thought, she simply stopped asking. Besides, weren't her mom and sister mad at each other since Meg always pestered Mom about leaving Chuck? From Meg's vantage point, Chuck was a jerk, and she couldn't understand why anyone would choose to stay in a relationship with someone that evil.

As if it were ever that simple.

"Listen, I don't have time to go into all the details right now." Meg lowered her voice as if she were worried about eavesdroppers. "But I want to talk to you soon. Can I come out there? I can shuffle some things around, drive out tomorrow ..."

She let her voice trail off. Kimmie tried to remember the last time she'd seen her sister. There had been one visit after Pip was born, which lasted long enough for Meg to drop off a few packages of diapers and two new onesies before she continued on her road trip to Denali with her husband and their cadre of rich, attractive friends. Then last December she pulled up in time to hand Mom a fruitcake and a pair of holiday socks before taking off toward the Fairbanks ice festival.

Apparently taking Kimmie's silence for reluctance or hostility, Meg added with a huff, "You know, it shouldn't take a death in the family to make us spend time together."

Kimmie wanted to remind Meg that she wasn't the one who left. It was Meg who stayed in Anchorage, Meg who abandoned her sister when she was arguably at her most vulnerable, leaving her and Mom to fend for themselves against Chuck's cruelty.

Kimmie recognized that her jealousy was misplaced. It wasn't like Meg could have done anything to assuage Chuck's anger. He would have been a terrible husband and a terrible stepparent and a terrible person whether or not Meg was there to share in the family's suffering. But the fact that Meg had gone on to attend college, found herself a successful husband to take her on so many exotic vacations, and was leading in every other way as functional and enviable a life as possible was an affront to Kimmie's sense of justice, immature and irrational as it might be.

Jade glanced out the door frowning, and Kimmie wondered just how long she'd been out here. It only felt like a few minutes, but of course a few minutes gave plenty of time to revive old grudges and poke at old scabs as far as her sister was concerned.

"Listen, Meg, I've got to hang up. I'm at work."

"Hold on. There's something I haven't told you." Meg was whining now, her voice rising in pitch. It was that same affected intonation that made her come across as cool and mature in high school but sounded grating and petty as an adult.

Jade was still staring at Kimmie, jerking her head now as if playing a game of charades, raising her eyebrows in some unspoken message. Goosebumps erupted at the base of Kimmie's neck, and she instinctively turned around. Her stepfather was just a foot behind her, glowering, his face somewhat droopy on account of all he'd had to drink.

"Just who d'you think you're talking to?" He grabbed Jade's cell phone. "Who're you?" he demanded coarsely, and Kimmie held her breath, straining to hear any response from the other line.

It was silent. Had Meg hung up?

All of Chuck's attention reverted back to Kimmie. "What're you doing with a cell phone? Didn't I tell you those things'll give you brain cancer?"

"It's not mine," Kimmie stammered. "I was just ..."

Jade rushed up, interrupting. "It was a prospective parent. A new family in town. They just had some questions about the daycare, and I was busy with the kids."

Kimmie felt her face heating up and didn't know if Jade's intervention made her feel more grateful or humiliated.

She winced when Chuck grabbed her arm, digging his dirt-crusted fingernails through her sweater. Dragging her away from Jade, he hissed, "Get the boy. You're coming home."

"It's not three yet," Kimmie protested. "I've got two more hours."

"Don't care," Chuck slurred. "And tell that big black gal you work with you quit. I can't find a single can of chili for lunch, and even if I did, I couldn't eat it because you lost the can opener. We're out of groceries, and the bathroom's a mess. You're coming home."

Kimmie didn't have the nerve to meet Jade's eyes but sensed her friend's gaze following her as she made her way into the daycare. Pip was still drooling on his cot, his hands tucked under his chin like a tiny cherub.

"Come on, Buster. Let's get you ready." She hated to wake him up. He looked so peaceful, and she knew he needed his sleep.

Pip stirred, and Kimmie smiled at him. "Wake up. It's time to go home."

Back at the trailer, she'd confront Chuck. She had to. She and Pip needed this job just as much as Chuck needed the paycheck. He'd come around.

Kimmie wrapped Pip's arms around her neck so she could carry him to the cubbies to collect their things.

"You okay?" Jade whispered. Kimmie hadn't even noticed her trailing behind them.

She sniffed. "Yeah. He's just ... you know, still having a hard time. After everything." She wrapped Pip's coat around his shoulders and wondered if he was about to fall asleep again in her arms.

Jade looked unconvinced. "You need something? I can help, you know. I even have a spare bedroom if you and Pip need some time away for a little bit." She let the last part of her sentence inflect up to a question.

Kimmie squeezed back the anger and mortification that were boiling inside her. "That's really sweet of you. But we're fine." She rubbed her brother's back and looked Jade square in the eyes. "We're going to get through this. We always do."

CHAPTER 14

Back home, Kimmie helped Pip get situated in their room with the handful of matchbox cars Mom managed to buy for him at the thrift store. Once Kimmie was sure he was adequately distracted, she headed to the bathroom and started cleaning. Chuck must have had a bloody nose again. Splatters of red filled the sink. She looked inside the cabinet. Great, no gloves, either.

She grabbed a few paper towels and balled them together in as thick of a wad as she could, hoping the barrier was big enough to protect her from coming into contact with her stepfather's blood. Who knew what kind of diseases he might carry? Her stomach retched, and she remembered she hadn't eaten any lunch. Oh, well. At least Pip was fed. Whatever Jade heated up for the kids that afternoon might have to last him until tomorrow morning.

If Chuck let them go back to the daycare at all.

He couldn't really force her to quit her job. They needed that money. Besides, he liked getting Pip out of the house. After three-day weekends when the daycare was closed for a holiday, Chuck would grumble and demanded to know when she would get that boy out of his hair.

A dozen times while she cleaned out the sink, Kimmie pictured herself walking into the living room, snapping off that stupid television set of his, and telling her stepfather he had no authority to make her leave her job. But then what? Even if he legally couldn't keep her from the daycare, he had every right to prevent Pip from going, and then what would be the point? She had to stay with Pip. She was his only protection from his father's violence. She would never leave the two of them at the trailer alone.

So if Chuck remained that stubborn about the daycare, if he said that he was withdrawing Pip from the program, did that mean she'd stay here, every bit a slave as her mom had been? The idea was unfathomable. She'd lose her mind. She'd go insane and kill herself like her mom had. Or kill her stepfather and wind up behind bars, with Pip imagining her a villain every bit as scary as the ones he saw on TV. No, she couldn't, she wouldn't stay here forever.

So what could she do?

She scrubbed at the sink fiercely until Chuck came in, pushing past her with a grunt. He unzipped his pants and started to pee.

Disgusted, Kimmie threw down her paper towel, stomped into the hallway, and slammed the bathroom door shut. People shouldn't live like this. It was cruel and inhumane to subject a child as young and impressionable as Pip to this kind of squalor and filth.

Chuck cleared his throat from the bathroom, loudly enough that Kimmie could hear through the door and above the sound of the wailing TV. She didn't know what was on, but it certainly wasn't appropriate for children. Sometimes she wondered if Pip retreated into his own mind like he did because his surroundings were too difficult to accept.

No kid should have to endure what he had, but what could Kimmie do? How could she help him? She thought about Taylor. She'd had the trooper on her mind even before he showed up at her work today. Fingering his card in her pocket, she wondered if there was any way he could help her.

But how?

If Chuck wouldn't let Pip go back to the daycare, that meant she couldn't go back either. She couldn't abandon her brother that way. As far as she knew, Chuck had never physically hurt Pip, but he'd threatened to. It was one of his go-to responses whenever Kimmie or her mom showed any sign of rebellion. If Mom let the coffee run out, Chuck would tell her he was going to bash Pip's head against the wall. If Kimmie didn't sign over her entire daycare check to him, he'd threaten to starve Pip for the week. Who could guess what would happen to her brother if Kimmie defied Chuck's orders and went back to the daycare?

She'd have to find another way to convince him. She could bring up the money, but she'd already tried that. There had to be something else.

Chuck threw open the bathroom door, jostling her as he squeezed his wide girth down the hallway. Scratching at his hairy belly, he mumbled, "Outta my way," and plodded back toward his recliner.

Kimmie glanced at him in open disgust. Her mom had spent a decade with this man, subjecting Kimmie and later Pip to his barbaric ways, his explosive temper. And now Mom was gone, and there was no way Kimmie was going to waste the rest of her life cleaning up her stepfather's messes and rolling over to be his punching bag whenever a violent mood came over him.

She was going to get away from here, and she was taking her brother with her.

CHAPTER 15

By the time Kimmie got the bathroom at least relatively clean, Pip had fallen asleep, content to finish his interrupted nap at home. It was just as well. She was sure he needed the sleep. She still didn't know how he was processing their mother's death. He'd cried when the ambulance came to carry her body away, but how much did he really understand? Kimmie had tried to explain to him, but what words do you use to tell a three-year-old their mother is dead?

Chuck was taking an afternoon snooze in front of the TV, and Kimmie tiptoed into the kitchen and scanned the cupboards. It was one of her regular pastimes, something she liked to call *let's see how much food there is and figure out how many days we can make it last.*

Today she was lucky. She pulled down two cans of chili from the back of the cupboard and the heels leftover from Chuck's white bread. She could feed Pip dinner after all.

Glancing around at her sleeping stepfather, she wondered how to make the best use of her time. If Pip were awake, she'd take him outside. It was chilly out, but the fresh air did both of them good. Every winter brought two or three major cases of sinus infections, and Chuck refused to let anyone see the doctor. The family could easily qualify for state insurance, but Chuck claimed the application process invaded their privacy and was convinced that Alaskan doctors were paid off for killing the most Medicaid recipients.

Kimmie hated feeling so helpless, and just a few months ago at work she'd printed and filled out the forms to get Pip onto Alaska's free health care for children. She used the daycare's address instead of their own and figured she'd keep the card there too in case Pip ever needed it, but the system was so backed up it would still be several months before she'd receive any kind of answer.

And Kimmie didn't plan to stay here that long.

All afternoon while she cleaned, she'd been thinking through her conversation with Taylor, running through each fact and insinuation.

Mom didn't write a suicide note. Or if she did, nobody had found it yet.

If Mom wanted people to read that note, she would have left it somewhere obvious. Kimmie had no idea how many suicide victims really did write letters for their families to find, but the trooper thought it was strange enough to at least mention its absence.

Mom had been in contact with Meg. About what? Chuck had sneaked up behind her while she was talking to her sister, interrupting their call before Kimmie could find anything else out. So what had Mom and Meg been talking about? How had Mom even reached out to Meg without Chuck finding out?

Meg didn't think Mom killed herself. Did Taylor actually say those words, or was that just the meaning Kimmie pieced together on her own? Meg had contacted the troopers. The troopers were investigating the case. Therefore, Meg must have given them some sort of information that cast suspicion on the suicide theory.

Meg didn't think Kimmie was safe. Meg asked her again to come to Anchorage, only this time it wasn't so she could sweep in and save the day and set herself up as Kimmie's parent-replacement, bossing her around and nagging her for all the ways she didn't live up to Meg's expectations. At least it didn't feel that way.

Not this time.

Meg wanted Kimmie to leave Chuck. That was nothing new. She'd wanted Kimmie to leave as soon as she knew or at least suspected what kind of man their stepfather was. There was nothing legally preventing Kimmie from leaving, and even though Chuck would be mad to lose a free source of domestic labor, he was too lazy to come all the way down to Anchorage to cause her any problems.

She could walk away now and never look back.

But what would happen to Pip? Relentlessly, her mind replayed the dozens of times Chuck had used Pip as a hostage to force Kimmie or her mom to do what he wanted. She could pass that information on to Taylor, but would anything happen? What if Taylor came back and said that he couldn't take any action unless she could prove Chuck actually harmed Pip? She was stuck.

But she wouldn't stay that way forever. There was some way out of this maddening prison. There had to be.

She just wished she knew what it was.

CHAPTER 16

Pip woke up from his nap crying. No, that wasn't the right word for it. Shrieking.

Kimmie had never heard any human make sounds like that, not in her entire life. She'd been heating up the last of the chili to get ready for dinner when she heard the shrill screams. Running to Pip's room, she braced herself for something terrible. His clothes were engulfed in flames. Chuck was stabbing him with the knife he'd used to butcher moose back in the days before he grew too lazy to go hunting.

But no. Chuck wasn't there, and as Kimmie knelt on the floor by the mattress, she couldn't see anything wrong. "What is it, Buster?" she asked, but Pip only continued to scream as if his intestines had caught fire. She examined his body, looking for injury, trying to guess where he hurt. Could it be his appendix or something else internal that she couldn't see? She had to get him to medical care, but how?

"Pip? Where do you hurt, Buster?"

He thrashed from side to side. She had to calm his movements. If she could just make eye contact, she could try to communicate. She curled him up on her lap, doing what she could to hold his head still so he wouldn't hurt himself with his wild flailing. When she saw the look in his eyes, her words caught in her throat. That wasn't her brother. It was someone else. Something else. His eyes were entirely vacant, reminding her mercilessly of her mother's corpse.

He stared at her, still unseeing, and shrieked again.

Terrified, she hefted him into her arms and raced him into the living room. "Something's wrong." She didn't care how worried Chuck was about money. She didn't care how much he hated the idea of doctors treating welfare patients. Pip needed medical attention. Now.

Chuck blinked at his son, and for a moment his face blanched. Kimmie didn't know if she should be grateful that he was taking Pip's condition seriously or if his reaction only freaked her out more.

"He woke up screaming," she explained, panting. "I don't know what to do." Her heart was racing, both from the physical energy it spent to keep her brother from flinging himself out of her arms and from her fear for his safety.

Chuck looked as bewildered as she felt, so she dared to squeak, "Should I take him to the doctor?"

The words seemed to snap Chuck out of his fearful reverie his son's behavior had cast him into. He scowled. "No." He stood up from the recliner, toppling Pringles crumbs and a crushed beer can onto the carpet.

He took a step forward and stared at his son. "Night terrors," he announced factually. "You've just got to wake him up."

Kimmie forced herself to look at those expressionless eyes again. "But he is awake. See?"

Chuck shook his head. "No, he ain't." He raised his fist in the air, and before Kimmie could react, he brought it down onto her brother's belly. Pip opened his mouth like a fish trying to gulp air, and in an instant the blank, glossy eyes took on an expression of fear and pain. He sucked in a noisy inhale then started to cry

"See?" Chuck turned back around and lumbered to his seat. "All you gotta do is wake him up."

Kimmie turned her back and hurried with Pip into the bedroom. She fingered the card in her pocket, where Taylor had written out his number, telling her to call if she ever needed help.

Through his tears, Pip clung onto Kimmie's shoulders but no longer flailed around or acted possessed. Kimmie took in a choppy inhalation and sank down with him on the mattress. Stroking his sweat-drenched hair, she fingered Taylor's card with her other hand and promised her brother, "I'm going to find us a way out of here. I'm going to get us some help."

CHAPTER 17

Dinner had been doomed from the start. During the entire time Kimmie was dealing with Pip and his night terrors, she'd left the chili on the stove. By the time she realized her mistake, half of the meal had turned into black crisp.

She would have never served it to her stepdad, but that was the last of the chili, so she added a few prayers and half a can of water, hoping to mask the burnt taste and stretch the meager offering out as much as possible. She scooped the top portion, the part that was the least scalded, into a bowl for Chuck and split the rest between herself and Pip. Even though Chuck never ate the heels of his bread, Kimmie couldn't serve the portions to Pip at the table without infuriating her stepfather, so she slipped them beneath her sweater to store for later.

Pip would sleep better with a snack before bed, anyway.

"This tastes awful," Chuck declared after his first bite. "What'd you do to it?"

Kimmie caught Pip's eyes on her. For her brother's sake, she'd try to avoid a confrontation. It would take every ounce of her patience and self-possession, but to keep Pip safe, it was worth the effort.

"I'm sorry." Kimmie eyed her own bowl, which contained nothing but black tar and a few beans. "It got a little burned."

Chuck spat, his saliva landing on the edge of the table instead of the floor where he probably intended. "What kind of stupid idiot can't even cook chili?"

She poked at the lumps in her bowl and offered another apology, one she mentally promised herself would be her last. She had to stop this, stop groveling. Mom had done nothing but cower before Chuck, and look where it had gotten her. For years, Kimmie had been plagued with both the urge to protect her mother and the unbearable frustration of knowing Mom was too weak to leave. Kimmie hated the way Mom refused to stand up to Chuck, the way she let him beat her up without offering up even the faintest of protests.

For years, Kimmie simultaneously despised, feared for, and pleaded with her mom, also vowing to herself that she would never let another man ruin her life the way Chuck had ruined her mother's. But now look where she was. It hadn't even been a full week since Mom's death, and Kimmie was falling into the exact same passive role, submissively trying to placate her stepfather because she was too scared to see Pip hurt.

It gave her an entirely new outlook on what Mom had experienced the last ten years of her life. What if the reason she stayed with Chuck wasn't because she was too weak to leave him but because she was scared of what he might do to her kids? By the time Pip came around, she must have felt even more trapped. For years, Kimmie wondered why her mom hadn't simply walked away, had cried herself to sleep at night asking God why her mom hated her and Pip enough to keep them trapped here.

Maybe Kimmie had been wrong. Maybe it was her love for her children that bound her mother to this monster.

Kimmie had vowed to never repeat the same mistakes her mom did, but wasn't she doing the exact same thing? Apologizing to Chuck because she didn't want him to get angry and possibly hurt her brother. Persevering in this purgatory of an existence because her only other option was to leave Pip alone with his father, abandoning the brother she loved.

"Why aren't you eating that, boy?"

Kimmie's spine stiffened while Chuck glared at Pip's bowl of burnt chili. Pip glanced to her, and she rushed to fill the silence. "They had a pretty big lunch this afternoon at work." Wrong thing to say. Why did she mention the daycare?

Chuck grabbed his son's bowl and shoved it under his chin. "You eat this food your sister made, or you're gonna be sleeping outside with the bears and the moose tonight."

Pip's eyes widened.

Chuck sneered, taking apparent pleasure in his son's fear. "That's right. Pretend like you understand what I'm saying. Pretend like you're not some stupid, idiotic ..."

Kimmie was clutching the sides of her chair to keep from jumping up and slapping him. Tears stung the corners of her eyes, not of anger or fear or even grief, but of sheer hatred. She wanted to see Chuck dead. She wanted to be there when he gasped his last breath, his ugly, gaping mouth hanging open, his curses finally silenced. The hatred coursed through her entire body, fueling her. She began to shake. The only thing that kept her from seizing whatever utensil she could grab hold of and attacking her stepfather was that she didn't want to scare her brother.

"Eat your chili, Buster," she whispered.

"That's right," Chuck mocked in an imitating falsetto. "*Eat your chili, Buster*, because you're lucky I even let you sit at my table. You know what most parents do to little boys who don't know how to talk by the time they're your age? They make them crawl on the floor and lick up their food like dogs." He jabbed his spoon toward his son. "That's what I'm gonna do with you if you don't eat every single bite from your bowl, you hear me?"

Kimmie turned toward her brother and scooped a small spoonful of chili into his mouth. Trying to shut out the sound of Chuck jeering at his son for having to be fed like an infant, she pictured a life free from everything. Free from Chuck, free from this revolting trailer. Free from her grief and her guilt, free from the questions about her mom's death that plagued her.

"That's right," Chuck taunted, his voice rising in pitch. "Feed the tiny little baby. Then don't forget to change his diaper too. Is your diaper dirty, you stupid little idiot?"

Kimmie kept her back to him. He was egging her on, a dinner game he'd played hundreds of times with her mother. Teasing and jeering until Mom started to cry or showed some other display of emotion, enough to fuel Chuck's sadism until he felt he had the right to heap physical abuse on top of the verbal. Kimmie refused to fall victim in this game of his. She wasn't going to give him the privilege of seeing her emotions, of sensing her fear. She wasn't going to show any sign of weakness.

He could beat her if he wanted, but her mind and soul belonged to her alone. She wondered what he'd do if he realized how much hatred she hid buried beneath her expressionless exterior, how many times she'd sat at this same table and visualized his pained and tortured death.

No, it wasn't a Christian attitude. Mom had taught her to forgive anyone who wronged her, but Mom wasn't here anymore, and her strategy of rolling over like a compliant dog welcoming its master's boot wasn't going to get Kimmie anything but injured. She knew that the Bible talked about love and grace and forgiveness, but there were also times for wrath.

And right now, the thing she prayed for most was for God to afflict her stepfather with every kind of disease and painful torment in his vast, almighty repertoire.

The thought fueled her determination, and she fed her brother in silence.

CHAPTER 18

It was Kimmie's good luck that the electric company decided to make good on their threat to cut off the power that night in response to a delinquent bill. Chuck's plot of land, like many others in the area, came equipped with a wooden outhouse, a remnant from Alaska's homesteading days, and as she led her brother outside, she had the chance to speak to him in private.

"The way your dad's treating us isn't right." She'd lost track of how many nights after a dinner just like this, or worse, her mom would hold Pip in her arms and croon, "Your father loves you. He just doesn't always know how to show it," or some other nonsense. Kimmie figured Pip was confused enough by his father's abuse that he didn't need anyone else making excuses for such unforgivable behavior.

"I'm trying to think of a way to get us to a safe place. Would you like that?" She searched her brother's face for any sign that he heard or understood.

"It's not always going to be like this. We can pray ..." She stopped herself. What was she trying to tell him? That they could pray and God would whisk them to safety as if he were a genie from a magic lamp? How many sleepless nights had Kimmie spent after moving in with Chuck, begging God to free her from that existence? To strike her new stepfather dead or make Mom brave enough to leave him or do something to stop the torture she constantly lived through.

But God hadn't answered her prayers. Ten years later, he still hadn't answered. She was still here, an adult but every bit as much dependent on her stepfather as she'd been in her teens. She wasn't mad at God, but she didn't want Pip to end up doing what she did, setting all her hopes on a prayer, a prayer that failed to come true. Kimmie still talked to God, but mostly it was to ask him to shield Pip from the worst of the horrors they had learned to endure.

She didn't have the strength to hope for anything more.

Mom was different. Mom had kept her faith until the very end. "God's got a reason for everything," she'd say while icing Kimmie's black eye so the bruise wouldn't raise quite as many questions at school. "We can always trust God to do what's best for us in any situation." That was another one of her favorites.

Kimmie didn't doubt God's goodness. She'd experienced waves of peace that swept over her during the depths of her turmoil and inner pain, signs of God's love she knew were divine. What she did doubt was her mom's simplistic expectation that if they remained steadfast and patient, God would usher them into some happily-ever-after dream world where Chuck was kind and their dilapidated, drafty trailer transformed itself into a home like her sister Meg's mansion on the Anchorage hillside.

If Kimmie wanted the fairy tale ending, she'd have to find a way to work out the details on her own. Sitting around waiting patiently had gotten her mom killed — yet another mistake Kimmie was in no hurry to repeat. She felt Taylor's card in her pocket, gleaning vicarious strength and courage. Just knowing someone else cared about her safety, someone with the authority of the state backing him up, gave her an unfamiliar sense of boldness and determination.

She would find a way. She would break free from this cage. She would find her happy ending, and she would give Pip the life he deserved.

Kimmie fingered Taylor's card. The outhouse was situated halfway between Chuck's trailer and their nearest neighbor. Mrs. Spencer was an elderly woman who sometimes let Kimmie use her phone. If she left Pip here and started to run ...

She glanced at her brother, who sat on the outhouse toilet. No, not yet. The last thing she needed was for Pip to follow her and slow her down or fall down the outhouse hole if she left him here alone. Her plan would have to wait. Tonight. Not so late that Mrs. Spencer would be in bed or alarmed by a knock on her door, but late enough that Pip would hopefully be asleep and Kimmie could come out here alone.

Thank God they'd cut off the power.

Her mind made up, she helped Pip off the seat and cleaned him up. Without any running water at home and nothing stored in bottles, they'd skip brushing their teeth tonight. You couldn't get a cavity from one act of negligence.

She held Pip's hand and shuddered as they made their way back to the trailer. An icy blast stabbed through her sweater. The sun was setting earlier and earlier each day, a sign of winter's soon arrival just as telling and ominous as the termination dust on the mountains. She wasn't going to spend another winter here in a trailer that could never heat up past fifty-five degrees, power that turned on and off based on when Chuck remembered to pay his overdue bills. By the time the winter solstice came, when it was dark by three and the sun refused to rise until after ten, she wasn't going to dig around for candle nubs because Chuck drank away their utility money.

She was going to be in a warm home by a roaring fireplace, making as much hot chocolate as she and Pip could ever care to drink, both of them tucked up in blankets and relaxing on the softest couch imaginable. She'd take Pip to the library, check out an endless supply of books, and read them all to him for hours at a time. Of course, she'd save her best voices for when it was just the two of them together.

They would be happy.

And they would be safe.

She gave her brother's hand a squeeze. "Come on, Buster. Let's get you home."

CHAPTER 19

Kimmie hoped that with the electricity cut off, Chuck would fall asleep early. Without his TV to keep him company, there wasn't much else for him to do. It was far too much to expect him to get up and attack that pile of dirty dishes in the kitchen, and besides, without the electricity the well didn't run. In the early days after Mom moved in with Chuck, the trailer was hooked up to a generator to prepare for Glennallen's sporadic power outages, but it had fallen into disrepair, and Chuck always maintained it was too expensive to fix.

Kimmie was looking forward to a quiet night. Chuck couldn't expect her to stay up and clean, not with the sun down and no running water. She might crawl in bed with Pip and cuddle for a while until it was time for her to go back out. She wasn't exactly sure what she'd do if she managed to make use of Mrs. Spencer's phone, but maybe the extra couple hours would give her time to think up a plan.

Back inside the trailer, she helped Pip take off his coat.

Chuck was in his chair, waiting for her. "Put the kid to bed then come out here."

She didn't know what he wanted, but at least Pip would be excused from whatever sadism Chuck might have in mind. It was the most Kimmie could ask for, at least at the moment. In a few hours, she'd tell Chuck she had to use the outhouse and head over to the neighbor's. Mrs. Spencer usually turned off her lights around nine, so Kimmie would plan her visit shortly before that. She'd call Taylor.

And then what?

The seed of a plan had started to germinate in her mind, but it would take time to fully form. She had to muse over it for a little while. It couldn't be rushed. Whatever Chuck needed her for, she hoped it wouldn't take too long. She helped Pip into his favorite pajamas, teaching him the names of the dinosaurs — at least the ones she could remember — while pointing to the pictures. Sometimes she wondered if any of her extra effort to coax Pip to talk was getting through, but she'd never stop. She was convinced that Pip had more to say, more to learn, more to achieve than those who just knew him as a speech-delayed child would ever give him credit for. With Mom dead, Kimmie was now her brother's only champion and advocate.

She knew she certainly wasn't ready for the challenge, but it had been thrust upon her nonetheless.

"God will always equip you to do the work he's called you to do," Mom used to say, but at the time Kimmie had been more worried about keeping her stepfather from knocking her out than she'd been about growing in her faith. Still, Mom continued to sprinkle these little devotional moments into their days, teaching her about the Lord and his plan of salvation. The spiritual upbringing in the family was now another task that rested entirely on Kimmie's shoulders. Had she ever talked to Pip about heaven and sin and forgiveness? She wouldn't know how to have a conversation like that with a neurotypical three-year-old. What was she supposed to say to Pip?

All that would have to wait. The longer she tarried in the bedroom, the angrier and more impatient Chuck would grow. She kissed Pip's cheek, but he struggled and clung to her when she tried to tuck him in.

"What's wrong?" she asked. "What do you need?"

He made a back and forth motion with his fingers near his mouth. The pantomime was easy to discern. "You want to brush your teeth?"

He responded with a grunt.

"There's no water tonight. It's okay. It won't be too bad to skip it for just this once."

Pip's eyes widened as if Kimmie had just confessed that she was the one who killed their mom, and she let out her breath. "Fine," she breathed, "just stay here for a little bit, and if you're still awake when I come back, we'll brush your teeth then."

She had no idea how she'd manage that without any tap or running water, but she'd figure something out. Prying herself free from his hold, she blew him a kiss and hurried to the door.

She'd kept her stepfather waiting long enough.

CHAPTER 20

Chuck was cleaning out his ears when Kimmie stepped back into the living room.

"You wanted to see me?"

He didn't turn to look at her. "Got these for you." He tossed a manila envelope by her feet. "Need them filled out by tomorrow when the mail comes."

She picked up the envelope as well as a few of Chuck's used Q-tips. "What's this?" She bent back the fastener.

"Disability application. You'll need that now you aren't working no more."

Kimmie's mom had never been one to gamble. She thought cards and dice were wicked, and she never took any risks. Kimmie wasn't like that, so she searched Chuck's face to try to detect how serious he was. This might all be some bluff. She could put up a tiny fight and be back at the daycare by tomorrow.

Or Chuck might be so set on keeping Kimmie at home that he'd do anything, even hurt Pip, if she defied his order.

Just how far should she push? And was she feeling lucky?

Like earlier, she decided to appeal to his greed and selfishness first. "You know, I think the state's really backed up right now on applications." She wouldn't mention her own firsthand experience applying for Pip's medical coverage. "It'd probably take a while for the money to start coming through." She also wouldn't mention the fact that no reasonable administration would label her unfit for work. Because Chuck had managed to eke money out of the system for years for no other disability than being a lazy alcoholic who preferred his drink over gainful employment, that didn't mean that anyone who filled out this packet could count on receiving a regular check.

Filling out his stupid application would get him off her back, but it wouldn't put breakfast in Pip's mouth.

"Another thing I started to wonder just now," she began, trying like usual to downplay her ability to actively think and reason for herself, "is if maybe we'd be better off in the long run keeping things the way they are." She didn't say the word *daycare*, didn't want to trigger him and set him off for a half-hour tirade. She could tell by the tightness in his face that she was walking on thin ice, but she'd have to venture out just a little further and hope it wouldn't crack.

"The nice thing about the current setup is it has Pip eating most of his meals outside of the home. It'd take quite a bit more grocery money to make up that difference." She watched Chuck warily, knew that he was still unconvinced. "He's usually really hungry by bedtime," she added hopefully.

It was this last comment that tipped the scale against her.

"You think I'm not doing my job as the man of this house in providing for my family?" His diction for once was impeccable, which only increased Kimmie's fear. Her stepfather was mean, violent, and sadistic whenever he was drunk, but he tired easily and soon lost interest.

When he was sober, on the other hand ...

"I didn't mean that at all." She opened the envelope and pretended to look through the first few pages. "I'm sorry. It's just, things have been a little difficult for us all ..."

"Difficult?" her stepdad roared. "You want to talk to me about difficult? Your mom had the nerve to hang herself in my garage, leaving me an idiot of a son who can't even say his own name and an ungrateful brat who stands in my house and tells me how to run my family!"

Kimmie shook her head vehemently. "I'm sorry. That's not what I meant."

He was out of his chair now, and Kimmie didn't know whether the first object to meet her body would be his fists, his boots, or some projectile. He grabbed her by the ponytail, snapping her neck back and twisting her head up to face him.

"Let's get one thing right, you spoiled little princess," he hissed into her face. For once, she wished for the familiar scent of beer on his breath. "This is my home, and as long as you live here, you better expect we're going to do things my way. If I say go on disability, you go on disability. If I say punch your brother for being a stupid, speechless idiot, you punch your brother for being a stupid, speechless idiot."

All day, Kimmie had been testing this thought in her head, this nagging suspicion Taylor had fueled with his speculations and questions back at the daycare. Was this the kind of outrage Mom witnessed before her husband killed her? Kimmie was smart enough to know that she was stupid not to feel scared. Stupid not to cower, to get on her knees, to beg for forgiveness.

But she wasn't ever going to grovel again. For the first time in her life, she saw her stepfather for what he really was — a pathetic, lonely man with no power except what people like her mom gave him. Mom fed his ego, bolstered his twisted sadism. If Chuck didn't have someone weaker to manipulate and terrify, he was absolutely nothing more than a potbellied man, a pathetic creature unable to wield any power whatsoever.

For the first time since she met Chuck, Kimmie wasn't scared of him. He could do what he wanted to her, then when he was done, he'd fall down exhausted and have to sleep until morning. She was younger, stronger, and more stubborn than he could ever hope to be. She was smarter too, which meant that she'd find a way to save both herself and Pip.

The torment would end, and Chuck would be left alone in a drafty, cold trailer, surrounded by beer cans and chip wrappers, with nobody left to terrorize, berate, or clean up after his pitiful messes.

Kimmie grinned.

And then realized from the glowing hatred in her stepfather's eyes that this single gesture of defiance might cost her very life.

CHAPTER 21

"You think this is a game?" Chuck punched Kimmie in the gut, his breath hot as he bellowed in her face. "You think you can come here and laugh at me in my own house?"

The anger that soared through her was as exhilarating as it was dangerous. Struggling for breath, she knew she couldn't irritate him further. She had to placate him. For Pip's sake.

But all she could think about was how pathetic he'd look in an orange prison jumpsuit, tired and weary, an old man who'd destroyed everyone around him and was finally reaping the benefits of his cruelty.

He slammed her against the wall and laughed as she collapsed to the floor. It wasn't until he unlocked his cabinet in the corner that cold fear chilled her whole body. He'd threatened each of them before with his rifle, even Pip, but that was always when he was so drunk he could hardly stand up straight.

She'd never faced him both armed and sober. All feelings of haughtiness and grandeur vaporized when he pulled out his hunting rifle. That's what he called it at least, because apparently before he found a woman he could send to the grocery store to buy canned chili, he actually had to work for his food. Kimmie was still on the floor, wondering if she'd have time to kick him and knock him off balance if he decided he was going to fire.

Please don't let Pip come out, she prayed and hoped that her brother was already asleep.

Chuck took a step forward. She'd already missed the opportunity to trip him with her leg. She was paralyzed, watching every one of her stepfather's movements as though through time-manipulating binoculars. Chuck himself was stuck in slow motion as he brought the rifle up to his shoulder and aimed, but everything else — her pulse, her eyes darting in every direction in search of escape, her choppy breaths — had sped up exponentially.

Chuck slid the bolt forward. He was going to shoot her. Right here as she lay cowering on the floor, he was going to shoot her. She didn't even have the courage to bring her hands to cover her face but instead stared at her stepfather, totally stupefied.

A defiant whine from the hallway was both grating and freeing. Kimmie jumped into action and sped toward her brother.

"Get him out of here," Chuck hollered.

Pip squealed angrily, pantomiming a toothbrush with his finger.

"He wants to brush his teeth."

"Just get him back in bed." At least Chuck had the decency to wait to murder Kimmie until Pip was safe in his room.

Heart still speeding, Kimmie led her brother down the hall. The electricity had been cut off so many times she always kept a small flashlight in the top drawer of the bathroom. She turned it on, wondering how to help Pip clean his teeth without any running water.

"Here. Open your mouth." She picked up his toothbrush, and he grunted in complaint, pointing to the tube of Colgate.

"No toothpaste," she told him, "not tonight. Now open up."

As she brushed his teeth, she brought her mouth toward his ear. "I want you to listen to me. No matter what you hear happening tonight, I want you to stay in your room, okay? If Daddy gets real loud, just stay in your room, and if he comes in acting mad ..."

She couldn't finish. What could she tell him? She wasn't even sure if Pip understood anything she said. If something happened to her and then Chuck came after Pip ... He could run. He knew where Mrs. Spencer lived. But what if he got lost in the dark?

"If Daddy's really mad tonight," she concluded, "it's okay to hide. You remember hide and seek at the daycare?" The thought gave her an idea. "Remember how you hid in that big house?"

Pip's eyes widened. Did he understand? She leaned in even closer. "If Daddy gets really mad and if I fall asleep or can't help you, I want you to hide. And if the sun comes out and you can sneak outside real quiet, go over to Mrs. Spencer. Can you do that?"

Wait. What if Mrs. Spencer just walked him back home to Chuck? It was too complicated. If Kimmie wasn't there to offer him every single direction like she'd spoon-fed him that night's chili for dinner, how could she expect Pip to remember everything?

Which meant that Kimmie had to keep herself alive through the night so that tomorrow she could find a way to get them both the help they needed.

By the time she got Pip tucked back into his bed, Chuck was back in his recliner. She glanced nervously around the living room until her eyes landed on the rifle leaning against the cabinet.

"Don't forget your application." Chuck nodded toward the pile of paperwork Kimmie had dropped on the floor.

If it helped her survive to see Pip through one more night, she'd go through the motions of obedience. Kimmie stooped to pick the file up and glanced again at the cabinet, promising herself that as soon as Chuck was asleep, she'd find a way to get a hold of that rifle.

CHAPTER 22

The temperature had dropped, but the sun still hadn't fully set. Another month or two and it would be dark before dinnertime, but for now the little bit of extra daylight still served in her favor. Pip had been snoring gently for about half an hour, and Kimmie's eyes were strained from filling out that paperwork with nothing but the dim twilight and a cheap battery-powered flashlight.

When she heard the front door shut, she strained her eyes and peered out the window. When Chuck had to pee and the power was out, he either filled up the toilet or sprayed the area right by the front porch, but this time she could make out his fat figure sauntering toward the outhouse.

Her whole body trembled. She'd already planned what she was going to do, but what if Chuck found out? What if they ran out of time? Then what would happen to them?

Before grabbing Pip, she ran to the gun cabinet. Chuck still hadn't put the rifle away. She'd never even handled the thing. Guns scared her, whether she was watching her stepfather aiming the barrel at her mom's chest or just seeing a gunfight on one of his violent TV shows. But this was the only way to make her plan work. She was faster than Chuck, but she certainly wasn't faster than a bullet.

She sprinted back into her room, trying to guess how long she had, begging God that it would be enough. Sometimes Chuck only needed a few minutes. Other times he could take nearly half an hour, although that was usually when he was in the house and had magazines to keep him busy.

She scooped Pip up, hoping he'd stay asleep until they were out of earshot. He'd be groggy and disoriented, and the last thing she needed was for Chuck to hear Pip crying as they made their escape. The biggest difficulty would be how to carry her brother and the rifle at the same time. She could just hide it. That way if Chuck went after them, at least he'd be unarmed. She didn't have a lot of time to make her decision. Instead of taking it with her and risking falling and hurting herself or her brother, she rushed it into their bedroom and shoved it under her mattress. All she needed was a few minutes' head start. She couldn't take Pip to Mrs.

Spencer's. That would be too obvious and one of the first places Chuck would look. They'd have to go in the other direction. Kimmie needed to end up at the highway if she wanted to find someone with a phone who could help, but her main priority would be to evade Chuck for as long as possible. That was the first goal. Everything else was secondary.

Kimmie yanked their blanket off the bed and covered her brother. Tattered as it was, it'd give Pip some extra protection from the cold. Thankful that he was still asleep, she hurried as quickly as she could toward the front door, grabbing her jacket. Where were her shoes? There wasn't any more time to waste. She threw them on her feet, snatched up her brother's tennies, and was out the door.

Chuck hadn't been hunting in over ten years, but Kimmie didn't know just how good of a sportsman he'd been in the past. Could he follow their tracks? Would he bother in this chilly twilight? She'd need to make her way to the trooper station, but first the long trek through the woods, away from the highway, away from the neighbors who might offer to help.

As soon as she stepped outside, she wished she'd brought that rifle. She wasn't even positive that she'd know how to fire it if she needed to, but at least she'd look imposing. Then again, she couldn't carry her brother and an awkward gun very far. Pip was getting heavy. The woods thickened just ahead. Once she was convinced they were concealed by the trees and the darkness, she'd wake him up.

She hoped she hadn't forgotten anything.

Going back was no longer an option. No second chances, no second guessing.

She had to go forward.

Even if it killed her.

CHAPTER 23

Pip woke up when a branch pulled back and slapped his shoulder. Kimmie was panting. She hadn't realized how tired she'd get carrying him for even this short distance. Wrapping the blanket more tightly around his shoulders, she leaned against a tree trunk and cuddled him close to her chest.

"It's okay, Buster," she said. "We're going to go on a little ..." A little what? What kind of name could she give to a situation like this?

"We're going on a trip," she finally explained. "And I want you to be strong and brave, all right? Can you do that for me?"

Pip was looking around at the trees in all directions. His eyes widened, and he clutched Kimmie's coat.

"It's okay," she crooned as calmly as she could. "I know just where we're going, and I'm going to stay with you." She wanted to promise that he was safe now, but how could she be sure it was the truth? Instead, she bit her tongue and started to sing one of Mom's Bible verse songs.

Thy word is a lamp unto my feet and a light unto my path.

It seemed appropriate for a night like this, when the deepening woods grew more and more menacing as twilight faded into darkness. Kimmie never had a great sense of direction, but without landmarks to guide her and only the light from the moon and stars, she felt even more lost. There was the big dipper, a staple in the Alaskan sky. If she followed it to Polaris, she was supposed to be able to find north, but the entire constellation tipped on its side and loomed so low on the horizon it hardly looked like it was pointing anywhere. And even if she knew were north was, that didn't tell her which direction the trooper station was from here.

The farther she got from her neighbors or the Glenn Highway, the more lost she and Pip could get, but what other choice did she have? If Chuck hadn't found out she was missing yet, he would any minute. Unless he was so tired he went right to his recliner after using the outhouse and fell asleep. It was possible. She doubted he was in the habit of spying on her and Pip at night to make sure they were both in their room.

Unless Chuck had a reason to suspect otherwise, wouldn't he just assume they were asleep? Then she'd have until morning to find her and Pip the help they needed. Taylor and the other troopers would offer their protection as soon as she told them about the way her stepfather had threatened her with his rifle.

The rifle. Why had she moved it? Chuck would notice it wasn't there. She should have left it totally alone. She and Pip could have been safe.

"Come on, Buster." She slipped on Pip's tennis shoes and tried to figure out the best way to keep him wrapped in the blanket without having him constantly tripping over the edges. "Look," she said after she wrapped it up. "It's a cape. You're like a superhero now."

Pip still looked as if he were on the verge of a meltdown. She needed help. Didn't God understand she couldn't do this if Pip was screaming and throwing a fit? Not that she could blame him. She was terrified, but she at least had the privilege of understanding why they were out here in the cold and dark. Pip must feel completely lost and clueless. She gave him one last hug before urging him on.

"Let's go, Buster. We've got to walk a ways, but you're big and strong and brave, right?" Even as she said the words, Kimmie wished she could feel any of those things at the moment.

A cold wind blew, and she cursed her thin jacket. At least Pip looked warm wrapped up in his blanket. She just hoped he'd be able to walk without tripping. She'd carry him farther if she had to, but right now all her energy was focused on keeping herself from hyperventilating from fear. She hummed a few lines from her mom's Bible verse song, coaxed Pip forward, and they were on their way.

CHAPTER 24

Kimmie couldn't believe it actually worked. She wasn't great with gauging time, but she figured it must have been close to an hour by now since they left Chuck's trailer. And so far, no angry yells or terrifying rifle blasts had pursued her and her brother.

She and Pip were deep in the woods now, but she'd followed a trail that was relatively straight. If she turned left and then circled back, she'd end up somewhere along the Glenn. Once she reached the highway, she'd be able to figure out where they were, and it was just a matter of time before they'd be safe at the trooper's station. In a way, she was grateful Chuck had pulled the rifle on her earlier in the evening. It gave her solid evidence she could pass on to Taylor and the others. Surely they'd agree with her that a three-year-old shouldn't be kept in a home with a father that volatile. She and Pip would finally be safe.

They would finally be free.

She continued to sing her Mom's little songs. Pip would whine restlessly if she grew quiet, and if she were being honest with herself, the Bible verses calmed her down too. Her body was shivering from cold, but she warmed herself with thoughts of a future safe with Pip. They'd move to Anchorage. Life wouldn't be a fairy tale squatting in Meg's home, but hopefully that situation would only be temporary. There must be daycares in town that needed a full-time worker and had room to enroll one more preschooler. It might not be the easiest way to make a living, but just about anything was better than staying in Glennallen with Chuck.

And no more canned chili for dinner.

Ever.

She could take Pip to church. Chuck thought all religion was nonsense and refused to let his family attend any services, but now that they were free, Kimmie could find a church in Anchorage with a good children's program where her brother could learn about the Lord. Even though she remembered her mom's lessons, she felt terribly inadequate to teach them to her brother. Pip would thrive in their new environment. He might even catch up on his language skills once he settled into a home and a routine that didn't involve watching his mom and sister get beaten up all the time.

It was happening. And Kimmie had done it. Her songs turned to psalms of praise.

Bless the Lord, o my soul, and all that's within me bless his holy name.

For the Lord is good, yes he is. The Lord is good, and his love endures forever.

I called on the Lord and he answered me. He saved me from my trouble.

Even though Kimmie had grown up singing these songs and listening to all of Mom's stories from the Bible, they'd never felt real to her until now. Kimmie was wrong to be angry at God for failing to answer her prayers. All this time, he'd been working out the details — all the way down to the electric company turning off their power and Chuck's having to use the outhouse — to secure their escape.

If only Mom had lived to see this day ...

But Kimmie couldn't think like that. Instead she shifted her thoughts to the future where she and Pip would have a nice place of their own. Nothing too outlandish. A two-bedroom townhouse would be fine. Anchorage had tons of parks. Her favorite playground while growing up sported a giant jungle gym, which was more colorful and complicated than what you could find at any of the other neighborhood parks. In fact, if she remembered right, that particular playground was located right across the street from a big apartment complex. That might be the perfect place to settle down, even more desirable than a townhouse. If she and Pip found a nice apartment, she wouldn't have to handle any of the snow shoveling or yard upkeep. It sounded better and better with each step that took them deeper into the woods.

Wait a minute. Wasn't she supposed to be leading Pip toward the Glenn? For as straight as the trail had seemed as she burrowed into the darkness to hide, she felt now like she'd been turned around a dozen different times like a kid spun around before hitting a piñata at a birthday party. This couldn't be right. She stared up at the sky. There was the big dipper, and if she were trained in navigation, she could probably use the North Star to figure out exactly where she was supposed to go from here, but the stellar map meant absolutely nothing to her now. It looked just like it had when she started her trek into the woods.

She stopped. "Hold on, Buster," she told her brother when he started to fidget. She checked to make sure his blanket was still wrapped tightly around his shoulders and then glanced up at the sky again. So that way was probably north ... But what did that tell her? She was so turned around she couldn't figure out which way she'd been walking, if she'd been walking in a single direction after all. While living at Chuck's trailer, the sun would rise above these woods, so did that mean she was supposed to head west to get back to the highway?

It was her best guess, but there were at least a dozen unknowns that kept her feet firmly planted where they were. What if the trail hadn't been as straight as she thought? What if turning around now meant landing straight back at Chuck's trailer? And since the Alaskan sun always rose at an angle and never due east, what did that mean for her calculations?

Not to mention the fact that she was only fifty percent sure that she'd figured out north correctly in the first place.

The temperature had dropped significantly when the last traces of sunlight disappeared, certainly not as bad as they'd get in the dead of winter, but this escape could have never happened in the dead of winter. It had to be now.

She held her brother close, borrowing a little of his warmth and refusing to accept that she might be lost. God wouldn't allow that to happen. He'd gotten her this far, which meant he wanted her to escape from Chuck's awful violence as much as she did. Which meant she would find her way to safety. The Lord would help her.

Wouldn't he?

She sank down with her back against a tree and held her brother close. "Let's just rest for a minute here." She wanted to unwrap Pip and cozy up beside him under the blanket, but it was so cold out she didn't want him to lose all that warmth he'd stored up in his little portable burrow.

"You doing okay?" She didn't wait for an answer. She knew it wouldn't come.

"Ma."

She paused. "What?" Kimmie was cold, but she was certain she wasn't imagining things. She stared into her brother's face. "What did you say?" She held her breath, waiting.

Nothing.

"Were you talking about Mommy?" Kimmie prodded, refusing to admit the sound might have been a random vocalization.

Pip stared at her blankly. He was tired. He should have been in a warm bed sleeping, not tramping through the woods. She pulled his blanket more tightly around his shoulders. "Do you miss Mommy?" she asked. Up until she said those words, she'd thought she'd been doing fine, but mentioning their mother brought a massive lump to her dry throat. She needed water. Pip must too, but there wasn't anything they could do until they got out of these woods.

Which meant she couldn't sit here wondering if her brother, whom everyone had considered nonverbal for the first three years of his life, had just spoken his first word or not.

She had to keep going. The more they moved, the more heat they would generate and the closer they'd get to the trooper's station.

The closer they'd get to safety.

Hopefully.

She stood up, glancing in all directions to make sure she was still on the same path she'd been on when she decided to stop. She couldn't be entirely sure that this would be the way to lead them to the trooper's station or not, but there was only one way to find out.

"Come on, Buster." She tried to make her voice sound as cheerful as possible. "Let's go see what's down this trail."

CHAPTER 25

If Kimmie had been able to plan her escape better, she would have left earlier in the month, before the termination dust fell, before the nights grew so frozen. Thankfully, it was clear out, and the moon kept the woods illuminated, but without the cloud covering, the night was bitter cold. She and her brother had no protection but a light windbreaker and one tattered blanket, and they were lost.

Kimmie was certain of it. She'd long lost track of the time, but it seemed to her that by now the moon was already on its way down in the sky. Which meant she'd been walking for several hours along the path she thought should have led her back to the Glenn Highway, and she had no idea where they were.

"Let's stop here for a minute, Buster."

Pip hadn't made any sounds for quite a while, no whining or whimpering. He'd stumbled a few times until Kimmie started to worry he was falling asleep while he walked. She tried carrying him but had to put him down every few minutes.

This wasn't going to work.

She was sweating beneath her jacket, even though her exposed face and hands burned with cold. She couldn't keep this up. It was too much for her. She was too tired.

She stopped to listen. If she could just hear one car or truck heading down the Glenn, she'd know which direction to turn. She'd been straining her ears for what felt like hours, but the Glenn was hardly traveled at this time of night, especially this far past tourist season. She heard the occasional rustling of wind, which only meant she had to brace herself for another onslaught of icy chill. Her legs ached, the pain in her feet reminding her that she and her brother had been walking way longer than they should have. How far was she into the woods now? She might be a hundred yards from the Glenn and wouldn't know it in this darkness, or she might be miles in the opposite direction.

What would happen if they didn't find their way out? She was too exhausted to carry Pip any farther. Each time she stopped to rest, she had to guess which way she'd most recently come from. Her mind was foggy, and even though it was convenient that Pip wasn't complaining or acting scared, she was worried by his complacency and her own mental confusion.

She held her brother close, and he nestled his cheek against hers. Her face was so cold she could hardly feel his skin. A moment later, his deep breathing told her he was asleep, and she wanted nothing more than to curl up beside him in their makeshift bed of spruce needles and forget herself until morning, but it was too cold. Neither of them would survive a night outside. Not if they stopped moving.

She watched her brother sleep, wondering how long she should wait before waking him up again. He needed his rest, but then again so did she. The problem was if she stayed here too long, she might lose the motivation to ever get herself back up. Then what would happen? Winter was closing in fast. What hikers would come out this way in that kind of weather? And the trappers who ventured this deep into the woods come wintertime might not even find their bodies if they were buried in snow or devoured by scavengers.

She tried to free herself from these oppressive fears, but they kept pressing in on her, weighing down on her chest, constricting her lungs until she felt like she could hardly breathe.

She had tried. God was her witness how hard she had tried. And in the end, it wasn't Chuck who did her in but this blasted cold and her own pathetic sense of direction. She thought of stories she'd heard of other unfortunate souls who met their demise in the Alaskan wilderness. Some were within a mile of the cabins or shelters or cell phone towers that might have saved them, but they had died nonetheless.

She couldn't let that happen to her and Pip. She had to find the energy to keep on going.

But not yet. After a short nap, she'd find her second wind. For now, she needed to rest. Just a few minutes, then she'd wake up.

Kimmie shut her eyes and let the heaviness and exhaustion sweep over her mind and carry her consciousness away into a merciful nothingness.

CHAPTER 26

She was at a birthday party in Anchorage. The kids were dressed up in pirate and princess costumes, laughing and drinking punch. Pip was sitting at the table, playing a puzzle game with two other little boys wearing eye patches and striped pants. He looked just as comfortable as the other children there, and even more amazing, he was laughing.

Kimmie excused herself from the chattering group of moms standing around with coffee cups in hand and stepped closer to her brother.

"My turn!" Pip exclaimed in a perfectly clear voice. "I get to go next."

Kimmie felt her entire core swelling with a pride so strong she wasn't sure her body could contain it all.

And then the fragments of her dream came crashing down around her like so many pieces of broken glass. She was awake. She was cold. And she was terrified.

"Pip!" she shook her brother, horrified by the feel of the stiff blanket around him. "Pip!"

She had only meant to rest. How could she have been stupid enough to fall asleep? "Pip?"

She threw the blanket down from Pip's shoulder so she could search out his neck and try to find a pulse. Nausea swirled within her stomach, and her prayer came out in a terrified, pitiful plea. *Help us.*

He was alive. The relief she felt was enough to warm her body and shoot her mind into action. They couldn't stay here. And her brother couldn't sleep any longer.

"Come on, Pip. Let's go."

He was nearly impossible to rouse, but the way he scrunched up his face in complaint at Kimmie's vain attempts proved he was still alive. Still with her.

"Wake up, Buster," she begged. "We've got to keep walking."

She'd been so terrified by the fear that she'd let her brother die in the middle of the night that she hadn't looked around her at all. The aurora was out, not the glorious teals and purple lights that raced across the Glennallen skies in the dead of winter, but a dull green glow shining near the horizon.

It was the answer to all of her cumulative prayers. The northern lights almost always ran parallel to the Glenn, which meant that if she followed them straight on, she'd find her way to the highway.

"Let's go, Pip." This time she didn't have to fake her cheer or enthusiasm. Whispering a prayer of thanks, she planted her brother on his feet then when he started to whine picked him up, strengthened by her newfound hope.

She would get help soon. She and Pip were going to make it.

They would be safe.

They would be free.

CHAPTER 27

When Kimmie finally stumbled onto the Glenn Highway, she realized that she was miles from where she'd started her circuitous meandering through the woods. She'd never have the energy to get all the way to the trooper's station. Not now. Not like this. But it didn't matter. She was safe. She'd make it. She and Pip were going to be fine.

She'd been carrying her brother, and now as the northern lights faded back to darkness, her last remnants of strength melted away to a deep, nearly paralyzing exhaustion. She was so close. She just needed to get to a phone. Some place where she could call for help.

But where?

If it was the summer, she'd have the light of the midnight sun to guide her, with sleepy tourists on their way to Fairbanks or Canada making their way up the Glenn. But now there was nothing. If it were the weekend, she might run into hunters coming back home with their spoils, but the night was dark and the highway deserted.

"It's okay," she told herself, speaking softly as if she were giving her sleeping brother a pep talk. "We're going to make it."

Walking to the trooper's station would take her too close to her stepfather's neighborhood. It wasn't worth the risk of getting caught. If Chuck was out looking for her, she shouldn't even be this close to the highway in the first place. Besides, she couldn't make it that whole distance. Not as cold and weak as she was.

The medical center was in the opposite direction, only a mile, maybe slightly more. It was a feasible distance to walk and still kept her away from Chuck's place. Besides, Pip really should get checked out. But with what money? Kimmie still didn't have her paperwork back from the state insurance she'd applied for, but it didn't matter. The people at the Copper River Clinic weren't going to turn her away.

She set her brother down. "Come on, Buster. Just a tiny bit more walking."

He made a miserable whine that was pitiful enough to wrench her soul apart, but she was at her physical limit.

"I can't carry you anymore," she tried to explain. "I just can't. Let's go see the nice doctor and get you taken care of, okay?"

She was terrified of what the folks at Copper River would find when they took off his shoes. What if he had frostbite? What if they needed to amputate?

No, she wouldn't think like that. She and her brother could both still walk. They were just cold. The clinic probably saw patients like that on a regular basis and had fast and effective protocols all set to go. The idea of a steaming shower and layer after layer of thick electric blankets fueled her legs as she slowly plodded forward.

Her brain was past the point of exhaustion, past the point where she felt she'd break if she didn't get warmed up and rested soon. But she had to keep going, and she had to keep Pip awake. He had to make this last little walk. It couldn't be more than a mile to the clinic. They were so close.

She heard a car behind her, saw the headlights illuminating the darkness. It was still too far back to have seen her, at least she hoped it was. She grabbed Pip by the shoulders. Did she dare flag it down? Who would refuse to help a three-year-old child in the cold like this? But what if it was Chuck? What if he was coming after them? She turned but was so blinded by the headlights she had no idea what kind of vehicle was speeding toward her.

Pip stood frozen beside her as well. "Let's go!" she panted. "Down to the ravine."

She and Pip stumbled down the small hill, where she crouched with her arms around her brother until the car sped past.

It wasn't Chuck.

Stupid. What had she done? If she'd just had the courage to flag that driver down, she and Pip could be at the medical center in a minute or less. *Stupid.*

She vowed that if another car came this way, she was going to stand out in the middle of the road, waving her arms until it stopped. Even if it were Chuck, it was better to live under his tyranny than watch her brother die from hypothermia.

But no other cars came. She was on her own. Pip started crying. She guessed from the way he bounced back and forth that his feet were hurting.

Was that just from walking all night, or had frostbite crept in?

Did frostbite even hurt? Her own feet were numb. Maybe it was a good sign that Pip felt something.

She couldn't carry him anymore, not in her arms like she had all night, but she couldn't watch him suffer like this either. She crouched down. "You'll have to climb on my back," she told him. That meant he couldn't have the blanket wrapped so tightly around his body, but they'd have to manage as best they could. They were so close to help; it was going to be okay. They were both going to make it. They were so close now.

CHAPTER 28

Kimmie pressed the nighttime buzzer outside the Copper River Clinic's emergency room and nearly collapsed while she waited for the door to open. When a young nurse in Bugs Bunny scrubs opened the door, all Kimmie could manage to say was, "We got lost."

Soon she was sitting in a wheelchair, heavy blankets draped over her shoulders, her feet soaking in a warm bath. Pip sat in her lap while the physician's assistant checked his vitals.

"I think you're both very lucky to have made it out of those woods when you did." He looked at her meaningfully. "Is there anyone you need to call? Anyone who'll be worried about your safety?"

Kimmie's memory flashed to Taylor's card, still secure in her pocket, and she shook her head. "No. I just wanted to make sure he was ..." Her voice caught when she thought about what might have happened to Pip. "I just wanted him to come in to make sure he was all right."

The PA smiled. "Well, in that case I can relieve your worries. He's clearly hypothermic, but I don't see anything that's going to prevent either of you from a full recovery. If you'd stayed out much longer ..." He left the thought unfinished, and Kimmie was grateful. Pip had perked up once he was inside, and she didn't want him to hear anything that would cause undo alarm.

The PA wanted her and Pip to stay here a few more hours. Every so often, the nurse brought in hotter water to fill her foot bath. Pip was wrapped in layers of blankets, with hot water compresses tucked around his body while he sat on Kimmie's lap, and the nurse popped in every so often to get a new temperature reading. The PA told her that if she wanted, she and Pip could rest here until morning. She was badly in need of sleep, but she couldn't relax yet. Not until she saw with her own eyes that Pip's temperature was back to where it should be.

Everything had worked itself out in the end. Everything was going to be all right.

The PA stepped out for a minute, and Kimmie tried to figure out a way to get comfortable in her wheelchair. She didn't need it anymore, but it was

197

the easiest way to keep Pip comfortable while she soaked her feet. She could think of worse things to worry about than starting tomorrow with a sore and stiff back.

She had just shut her eyes when someone knocked from outside her room. "Come in." Her voice was so weak, she doubted even Pip heard it let alone someone in the hallway. Her door swung open, and the nurse poked her head in, frowning apologetically.

"Someone's here to see you."

Kimmie's lungs seized up, and her heart rate soared. Chuck? How could he have found her? He had no idea where she and Pip were. What could she tell the nurse? How could she let them know not to let him in?

"It's a trooper," the woman announced, and Kimmie stared at her blankly.

A trooper?

The door opened wider, and Taylor stepped inside. He looked far more casual out of uniform but just as confident in his dark blue jeans and crisp flannel hanging open to reveal the vee-neck T-shirt beneath. He offered a smile that looked both tired and caring. "Sounds like you've had quite the adventure tonight."

Kimmie felt herself return his smile. "That's one way of putting it."

"You have a few minutes?" He ran his hand across the faint stubble on his jaw.

"Of course." She glanced around, trying to figure out where he could sit. Even without his trooper hat, Taylor was over six feet tall, and she felt like she'd get a kink in her neck if she had to stare up at him from this wheelchair for very long.

He reached out his long arm to shut the door then leaned against the exam table. He still wasn't sitting, but at least his relaxed posture made it easier for Kimmie to meet his eyes. He grinned at Pip. "How's the little guy? Is he doing okay?"

She nodded. "The PA says he'll be fine."

Taylor leveled his eyes. "And what about you?"

His question caught her off guard. Warmth flushed to her cheeks, warmth she probably couldn't attribute to her piles of blankets. "I'm fine, too. Thanks."

"Good. That's a real answer to prayer."

She waited for him to say more, still slightly confused why he was here. How had he heard about what happened to Pip and her unless Chuck had called the station when he found them missing? And what did it mean that he wasn't in uniform? Was he working tonight, or had he heard she was here and come in to check on her?

He reached down and brushed some hair off of Pip's forehead. "You look tired, little buddy."

Pip blinked his drooping eyelids once before they closed shut. Kimmie was relieved to feel him relax in her arms.

"I just got out of a meeting with your sister." Taylor's words didn't make any sense. Her sister?

"She's here? In Glennallen?"

Taylor nodded. "She showed up at your home to check on you. Your stepdad told her you were already asleep and refused to let her in, but she had a bad feeling about it all. She went around to the window and saw your empty room from the outside. She said there was also a rifle poking out from under the mattress."

Kimmie tried not to blush. She thought she'd done a better job hiding it.

Taylor was staring at her with a gaze full of compassion. "Are you still cold?"

She hadn't realized until then she'd started shivering. The nurse said it might happen as her body regained heat, but she suspected the reaction had more to do with the thought of her sister sneaking around Chuck's trailer like some sort of amateur sleuth. Meg had no idea what kind of man she was dealing with. What was she thinking? If Chuck had found her snooping through the windows, who knew what he might have done?

"I'm all right." Kimmie smiled in an attempt to appear more convincing. "It's just been a really long, hard night." She swallowed down the lump that had formed in her throat. Why did it always feel like when she was with Taylor she was going to break down into tears? He was strong and confident, the kind of man who should make a woman feel at ease. Instead, his strength only heightened her own sense of vulnerability, and the compassion and gentleness of his demeanor reminded her that she and

Pip deserved so much more love and happiness than life had given them.

Taylor leaned forward and tucked in one of the blankets that had fallen off Pip's shoulder. "Here." He wrapped Kimmie and her sleeping brother closer together. "Is that better?" As he pulled away, the back of his hand brushed against her cheek. She jumped involuntarily.

If he noticed her reaction, he didn't show it.

Taylor sat in the PA's swivel chair. Rolling it a little closer to her, he held her gaze steady. "A lot of people were really worried for your safety."

She tried to read from his expression if he'd been one of them.

He lowered his voice. "Can you tell me what happened tonight?" She didn't know what he was asking. She had no idea how to respond. What did Taylor already know? What did he suspect? According to the story Kimmie told the clinic staff, she and Pip had gone for a walk to look at the stars and gotten lost in the woods. It was on the far side of believable, but nobody had asked for any corroborating details.

Taylor looked stern. "I want to help you, Kimmie. And I think you need it."

She didn't bother contradicting him. It was true. She had risked her life tonight to get Pip to safety. Now here she was, only a few miles from home, but she was with someone who could help her. Taylor would know what to do.

"You don't have to be afraid." He reached out and took her hand. It wasn't until she felt the steadiness of his touch that she realized how much she was trembling. "You can trust me." His voice was earnest. "I want to help you."

She glanced down at her brother, soundly asleep in her arms, reminding herself that she would do anything to keep him safe.

Kimmie told Taylor everything.

CHAPTER 29

Kimmie was shaking so hard that a few minutes into her story Taylor reached over and helped her settle Pip onto the hospital bed. "I don't want you to drop him," he explained gently.

Kimmie felt even more vulnerable and exposed without her brother on her lap. It was as if her entire body was a window into the pit of her psyche, and as long as she had Pip shielding her, the curtains were at least partially drawn. Now there was nothing to separate her and Taylor, nothing to filter out the awful truth.

She clutched her blankets around her shoulders and told him everything, not just about tonight when Chuck had threatened her with a rifle but all that she and her mom had endured. Horror stories she hadn't recalled in years came tumbling out like a tangled mass of words, but instead of bringing healing and catharsis, she felt defiled having to relive those haunting memories, victimized all over again in the retelling.

Taylor was a patient listener, asking a few pointed questions that kept Kimmie focused, making compassionate *mmm*s at the right times, nodding his head in sympathy. When Kimmie had drained her memory banks completely dry, Taylor held her gaze. "Thank you for being honest with me. I'm sure that wasn't easy."

She was still trembling, but he didn't mention it. She stared at him, wondering what was supposed to happen now. She'd done her job. She'd gotten Pip out of Chuck's house and managed to tell the trooper about all the abuse they'd suffered. Her mission, as gruesome and excruciating as it was, had been a success.

Taylor sighed heavily in his chair, and Kimmie wondered if she'd depressed him with her stories. He was so engaged while she was talking, but now that everything was disclosed, he looked tired. For a second, she wondered if she'd made a mistake. What if he came back and said there was nothing he could do? If not even a state trooper could free her brother from Chuck, her dreams of freedom and safety were nothing but an illusion.

The thought led to a terrifying conclusion.

What if Taylor couldn't help her? What if he told her it was out of his jurisdiction? What if he told her that since Pip himself hadn't been the victim of physical abuse, he had to go back home and live with his dad?

Kimmie braced herself, certain that the next words out of Taylor's mouth would tell her that everything she'd suffered through tonight was in vain. She and her brother would never be free.

Instead, he reached out toward Pip, who'd rolled out of his blankets, and tucked him back in carefully. Taylor looked at Kimmie with a gaze full of sympathy and trust. "I'm glad you were able to talk about these things. All your stories are going to help us build our case."

"What case?"

Taylor was gazing at Pip while he slept peacefully in the hospital bed. "The case against your stepfather. We've put out the warrant for his arrest."

"Because you thought he hurt us and that's why we were missing when my sister came by?"

Taylor shook his head. "No. Because we've received solid evidence that implicates him in your mother's murder."

CHAPTER 30

Kimmie stared at the trooper, wondering why Taylor's words didn't cause any of the emotional reactions she might have expected.

"So you found proof?" She realized that she sounded clinical and unmoved, but that's also how she felt. Taylor suspected that Chuck was involved in her mom's death. Was she truly surprised, or was he simply telling her the truth that she'd been trying to deny?

He nodded. "Your sister ... well, maybe I should let her explain it to you."

Kimmie wished he wouldn't. Taylor would never understand the kind of relationship she had with Meg. "I think I'd rather hear it from you," she admitted, hoping she didn't sound too rude.

He nodded in understanding. "Well, I guess your mom was making plans with your sister. Meg was going to drive out to Glennallen to pick up you and your mom and your brother and take you to her house in Anchorage." He leveled his gaze. "Your mom was getting ready to leave Chuck."

No matter how much Kimmie might have wanted to believe those words in the past, she still couldn't believe them to be true. Mom was scared. She was timid. How would Meg have convinced her to find the courage to leave?

Jumbled thoughts and half-formed arguments raced chaotically through Kimmie's mind. Meg had always disliked their stepfather. She could have made something up. If Mom were ever going to leave Chuck, it would have happened years earlier, before things got as bad as they had. Meg didn't know what she was talking about. She was just trying to find a way to take charge over the family that she'd abandoned so long ago.

Of course, Kimmie would be stupid to defend Chuck of all people. He'd certainly shown himself over the years capable of a rage that could turn murderous, but there was a part of her brain that still wanted to believe Mom decided to end her life on her own terms. If Chuck really had killed Mom, there must have been something Kimmie could have done to intervene. Something she could have changed. She could have fought harder to get Mom out of that trailer. She could have told somebody about the abuse that was going on back when she was in high school. Her teachers would have had to get protective services involved. Kimmie could have done something differently.

She could have saved her mother.

"Are you all right?" Taylor asked. "It's a lot to take in."

She wanted to yell at him. Wanted to scream that her sister was a liar. But Meg had no reason to make a story like this up. Hadn't she told Kimmie she had more information about Mom's death?

Taylor wrapped his arm around her, which only made her tremble harder. "I'm so sorry," he whispered. "But the good news is you're here now. You and your brother are both going to be safe."

"So you found him then?" Kimmie asked.

Taylor shook his head. "He wasn't home when our men went by earlier, but don't worry. Soon your stepfather will be behind bars, right where he belongs."

Kimmie looked into Taylor's kind and earnest eyes and trusted him. She didn't have any other choice.

CHAPTER 31

"Thank God you're safe." Meg threw her arms around Kimmie's shoulders in the hotel lobby then flung a smile at Taylor. "Thank you so much, officer, for all you've done for our family. You're an angel."

Kimmie bristled at the flirtatious tone her married sister had adopted, and she reached for her brother, asleep in Taylor's arms. "I can take him from here."

Taylor shook his head. "You've had enough physical exertion for the day, I think. Let me carry him up to your room. It's no problem."

Meg draped her hands over his bicep and crooned, "You're right. I bet to you he's no heavier than a piece of paper, right?"

Taylor smiled and raised his eyebrows at Kimmie as if to ask, *is your sister always like this?*

She shrugged. *Unfortunately, yes.*

Meg led the way up the hotel staircase and to their room on the second floor, past several moose and caribou heads mounted on the wall, their sad and mournful eyes seeming to follow the procession. Meg fumbled with her key card, laughing airily when she realized she'd been trying to insert it upside-down.

"Which bed is his?" Taylor asked. Kimmie glanced at the two doubles in their room. If Chuck found out where they were hiding and barged into the hotel, where would Pip be safest? A dozen scenarios ran through her head, pictures of her stepfather breaking into their room, rifle aimed to kill.

"Let's settle him down here." Kimmie pulled down the blankets on the bed by the window, but Meg shook her head.

"You don't want him sleeping that close to the heater, do you? It can't be good for his breathing, all that dust blowing around in the air. Why don't you put him here? He'll stay warmer if he doesn't catch a draft."

Taylor looked from one sister to the other, still holding Pip in his arms. He raised his eyebrows questioningly at Kimmie.

"Fine," she answered. "He can sleep there."

Meg grinned smugly as Taylor lowered Pip into the bed by the door. Kimmie would sleep on the other side of him, so at least if Chuck barged in he'd have to get through her first.

Was this what her life was reduced to? Hiding from Chuck in a cheap hotel room, wondering when he'd attack? Maybe she'd feel better when they got to Anchorage. But would she ever be truly safe?

Meg stepped between her and Taylor. "Thanks again for all you've done, officer. You're so brave. I'm just so thankful we have people like you looking out for all us little guys." She let out another girlish giggle.

Kimmie studied Taylor's expression, trying to figure out if he was the kind of guy who would immediately fall under Meg's dazzling spell. Twenty-seven and rich enough to afford her own personal trainer and year-long visits to the tanning booth, Meg looked like she came off the pages of a beauty magazine even wearing her simple designer jeans and casual blouse that clung tightly to her figure.

Surprisingly, Taylor offered a quick word of thanks then turned his attention to Kimmie. "Are you going to be all right here for the night?"

She thought it was weird that he was asking her. Wasn't it his job to know how safe she was? Shouldn't he be able to answer that question far more readily than she would?

"We'll leave for Anchorage first thing tomorrow." Meg took a step closer to him and flung her shoulders back. Kimmie wondered if her sister realized how silly she looked trying to catch the gaze of a near stranger or if her filthy-rich husband had any idea how she acted around other men when he wasn't around.

Taylor glanced at Pip curled up on the hotel bed, and Kimmie watched his gentle features soften even more. "I think that's good." He was talking to Kimmie, staring at her now with an intensity that made her face heat up. "You'll be safe in Anchorage. Does Chuck know where your sister lives?"

"I don't know how he could," Meg answered, clearly waiting for this chance to insert herself into the conversation. "He never let Mom come and visit. I don't think Mom even had my address."

"That's good." Taylor looked relieved. He lowered his voice, leaning in toward Kimmie. "Do you still have my cell number?"

She nodded. Kimmie didn't have to put her hand in her pocket to know it was there. All night long, she'd been fingering its wrinkled corners, trying to muster up the last of her courage and strength while she was trying to lead Pip out of those cold woods.

Taylor smiled. "Why don't you give me a call once you feel settled and let me know how you're doing."

Behind him, Meg raised her sculpted eyebrows, and her mouth dropped open into a tiny O before spreading into a grin that made Kimmie feel queasy.

"Officer," Meg sang out in her most melodic voice, "I'm sure it's going to be hard for Kimmie to leave everything she knows behind here in Glennallen. I bet it'd be a real treat for her if you'd come have dinner with us one night. We're up on the hillside, and we'd love to have you."

Kimmie wanted to join her brother in bed and throw the blankets over her face, but Taylor was still gazing straight at her, holding her captive by the intensity of his stare. "I'd like that," he said.

Kimmie ignored the sloshing feeling in her gut, the skipping and erratic heartbeat in her chest. He'd fallen prey to Meg's charm, and that was all. There wasn't a single member of the male species who could refuse her anything.

Meg was wiggling her eyebrows up and down when Taylor wasn't looking. Kimmie had no idea what information her sister was trying to convey or why she was making such a fool of herself. Whatever it was she suspected, Meg was reading the situation wrong. Taylor wouldn't drive all the way to Anchorage just to visit some fancy home on the hillside. He was only saying that to be nice, the same way an adult smiles at the little kid who says they're going to grow up to become an astronaut or the president. Taylor was doing what any polite person in his situation would do, but unless he had to relay more information regarding her stepfather's case, Kimmie knew she wouldn't see him again.

Meg had no idea how much she was humiliating herself when she put her manicured fingers on Taylor's shoulder and giggled, "It's a date then."

Kimmie wanted to apologize for her sister's behavior, but when she found the courage to glance at Taylor's face, she was surprised to find a gentle bemusement where she expected to see impatience or irritation.

"Funny coincidence," he said. "But tomorrow's my day off, and in the afternoon, I've got to drive my friend to the airport. Any chance you ladies would be free around six?"

"Tomorrow?" Meg asked.

Taylor looked at the alarm clock by Pip's bedside. "Actually, it's today if you wanted to be technical."

Kimmie had about two dozen different arguments. She and Pip were still exhausted. A few hours of sleep in a strange hotel followed by a four-hour drive to her sister's wasn't going to leave anybody with energy to play hostess. Pip would be confused enough being in a new place surrounded by new people. The last thing he needed was Taylor stealing Kimmie's attention away from where it really needed to be.

Kimmie shot her sister an imploring look, one she was certain Meg was going to ignore.

Meg frowned. "I'm sorry, officer. My husband's in real estate. He's got a really important meeting at six tomorrow that we can't miss."

Relief washed over Kimmie's whole body until her sister's face broke out into a mischievous grin. "But while Dwayne and I are out, I'm sure Kimmie's free. Why don't the two of you have dinner together?"

Each and every argument that ran through her brain died on Kimmie's lips when Taylor leaned slightly toward her. "I'd like that. I'll bring takeout. Does Pip like Chinese food?"

Did he? If it wasn't chili from a can, white bread, or one of the frozen meals he ate at the daycare, Pip had likely never tried it.

"You've got my number." Taylor continued to smile. He looked so genuinely happy Kimmie couldn't bring herself to mutter some excuse to free him from this embarrassing arrangement. "Why don't you plan on texting me your sister's address once you and Pip are settled."

She refused to tell him she didn't even have a cell phone and had never sent a text in her life. For all the joy her sister derived from playing matchmaker, Meg could lend Kimmie her phone for something as simple as that.

Meg flung her hair over her shoulder like she was auditioning for a shampoo commercial. "Well, then, it's a date. We'll see you tomorrow night."

Kimmie plopped onto the bed as soon as Taylor closed the hotel room door behind him. Meg sank down next to her and elbowed her in the ribs. "Well, come on now, a date with Officer Chiseled? No need to thank me.

Just be sure to invite me to the wedding."

Kimmie pulled the blankets over her head. She was dying to sleep, but if truth were to be told, she was too embarrassed to let Meg see the girly grin that had spread across her face.

CHAPTER 32

That night, Kimmie dreamed she was strapped in the passenger seat of a car speeding recklessly over a bridge. "Slow down," she shouted at the driver.

Chuck's menacing laugh answered back. "You think this is fast, girlie? You haven't seen fast yet."

Pip squealed in the back seat, but Kimmie's seatbelt was so tight it was digging into her shoulder bone. She couldn't turn around to offer her brother any comfort.

"You're scaring him," she yelled, hoping Chuck would feel some degree of pity for his own child. Instead, he laughed again, filling the front seat of the car with the scent of stale beer and sunflower seeds.

"How's this for scared?" He spun the wheel back and forth, sending their speeding car careening from one lane to the other. The bridge swayed beneath them. Kimmie gripped her seat, praying for rescue. If she reached out, if she were able to seize hold of the wheel ... No, it was too dangerous. There was nothing to do. Nothing to do but pray and wait and hope that she and Pip survived.

She woke up drenched in sweat. Meg was staring down at her with a frown. "Sorry to wake you, sleeping beauty, but if I'm going to get my house ready for your hot date tonight, we need to get on the road."

Kimmie glanced at the clock. Seven thirty? After everything they'd gone through last night, Meg thought it was appropriate to wake her and Pip up at seven thirty?

"Come on," Meg urged. "I've got a hair appointment in town at noon, and I don't want to cancel."

Kimmie rolled her eyes. At least Meg's real reason for waking her up this early was more in line with her character, easier for Kimmie to accept. She glanced at her sleeping brother, hating to break his rest.

Meg flung a suitcase on the bed and started to fill it. "Let's go. He can sleep in the car."

Kimmie didn't have the energy to argue. Besides, she and Pip probably shouldn't linger in Glennallen any longer than was necessary, not with Chuck still running loose. She reached out her arm to give her brother a gentle shake. "Come on, Buster. Time to wake up."

"You call him Buster?" Meg paused with a pair of heels in her hands. Who packs heels to take a four-hour drive to do nothing but pick up their sister?

Kimmie continued to focus on Pip. "Yeah. Why?"

"That's what Mom used to call Dad when they were being silly. Don't you remember?"

Kimmie shook her head. Back when they'd lived together, one of Meg's favorite pastimes was playing *Don't you remember*, a game in which Meg received the inherent bragging rights that came from having far more recollections about their dad than Kimmie ever would. The superiority that went along with her status as *eldest daughter with the best memory* was as infuriating as it was unjust. Why should Meg be the one with all the memories?

"Hey, is he always this hard to wake up?" Meg asked, studying Kimmie and her failed attempts to rouse Pip.

She shrugged. "Not always. But he's had a hard night." There was an edge in her voice she didn't try to mask. What did her sister expect? Meg had no idea what Pip had gone through lately, and she never would. Yet another case of Meg's getting all the family's allotted dose of good luck. It wasn't enough for her to be the prettiest, the smartest, and the one with all the memories of Dad. She was also the one who'd never had to deal with Chuck, never had to clean up his snotty paper towels or fetch his coffee sludge. As far as Kimmie knew, Meg had never been hit a day in her life, and her most pressing worry was whether or not she could keep her figure trim enough to warrant her position as a trophy bride for one of Anchorage's most successful real estate moguls.

"Maybe you should just take the blankets off him and let the cold wake him up."

Kimmie glared at her sister. Did driving four hours to meet her half-brother make Meg some kind of parenting expert all of a sudden?

"Come on, Pip," Kimmie pleaded. "You've got to wake up."

"If you keep snuggling him like that, he won't have any reason to get out of bed."

Kimmie ignored Meg's nagging, and eventually her sister took the hint and went back to her packing. Kimmie brushed Pip's forehead. "Does he feel hot to you?"

Meg reached out then shrugged. "Little bit, but you've kept him buried under those blankets all night."

"I wonder if he's getting sick. It wouldn't be a surprise after he spent so much time outside."

Meg rolled her eyes. "Is that still what they're teaching in these Glennallen schools? The cold can't make you sick. It doesn't work that way. It's just an old wives' tale."

"Shut up." Kimmie flung the blankets off her brother. The PA at the clinic hadn't warned Kimmie about overheating. Had she bundled him too tightly in her worry for his safety?

"I'm serious," Meg went on. "If anything, all the cold does is lower your immunity. It can't actually give you a virus."

"I said shut up." Kimmie stood Pip on the ground and watched anxiously while he blinked his sleepy eyes awake. "Are you all right, Buster?" She wished Meg hadn't mentioned that being one of their mom's pet names for their dad. She was going to feel self-conscious now each and every time she used it. "Pip? Are you all right?"

He scrunched up his face.

"I think he needs to see a doctor," Kimmie announced.

Meg threw a fancy handbag into her suitcase. "He's probably just tired."

"He looks like he's in pain."

Meg shrugged. "That's how I look every morning before I put on my makeup."

I bet it is, Kimmie thought to herself. She sat down on the edge of their bed and took Pip into her arms. "Does something hurt," she asked him, "or are you just tired, buddy?"

He winced.

"Can you show me what hurts?" Kimmie ignored her sister's melodramatic sigh. Meg was probably worried about that hair appointment she'd miss if they didn't get on the road soon. Hair like that probably had to be touched up once or twice a month. With as much as Meg was sure to be paying her stylist, the hairdresser could afford to reschedule.

"Something's really wrong. I think we better get him checked out."

"Fine," Meg huffed as she zipped her overstuffed suitcase shut. "But you don't want to take him to this Glennallen hole in wall. I mean, it's fine for something like last night when you need quick attention right away, but for childhood illnesses, you really should see a specialist. Does that tiny little clinic here even have a pediatrician on staff?"

Kimmie had spent all of Pip's life worrying herself sick over every minor injury or sniffle, hating that his father was too cheap to allow him to get proper medical care. Now that Chuck was out of the picture, there was no way Kimmie was going to relinquish her decision-making authority, handing the responsibility over to someone who hardly even knew her brother.

"The Copper River Clinic's closest," she argued. "Let's just stop by there on the way out of town." She thought about the Cole twins who'd been out of the daycare with strep throat and hoped Pip hadn't picked up something like that.

She put her finger on his chin. "Open your mouth like this. "Let me take a look."

"Good grief, Kimberly," Meg whined. "You're not a nurse."

No, but I'm his sister, which is more than you're acting like at the moment. She kept the retort unspoken and tried to look in Pip's mouth.

All she could see was black. "You have a flashlight or something?"

Meg crossed her arms. "Do you even know what you're looking for? Does working part-time at a daycare all of a sudden make you an expert in childhood illnesses?"

"Do you have a flashlight or not?" she repeated. "All I need is a simple yes or no."

Meg rolled her eyes. "Use my cell." She tossed her phone onto the blanket and then let out a loud and frustrated sigh when Kimmie asked her how to turn on the light.

"I can't believe you don't even know how to use a cell phone."

Kimmie ignored the remark. "Now say 'ah,'" she told her brother.

"Do you even know if he understands a word you're saying?" Meg asked as she stared into the mirror above the dresser applying her mascara.

Kimmie heard the question, but as she shined the light, she realized Meg was right about one thing. She really didn't know what she was looking for. Pip's throat was bright red, but maybe that's the color it always was.

She tried to figure out how to turn the light off when Meg finally yanked it out of her hands and did it herself. "Did you find what you were looking for?"

Kimmie ignored her sister's sarcasm. "I want to take him to the clinic before we head out of town."

"If you wait a few hours, I have a friend with a kid about that age. I actually borrowed her car seat for Pip's drive to Anchorage. She takes her son to a naturopath in Eagle River, says she's a miracle worker."

"I don't want a naturopath," Kimmie snapped. "And I don't need a miracle worker. I just want someone to check him out and let me know if something's wrong."

"Of course something's wrong," Meg replied. "The kid's three and doesn't even talk yet. Which reminds me, I have a number for you to call once we get you settled in. There's a state program for kids with special needs, where they'll come right to your house."

"That's not what I'm talking about." Kimmie wondered how she and her sister would survive the long drive to Anchorage, let alone coexist under the same roof until Kimmie found a place of her own. It was a good thing Meg had a mansion where they'd have plenty of space so hopefully Kimmie and her brother could keep to themselves.

Meg stared at Kimmie, who felt like she was now expected to apologize for her outburst. Instead she gave Pip a little squeeze, straightened out his rumpled clothes, and said, "Let's find where that nice trooper put your shoes last night and then we'll take a quick visit to say hi to the nurse." She shot a look at her sister, who managed to roll her eyes while applying her eye makeup.

"Fine with me. While you're in with the nurse PA or whoever they've got working there, I guess I'll call my hairstylist and cancel that appointment."

CHAPTER 33

The clinic was only a few minutes away from the hotel, but Kimmie was shaking by the time Meg pulled up in front of the building. She didn't know if it was her body reliving last night's trauma or the adrenaline in her system from fighting with her sister. Maybe both.

"You coming in?" she asked Meg, who was still buckled in the driver's seat.

"Go on ahead. I've got some phone calls to make." Meg adjusted the rearview mirror so she could look at herself as she reapplied her lipstick. Ignoring her, Kimmie helped Pip out of his car seat. "Come on, Buster," she whispered in his ear. "Let's see if the nurses here can do anything to help you feel better."

After checking her brother in, Kimmie sat down with Pip on her lap and started reading a magazine. In the corner, two kids around Pip's age were playing in the children's area, stacking blocks and coloring while their mom scrolled on her cell phone.

Kimmie was exhausted. One nice thing about driving all the way to Anchorage with Meg was her sister was a coffee snob and probably knew the best place in the area to get a hot drink.

"Well, fancy seeing you two here."

Kimmie turned around at the familiar voice as a smile worked its way to her lips. "Look, Pip. It's Trooper Tanner."

"Call me Taylor, okay?" He stood above them, staring down in a way that reminded Kimmie just how tall he was. He grinned and sat down next to her, and she wondered if she smelled as gross and looked as tired as she suspected.

Taylor reached over and offered a playful pout to Pip, who was frowning and leaning against Kimmie's chest. "Everything all right?"

"He woke up with a little bit of a fever," she explained.

Taylor tousled Pip's hair. "Poor little thing."

Kimmie wondered what else she was supposed to say. It wasn't like she had any practice running into handsome troopers in doctor's offices, but she figured it wasn't polite to ask something like, "So, what are you doing here?" She stared at her hands resting on Pip's legs.

"Did you both sleep okay at the hotel?" Taylor asked.

She nodded, pressing her lips together, trying to figure out why her brain had suddenly grown incapable of carrying on a simple conversation. Behind them, the two kids argued over a broken crayon until their mom barked at them.

Taylor stretched out his legs, looking perfectly at ease. "So, we still on for dinner tonight?"

Kimmie flushed. "Oh, I'm sorry about that. My sister can be kind of a handful."

"Well, that doesn't seem like something you need to apologize for, does it?" Taylor asked with a grin.

"No." She tried to smile. "I just didn't want you to feel like you were forced into anything you didn't want to do."

Taylor chuckled. "I hate driving to Anchorage. I rarely go in. I'm only doing it because I owe my buddy a pretty big favor. He doesn't have anyone else to take him in time to catch his flight."

"Does he need a ride?" Kimmie asked. "We've got room in the back seat."

Taylor shook his head. "That's not what I meant. I wasn't asking you to drive him in. I'm just saying that knowing I'll be ending the day with you and your brother and some great Chinese food is going to keep me from getting grumpy on the road."

Kimmie smiled and forced herself to look away before her flush deepened.

"Pippin Jenkins?" The nurse called out. "Ready for you now."

Kimmie set her brother down and stood up, facing Taylor. "Well, I guess I'll see you tonight." She felt silly stretching out her hand as if she were an applicant who'd just finished a job interview, but Taylor pressed it warmly.

"I'll be looking forward to this evening." His smile made her warmer than she'd been all fall.

As she walked with Pip toward the nurse, she felt Taylor's kind gaze following them, somewhat surprised to realize that she was looking forward to their dinner tonight just as much as he was.

CHAPTER 34

"We'll get those results from the strep test back in a few minutes," the PA explained. Kimmie was still sweating from having to hold Pip down while the physician's assistant tried to swab the back of his throat.

Tabitha scowled at her pad of paper. "May as well write him a prescription now, because I can pretty much guarantee it's going to come back positive."

Kimmie felt much more comfortable with the PA she met last night than the one examining Pip today. Tabitha was old and ill-humored and made Kimmie wonder if she had outlived her lifetime dose of both compassion and bedside manners. She stopped scribbling and looked up.

"How old did you say your son is?"

Kimmie had explained earlier that Pip was her brother, but this was the second time since then Tabitha had made the same mistake. It wasn't worth correcting the PA again, so Kimmie just answered, "Three."

Tabitha still stood, frozen, with her pen poised over her pad. "Three years and how many months?"

"He'll turn four in November."

Tabitha narrowed her eyes. "Three years, ten months." She glared at him while emphasizing these last two words.

"Ten months?" Kimmie repeated. "Yeah, I guess that's right."

The way Tabitha rolled her eyes reminded Kimmie of how her sister might look in another forty years if she ran out of money for all her anti-aging skin treatments.

"And he doesn't talk at all?" Tabitha asked.

Kimmie searched for a polite way to remind the provider that her patient was sitting right in front of her, listening in.

"He does use some words," Kimmie stated defensively, stretching the truth just a little.

Tabitha raised a single eyebrow. "Single words, I assume?"

Kimmie stared at her blankly.

"He's not stringing words together yet to form sentences?" the PA pressed.

Kimmie shook her head, feeling just as ashamed as her brother would be if he understood this conversation. "No sentences. Not yet," she added as a hopeful aside.

Tabitha reached for a brochure. "And who's his pediatrician? You're taking him to someone in town, I assume?"

Kimmie felt far too intimidated and bewildered to admit that Pip had never seen a healthcare provider until his trip to the emergency room last night. "There's a naturopath in Eagle River," she answered, careful to word her statement in a way that was not technically a lie.

"Well," Tabitha went on, "I'm sure I have no idea if a naturopath utilizes the same developmental screening methods as a real doctor, but it's clear to me that this child is lacking in his development and could benefit from speech intervention services."

She reached into a drawer and pulled out a brochure. "In all honesty, I was surprised when you told me he wasn't receiving any therapy already. They'll do free home visits through the state for all income brackets," she added, carefully eyeing Kimmie.

She took the brochure with a humble, "Thanks," and was relieved when a nurse popped in.

"The test came back positive," he announced.

Tabitha nodded at him with a smug look then handed Kimmie a prescription form covered in scribbles. "Take this to the pharmacy. Expect it to take them ten or fifteen minutes to get everything ready. Follow the directions on the bottle, and you really should make that call for speech services. Most experts say that intervention before the age of two is most ideal. After that the window of opportunity shrinks exponentially as a child ages."

Shutting her ears to Tabitha's ominous prognosis, Kimmie sighed with relief when the PA stepped out.

Kimmie ran her hand across Pip's forehead. "You doing all right, Buster?" She searched his face for clues that might indicate how much, if any, of the conversation with Tabitha he'd understood. Kimmie knew there was far more to her brother than the PA gave him credit for, but she also knew that Tabitha was probably right about some things. If Kimmie had known Pip could get free speech therapy through the state, she would have convinced her mom to make it happen. Instead of a home visit, maybe the specialist could have worked with Pip at the daycare. How much farther along might he be if Chuck hadn't kept them slaves in his trailer, unable to reach out to anybody on the outside for help?

She shouldn't have wasted precious minutes in the waiting room, staring at Taylor, acting like a starstruck schoolgirl. She should have been telling the trooper more about Chuck, helping with the investigation by brainstorming where in the world her stepdad might be hiding out. At least she'd be seeing Taylor again tonight. This time, instead of acting like a stupefied idiot, Kimmie would do everything she could to help him with the case. She would make sure that Chuck was never free to hurt her or her brother again.

CHAPTER 35

Leading Pip back toward the lobby, Kimmie heard her sister's abrasive giggle even before she stepped into the waiting room. What was Meg doing? Didn't she know how rude it was to talk that loudly on the phone in a public area?

Except that Meg wasn't on the phone.

Her sister stood and smiled brilliantly when Kimmie stepped forward. "So," Meg said, drumming her perfectly shaped, long fingernails on Taylor's shoulder, "you're back. Did the doctor give you the answers you wanted?"

Kimmie fought back an unjustified wave of jealousy when she saw her sister with Taylor. "Pip's got strep." She shot a haughty glance at Meg.

"Poor little guy." Taylor reached out and ran his fingers gently through Pip's hair.

"Well, you ready to go?" Meg adjusted the strap of her handbag and glanced at the clock hanging above the pharmacy window.

"No," Kimmie answered, "I've got to wait for Pip's medicine."

Meg sat back down next to Taylor and bumped her shoulder against his. "I guess it's a busy day at the pharmacy then, isn't it?"

"I'm waiting to get a prescription filled too," he explained. He patted the empty chair next to him. "Have a seat."

Kimmie held up the piece of paper Tabitha had given her. "I think I need to drop this off first." She would never admit it in front of her sister, but she was glad someone was here who knew how to use a pharmacy. She found herself wondering what kind of medicine someone as strong and apparently healthy as Taylor needed and fought down another surge of jealousy as she realized that her sister was so nosy that it was probably the very first question she'd asked him.

Taylor showed her where to drop off Pip's prescription, and then she sat down next to him, waiting. Hadn't Meg said she wanted to make phone calls from the car?

"So," her sister crowed in her obnoxious, singsong voice that was far too loud, "Taylor and I have been talking all about the East Coast."

"Oh yeah?" Kimmie asked. "You have family there or something?"

Meg let out a giggle. "That's where he's from, silly." At least she didn't revert back to her favorite childhood taunt by adding *don't you remember*, but her tone and the expression on her face said the exact same thing.

"I worked on a police force in Massachusetts, but the suburbs felt claustrophobic."

"That's why you moved to Alaska?" Kimmie asked.

Meg nudged him again. "That wasn't the only reason." She batted her eyes as if fleas were threatening to land on her eyeballs.

Taylor looked pensive. "Well, that was one of the reasons."

Kimmie waited for more, hating to imagine there were things about Taylor's life her sister knew that she didn't. She might have asked him for further details, but a woman in a lab coat called his name, and he stood up to walk to the counter.

"What kind of medicine do you think he's on?" Meg whispered as soon as his back was turned.

Meg wasn't talking nearly as quietly as she probably thought, but as humiliating as her question was, Kimmie was simultaneously grateful to learn that Taylor hadn't told her sister everything.

Holding a paper bag with a receipt stapled to the top, Taylor gave a little wave. "It was nice running into you," he said, and this time Kimmie was certain all his attention was focused on Meg. It was just like her sister to monopolize the spotlight, just like she always had.

Meg wiggled her fingers in a playful goodbye, but Kimmie grimaced at the sound of her sister's fake fingernails clanking against each other.

She watched Taylor step toward the exit, still wondering what he had in his paper bag. "See you tonight," she mumbled.

As soon as he was out of the lobby, Meg elbowed her in the side. "You're lucky I'm married, or I would totally be all over that."

Kimmie rolled her eyes. With as shamelessly as Meg acted, nobody would suspect she was married if it weren't for that huge rock on her left hand.

"You really should try to find out what kind of pills he's on," Meg whispered.

Kimmie crossed her arms and waited for Pip's medicine.

CHAPTER 36

"Oh my goodness," Meg squealed as she slid her trim and athletic frame behind the steering wheel. "I still can't get over how cute that trooper is. Did you see those shoulders of his? And he knows how to dress the part, too. Alaska casual looks really good on a man that sculpted."

Kimmie buckled Pip in the back and wondered if now was the right time to remind Meg about her husband in Anchorage.

Sitting down in the passenger side, Kimmie sighed. The PA, unfriendly as she'd been, had ordered antibiotics that should help Pip feel better by the end of the day. He needed one dose now and another at bedtime, but since Kimmie didn't want to do anything to upset his stomach, she decided to wait until he'd had some breakfast.

Meg made a quick stop to Puck's grocery store, and while Kimmie was waiting for her sister, she turned around to glance at Pip. "You hanging in there, Buster?"

Pip refused to look at her. What was wrong? Did he miss Mom? Was he mad at her for not paying attention to him now that Meg was here hogging all the conversation? She still had that brochure from the PA, along with Tabitha's stinging words. *Shrinking window of opportunity.*

She shouldn't feel guilty. It wasn't like Chuck was a reasonable kind of father who would permit his son to get regular therapy, especially since he assumed Pip was stupid and wasn't worth teaching anyway. The problem was that Kimmie hadn't even tried. She should have at least done what she could to change Chuck's mind. She should have died trying. Now even if Pip started receiving intervention services once they got settled in Anchorage, he might never catch up to where he would have been. She thought back over every interaction with her stepfather, every terrible hungover morning and late drunken evening. There must have been some point in time when she could have brought it up.

Either that or she could have convinced Mom to leave him. Meg managed to change Mom's mind, however surprising it was to think about. Strange that Kimmie and her sister had talked about naturopaths and the immune system and Meg's obsession over Taylor, but they hadn't even talked about what evidence Meg had to show the troopers that Mom was planning to leave.

The evidence that proved Chuck's guilt.

She hated thinking about him, hated the way that even his memory made her skittish. She locked the car doors then felt like a baby. Did she really think Chuck would come here and hurt her or Pip in broad daylight in the middle of a grocery store parking lot?

The truth was she did.

And she was scared.

She turned around in her seat. "You're being such a good traveling buddy." Pip looked tired, and she hoped that after he got a little bit of breakfast and his first dose of medicine he'd nap for most of the trip. He had a lot of sleep to catch up on. She also hoped Meg wasn't going to spend the entire drive to Anchorage lecturing her on the deplorable evils of antibiotics, but it would be just like her. Meg, who never had a kid because she refused to ruin her figure.

Meg came back to the car carrying groceries loose in her arms.

"Did they run out of bags?" Kimmie asked.

Her sister shook her head. "No, but I never use plastic, and I didn't bring my cloth shopping bag in with me."

Kimmie didn't respond.

"I got him some yogurt," Meg said. "Does he like yogurt?"

Kimmie found herself wishing that Meg would ask Pip herself but instead just answered, "He likes it." She took the container from her sister and popped open the door of the backseat. "You hungry, buddy?"

Pip reached out for the yogurt, a good sign.

"Got a spoon?" Kimmie asked.

"I knew I forgot something," Meg exclaimed. "I'll go back in. I need a drink too."

While she waited, Kimmie pulled the antibiotics out of the paper bag she'd gotten at the pharmacy. "All right, Buster. Let's get you healthy again." She shook the bottle, and Pip eyed her warily as she filled the syringe with the chalky white liquid.

Kimmie studied her brother strapped into his toddler seat and decided she'd need to better angle herself. She stepped out of her seat then opened the back door of the car, trying to find the position that would get her closest to her brother while still offering the most protection from his feet and fists if he refused the medicine.

"This is going to make you feel lots better." She heard the trepidation in her own voice and prayed Pip wouldn't throw a fit. She glanced up at his tight lips and knew she was in for a battle.

"Please, Pip, just take this little bit for me, okay?" Her voice turned whiney, but not even her pleading could convince her brother to open his mouth for the syringe.

She lowered herself closer, getting kneed in the chest a few times until she managed to use her body weight to pin his legs against the seat. He gave a loud shriek in protest.

"Please, just take the medicine," she begged.

A woman walked by, and Kimmie wished the car door was shut. The last thing she needed was for some stranger to assume she was abusing her brother and call the troopers. Trying to shush his shouts, she reached out with one hand to try to keep Pip's arms from flailing and held the syringe with her other. Pip's limbs were secured, but he squirmed so much it took all her focus just to keep him pinned down without hurting him.

She wanted to yell even louder than he was, but that would only intensify Pip's reaction. He thrashed his head from side to side, colliding with Kimmie's nose.

"Ouch!" she roared. Tears of frustration threatened to spill out of her eyes. "Just take the stupid medicine." She shoved the syringe into his clamped lips, unsure how much of the liquid was actually going in his mouth and how much had sprayed out over them both. She was breathing heavily when she released his arms and legs. The woman who'd passed her earlier was standing on the sidewalk glaring at them. Kimmie lowered her gaze. She wanted to find a way to explain, to let this stranger know she would never intentionally hurt her brother. But he needed the medicine if he was going to get better, even if his screams made it sound like she was trying to murder him.

She pictured herself forced to repeat the same routine twice a day for a whole week. Why couldn't Pip understand she was trying to help? Kimmie smoothed her hair into place, gave the nosy woman what she hoped was a friendly wave, and got back into her seat.

Meg arrived back at the car, bouncy and breathless. "Got the spoon." She tossed it to the backseat, and Kimmie had to turn around one more time to help Pip open his yogurt container and eat his breakfast. "Does he like that flavor?" Meg asked.

"Yeah. Thank you."

"Well, I figured that since he's going on antibiotics" — she spoke the word as if it were a medieval curse — "we may as well try to build up his digestive tract with as many probiotics as possible. I got him a kombucha too. Does he drink those?"

"I've never heard of it."

Meg shrugged. "Well, it's super good for you. But you might want to check. It could be slightly alcoholic. Hmm. Didn't think about that. I guess maybe you shouldn't give it to him after all. Do you drink coffee?" She handed Kimmie a steaming Kaladi Brothers cup, which she grabbed gratefully.

"Here's some creamers." Meg tossed a few packets into Kimmie's lap. "I have no idea how you take it." She spoke the words spitefully, as if it were Kimmie's fault Meg was never around.

They pulled out of the driveway, and Meg checked the time. "Hmm. I think I probably better cancel that hair appointment after all. Siri, call Denise."

Kimmie crossed her arms while Meg held a conversation with her cell phone and then with her stylist. Wasn't Meg going to take care of that at the clinic? Oh, well. Ninety percent of what Meg did Kimmie would never understand. Like how she could stand to live with a man whose only ambition was to sell houses and have the most bleached blond hair and darkest tan in Anchorage.

Or how she'd finally convinced Mom to find the courage to leave Chuck.

Once they got back on the Glenn, Kimmie turned around in her seat, checking every so often until Pip fell asleep. After his eyes closed, she waited a little longer just to be sure then faced her sister.

"All right," she said. "I want to hear about Mom, and I want you to tell me everything."

CHAPTER 37

For a woman who had always exuded confidence and haughtiness, Meg seemed the slightest bit uncertain. "Are you sure you want to get into all this now?"

Kimmie crossed her arms. "I'm sure."

"Really? Because I know you had a hard night last night, and you probably still need to catch up on your rest. Why don't you take a nap first or something?"

"I just had all that coffee. Now tell me. You and Mom made plans for her to escape. That's what you told Taylor."

"Who?"

Kimmie rolled her eyes. Really? For as long as Meg had been flirting with the trooper after setting him up on a forced date, she had already forgotten his name?

Typical.

"Taylor," she repeated with emphasis. "The trooper."

Meg grinned. "Oh, yeah. Him. I still think you need to find out what meds he's taking before you let things get too serious. But he's crazy hot. I'll admit that. I could totally see the two of you together."

Then why in the world did you have your paws all over him? Kimmie wanted to yell, but she held her tongue. She wasn't charging into this conversation to get news about Taylor. She needed to hear about Mom.

Now.

"What happened? What haven't you told me?"

Meg took in a deep breath. "Well, I can tell you, but I still think you should rest a little bit and we can talk when you're feeling a little better. I could wake you up once we get to Eureka ..."

"Just get it over with," Kimmie snapped.

"Fine." Meg was clearly annoyed and saw no need to hide it. "Mom called me a couple weeks ago. Asked if I knew of any good lawyers, someone who could help her fight for custody of Pip. I told her Dwayne's got connections. We could figure something out."

"How did she even get in touch with you?" Kimmie asked.

"On her cell. The one I got her last Christmas."

"Mom had a cell?" For a minute, Kimmie wondered if they'd stopped talking about the same person.

"Yeah. I'm surprised she didn't tell you."

Apparently, there were plenty of things Mom hadn't told her. Kimmie found herself yet again facing pangs of jealousy when she thought about her sister and the secret conversations she had with their mom.

"I thought you two were still fighting over Chuck."

Meg waved her hand in the air dismissively. Kimmie wished she'd keep it on the wheel. "What, that? Water under the bridge. We talked once or twice a week. Even more once I got her that phone."

None of it made sense. "When did she find a way to call you? Where did she go to get reception?"

"You really haven't been keeping up with the times, have you?"

Kimmie blinked at her sister.

"Coverage isn't what it was three or five years ago. The whole trailer's a hot spot. Mom even got herself a Facebook account. Used it on her phone all the time."

"What? You're serious?"

Meg chuckled. "I know. It was ridiculous, someone her age learning Facebook. But it was adorable, I swear."

"Why didn't she tell me any of this?"

"She probably didn't want you to get in trouble with that jerkface she was with. Oh, by the way, is the kid asleep?"

Kimmie glanced back again. "Yeah, he started dozing off right after we passed Mendeltna."

Meg let out her breath. "Good. I mean, I know he doesn't talk and all, but I'd hate to have him hear what I've got to say about his dad."

"You can skip that part," Kimmie said curtly. "I'm pretty sure I know more about that than you."

"Right. Well, so I got Mom that cell phone at Christmas ..."

"What'd you do?" Kimmie interrupted. "Hide it in the fruitcake?"

Meg looked appalled. "No. I told her I'd left it with Mrs. Spencer next door."

"Mrs. Spencer knew Mom had a cell phone?" Kimmie thought back to all the times she'd trekked to her neighbor's house to make a call. What kind of dysfunctional family did Mrs. Spencer think she was living next to?

"You're missing the point," Meg complained. "The point is once Mom got her phone, she and I were able to stay in touch. She'd call me whenever Bozohead was taking a nap, and that's how I found out just how bad things were."

Kimmie stared out the window at the mountains in the distance. Right now, their snow-dusted peaks felt closer to her than either her sister or her mom.

"Hey, it's not like she wanted to keep secrets from you." Meg sounded defensive. "You know how things were at that home. Everyone had to keep everything from everybody. That's just the way it was for you guys."

For you guys. Kimmie wondered how easy it was for her sister to throw around those kinds of phrases. *For you guys.*

Apparently taking Kimmie's silence for further offense, Meg ran her hand through her hair and huffed. "It's not like it was easy for me either, Cinderella. You think I liked to hear about the things that creature was doing to you?"

Kimmie bristled. Whatever happened to her under Chuck's roof wasn't her sister's business. And the fact that Mom blabbed everything to such a snotty, stuck-up, plastic Barbie doll like Meg doubled the sense of betrayal.

"Finally, Mom called me and said she wanted my help getting away."

Kimmie bet Meg just loved that. The chance for her big sister with the huge bank account and just as massive messiah complex to whisk in and save her wretched family from the clutches of evil. How grandiose. It must have given Meg quite the rush to be involved in anything more important than filing papers for her snotty husband.

"Why are you glaring at me like that?" Meg finally demanded.

"I'm not glaring." Kimmie glowered out the window.

"Yes, you are. You asked me a question. Now I'm telling you the answer, and you're acting all hurt and depressed. It's not like it's something I like to talk about."

"You certainly had no problems telling everything to that trooper," Kimmie blurted.

"So that's what this is about?" Meg had a bad habit of flaring her nostrils when she got angry, one of her only physically unattractive qualities. Kimmie reveled to see that her picture-perfect sister wasn't quite as put together as she wanted everyone to believe. "Listen, if you're upset because I went to the authorities to get you the help you obviously needed ..."

"I'm upset because you never cared!" Kimmie raised her voice, surrendering to the anger that gave her entire psyche a sense of power she'd rarely felt before. "You never cared. You ran off as soon as Mom got together with Chuck, and you never looked back."

Meg swerved to avoid hitting two ravens pecking at roadkill in the middle of their lane. "Is that what you think happened?" Her nostrils flared even more wildly.

"That's not what I think happened. That's what I know happened."

Each time Meg spoke, her volume escalated. "You know nothing. Hear me? I died when I found out what that oaf was doing to Mom. I literally died. Want me to prove it?"

She yanked up her sleeve. "See? That's what I did when I heard. By the time Dwayne called the paramedics, I didn't have a pulse. So don't even think about talking to me about who's suffered more or who put up with what or who hurts the most now that Mom's gone. Because you don't even know the half of it."

Meg gasped for breath as tears rolled down her cheeks. For what felt like minutes, Kimmie was too stunned to say a word. Finally, she forced herself to open the glove compartment where she found a travel packet of Kleenex. She pulled one out and offered it to her sister as a gesture of goodwill.

"Thanks." Meg blew her nose loudly then dabbed at her eyes. "I knew I shouldn't have put on all that mascara." She choked out a laugh. Kimmie joined in, feeling even more awkward and embarrassed than she'd been the day when she was ten and got caught trying on her sister's pushup bra.

"Mom never told me," Kimmie finally confessed.

Meg shrugged. "Of course she didn't. She never knew."

Kimmie didn't know what else to say. Staring at the snow capping the mountains ahead, she imagined how lonely and isolated it would feel to be up there looking down at a single car edging its way down a deserted highway.

The termination dust glistened in the sunlight.

CHAPTER 38

Kimmie woke up when the car rolled to a stop. "Where are we?"

"Just past the air force base," Meg answered. "Looks like you got bored playing Cinderella and tried to be Sleeping Beauty for the day."

Kimmie wasn't amused at her sister's little joke. She must have crashed shortly after their fight about Mom because she didn't remember anything else from the drive.

"Has Pip been napping this whole time?" She turned around as best she could in her seat.

"He's fine. Poor kid needs his sleep."

Kimmie glanced at her sister and whispered, "Sorry."

Meg shrugged. "Me, too."

Kimmie wanted to say more. Needed to say more. She still didn't know the details of Mom's escape or anything else Meg had talked with the trooper about.

"We'll be home in a half an hour. Maybe a little less if traffic stays this light."

It had been years since Kimmie's last trip to Anchorage. Pip had never been to a city this size, and she wondered if he'd be mesmerized by the traffic and crowds or terrified. She should warn Meg. Find a way to tell her about how Pip could freak out if too many changes were introduced at once. Maybe this move had been a bad idea after all. Then again, it's not like they could have stayed in Glennallen. So much had happened since yesterday, she realized she hadn't even called Jade to tell her she wasn't coming in to the daycare.

She winced in disapproval. "I can't believe it."

"What's wrong?" her sister asked.

"I missed my shift at work. I didn't let anybody know I wouldn't be able to make it."

Meg tossed her hair over her shoulder. "I'm sure everyone will understand once you tell them about last night."

"Yeah, but I don't even have their phone number," Kimmie whined. Compared to nearly losing her brother to hypothermia and getting lost

231

with him in the woods escaping from a murderous stepfather, missing work was a relatively minor burden, but she'd never flaked out like that before. She shook her head. "Jade's going to hate me."

"Jade?" Meg repeated. "Is that the one whose phone you were borrowing the other day?"

"Yeah."

"Then her number's still in my cell. You can call her and save your conscience." She tossed the phone onto Kimmie's lap. "Here you go. Have at it."

Kimmie tried a few times but wasn't even sure how to turn it on.

"Wait," Meg huffed, then softened her voice to add, "Let me do it."

"Can you do that while you're driving?" Kimmie asked when her sister took her phone back.

"Of course I can. It's not like I'm dialing or anything." She held the phone close to her mouth. "Siri, open recent calls."

Her request was met with a mechanical beep as the phone lit up.

Meg passed it over. "Just find the one from yesterday and hit that green phone icon."

Kimmie still couldn't get her mind around her own mother having a contraption this fancy. All those months and Chuck never found out? A second later, Jade was on the line, and Kimmie gave her the very abbreviated rundown of why she had to leave town.

"Everything okay?" Meg asked when Kimmie ended the call.

"Yeah," she answered, feeling sheepish for being so worried earlier. "I guess strep's going around the whole daycare, so Jade's only got four kids in today anyway. She's doing fine."

Meg didn't say *I told you so,* but her smug smile spoke volumes.

"Now that we're back in civilization, mind if I turn the radio on?" Meg reached out toward the dial. Soon her loud, booming music stole any further chance Kimmie had to ask her more about their mom. Unfortunately, the noise didn't manage to drown out her feelings of confusion and fear.

CHAPTER 39

Mom had bragged about Meg's house, but Kimmie had thought she'd been exaggerating until they pulled up into the winding driveway. At one point, Meg had to stop and put in a code that automatically opened a heavy brass gate. To the right was a tiered landscape with shrubs and mulch that looked as fresh as if it had just been poured out of the bag. To the left were tall brick pillars every few feet covered in some kind of lavish ivy.

"This driveway must take the entire day just to shovel in the winter," she commented.

It wasn't until her sister started to laugh that Kimmie realized Meg and her husband would pay someone to plow any snow that accumulated in front of their house.

Meg pushed the button on her sun visor that opened an immaculate garage, cleaner than the interior of most people's houses. A few garden tools with matching pink handles hung on one wall, bikes and tennis equipment on another. A golf bag in the corner was the only item that wasn't hung or somehow suspended above the perfectly swept concrete floor.

"Come on in." Meg stepped out of the car and tilted up her chin, probably waiting for Kimmie's gushing words of praise. The problem was Kimmie couldn't even find her voice.

"Wake up, Pip." Kimmie wondered if he was going to spend the whole day sleeping. Was it normal for him to be this tired? She shouldn't overreact. He was going to be fine. Everything was going to be fine.

She thought about the ornate gate with its automated code. She didn't even know people had homes like this in Anchorage but was thankful for the extra security it would afford. For the first time since her mom died, she wondered if things were actually going to start getting better.

"Take off your shoes," Meg called behind her shoulder as she stepped into a kitchen with massive windows and a vaulted sky roof. She turned around, beaming, but Kimmie still had no idea what she was supposed to say.

"Wow," she stammered, which was apparently enough to loosen Meg's tongue.

"Dwayne designed this place as an early wedding gift for the two of us. He told me I could either have the skylight in the ceiling or a honeymoon in Greece, and then when I told him I just couldn't make up my mind, he surprised me and gave me both." Her giggle was even more grating and airy than usual.

"Sweet cakes, is that you?" A tan Ken doll lookalike stepped into the kitchen and gave Meg a kiss on the cheek. "I didn't know you were bringing company over." He stretched out his hand. "Hi. I'm Dwayne."

Kimmie blinked at him, surprised to find that he looked exactly like he did in the wedding picture Mom had hanging on the fridge back home, right down to the last pixel. She was also surprised that he didn't seem to know who she was.

"Kimberly," she told him as she shook his hand.

"Nice to meet you, Kimberly. It's always lovely meeting one of my bride's friends."

Kimmie glanced at her sister who swatted him playfully with her handbag. "Bunny-boo, this is my *sister.*"

Dwayne's eyes widened. "*You're* Kimmie?"

Meg laughed, but not convincingly enough to keep Kimmie from picking up on the slightly nervous edge. "I told you she might be coming here to stay for a little while."

"Oh, great." Dwayne's smile hadn't changed once since he stepped into the room. Kimmie wondered how he managed without giving his cheeks some massive cramps. He bent down to kiss his wife again, whispering loudly, "She staying in the upstairs guest room or downstairs?"

"Downstairs," Meg answered just as conspiratorially.

Dwayne nodded. "Well, I'm off."

"Where you going, baby-bear?" Meg asked with an exaggerated pout.

"Work, work, work." He stuck out his finger and pressed in Meg's petite button nose.

"Boop!" she responded with a giggle, and after a fair amount of nose-kissing, cooing, and name-calling, he was gone.

Meg let out one last laugh when he left. "So that was Dwayne."

Kimmie hadn't realized until she saw her sister relax that Meg's smile had been just as huge and just as unwavering as her husband's during their entire exchange. Her sister sank down onto one of the tall barstools around a marble island countertop, moaning something about being too early in the day for wine.

"Can I do anything to help around the house?" Kimmie stared at the immaculate kitchen, wondering how her sister managed to keep herself from getting lost in her own home.

Her words seemed to sweep away whatever exhaustion cloud had covered her sister. Meg lifted up her head. "No, no, everything's taken care of here. Come on. Let me show you to your new room."

CHAPTER 40

"Sorry," Meg said, staring at the sparse bedroom. "I really had no idea what kind of toys a typical three-year-old would play with, and even if I did, I wasn't sure what would be appropriate for Pip."

Kimmie tried not to let her annoyance show. Meg was trying. The two women hadn't fought since their spat in the car, but every sentence felt strained. Like they both knew this was some kind of an act, but even the stress of keeping up such a complicated pretense was easier to deal with than the bickering and jealousy that had polluted their relationship for years.

Meg had already given them a tour of the house, explaining which rooms Dwayne considered on and off limits. Kimmie figured if she stuck with the guest room, the attached bathroom, and the kitchen, she'd be perfectly safe. She didn't even know where Meg and her husband slept.

Kimmie watched her sister shuffle from one foot to the other and felt a little bit sorry for her. It wasn't her fault that she was trying so hard to impress them.

"Any idea how you want to spend the rest of your afternoon?" Meg asked. "We could take Pip out for lunch and go to the park."

Kimmie wondered if Meg remembered the playground Mom used to take them to a lifetime ago. "Is there still that playground with the giant jungle gym?"

Meg frowned. "Which one do you mean? The one on Tudor and Lake Otis?"

"It was red and green and blue, and it had a swing coming down from the center and games like tic-tac-toe and stuff you could play on the sides."

Meg shook her head. "I don't remember any like that, but I know a nice one with a little foot bridge and a stream. It's getting cold, but the ducks were still there the last time I drove by. Does Pip like feeding ducks?"

Kimmie wished her sister would stop asking questions like that. Didn't she understand that for his entire life, Pip's existence had been relegated to his bedroom and the daycare? The only playground he'd ever known was the cheap plastic one at work. It was small, only room for two or three at a time, and other than a two-week period where he decided he loved the swings, Pip had never shown any interest in it at all.

"Let's not worry about a park today," Kimmie decided. Pip didn't act like his throat hurt, but she figured it was still too soon to take him out for a lot of running around.

"You sure? I could ask some of my mom friends. They might know of one with a jungle gym. Does he like to climb or something? Maybe we could set up a playdate."

Kimmie shook her head. The last thing she wanted to do was sit with dozens of other kids whose obvious developmental advancements just made Pip's delays seem even more exaggerated. And since he'd just gotten diagnosed with strep, she doubted parents would want him around their kids either.

"I think that we just need some downtime for a while. Is that all right with you?" She wasn't used to tiptoeing around her sister's feelings, but she asked the question gently, uncertain exactly what it was that she was trying to protect Meg from.

Meg nodded. "That sounds good. Does he have a favorite movie? We've got Netflix and Amazon and Hulu if there's something he wants to stream."

"Let me get him settled in for a little bit," Kimmie said even though she and Pip didn't have a single bag of personal belongings between them. She'd probably have to ask Meg to take her shopping soon, an excursion her sister would adore and Kimmie despise. But right now, she needed a few minutes alone. A few minutes with her thoughts and with her brother without anyone else staring over her shoulder or worrying about her.

She offered Meg an unconvincing smile. "It's going to be all right," she promised. "I just think Pip needs a little bit of quiet, and then we can decide what to do with the rest of the day."

"Okay." Meg lifted her hand and gave a little wave before shutting the door behind them, and Kimmie spent the next several minutes staring at the flowered wallpaper in silence.

CHAPTER 41

Meg came home with Subway sandwiches a little over an hour later.

"It doesn't look like that fever's done much to suppress his appetite, does it?" Meg asked, glancing at Pip.

Kimmie hadn't seen her brother eat so much before in a single sitting. Then again, between the rationed meals at the daycare and Chuck's bread heels and chili leftovers, this may have been the first chance Pip ever had to eat however much he wanted. How sad would it be to learn that all of his delays were simply a symptom of malnourishment? Then again, maybe that would be good news because his body and brain would catch up as soon as he got the calories and nutrients he'd been denied for so long.

It was nearly impossible for Kimmie to keep up any sort of conversation while they ate. She wanted to ask Meg more about their mom, but she'd have to wait for a time when Pip wasn't within earshot. Given how long he'd slept in the car, Kimmie doubted he'd take his regular afternoon nap. His schedule, his whole life, was thrown off balance, and she was both surprised and grateful he hadn't started throwing fits yet. Maybe that was another symptom of the strep. Maybe he was too tired to act up.

"So, work's going well for Dwayne?" Kimmie asked after an awkward silence.

Meg took a bite of her vegan wrap and shrugged. "You'd have to ask him. It's not like he talks to me about any of it."

"I thought you were his assistant or something."

Meg shrugged again. "Just because you work for somebody doesn't mean you know what they're up to." Her words were strangely cryptic and her expression somber enough that Kimmie tried to think of some way to change the subject.

"You sure it'll be okay for Taylor and me to have dinner here tonight? That won't be weird since you'll be out?"

Meg laughed. "What, are you young enough that you still need a chaperone on a date? Or are you worried about being alone with someone who's on prescription meds and you don't know what they are?"

Kimmie felt herself blush and tried to hide her face behind her sub.

"Will you get off his stupid prescription?"

"Fine. Then you tell me why you all of a sudden want to back out on a date with Alaska's most eligible trooper."

Kimmie rolled her eyes before taking a bite. "I just wanted to make sure it's not weird for you or anything."

"Not at all. I think it's adorable. You should've heard all the questions he was asking about you when you and Pip were with the doctor. I think he really likes you."

"You're just saying that." Kimmie tried to ignore the heat in her cheeks and the fluttering of her heart.

"No, I'm not. He asked all kinds of things. If you had a boyfriend, what kind of guys you typically date."

"What did you tell him?"

"The truth, of course. I told him that you only date guys with hard, chiseled jawlines, trim and athletic physiques, and that you once told me there was nothing in the world sexier than a man in uniform."

Kimmie stared at her sister, too mortified to speak.

Meg chuckled and took a sip of her bottled water. "Don't worry. I didn't really say all that. Although I might've mentioned something about uniforms."

Kimmie wasn't sure if Meg was still joking and decided that it might be better if she let the subject drop.

"I'm really happy for you," Meg finally said. "He seems like a decent guy, and he obviously cares about you and Pip. Even if he is on meds." Kimmie finished her sandwich in silence.

After lunch, Meg turned on the Pixar movie *Cars* for Pip. It was one of the ones he had already seen and seemed somewhat interested in at the daycare. Kimmie figured that with everything else going on right now, anything she could do to surround him with the familiar would be beneficial.

Once he was settled comfortably in the living room, Kimmie and Meg sat at the tall kitchen barstools and started brainstorming a shopping list.

"I have tons of clothes that you can have, so other than socks and underwear, I think you'll be set. What about shoes? If you're still a seven, mine will be a little big for you."

Kimmie glanced down at her feet. "I just brought my tennis shoes, and that will be fine for now." She didn't want to think about the approaching winter, the fact that before long she'd need snow boots and hats and gloves. She thought about one of mom's favorite Bible verses. *Do not worry about tomorrow, for tomorrow will worry about itself.* If God could get all of the Alaskan plants and animals and wildlife ready for winter, he could do the same thing for her too.

With Pip, on the other hand, it would be a little trickier not to worry.

"My friend Shannon's got a boy who just turned four, and she's not planning on having any more kids, so she's going to bring a few big bags of clothes, but she can't come until tomorrow. Do you want me to pick him up an outfit or two to wear until then? And what about pajamas?"

Kimmie didn't mention that with as difficult as it was to make it to the laundromat, Pip usually wore the same clothes several days in a row.

"I think he'll be fine until then, but I guess if you find any dinosaur pajamas, he really liked his pair from back home." She ignored the tightening in her throat when she thought about everything her brother was forced to leave behind. "They were green," she added quietly.

Meg gave her a sympathetic glance, and for a moment Kimmie worried that the dam she'd erected around her emotions since her mom's death was about to break. She would tell Meg everything, all about those years of torment, the shame and fear that now felt just as much a part of her as her DNA. She wanted to cry, to tell her sister how much she missed Mom, how impossible it was to think that someone so loving could kill herself or end up murdered.

She wanted to asked Meg what she thought about their time together as children. Was she disappointed that they had drifted so far apart? Did she secretly hope that this time of living under the same roof might be the first step toward healing that giant rift that had come between them?

Instead, she rattled off some of the toiletries she and Pip might need.

"Seriously?" Meg looked at the list she'd just written. "That's all you want me to get? Just toothbrushes, toothpaste, and a hairbrush?"

Kimmie stared at her lap. If she asked for more, she was afraid of overtaxing her sister's generosity. If she stuck with this list of the bare necessities, though, Meg might feel insulted as a hostess.

Maybe sensing Kimmie's discomfort, Meg smiled. "I guess you're right. Our skin tones are so close to the same that whatever I use for makeup I'm sure will work for you too. What about snacks? Dwayne and I are so busy we usually eat out or just pick up some takeout on our way home from the office. With Pip not feeling good though, I thought maybe I could get a few snacks and some easy breakfast stuff just to keep on hand. Should I get more yogurt?"

"Yes, please," Kimmie answered, once again feeling overwhelmed by this display of opulence, privilege, and generosity.

"What about for breakfast? You know me. I'm no cook, but I could grab something easy. Does he have a favorite cereal? Does he like granola? Hey." Meg reached out her hand and gave Kimmie's shoulder a squeeze. "What's wrong? Did I say something?"

Kimmie sniffed and wiped the tears from her eyes.

"What's the matter?" Meg asked the question so directly that Kimmie didn't have time to think up a lie.

"I don't know what he likes to eat for breakfast."

Her sister stared at her blankly. Of course it wouldn't make sense to someone like Meg, someone who could eat out or call for delivery or hop in her fancy car and drive to any grocery store or restaurant she wanted. Meg would never know what it was like to be so poor that a single crust of bread would be split between three people. She and Meg were born and raised by the same woman, but they were from completely different universes. Today was the first time Pip ever had a choice about what he ate, which only made the fact that he couldn't talk even more heart wrenching.

Kimmie sniffed. "I'm all right. It's just been a long day."

Meg looked at her quizzically, her pen still hovering over her pad of paper. "So, something simple like Cheerios, maybe?"

Kimmie sunk her head into her hands, wondering how something as simple as making a shopping list grew to be so draining. "Yeah," she answered, finding each word laborious to croak out. "Cheerios sound fine."

CHAPTER 42

Kimmie lost track of how many times she'd checked in on Pip in the living room while Meg was out shopping. The moment her sister said goodbye, Kimmie realized she should have asked Meg to pick up a few cheap matchbox cars, but she felt too silly to chase her down in the garage and add one more item to her list.

Kimmie had no idea what Pip could do here to occupy his time besides watching movies, but they'd think of something. Anchorage wasn't quite as cold as Glennallen. Maybe she and her brother could spend some time outside. The neighborhood was quiet. Kimmie could get used to living here.

If she had to.

Hopefully, the arrangement would be temporary. As soon as Kimmie found a job, she'd start looking for a place of her own. Meg's house felt more like a museum on display than a home where a kid would be free to run and jump and play. If Pip ever did any of those things.

She'd felt her brother's forehead on at least five different occasions in the past hour. How long was Meg going to take grabbing a few snacks and toiletries? Then again, Anchorage wasn't like Glennallen with its one grocery store. From Meg's home, it took at least a quarter of an hour just to get off the hillside. Driving to downtown Anchorage would probably take an hour if you ran into traffic.

But there were advantages to living in a city, advantages that Kimmie was prepared to seize. On the drive to her sister's, they'd passed two different storefronts with speech therapy signs. Pip would be in good hands. And hopefully Kimmie would find a job soon.

A door slammed. Kimmie turned around. "Hello?"

She checked the garage, but her sister wasn't home yet.

"Is someone here?" She hurried to the living room, where Pip was wrapped in blankets watching *Cars*. She checked his forehead once again out of habit. At least his fever was going down. "Do you need anything, Buster?" she asked. "Do you have to use the bathroom?" She glanced around, wondering if he'd wandered off in search of a toilet, but from what

242

she could tell, he hadn't moved since the last time she checked on him.

Maybe she was hearing things.

She eyed the front door. It was still locked. Which was generally a good sign, but only if you weren't trapped in a house with doors that closed on their own.

And a floor that creaked like someone was walking right behind her.

"Dwayne?" Kimmie's voice was shaky and uncertain. Even if someone had been in the next room, they probably wouldn't have heard her. She peeked out the front window to see if there were any cars in the driveway. But how could anyone get past that big iron gate?

Another sound, this one from the level above. Something moved upstairs. Suddenly, Kimmie's lungs started to seize up. What if it was Chuck? How hard would it be to find Meg's home address? He knew where Kimmie was, and he was coming after her. That had to be it.

She shoved her hand into her pants pocket, where Taylor's business card was crumpled from all the times she'd handled it. She had no idea what kind of long-distance rates Meg got on her landline, but whatever it was, she and Dwayne could afford it. Kimmie hurried to the kitchen, and her fingers shook while she dialed the number.

"Hello, this is Taylor." He sounded so casual. So happy.

She wet her lips and tried to steady her voice. "Hi. It's Kimmie. I'm at my sister's."

"Oh, yeah." From his jocular tone, Kimmie could almost see Taylor's warm smile. "You calling to give me her address? I'm on the road still, so I won't be able to write it down."

Kimmie's neck tingled with the vague sense she was being watched. She lowered her voice and took the phone closer to the hallway where she could keep an eye on her brother. Pip hadn't moved. So what was making all that noise?

"Kimmie? You still there?"

"Yeah," she whispered.

Taylor chuckled. "Good. I thought you had cut out on me for a minute. Reception's not great around here. Mind if I call you back in a little bit? We're about an hour still from the airport."

"I think someone's in the house."

Taylor paused, and when he spoke his voice was deadly serious. "You're at your sister's?"

"Yeah. She went to get some groceries, but I think I heard a noise upstairs."

A staticky noise garbled his words when he asked, "What kind of noise?"

"A door shutting. Someone making the floor creak." She held her breath, waiting for Taylor to tell her that all Anchorage mansions creaked, that they all had drafts that could blow doors shut unexpectedly. She wished she could look at him right now, wished she could borrow a little of the strength she always managed to find when he was nearby.

"Given everything you've gone through, you can't be too careful," he said, his voice taking on a mechanical quality. "I think you should ..." His next words were even more garbled.

"What?" She gripped the phone, straining to make sense of his words through the static. "Taylor? Are you there?"

Her sister's phone beeped in her ear. She'd lost the call.

CHAPTER 43

Kimmie stared alternatively at her brother and the phone in her hand. What should she do? She tried calling her sister's cell, but it went straight to voicemail. In a way, she was glad. She didn't want Meg to see her freaking out like this.

Every house made noise. She glanced out the window. The trees at the back of Meg's property swayed their branches grandly. It was probably just the wind.

Kimmie glanced around, wondering where she could take Pip if they needed to lock themselves in somewhere. The thought was silly. She was free now. Chuck had no idea where she was. Besides, there were troopers looking for him all around Glennallen. He couldn't have made it all the way to Anchorage, could he? She doubted his truck would even run that far.

No, it wasn't Chuck, and she didn't need to rush into a closet with Pip and hide. She was an adult who was acting like a child staying home alone for the first time. She marched back to the kitchen, listening at the same spot where she'd heard the door slam earlier. Nothing. The wind or her imagination. That was all. She glanced down the hallway and up the carpeted stairs leading to the second story. What could stop her from checking things out, just to be safe? She was tired of running, tired of hiding, and tired of being scared. Clutching her sister's phone with one hand, she rummaged through Meg's drawers with the other until she found a large cutting knife.

Nobody would catch her unprepared. Because nobody was upstairs. Still, having a weapon gave her a sense of power.

Not that she'd need it.

"I'll be back in a sec," she told her brother as she passed by the living room. He didn't glance up from the TV.

Tiptoeing up the stairs, Kimmie steadied her breath. She was going to confront her fears head-on this time and prove to herself that nobody else could be in this house.

She'd only been upstairs once, and half the doors had remained shut when Meg gave her the grand tour. Should she open each door one at a time to prove to herself that she was alone?

A thumping noise from down the hallway. This time Kimmie was certain of it. She stared at the knife in her hand. What good would it do against armed robbers? What good would it do against Chuck and his rifle?

A whispered voice. More than one person?

She still held the phone, but if she turned it on the beeping noise might alert the intruders. She had to get back down to Pip. Had to get him to safety.

Kimmie strained her ears, expecting almost anything — gunfire, Chuck's angry curses. What she didn't expect was a loud, shrill giggle.

She froze in the hallway, unable to move her legs as the far door opened and her brother-in-law poked his head out. "Kimmie?"

She tried to hide the phone and the knife behind her back but was certain he saw them both. Heat rushed so fast up to her face she felt dizzy. "I didn't know you were home," was all she managed to stammer.

"Just for a minute. I had to grab something I forgot." He cocked his head to the side. "Are you okay?"

Kimmie's hands were sweating so much she was afraid she might drop the knife. "I'm fine. I just heard a noise and got a little startled. That's all."

He smiled at her, but his expression did nothing to dull her sense of fear mingled with mortification.

Kimmie thought she heard another noise coming from the back room, but she wasn't about to step forward and investigate. She turned to head back downstairs when Dwayne called after her. "Hey, Kimmie?"

He'd plastered on that same fake smile he'd worn when they first met. She didn't know why the look should disgust her so much, but it did.

"Yeah?" Why couldn't he leave her to die of humiliation in peace?

"Meg's always getting on me for leaving things at home, so I'd love it if you didn't mention I was here." He winked. "Sorry for scaring you."

She turned away as his door clicked back in place to the sound of a stifled giggle.

CHAPTER 44

Kimmie didn't hear when or if Dwayne left, but the house was quiet when *Cars* ended, and she figured whatever business he'd wanted to get done at home was accomplished. Pip was restless, wandering from room to room. Kimmie followed him mindlessly. What else was there for her to do?

Meg came home a little before five, carrying at least half a dozen fabric shopping bags, which she dumped on the counter before racing upstairs. "I'm so late. I've got to get ready for that thing with Dwayne tonight. Follow me upstairs, and we can talk while I get ready." She rattled off the things she bought, and Kimmie was amazed that her sister could turn a seven-item list into a several-hundred-dollar shopping spree.

"Oh, and I know I said you could wear my clothes, but I saw this cardigan sweater and figured it'd look really good with some black slacks for your date tonight. You'll have to let me know if it fits." Meg tossed it to her and scurried into her bathroom, where she immediately began emptying her drawers haphazardly. "You excited about spending time with that cute trooper? Have you noticed how sexy he sounds when he laughs? You better tell me everything that happens tonight, or I'll totally die of jealousy. By the way, how'd things go while I was gone? Were you bored? Did you figure out how to use the TV remote? Is Pip feeling any better?"

Kimmie glanced at Meg's bed, where Pip had been fingering the raised patterns of her quilt, but he wasn't there anymore. "Pip?"

Kimmie retraced their steps downstairs, her heart high in her throat. Finally, she found Pip pulling a bag with dozens of matchbox cars out of one of Meg's shopping bags.

"Are these cars all for him?" she called up the stairs.

Meg appeared at the top of the landing. "Yeah. I remember Mom mentioned that he liked them."

Kimmie was touched by the gesture and glad that now Pip would have something to do to occupy his time besides wandering from room to room, feeling up the different blankets and pillows and upholsteries. She had to pull the butcher knife back out of the drawer to cut the box open, which reminded her of how scared she'd been when she'd heard her brother-in-law upstairs. She needed to call Taylor too and let him know she was all right. The afternoon had whizzed past.

She carried the new toys upstairs where Pip could play with them in Meg's room, hoping her sister wouldn't mind the mess.

Meg was in front of her mirror, running a flat iron through her hair. "I can't believe it took me that long just to get everything. I hope I'm not late. Dwayne throws a fit about that."

Kimmie still hadn't decided what, if anything, she'd tell her sister about seeing Dwayne at the house. It wasn't her business for one thing, and it would make things awkward for the rest of her stay if she and her brother-in-law started this visit on bad terms. On the other hand, Kimmie was sick of secrets, sick of having to pretend. She had no idea what Dwayne was doing this afternoon at home, and even though she had her suspicions, she doubted Meg would listen even if Kimmie did decide to share.

She'd have time to think through things later. She'd met Dwayne for all of two minutes. She shouldn't jump to conclusions.

Meg brushed her hair into place, pouting until she got it just right. She glanced at Kimmie's reflection in the mirror and asked, "So what time's Officer Cutie coming to dinner?"

"Around six," Kimmie answered. "I still need to call and give him your address."

"Use my cell." Meg pointed to her handbag on the bed. "I already put his name in there."

Kimmie was impressed that she managed to get the phone turned on, but after that she was lost.

"Here, give it to me," Meg ordered, then taking the phone said, "Siri, call Taylor's cell." She shoved the phone back to Kimmie when it started ringing.

"Kimmie?" His voice sounded panicked. "I've been really worried about you. I kept trying to dial the number you used to call me earlier, but it went straight to voicemail."

Meg leaned over and called out, "That must have been the landline. I've got the ringer turned off."

Kimmie blushed, realizing she was on speaker, and walked down the hallway where she hoped she could find a little privacy. For all she knew,

Dwayne was home again and about to pop out of the room at the far end of the hall.

"Are you all right?" Taylor asked. "I was worried. I almost called the local police to check on you."

"I'm sorry." She should have called him right back, but she was so embarrassed to have let her brother-in-law freak her out that she'd conveniently forgotten. "Did you get your friend to the airport all right?"

"Yeah. You still free for dinner?"

Kimmie thought of all the reasons why Taylor shouldn't come over. She hardly knew him, for one thing, and she didn't like the thought that he was paying her attention just because he was sorry for her. It felt strange and somewhat rude hosting someone at her sister's house, especially with Meg out for the evening. Besides, she had Pip to worry about. What if his fever spiked?

"I hope you like Chinese." Taylor's voice was playful, and Kimmie's arguments died on her lips.

"That sounds delicious."

"Where should I meet you?"

Kimmie stepped back into the bedroom where Meg shouted him her address through her closed closet door while she dressed.

"Did you catch that?" Kimmie asked with a laugh. She nearly tripped over one of Pip's cars as she stepped back out of the room.

"I got it," Taylor answered. "I'll see you pretty soon. And Kimmie?"

"Yeah?" She waited, her heart a fluttering bird in her chest.

"I'm really looking forward to spending some time together."

CHAPTER 45

Aside from Pip's throwing a minor tantrum when Kimmie moved his car collection back downstairs to the living room, the evening went smoothly enough. Meg was a bundle of nerves and motion until she swept out at quarter to six, complaining about how late she'd be, wishing Kimmie good luck on her big date as if it were a final exam at school.

The door slammed shut behind her with an echo, and then the house fell silent. Kimmie had showered and changed into a pair of her sister's black slacks and a black shirt. It was darker than what she'd normally wear, but the burgundy cardigan and a turquoise necklace from her sister gave a cheerful splash of color. She'd lost track of how many times she'd opened and shut the kitchen cabinets just so she could remember where everything was when Taylor arrived with the food.

Pip adored his new dinosaur pajamas from Meg and was already dressed for bed. Kimmie was glad he was happy playing with those cars. Her sister might never know what a genius purchase that was. Kimmie wandered from room to room, wondering what she could do to make anything look more attractive. The house was spotless, and the decorations were sparse but tasteful. She hoped it wasn't too opulent for Taylor. She didn't want to make him uncomfortable, didn't want him to think she came from the kind of family that had nothing better to do than flaunt all their wealth to make others jealous.

She tried to imagine how the night would go. She'd never been on a date before. Even though she and a boy in high school had crushes on each other for a while, she'd never been allowed to see him outside of school. She wondered if Meg was this nervous before her first date with Dwayne.

Kimmie glanced once more at the mirror, hardly recognizing herself. From one angle, she looked tired and old, like you'd expect from someone who'd just lost their mother. But when the light caught her face a certain way and when she gave a faint smile, she glowed with maturity. She hoped Taylor wouldn't think she'd spent too much time getting ready. Meg insisted on putting some makeup on her even though Kimmie had never worn anything besides chapstick and blush before. The foundation did wonders at hiding the smudges beneath Kimmie's eyes, but when she met with Taylor she still wanted to look and feel like herself.

Meg had fixed the house phone, and Taylor had called a few minutes earlier to let her know he was running late. Apparently dozens of other hungry Anchorage residents were also in the mood for Chinese, and the wait for takeout would be longer than he'd expected. Kimmie paced the downstairs hallway, trying to calm her nerves, trying to keep from feeling guilty. What kind of daughter goes on a date the week her mother dies?

She hummed one of her mom's Bible tunes. *Surely I am with you always, even to the end of the ages.*

How much longer was Taylor going to take? She'd forgotten to ask Meg how to let him through the iron gate up the driveway. She checked the window every few seconds to see if he was on his way, ready to meet him.

From the living room, Pip let out a squeal. When she got to him, she saw him struggling to separate two cars whose bumpers had gotten stuck together.

"Let me help," she urged, but her brother refused to let either of them go.

"If you give them to me, I can fix it." She felt bad for sounding irritated. It wasn't Pip's fault he got frustrated so easily.

She finally managed to yank the cars out of his hands, ignoring the angry shrieks that died down the moment he realized his toys were free. She wondered what Taylor would think if she tried to wrestle her brother's medicine into him after dinner. It would probably be best to wait until he was gone.

The doorbell rang, and Kimmie sprinted ahead, reaching it in just a few strides. Suddenly feeling foolish, she waited until she caught her breath so Taylor wouldn't think she'd been running, then flung the door open.

The smile froze on her lips.

It wasn't Taylor at the door.

CHAPTER 46

"Hello, Kimmie. You're looking grown-up tonight." Chuck leered at her and shoved his way into the entrance, locking the door behind him.

"What are you doing?" Kimmie could barely stammer the question.

"Just checking up on my favorite stepdaughter." He let out a grating chuckle as he glanced around the foyer. "Too bad you're the ugly one of the sisters. You could never get a rich man to marry you and set you up in a home like this. Not with a face like that."

Kimmie was bombarded with a dozen thoughts at once, which all finally managed to clear their way through the chaos into the single realization: *I have to protect Pip.*

She figured the longer she could keep Chuck here in the foyer with her, the more chance her brother would have of staying safe. Maybe he'd recognize his father's voice and hide. Kimmie wished there was a clock somewhere. If she stalled long enough, Taylor would show up. He'd know what to do.

Deciding that the best way to protect herself and her brother was to keep Chuck as calm as possible, she led him to the kitchen, taking the long route so he wouldn't pass the living room.

"Where's Pip?" Chuck asked, glancing around as if his son might be hiding in one of the kitchen cabinets.

"He's not feeling well. He's got strep throat."

Kimmie eyed the drawer where the meat knife was kept, trying to edge her way closer to it.

"Is that a phone behind you?" he asked with a snarl.

She nodded.

"Unplug it and slide it over to me."

She didn't argue. The movement allowed her to sidle up to the knife drawer, which is where she hoped to stay for the remainder of this conversation.

Chuck slammed the phone against the counter, chuckling as the batteries flew out, then he did the same with the base. "There now." His eyes glinted in the sunlight streaming in from the windows in the vaulted ceiling. "Any other phones I need to know about?"

Kimmie shook her head.

"I suppose you know why I'm here."

Kimmie blinked at him. Why was he here? To kill her? To kidnap Pip? Whatever it was he wanted, he wouldn't succeed. She inched her hand behind her toward the handle of the knife drawer.

"Your sister's got something that belongs to me."

Kimmie didn't know what he was talking about, and she flinched when Chuck snarled, "Where is it?"

"I think it's in her room," she lied, hoping he might turn around, distracted enough to let her get at the knife.

Chuck took a step toward her and grabbed her arm, pinching until she sucked in her breath from the sharp pain. "Take me there."

She took the long way again, praying that God would send his angels to protect Pip. As long as her brother stayed safe, it didn't matter what happened to her.

Halfway up the staircase, she paused and glanced behind.

"Hurry up," Chuck snarled.

She led him into her sister's room.

"Where is it?" he demanded.

"In one of her dressers. She didn't say which."

Chuck started ripping out the drawers of Meg's bureaus, flinging undergarments and shirts and gym clothes across the floor. Kimmie bit her lip. She didn't know what he was looking for, but as long as he stayed busy, nobody would get hurt. She glanced around her sister's room, wondering if there might be another phone in here.

"I don't see it," Chuck growled, flinging the last drawer against the bedpost.

"She said it was in here, I swear it." Kimmie had to keep him distracted. He glowered at her, and she realized the sickening truth. He was sober. This wasn't some kind of drunken rage. This was methodical, premeditated.

Pip, I hope you're hiding somewhere ...

"Stop lying to me and tell me where that brat put it." Chuck stepped toward her, and Kimmie automatically inched her way toward the wall.

"There's another room. Her husband's. I might have made a mistake. It might be in there."

With as many rooms as Meg had in her home, hopefully Chuck's search would keep him busy enough until Taylor arrived or Kimmie found some way to call for help.

She pointed to the door Dwayne had popped out of earlier today, and she marveled that someone like her brother-in-law could have ever frightened her. After what Chuck had already put her through during the past ten years, she should be immune to silly fears.

Her legs were steady as he pulled her behind him, striding toward Dwayne's door.

"If you don't find me what I'm looking for, I swear I'll kill you." His voice was low and menacing, and Kimmie had no problem believing every word.

Dwayne's room was different than his wife's. His king-sized bed took up most of the floor space, and the only other furniture was one small end table. Chuck yanked out the drawers, spilling their contents onto the bed. Just a few sports magazines, a bar of deodorant, and a plastic wrapper.

"Where are those blasted letters?" Chuck was bellowing in her face, and Kimmie felt herself shrink as she tried to inch farther and farther away from his fury.

"You think you can get away with hiding them from me like that?" he yelled. "I told you I'd kill you if you didn't hand them over."

He grabbed her hair and yanked down. "You think you're so clever? I'll show you who the smart one is around here."

She shut her eyes as he kneed her in the gut and then the face. Blood spilled from her nose. She tried to swing her arm to push him away, but he grabbed it and kept it pinned behind her back. One small jerk and he could snap her shoulder out of place.

He let his fist fall on her back. She let out a pained gasp as the wind rushed out of her lungs, and Chuck mocked her in his grating falsetto. "Is baby girl hurting? Did precious little princess get a boo-boo?"

Kimmie tried to not to make any noise. Chuck had threatened to kill her in the past, but tonight he clearly possessed the physical stamina and clarity of mind to carry out his plan.

"Tell me where those letters are." His fist found its way to her gut, driving her to her tiptoes with its force.

She collapsed onto the ground, and he straddled her in an instant. *Stupid, stupid, stupid.* What had she been thinking? That she could outwit him? That there was any way to get the upper hand? There was no way to escape this. Chuck wrapped his beefy hands around her throat. He was too strong. She couldn't protect herself. But maybe it was better this way. If Chuck killed her, at least she could join her mom in heaven.

The thought sent a wave of peace spreading through her broken body. As long as she didn't give way again to fear, it was going to be all right.

Warmth flooded her spirit. A peace far more poignant than anything she'd ever known overcame her senses. Her body flailed beneath Chuck's weight, but her physical survival instinct was something separate, something distinct. It wasn't her at all. She watched it as if from above. So this was what it felt like to die. She thought about how many times in the past she had struggled in vain against Chuck and his violent outbursts, striving with a purely animalistic instinct for her own survival. If she'd known death was anything like this, she would have never been so afraid.

I'm going to see my mother again. The realization flooded her with joy, a sense of lasting happiness and contentment unlike anything she'd experienced in the past ten years.

I'm going to be with Jesus soon. No, not even soon. God was here. Right here. Right now. She knew it just as clearly as she knew that once Chuck killed her, she would be in the presence of a Majesty more holy and powerful and personal than any mortal could dare imagine. That glory was hers. It was waiting for her. She could almost hear the sound of her heavenly Father's voice ready to welcome her into paradise.

Somewhere in the distance, Chuck was roaring at her, cursing her as he drained the life out of her with his meaty hands.

Her body seized. Her brain jostled awake. *Wait.* What was she thinking? She couldn't die. She had to help her brother.

She struggled. Strained even though she knew the battle was already lost.

God, help me. I need to save him.

Chuck's sweat beaded onto his forehead and dripped down on her. She had to get away from him, but it was impossible.

I'm sorry, Pip.

A few more seconds, and it would all be over. Maybe it already was. Through her blurred and blotchy vision, she saw Chuck stand up. He was done?

It was just as well. Just a few more minutes. Then she'd be home.

At the doorway he turned. Something small was in his hands. He aimed it at her.

Kimmie didn't even hear the gun's explosion. Chuck's words and threats meant nothing anymore. She closed her eyes. She was ready to go home.

CHAPTER 47

It was everything her mother told her it would be. The streets were made of glass, the gates of the most exquisite jewels.

He was there. She could sense him even though she didn't see him, the warmth of his fatherly love soothing over any pain, silencing any fears. She wanted to run to him, but something was stopping her.

She didn't understand. She could hear the distant music and wanted to join in the majestic chorus, but she was too far away. She couldn't make out the melody, could only faintly hear it, sense it as a vague echo of what might have been.

It was getting quieter now, fading further off into the distance. Kimmie was frantic to find out what she had to do to get it back.

Is someone there? Is that you, Mom?

The music stopped, and the pain that battered every inch of her body immediately stole away any memory of the joy or peace she had previously felt. It had all been a dream. There was no heavenly bubble of protection, no glorious music, no majestic homecoming.

She was still alive. For all Chuck's threats, he hadn't managed to kill her after all.

Someone was with her, someone watching over her, trying to wake her up.

Mom? Are you here?

As soon as she tried to speak the words, Kimmie remembered her mother was in a different place, the paradise that Kimmie had only managed to glimpse from the other side of an unscalable chasm.

Her mom couldn't help her now. Nobody could.

Kimmie shut her eyes again, wondering just how much longer she'd have to wait before she heard that heavenly music once again.

CHAPTER 48

It was hard to guess how many times Kimmie had drifted in and out consciousness, begging to wake up in the paradise she'd envisioned, only to find herself still lying in a broken heap on a bloodstained carpet. Where was Pip?

That one thought alone gave her reason to try to rouse herself. She had to find out if her brother was okay. Searing pain in her shoulder made crawling impossible, so she used her legs to scoot, inch by inch, collapsing every few feet from the effort. Through the roaring in her ears, she heard the Bible songs her mother used to sing.

I can do all things, I can do all things, I can do all things through him who gives me strength.

She didn't know how far she'd moved. It felt like miles, except she was still in Dwayne's bedroom. She had to make it downstairs. Had to check on Pip.

I can do all things, I can do all things, I can do all things ...

Throughout the past ten years, the bulk of Kimmie's prayer life had been spent asking God to release her and her family from Chuck's tyranny. When the Lord remained silent, she eventually grew tired of asking. But now, the instinct to pray, to plead, to call on the Lord for help, was just as strong as the urge to survive. She had to keep going. Had to make sure her brother was okay. She didn't know the extent of her injuries and wasn't sure if she was putting herself in more danger by trying to move. All she knew was that if Chuck had been angry enough to do this to her, he might have done anything to Pip. She had to find out. And if her brother was still in danger, she would fight her stepfather until her dying breath to keep Pip safe.

Down the hall, a trickle of wet blood following behind her, she pressed on to the staircase.

What now?

She couldn't think about the pain. Couldn't even think about her own survival. All she had to push herself forward was the image of her brother's scared face. She had to get to Pip.

She tried to call out to him, but it hurt too much. She couldn't inhale enough air. She blacked out on the top of the staircase, and when she opened her eyes again, they stung.

Smoke.

She did her best to look behind her but could only turn her head a few degrees before the pain rippled down to her ribs and radiated through her entire body. The smoke was coming from upstairs. She had to go down. She had to get to Pip.

Scooting on her bottom like a tiny toddler pretending the stairs were a giant slide, she grimaced against the pain and worked her way down. She nearly passed out once more on the center step but forced her eyes to stay open even though her mind registered nothing but the pain.

Pip. She had to save Pip.

Whatever Chuck had done, the fire was upstairs. She still had time. She had to save her brother.

At the bottom step, adrenaline soared through her, and she managed a few whole steps before tottering down. Her head was light. The pain in her shoulder made it nearly impossible to focus on anything else.

Help me, God.

She was moving again. It wasn't graceful or efficient, but she struggled forward inch by painstaking inch to the living room, her lungs stinging with every breath she took. Whatever flames upstairs were causing the smoke, she couldn't hear them over the roaring of her pulse in her ears.

Just another ten feet to the living room.

"Pip," she croaked, steeling herself for whatever she might find. Would he be injured too? She had no idea how she'd carry him, but she'd muster the strength to get him out of this house and to safety. That's all that mattered. She might be dead in ten minutes, but as long as she got Pip outside, it would be okay.

She grabbed onto the doorframe and pulled herself forward with a groan.

She was in the living room.

But her brother wasn't there.

CHAPTER 49

Kimmie woke up from another blackout, trying to remember what she was doing on the floor in a room full of smoke.

Someone was calling her name, someone muffled and far away.

Where was Pip?

She tried to push herself up, but there was no connection left between her brain's demands and her body's ability to comply.

"Pip!" She was screaming the word, or at least she thought she was, but she couldn't hear herself.

Smoke stung her lungs. She tried to cough, but the hot pain streaking from her ribs immobilized her completely.

What had Chuck done to Pip?

"Kimmie." She ignored the voice. She had a job to do. She couldn't fail her brother. If only she could remember how to move.

A man's face frowned down at her. Fingers touched her face, but she didn't feel them. He was saying something to her, but she couldn't understand the words. It wasn't until he tried to move her that she fought him off. No, she needed to save Pip. He couldn't take her anywhere.

She thrashed her body, fighting him off, confusion and pain clouding out any higher reasoning. She screamed her brother's name, the first time she'd managed to make her own voice heard.

He whispered something in her ear, but she couldn't hear it over the deafening roar of flames.

CHAPTER 50

Kimmie blinked her eyes open.

"Can you hear me?" A kind face gazed down at her, the relief evident in his eyes.

Her lips were dry and cracking.

"Don't try to talk," he told her. "They're taking you to the hospital. You're going to be all right."

She didn't believe him. He was lying to her. She was dying. There was no way to recover from injuries this severe. And she'd failed to save her brother.

The stretcher she was lying on bounced as it was wheeled down her sister's walkway. Ahead of her she saw the iron gate wide open and wondered how the ambulance had managed to get inside. The stretcher turned as they approached the vehicle, and she saw her sister's home engulfed in flames.

"Pip!" The sound was deafening, a roar of pain and terror and trauma and disbelief. "Pip!" Her soul screamed out the words, but all she could hear were kind assurances from the man beside her.

"Everything's going to be okay." Yet another lie.

The stretcher was hefted into the back of the ambulance. She shut her eyes, but all she could see were the flames that had claimed her brother's life. She hadn't reached him in time. It didn't matter what happened to her now. They might as well let her die as quickly as possible.

She was ready.

There was nothing left for her on earth.

CHAPTER 51

Kimmie woke up to the sound of a muffled conversation.

"... captured right near Northern Lights Boulevard ..."

"... arson and attempted murder ..."

"... still can't believe how this could have happened."

She opened her eyes. "Hello?"

Her sister was at her bedside in an instant. "You're awake. Hey, over here. She's awake. Someone go get the nurse. Wait, I'll use the call button. Do you need more morphine?"

Kimmie squinted her eyes in the blinding overhead light and wondered if this was how Chuck felt when he woke up with a hangover.

"How are you doing?" Taylor was beside her. There was something familiar about his presence. Memories of smoke and flame flashed in her mind.

"That was you?" Her voice was hoarse and untested, unfamiliar even to herself, but he smiled.

"Yeah. That was me."

"Wasn't he heroic?" Meg crooned.

He reached out and took Kimmie's hand. She squeezed as tightly as she could. She wanted to hear the truth from him. Meg would just ruin it all with her tears and emotionalism. Taylor would tell her the truth. He'd help her accept what happened.

"Was Pip ...?" She couldn't bring herself to finish the question but continued to hang onto him, praying he'd understand.

Taylor glanced at Meg. No, Kimmie wanted to hear it from him. She gave his hand one last, pleading squeeze, and Taylor cleared his throat. "You want to hear everything?"

"I think she should rest," Meg inserted.

Shut up, Kimmie wanted to say but kept her eyes focused on Taylor.

He set his other hand on top of hers. "Pip was in the house when your stepdad started that fire. We think Chuck was looking for letters your mom sent Meg, letters depicting the kind of abuse you and your family suffered, letters indicating she was planning to run away but was afraid if Chuck

262

found out, he'd kill her. He wanted to destroy what evidence he could, and when he didn't find what he was looking for, we can only assume he torched the place in hopes of covering his tracks."

Kimmie didn't care about motive or method. She only wanted to know how much her brother had suffered.

"Pip was a very brave, very smart little boy," Taylor went on. "When I got to your sister's place, I called the fire department and saw you in the living room. I got you out but you were worried about Pip so I went back to look for him. I found him hiding in the bathtub, surrounded by his toy cars."

Kimmie's throat seized in pain when she asked, "Was he hurt?"

Taylor shook his head. "He's doing great. The doctors want to check him out, but from everything we can tell, your stepdad never laid a hand on him. Besides a little smoke inhalation, he's going to be just fine."

CHAPTER 52

Five days later

"Come on, hot stuff. Recovering from shoulder surgery is no excuse to miss your big date." Meg dumped her bag full of cosmetics onto Kimmie's hospital bed. "You know, there's absolutely no way this guy would drive four and a half hours one way on his day off if he wasn't already totally into you. Not to mention the fact that he singlehandedly broke down my door and rushed into a burning building to save your life."

"And Pip's," Kimmie added weakly.

Meg grinned. "Right. And Pip's. Which reminds me, you know that daycare he's been going to? They actually have a worker going on maternity leave in exactly four weeks, which means if you want the job, it's yours."

"Really?"

"Yeah, but you can thank me later. Right now, I just need you to shut your eyes so I don't poke you with my liner. No, don't scrunch them up like that. Just look down. Like this."

"Did anyone ever tell you that you're bossy?"

"Thank you. Oh, speaking of bossy, you're not going to forget to ask him about that prescription, are you? You can learn a lot about a man by what drugs he takes."

"No, I'm not going to ask about his prescription. That's his business."

Meg shrugged. "Well, then, don't come whining to me when you find out he's got some fatal illness right when things are starting to get serious. Or have you ever considered that he could have an STD?"

"Will you cut it out?" Kimmie snapped.

"Fine. Fine. Now are you going to let me do your makeup or what? This man risked his life to save you. The least you could do in return is let me make you presentable."

Four days later

"So you ready to be back home? Or at least back at your sister's?" Taylor asked.

Kimmie held the hospital phone close to her ear in order to hear better over the sound of Pixar's *Cars* playing loudly on the TV. "Yeah. It'll be good to spend more time with Pip."

"Is he enjoying that daycare?"

"Yeah. It's a really nice place. I've talked to the director there a few times. She said her daughter was a lot like Pip, didn't talk for the first few years, things like that, and now she's a senior at Dimond High and planning to become a speech pathologist."

"That's awesome. Hey, is Pip there with you now?"

"Yeah."

"Let me talk to the little Buster."

Kimmie called Pip over, wincing when he jostled her injured shoulder as he made his way to his perch on her pillow, his favorite seat in her hospital room. "Trooper Taylor wants to say hi."

She handed him the phone and could hear Taylor's voice on the other end. "Hi, buddy. Are you having a good day?"

Pip stared at the receiver then ran his favorite car up and down it.

"What's that noise?" Taylor asked. "What's he doing?"

"He's driving his car on the mouthpiece," Kimmie explained. Giving her brother a kiss, she brought the phone back to her ear.

"That was one of our best conversations yet," Taylor joked.

"I think he likes you."

"Yeah?" Even across the miles, she could hear the grin in Taylor's voice. "What makes you think that?"

"That was his favorite car. If he didn't like you he would have used the dump truck."

Twelve days later

Meg stood at the top of the staircase, shaking her head. "No. Absolutely not."

Kimmie looked down at herself. "What's wrong?"

"Nobody goes to La Mesa's in flats and a plain brown sweater."

"You're the one who gave me this plain brown sweater."

"And it'd be fine if he were taking you out for McDonalds. This is La Mesa. Sheesh. Super high-end."

"I didn't know."

Meg rolled her eyes. "You've got to keep up with the times. Now go change"

Kimmie glanced at her clothes. "But I like this sweater."

Meg rolled her eyes. "Sometimes I think you're totally hopeless. You have no idea how into you this guy is. First he saves your life, then he spends every single day off driving all the way out here to take you to the fanciest restaurants in Anchorage. How clueless do you have to be?"

"About as clueless as the woman who didn't know her husband was having an affair with the office assistant?"

Meg waved her hand in the air dismissively as she hurried down the stairs. "Touché. But I did know about it, for the record. I just didn't want to say anything until we'd been married five years. And the timing couldn't have been better. I'm getting my share of the insurance money from the fire, and he can have the rest. Including Miss Secretary. And hey, if Taylor wants you to sign any prenups before you guys tie the knot, tell me and I'll have my lawyer look it over for you. That guy literally saved my life."

Kimmie rolled her eyes. "It's our second date. The only knots I'm working on right now are the ones in the back of my head. Even with the physical therapy, I can't manage to reach back there to get it brushed out."

"That's what you have me for. That and making sure you don't walk into La Mesa's looking like a thrift-store special. Come on. Let's get you back to your room. I hate to say it, but we have a lot more work to do. By the way, did Officer Hard Abs ever respond to your text? What did he say?"

"It wasn't *my* text, and I'm still mad at you for stealing my phone like that. You had no right, you know."

Meg pulled Kimmie into her bathroom and started attacking her hair with a brush. "Ok. Sorry, not sorry. Now what did he say? Did he tell you what meds he's on?"

"Actually, he told me he takes nothing but a multivitamin."

"What about his prescription he picked up from the pharmacy?" Meg was yanking her hair mercilessly, but Kimmie still wanted to stretch the story out a little longer. Her sister deserved it.

"The day we ran into him in the clinic, he was picking up flu medicine for a little old lady who was too sick to leave her home."

Meg stopped assaulting her with the brush and stared into the mirror. "Seriously? You're not pulling my leg?"

Kimmie grinned. "I might be. Guess you'll never know, will you?"

Meg reached into Kimmie's pocket. "But I can look at your phone, can't I?"

Kimmie giggled as she tried to push her sister away. "You can try, but I already deleted the text."

"I should have never taught you how to use a cell."

"You should have never texted my boyfriend and asked about his personal business."

"Wait, he's visited you at the hospital and he's taking you out to dinner at La Mesa's, and he's your boyfriend all of a sudden?"

Kimmie smiled and shrugged. "Yeah. A lot can change in two weeks. You've got to keep up with the times."

Three hours later

"You're looking lovely." Taylor raised his water goblet and smiled at her warmly.

"Thanks."

"How's Pip?"

"He's great. He had his first meeting with the new speech therapist yesterday. She's been working with kids like him for almost twenty years, and she specializes in the four and under age range, so I think it's going to be a perfect match."

"Speaking of perfect matches," he said, reaching for her hand, "I'm really glad we've been able to spend this time together."

She smiled back at him. "Me, too." Kimmie still didn't understand what Taylor saw in her, but it must be something since he was calling her every day on her new cell phone and making plans to drive to Anchorage to see her on almost all of his upcoming weekends.

"I know we weren't going to discuss the trial at dinner, but I did want to tell you they set the date."

"What's that mean?"

"For right now, nothing. Even without your testimony, they're already building up a solid case. Everyone's sounding pretty confident he'll be tried not only for the house fire and your assault but for your mom's murder as well."

Kimmie wondered if she'd ever get used to hearing the words *mom* and *murder* together. With everything that had happened — her injuries coupled with her long physical recovery plus the relief at having Pip safe — she was still processing her mom's death in choppy spurts and pieces. She was grateful that Taylor felt comfortable with her sudden bursts of emotion, grateful to finally have someone to talk to, someone who allowed her to feel secure enough to be her true self. Until she met Taylor, she wasn't even sure she knew who that was.

The waiter in his flawless tuxedo served their appetizer dish, and Taylor took both her hands in his. "Shall we pray?"

She nodded. In spite of all she and her family had gone through, there were still hundreds of reasons to give thanks.

CHAPTER 53

Spring

The Copper River Basin had broken out into spring, the season where the roads turned to slush as the snow melted, leaving acres of puddles and perfect breeding conditions for raising next summer's batch of mosquitoes.

Kimmie was nervous. It wasn't her first trip back to Glennallen. She'd already returned to speak several times with the prosecuting attorney assigned to her stepfather's murder and arson trial. She was also here last Christmas, when Taylor drove her out so she could attend his work Christmas party and meet all the colleagues he'd talked so much about. But this was the first time she'd step foot in Chuck's old trailer since the night she and Pip fled through the woods.

"You sure you want to do this?" Taylor asked, holding his arm protectively around her waist.

She nodded. After Kimmie healed from her physical wounds, her sister talked her into trying out the same counselor Meg had seen after slitting her wrists. Kimmie had balked at the idea, but Meg had so many nice things to say about the woman and wouldn't stop nagging, so Kimmie finally agreed.

Half a year later, she was still seeing the same therapist, who agreed that this one last pilgrimage home could play a large role in Kimmie's healing process.

She was glad to have Taylor with her and glad that Meg had taken time off her new job as a fitness director to watch Pip. After spending the day with Taylor, Kimmie would head over to Jade's and crash on her friend's couch before Taylor drove her back to Anchorage tomorrow. With as close as they'd become over the months, it was surprising to think that this was the longest stretch of time she'd spent with him without either her sister or Pip around.

He gave her a reassuring squeeze. "Want me to wait out here?"

She shook her head, certain that there would be no way she could confront these memories of her past if Taylor weren't here with her.

"Got your letter?" he asked.

She took the single sheet of paper out of her pocket and unfolded it.

When she and her therapist had come up with this idea, Kimmie thought she'd be too embarrassed to read something out loud, but now with Taylor here by her side, she felt safe.

She could do this.

The trailer was almost exactly like she'd left it. Nobody had come to clean it out. There was Chuck's recliner, with the trash and litter he'd left there before he went after Kimmie and her brother in Anchorage.

There were the used napkins on the floor. If she walked into the kitchen, she was certain she'd find the same pile of dirty dishes in the sink that she'd left there the night she ran away.

But she didn't need to go that far. Everything she wanted to do could take place right here in the living room.

She spread out her letter and with trembling hands began to read.

Dear Chuck, to say you ruined my teen years and early adult life would be a gross understatement. Because of you, I lived in constant fear, hunger, and emotional turmoil. I wasn't able to form any meaningful friendships with others my age because I was too afraid to let anyone get close, embarrassed to think that someone might discover the squalor and terror in which we lived.

Your abuse touched every aspect of my life, and as a result I lacked confidence and never felt like I had any sense of control over my future, my will, or my body. The fact that you killed my mother and then blamed her death on suicide has haunted me for months. I've lost untold hours of sleep and am afraid of the dark now because of you. Even worse is the way you treated my brother. No child should have to grow up knowing his own father is a heartless murderer.

But in spite of all the ways you deprived Pip of the things a healthy child needs to mature, he is thriving without you. With his speech therapist's help, he's stringing words together now and knows over three dozen signs. If your goal was to make your son as miserable as you made me, you have already failed. He is happier, healthier, and better off without you.

I wasn't exaggerating when I said you ruined my life, but just like I refuse to watch you hurt your son anymore, I also refuse to let you ruin or dictate my future. The coping mechanisms I learned while I was under your roof were survival instincts that helped me endure life in your home, but I don't need to rely on those bad habits anymore. I am surrounded by a vivacious and fun-loving sister, an adorable little brother, and a boyfriend who has supported me through each and every step of my healing journey.

I suppose if I had the time and the energy, I could sit and ask you why you did the things you did. If you despised the person you were just as much as you made us despise you, if there was a deep sadness or trauma in your past that made you turn into the monster you became. But I don't want to know those answers. And I don't want to ask you those questions.

I forgive you for what you've done to me and my family. I forgive you, but that doesn't mean I'm free from anger. It's something I know I need to pray about more, and it might be something that takes a lifetime to heal from. This is my journey. I'm far from whole, but I'm thankful that my family and I can finally live in peace.

And maybe the more I heal, the more forgiveness I can find in my heart toward you for all you did.

Kimmie glanced up at Taylor when she finished reading. What was supposed to happen now? What should they say?

He leaned down and kissed her on the forehead. "That was perfect. I'm so proud of you."

He took her hand in his and squeezed. "Before we go, I have a letter of my own."

CHAPTER 54

Kimmie was surprised when Taylor took a folded piece of paper out of his own pocket.

"What are you doing?" she asked.

"You'll see." His voice was loud, stronger than hers, when he started to read.

"*Dear Mrs. Jenkins, I'm Taylor, and I'm so sorry that we never had the privilege of meeting in this life. I have, however, had the privilege of dating your daughter now for almost nine months, and I'm sure you already know this, but she is a true delight. She's made my life so full, and I'm a better man for the time we've spent together. She's also told me what a great mother you were, and in a way, I feel like I already know you.*

"*That's why I hope that if you really were alive you'd give your blessing to what I'm about to ask. See, I want to make Kimmie my wife, but my mama raised me old-fashioned and told me I had to get the parents' permission before asking a girl to marry me. Since we all know that a solid marriage isn't based just on how poetically you can claim your love for someone, I'd like to tell you what my prospects are.*

"*I'm a trooper living in Glennallen, but that's caused a few problems for Kimmie and me. See, she's in Anchorage, where she's got a great job and where Pip is getting all these fabulous services, so I really can't find it in me to ask her to uproot herself from all that and come back here where she'll be met by so many painful memories. And I doubt your daughters would admit it, but I think Kimmie and Meg would miss each other if I tried to tear them apart.*

"*Which is why I ended up getting a new position lined up, and I'll be starting at the Anchorage police academy in six weeks. Assuming your daughter says yes, I'd like to make her my wife sometime this summer. I might not be able to afford a mansion on the hillside, but I'd like to see her settled into a nice house, her and Pip both, and I'd just like to mention that if the opportunity comes and it feels like the timing's right, I would consider it a blessing and an honor to officially adopt your son because I love that little boy, and I'm already so proud of the developments he's made.*

"*To be quite honest, Mrs. Jenkins, I've been meaning to find a way to ask your daughter to marry me for quite some time now, and being the big chicken I am, this is the best idea I could come up with. I promise that if she agrees to my proposal, I'll spend every day providing for her, protecting her, and giving Pip the happy childhood a boy like him deserves."*

Kimmie stared up when Taylor finished reading. Was he actually shaking?

He folded the paper up and tucked it back into his pocket. "Well?" he asked.

She stood up on her tiptoes and wrapped her arms around his neck. "Of course," she whispered and melted into his kiss.

Frost Heaves
a novel by Alana Terry

Note: The views of the characters in this novel do not necessarily reflect the views of the author, nor is their behavior necessarily condoned.

Frost heaves (noun): Upward swelling in soil or roads during freezing conditions, caused by water expanding as it turns to ice.

"So do not fear, for I am with you; do not be dismayed, for I am your God. I will strengthen you and help you; I will uphold you with my righteous right hand."
Isaiah 41:10

CHAPTER 1

Jade was being ridiculous. She had no reason to be this nervous. And for what? A testimony? She'd talked about her past plenty of times. Why should doing it on stage in front of her entire church be any different?

Staring at her reflection in the mirror, she wiped her sweaty palms on her pants. *Come on, girl. You've got this.*

The bathroom door swung open, and Jade jumped as her daughter burst through.

"Dezzirae Rose Jackson," Jade snapped, then paused to collect her breath. "You nearly gave me a heart attack."

"I'm sorry, Mama."

"Forget it." Jade let her daughter cling to her leg and adjusted a barrette holding one of Dez's corn rows. "What are you doing here scaring me half to death? Aren't you supposed to be downstairs playing?"

Dez shrugged. "Got bored."

As cute as Dez looked in her *God is my Superhero* T-shirt and sparkling light-up tennis shoes, Jade didn't have time for any extra drama tonight. She gave her daughter a well-rehearsed scowl. "You know you're not supposed to be bugging me right now. I've got to get ready for my talk. How many times do I have to tell you?"

Another shrug.

"Aren't there any other little kids down there?" Jade asked.

Her daughter rolled her eyes dramatically. "Just Mrs. Spencer's grandkids, and they're still babies."

"They're a year younger than you are," Jade huffed.

"Two years." Dez jutted out her lower lip and cocked her head to the side. "And besides, if I stay downstairs, Mrs. Spencer's gonna make me practice my angel lines for the Christmas play, and it's just too hard. Can't I stay up here with you? Mrs. Spencer said it's all right with her."

"Well, it's not all right with me."

"How come?"

"Because I've got to focus on what I'm going to say, and I can't worry about whether or not you're sitting there squirming in your seat." She kissed the top of her daughter's head then pushed her out the door. "Now get yourself back downstairs. And march."

Dez stomped out, staring at her feet. Soon, her light-up tennis shoes distracted her, and she bounced away.

"Oh, that girl," Jade groaned and checked to make sure the backs of her earrings hadn't fallen out. She'd checked them half a dozen times by now, but it was the only thing she could think of to do to get her nerves to settle down.

Lord, you've got to help me get through this.

Her hands were a clammy, sweaty mess, and she washed them again at the sink. After giving herself one more glance in the mirror to make sure everything was right where it was supposed to be, she walked out the door. She had to head downstairs to have a talk with Dez's Sunday school teacher. Mrs. Spencer had agreed to come tonight to watch the kids, and Jade felt it was only right that she give Mrs. Spencer fair warning. Dez had been a handful and a half all day. She was already five but had missed the cutoff for kindergarten by a week and a half. It wasn't even Christmas yet, and already Jade regretted not making a bigger push with the elementary school to accept Dez early. She was acting up nearly every day at the daycare where Jade worked and even gave one of the smaller boys a white-wash when she pushed him down in the snow. Jade had put up with enough of other people's drama in her own life. There was no way she was going to see her daughter turn into a bully.

She was halfway to the stairs when someone called her name.

Jade turned around. "Hey, girl." She might weigh twice as much as her petite friend, but she didn't worry about squeezing too tight as she wrapped Aisha up in a hug. "I'm heading on downstairs," Jade explained. "Got to talk to Dez's teacher."

"Hold on," Aisha said. "There's someone here to see you."

Jade followed her friend's darting eyes, which landed on a tall white man in a crisp navy blue trooper's uniform. Jade scowled. "Who's that?"

"New trooper," Aisha explained. "He just moved to Glennallen from the bush."

"Is he joining the church or what?" Jade didn't like the way he was staring at her.

The trooper took a few steps closer, and Aisha shuffled nervously. "Sorry, I should have told you sooner," she whispered, but Jade didn't have time to figure out what she was talking about.

The trooper descended on her, hand outstretched enthusiastically. "I'm Ben. You must be Jade."

She gave him a glower. "What makes you think that?"

He gave Aisha a nervous glance, and Jade frowned at him disapprovingly. There were a dozen things annoying about being the only black person in a town as small as Glennallen. Having strangers presume to know her identity was toward the top of the list.

"Aisha pointed you out," he answered.

Oh. That made more sense. Jade cleared her throat and took Ben's hand into her sweaty palm. "Okay. Well, then, what can I do for you, officer?"

"I know you're busy getting ready for tonight's service, but can I talk to you? Won't take more than a minute."

Jade made a point of turning to look at the bear-shaped clock hanging in the church foyer. "Good, because a minute's all I got."

"Is there some place where we could sit down?"

Jade shrugged. "It's a free country, right?" She decided Pastor Reggie wouldn't be needing his office tonight, seeing as how he was on vacation with his family in the Lower 48. She started to head that way then stopped when Aisha touched her arm.

"Sorry," she whispered again. "We started talking outside, and I mentioned that letter. I should have asked you first."

"Yeah, you should have." Jade brushed passed her friend, holding the door open for the trooper. Once they were situated in her pastor's office, she crossed her arms and stared at him. "Like I said earlier, I don't have a lot of time. What's this all about?"

CHAPTER 2

Ben seemed to take a lifetime to decide where and how to sit.

"Are you comfortable?" he asked once they were finally situated.

Jade didn't answer. As far as she saw it, she'd never be comfortable. Not held up by some white cop ten minutes before she was supposed to stand up and share her testimony in front of her whole church.

And for what? That letter was just some stupid ploy. It didn't mean anything. Jade had lived her life in fear. She was an expert on the subject and had eventually learned that fear can't kill you.

And that you don't go to the police when you've got a problem. It was bad enough the daycare where she worked invited the troopers in once a month to read stories to the kids. It was just as well the men who came couldn't read her mind, or they'd never come back.

Jade still had her arms crossed, but Ben didn't seem to know what to do with his. "I saw the announcement in the newspaper," he finally explained. "Thought I'd come hear you."

Is that all he had to say to her? She stared at Pastor Reggie's stack of *Alaska Fishing* magazines and waited.

He cleared his throat. "I'm new to the area and heard a lot of good things about the church."

"Mm-hmm. I'm sure you did."

Ben glanced at her questioningly. She held his gaze until he looked away.

Finally, she decided it was time to put this conversation out of its misery. "Listen, if Aisha told you about that letter, I want you to know it's all under control. It's totally fine."

"Your friend seemed pretty worried about it."

Jade shrugged. "She gets like that, but trust me. It's nothing. Is there anything else I can do for you?"

Ben leaned forward earnestly, his eyes nearly as large as Pastor Reggie's mounted moose head behind him. "I want you to know this is the kind of thing we take seriously down at the trooper station."

"I bet you do." Jade stood up. "Well, if there's nothing else, officer, I need to get ready."

Ben nodded. "Will you let me know if there's anything I can do to help?"

Help? There was a new one. As far as Jade could tell, policemen like him had *helped* her family far too much already.

She opened the door of the office, mumbling, "I'm sure I'll be all right," as she let herself out.

CHAPTER 3

Before Jade could head downstairs to check on her daughter, Aisha hurried toward her. "Listen, I'm sorry about that trooper. I didn't know he'd want to talk to you right away. I just kind of mentioned it in passing ..."

Jade rolled her eyes, figuring it must be their differences that kept her and Aisha close. Jade had given up any desire for romance or even casual dating, but Aisha would flirt with anybody under the age of fifty. Men in uniform were one of her special weak points. Jade was certain that Ben's trooper's badge was all Aisha had to see to start fawning all over him, and what better way to snag his attention than to blab about some threatening note Jade received in the mail?

"Don't worry about it," Jade mumbled. She couldn't afford to stand here all night and convince Aisha that everything was fine. She'd lost enough time already. Men and women were filing to their seats, smiling at Jade as they passed the family of carved bears welcoming congregants to the service.

On with the show.

She straightened her shirt, smoothed out her pants, and walked into the sanctuary with her head held high, resolving to forget about Aisha and that silly trooper. Jade would bet her paycheck from the daycare that Ben would ask Aisha out before Christmas rolled around. She could have him. Jade had a testimony to focus on.

She made her way to the front row and bowed her head, partly because she wanted to pray and partly so people wouldn't come up and try to strike up any conversations. She clasped her hands in her lap. Were they still shaking? What was it about tonight's testimony that had her so worked up? This was Glennallen. There was hardly anyone she hadn't met in this town, and most of them were already familiar with her story. If anything, tonight was her chance to tell her testimony in her own words so her neighbors wouldn't have to rely on second- and third-hand information.

Nothing like a small town in rural Alaska to get the gossip fires roaring like mad.

Jade shut her eyes. She had to focus her attention on what she was going to say. Had to make sure that her spirit was in the right place.

Help me, God, she prayed when a shrill, whiny voice interrupted.

"Mama!"

Jade snapped her eyes open. "What did I tell you about bugging me when I'm up here?" she hissed, hoping that since she was in the front row, the people behind couldn't detect the annoyance in her expression. If they knew how exasperated she got with her daughter, they might all think twice about inviting her to share tonight.

"I'm so bored down there," Dez groaned and plopped into a chair with a melodramatic sigh.

Jade pinched her arm. "You get yourself back downstairs, or I'm taking away those new light-up shoes, got it?"

Dez turned to her mom once more with wide, pleading eyes. "But I'm old enough to be up here, and I promise to be real quiet."

"Well, you and I both know it's impossible for you to be real quiet. Now get downstairs." The last thing Jade needed was for Dez to hear her testimony tonight and start asking a thousand questions about their past. Jade forced a stern expression as her daughter tilted her head to the side and stuck out her lower lip.

"None of that now." Jade cracked a smile and gave her daughter a playful swat on the arm. "Go get yourself downstairs or I'll tan your behind."

"No you won't." Dez was smiling now. "You're always saying that, but I don't even know what it means."

"If you don't know what it means, then you should be a lot more worried than you are."

Dez rolled her eyes again, but it was clear to see she was trying hard not to grin.

"Go downstairs, baby," Jade repeated.

"But Mrs. Spencer's gonna make me practice my angel lines."

"Then practice your angel lines, baby. I swear, I've never seen a child more stubborn than you." She let out her breath, softening her voice. As a new Mom, Jade had resolved to never resort to bribery, but that was before she had any idea what it was like to negotiate with a precocious preschooler. "Tell you what. If you're real good, I'll take you out for ice cream after the service."

"But it's too cold," Dez complained. "You can't eat ice cream in the middle of winter."

Jade found herself wondering for a moment if Dez really was her flesh-and-blood child. "Of course you can. Who's been raising you, my little Eskimo baby?" She tickled her daughter's ribs. Dez squealed and ran down the aisle. Jade just hoped she wouldn't trip anyone on her way out of the sanctuary.

With Pastor Reggie out of state, Jade wasn't sure who was going to start the service. These Tuesday night meetings had started out as just a prayer service, but then they added a worship band. Next, Pastor Reggie started to ask people to share their testimonies until finally it was like having a second church meeting in the middle of the week. Jade didn't mind. With the sun setting by 3:30 at the latest during this phase of the Alaskan winter, it wasn't as if there were a whole lot else that she and Dez could be doing. Still, with its being so close to Christmas, she would have thought more people would be out of town traveling, but the sanctuary was as full as it was on a typical Sunday.

Great. On top of the crowd, the couple who usually led worship was out with the flu, and Reggie and his family were out of town, so Jade's talk was going to be the focal point of the evening. It was hard to think that all these people had come just to hear her. Up until recently, Jade hadn't thought of her testimony as anything special, especially when you compared it to the stories of Christians who were saved out of lives of alcoholism or addiction or truly destructive behaviors. She didn't feel ready to talk in front of a group this large, and she certainly didn't feel like she'd had enough time to pray and prepare herself spiritually, but there wasn't anything she could do about it at this point.

One of the elders welcomed everyone to the meeting, offered a quick word of prayer, and then Jade was standing before a church full of people waiting to hear her story.

CHAPTER 4

For all of its rocky start, Jade's testimony picked up until she almost forgot that she was the one speaking. Explaining her history, it felt more like she was one of the dozens of church members sitting in the rows of chairs, listening to her talk about the way God had worked in her life.

She sensed the general interest in the room, and when she talked about the church she grew up in while she was still living in Palmer, Alaska, she saw her audience leaning in as if refusing to miss a single word. She painted them a picture with her words, a picture of the extreme control the leadership at Morning Glory International held over her family, over their congregation. At one point, her eyes landed on Ben, the trooper sitting in the back row, and she saw the same interest and curiosity in his expression as she felt from the rest of the church.

Her hands clammed up for an instant, making it hard to hold onto the microphone. She pried her eyes away from his and avoided looking at that section of the sanctuary for the rest of her speech.

"The funny thing about it," she explained, "is that we would have never used a word like *cult* to describe ourselves. Even though it sounds pretty obvious to other people that what we were involved with was definitely not a healthy Christian church, we didn't know that. We were all taught, not just the kids but our parents too, that it was a grave sin to disrespect our leaders or question their authority in any way. Since we all upheld and respected the Bible, we believed that it would be wrong to go against anything our pastor said. At least once a month the preacher would talk about how Miriam bad-mouthed Moses and was struck with leprosy. The moral was always that we should never question God's leaders. I asked my five-year-old about it a few weeks ago, and that particular part of Scripture hasn't even come up in her Sunday school lessons. She's never even heard of it, but it was more common at our church than Noah's ark or Easter Sunday or any of the other Bible stories.

"It wasn't just Sundays either. We had meetings just about every night of the week, and if you missed something, you needed to have a really good reason or the elders would start to question if you were backslidden. You couldn't miss a service if you were sick, either. You were supposed to come even if you were throwing up a lung and have the elders pray for you and anoint you with oil, right there in front of everybody. And if you didn't recover by the end of the service, that was another time where people would question if you were backslidden. My mom pushed vitamins on all of us like we'd die without them because she knew people would question her spiritual health if her family ever caught a cold."

Jade's hands were still sweaty, but that wasn't because she was staring at the trooper anymore. It was because she knew what part of the story was coming up. She swallowed once, trying to recapture the sense of calm she'd had just a moment earlier.

Unfortunately, she knew that this part of her testimony wouldn't be nearly so easy to get through.

"The biggest problem was that there was no accountability for the elders or the head pastor. If they did something wrong, nobody would dare call them out on it. There was abuse of all kinds. If it's a kind of abuse you can imagine, it was probably happening at Morning Glory, and most of the leaders knew about it. Some of them were honest and God-fearing, but some were the actual perpetrators. Due to this whole idea that you can't question what your leaders do, lots of people got hurt, including children."

She winced, hating to even say the words, hating to remember what she went through.

She was staring at her hands now, wondering if anyone else could see them tremble. She glanced up once and caught Aisha's eye, gleaning an extra dose of strength. If she told her story — even the humiliating and painful parts — maybe she'd help someone else in the future, someone going through the same thing.

"The pastor of Morning Glory took an interest in me, and I got pregnant when I was seventeen. I've since then learned that I wasn't the only underaged girl who found herself in that situation, but the others were encouraged to go have abortions. I refused. I knew what had happened to me was wrong, but the idea of an abortion terrified me. So I told my parents."

She swallowed down the lump in her throat. A few members of the congregation were looking at her with so much sympathy it was like they were trying to squeeze the tears straight out of her body. One woman toward the front was silently weeping.

Jade felt bad for making everyone else depressed. Weren't testimonies supposed to be uplifting? She forced a smile. "Thankfully, my parents believed me and took action. We left the church, which is a whole long and complicated story in and of itself." Jade took in a deep, choppy breath. She wanted to tell them everything. She'd never skipped over this part of her testimony before, but tonight she couldn't get the words out. Couldn't tell them what it really cost her family when they filed charges against the Morning Glory leadership.

She raised her head and glanced at the clock. Mercifully, her time was almost over.

"I won't get into all the details, but the short version is I ended up delivering my healthy daughter, Dezzirae, right before I started my senior year of high school. I later grew to realize that all believers have access to the same God. We don't need a pastor or an elder telling us when we have to go to church or how we should raise our kids or what we should do with our futures. We can all talk to God on our own. And that's not to discount how important it is to have a church family and to have mentors who can give you wisdom and support, even though I'll be the first to admit I still really struggle when it comes to issues of authority after everything we went through."

She glanced once at Ben, who was studying her attentively.

"I'm just really thankful that my parents had the courage to stand up to the leadership like they did because I have other friends whose parents were too afraid to do or say anything." Jade's mouth turned dry, and her words caught somewhere in the back of her throat. A picture of her dad, smiling and serene, flitted uninvited into her mind.

She blinked, forcing herself to stay composed. "I guess that's what I want to end with tonight. A reminder that we're all children of God, whether or not we're a pastor or an elder or have any kind of fancy title, and we all are given the Holy Spirit to lead us and guide us."

She gave the audience a brief nod and turned off the microphone. She wasn't sure if one of the elders was going to close the meeting right away or if they would take a little time for prayer requests before everyone left, but she didn't care.

Walking down the side aisle to keep from distracting anyone, Jade hurried out of the sanctuary. She turned on her car's autostart as she made her way downstairs. If she was lucky, she could grab Dez and have the car warmed up before the congregation was dismissed. The last thing she felt like doing was making chitchat with three dozen people who wanted to talk to her about her life's deepest pain.

Breathless and impatient, she swung open the door of the church nursery, hoping that Dez might have forgotten the promise of ice cream and instead would settle on some hot chocolate back home.

"How'd it go upstairs?" Mrs. Spencer asked, glancing up from the book she was reading to her twin grandchildren in the rocking chair.

"Fine. Thanks so much for being down here."

"My pleasure."

Jade glanced around the room. "Is Dez ready to go?"

Mrs. Spencer blinked at her. "I'm sorry?"

"I've got the car running," Jade explained as she picked up her daughter's jacket from the nursery coat rack. "Is Dez ready?"

"I thought she went upstairs with you. She told me she was going to ask if that was okay." Mrs. Spencer stood up, setting her girls down on the ground.

"No," Jade answered. "She came up to ask if she could stay, but I sent her back down here." She mentally rehearsed everybody she'd seen in that sanctuary. It was a larger crowd than she'd expected but certainly not big enough that she would have missed seeing her own child.

The dry lump returned to her throat, and her heart started pounding high in her chest.

Where was her daughter?

CHAPTER 5

Jade's voice was hoarse, not from giving her testimony but from shouting into every bathroom stall, storage closet, and hiding place in Glennallen Bible Church. Initially she ignored the terrified feeling in the base of her gut. Dez was just throwing a silent fit somewhere to protest being sent downstairs with old Mrs. Spencer and the "babies." Either that or she was playing an elaborate game of hide-and-seek.

It was what Jade had to believe, and instead of focusing on her fears, she rehearsed all the ways she'd lecture her daughter.

Jade had just finished checking the men's room when Aisha trudged up the stairs, shaking her head. "I checked the nursery rooms and the cleaning closet downstairs. Do you think she went out to the car?"

"I looked there already." Jade glanced around. She didn't want Aisha to see the fear in her eyes. There had to be somewhere they hadn't searched yet. A five-year-old didn't just disappear, especially not on one of the darkest nights of the year. It wasn't even Dez's bedtime, but the sky had been black as midnight for hours already.

Mrs. Spencer hurried toward them. "I just went over everything with Jerry, since he's the go-to guy on maintenance here," she said. "Neither of us could think of any other places in the church that haven't been checked."

Aisha stared at the exit. "People are starting to leave. If we're going to ask for help, we better do it before they're all gone."

At first, Jade had been content searching the church with Aisha and Mrs. Spencer, but if not even the maintenance man could find her daughter, it might be time to recruit more volunteers. She gave a resigned nod, and Aisha scurried to the doorway.

Mrs. Spencer reached out her hand and rubbed Jade's back. "Are you all right, dear?"

Jade nodded. Dez was bright, precocious, and far too intelligent for her own good, with enough common sense to stay indoors when it was negative twenty degrees and pitch-black outside. She also knew how to get on Jade's nerves. "I'm sure she's just hiding out or something." Even as she said the words, she sensed how uncertain they sounded. She tried to force more confidence into her voice. "She does stuff like this all the time."

"I'll go check downstairs again," Mrs. Spencer finally announced. Jade imagined the possible ways she'd punish her daughter once they finally found her. Did Dez have any idea how many people she had worried?

Aisha hurried up with Ben behind her. Of course, she would have turned first to Mr. Trooper. This time, however, Jade couldn't afford to be haughty.

"I hear your daughter's missing?"

Jade forced herself to meet his gaze. "Yeah, I'm sure it's nothing. She likes to be dramatic. But it's so cold outside ..." She let her voice trail off.

"How long has it been since anyone saw her?"

Jade wanted to laugh off his question, but she couldn't. "She came upstairs right before the service started. She wanted to sit with me, and I sent her back downstairs. So the nursery worker thought she was up here, and I assumed she was down there ..." Jade wanted to kick herself. What kind of a mother would take a full hour to realize her daughter was missing? If Dez was outside, she could already be suffering from hypothermia.

Aisha offered her a sympathetic side hug. Ben, however, was far more formal. "You've searched everywhere in the church? You're convinced she's not in here?"

Jade shrugged. "We had three of us looking, and then we got the maintenance man to help. So as far as I know we've checked everywhere."

Aisha kept her arm around Jade's waist, and Jade felt like her tiny friend was the one supporting her. They both looked to Ben, who pulled out a small radio.

"It's cold enough outside and dark enough that I don't want to mess around. I'm gonna call this in." He turned to Aisha. "Why don't you run outside and ask anyone who's able to stay to stick around. We're going to need all the manpower we can get."

Jade couldn't stand the thought of standing by like some helpless damsel. "I'll go with you."

Ben shook his head. "No, you stay. I need you here to pass information on to dispatch. Then you're going to tell me everything you know about that letter."

CHAPTER 6

Jade refused to answer Ben's questions until she could start actively helping with the search. Once she was bundled and outside, Ben began his interview.

"Your friend told me you received a threatening letter. Can you tell me exactly what it said?"

"Yes, I can." Jade hid her hands inside her coat sleeves since she didn't have any gloves. "It said, *Sorry about your dad. You better make sure your little girl's not next.*"

He watched her fidgeting with her sleeves and then handed her his own gloves. She was too tired and cold to refuse them.

"What did the reference to your dad mean? Did you understand that part?"

"Yes," she answered flatly and stared at Ben. He was the real reason why she hadn't shared that part of her testimony at church.

A trooper car pulled into the church parking lot, and Ben excused himself to fill his colleague in. Not a moment too soon. Jade caught Aisha standing under a street lamp and hurried toward her.

"What's going on?" Jade asked.

Aisha's teeth were chattering. "We've looked in all the cars, under all the cars, and around the church. I don't know what else to do but start searching along the road and behind the buildings."

"She wouldn't have come out here. Not without her coat." Jade shook her head. This search was a waste of time. Her daughter had probably found some hiding place in the church, maybe even fallen asleep, and she was going to be grounded until her eighteenth birthday if she didn't show herself soon.

Aisha frowned sympathetically. "Are you doing okay? Do you need anything?"

Jade shrugged. "I need to find out what that girl is doing. I swear, she can be so stubborn."

Ben raced back up. "We've got two men coming out now, and the search and rescue team is standing by in Fairbanks."

"Fairbanks?" Jade wished she could explain what she already knew. Dez wouldn't be out here in this cold.

Ben nodded. "It's a cold, long night. We've got to act fast."

"Well, thank you, Mr. Optimism," Jade muttered under her breath before turning away.

"Wait a minute." Ben reached out his arm, shying away just before touching her elbow. "I still need to know more about that note. You were saying something about your father."

Jade cast her glance over to Aisha, but her friend was already heading off to join the volunteers in the wooded area behind the church.

"What do we need to know about your father?" Ben asked. "What's this letter mean?"

Jade wanted to tell him to mind his own business, but everything regarding her dad was public record anyway. If she told Ben everything now, it'd free up his time to keep looking for her daughter. She took off, following Aisha toward the woods, and Ben hurried to keep up beside her.

"You were listening when I was talking tonight, I assume?" Jade asked, hoping she could save even more time by not having to repeat everything she'd gone through earlier.

"Yeah. I'm so sorry for what happened to you."

Jade didn't have time for sympathy right now. Not from a cop. "My parents went to the police. They pressed charges against the pastor of Morning Star."

"Good," Ben inserted forcefully.

His comment derailed her concentration, and it took a second to remember what she was saying. "Well, we did it all. Went to the police, talked with the lawyers. They looked for other witnesses to come forward, but everybody else refused to testify against him."

"They weren't brave enough?"

"No," Jade replied. "They weren't stupid enough. Pastor Mitch had connections all over the Mat-Su valley. The longer the pre-trial period spread out, the more we realized he was going to get away with it. If we got ourselves a miracle, he might get charged with statutory rape, but even that didn't seem too likely. With Pastor Mitch being on a first-name basis with nearly everyone in Palmer, my dad lost hope that he'd ever see the inside of a jail cell."

"That must have been disheartening."

Jade wondered if Ben had taken police training in the art of understatement.

"It was ridiculous," she spat. "And the whole time, we were getting death threats from the people we thought had been our friends, even from some of the parents of girls who went through the exact same thing I did. They treated us like we were turning our backs on God, like we'd lose our salvation if we testified against a monster like that."

Jade gritted her teeth. This wasn't the time to get weepy and weak. This was the time to be angry. Angry, determined, and focused.

"So what happened?" Ben asked the question so softly, Jade wondered if he already knew or maybe suspected the answer.

"My dad attacked him. Confronted him one night when he was coming home and assaulted him with a baseball bat."

She paused to see if Ben had any interjections, if he was going to lecture her about the need to let justice follow its own slow course of action. He remained silent, which wouldn't make telling him the rest of the story any easier.

She was trying to figure out how to continue when someone called out, "Hey, over here!"

Jade raced ahead, panting by the time she made her way through the snow to where the maintenance man was shining the flashlight of his cell phone. "Does this look familiar?" he asked.

Jade's heart was pounding as she stared at the red scarf in the snow. She studied it for a full second before answering, "That's not hers."

"You sure?" Jerry asked, as if Jade might not recognize her own daughter's scarf.

She nodded, too disappointed to think up any caustic remarks. "And look." She pointed at the lower fringes. "It's been out here a while." She tried to pick it up, but it was frozen to the snow. "See?"

Jerry nodded. "Yeah, I guess you're right. False alarm."

Jade stared around at the towering spruce trees. The snow lay in uneven heaps, without any trace of footsteps. They were wasting their time. "I don't think she's back here."

Jerry shined his flashlight around. "Yeah, I thought she might have left some tracks, but I don't see any."

Jade swallowed hard. "No. No tracks." She had to keep control over her emotions. She had to be strong. It was the only way she was going to find her daughter again.

Lord, show me where she is, she prayed and thought about that letter she'd gotten in last week's mail.

Sorry about your dad. You better make sure your little girl's not next. Would someone from Morning Glory come all the way out to Glennallen from Palmer to hurt her daughter? Was that the way the church was going to get back at Jade for speaking up against their pastor after all these years?

It was far-fetched. It was insane.

But right now, it sounded like the most plausible explanation.

CHAPTER 7

It was nearly eleven before Aisha and Ben forced Jade to warm up indoors. The church had been set up as the search and rescue crew headquarters and was teeming with volunteers and first responders. A helicopter with search lights was circling the area, and the pararescue team from Fairbanks was due to land any minute. Wilderness search and rescue dogs were on their way, and Aisha had already run to Jade's home to get a sample of Dez's dirty laundry so the canines could try to pick up her scent.

Jade couldn't believe any of this was happening.

"If your daughter wandered off, we're going to find her." Ben pulled a pen out from his breast pocket. "But until then, we need to examine every possible option. I want you to think of anyone who may have wanted to hurt you or your daughter. We need to make a list of possible suspects."

Jade's hands were so cold even after wearing Ben's gloves she could hardly hold onto her mug of coffee. She blinked at him.

Aisha gave Jade what must have been her fiftieth hug of the night and stood up. "I'm going to see if I can call in a few more volunteers. Be back soon." Jade watched her friend depart, feeling a wistful longing for something she was too tired and confused to name.

"Suspects," Ben repeated. "Who might have sent you that letter, for one thing?"

That one wasn't hard to answer. "Anybody back at Morning Glory."

"No good. It's too broad."

"Well, what do you want?" Who did this cop think he was, making Jade feel like a criminal being brought in for questioning?

"I need names. Specific names. And details. Where they live. Who had the most motive to hurt you or your family."

"I don't know." Jade didn't try to hide her exasperation. She focused on a small speck of dirt beneath her fingernail, begging herself to stay composed. Once she got her daughter back safely, she'd allow her tears to fall. Until then, she had to seize control of her emotions.

Ben sighed and softened his expression. "Look, I know how hard this is for you."

Jade didn't believe him, but she had no energy left to argue.

"Let's back up a little bit, okay? Can I assume the note you received was from someone at your old church?"

She sniffed and nodded. "Yes." Who else had that much reason to hate her as well as her father enough to send a letter like that?

Ben nodded. "I'd have to agree."

She tried not to let him see her roll her eyes. Did he think that listening to her testimony once and spending some time together outside in the cold made him an expert on her and her family situation all of a sudden?

"Do you think it could be the pastor retaliating?"

Jade scoffed. "I seriously doubt that."

"We can't take anything for granted," Ben reminded her, as if she wasn't already keenly aware of the gravity of her situation. He frowned. "I hate to be indelicate here, but putting together what you said in church this evening, would I be right to assume that this pastor, this ..."

"Pastor Mitch." Jade supplied the word for him.

"Pastor Mitch," Ben repeated. "Am I right to assume that he is your daughter's biological father?"

Jade kept her eyes on his shoulder. "That's correct." Next thing he'd do was find two dolls and tell her to show him how it happened.

Ben sighed. "Well, if you ask me, that makes him a pretty significant suspect right there. Your father attacked him, you exposed him for what he was, and your daughter is his biological offspring."

Jade stared at him. Had he come up with that all by himself?

He looked at her, waiting.

"Problem with that line of reasoning is that he's dead." Jade's voice was flat.

"He is?"

"Yeah. As of last fall." Jade had read the obituary herself, two paragraphs posted online. *Pastor Mitch Cobb, beloved church leader, husband, and friend is now rejoicing eternally in the kingdom of heaven ...*

The irony wasn't lost on Jade to see the pastor who'd preached nothing but faith healings succumb to cancer. She stood up.

"I'm going to see if Aisha needs help making those phone calls." She took a step away, but Ben grabbed her by the hand.

She yanked herself free instinctively and hissed, "Don't touch me."

"I'm sorry. I know this is difficult for you."

"Actually, officer, I don't think you do." She refused to meet his eyes, knowing that if he was staring at her with even a fraction of the compassion she could detect in his voice, she'd break down and never make it through this night.

"I really want to ask you a few more questions. Do you need a break first?"

The last thing she wanted to do was to sit here with her daughter missing and talk with this trooper, but she was too tired to argue. She shook her head. "No, I'm okay."

"You're sure?"

"Yeah." The sooner they got this meeting over with, the sooner she could go back and join the citizens of Glennallen who right now were braving the ever-dropping temperatures to look for her daughter. It was only a few questions. What was she so afraid of?

She took in a deep, choppy breath and gave him a nod. "I'm ready. Let's do this."

CHAPTER 8

Once she started, it was easy for Jade to come up with name after name of members of Morning Glory International who might want to hurt her family. There was Elder Keith, formerly one of her dad's best friends and the one who'd been the most vocal about trying to cover up the abuse. He even offered to pay the family five thousand dollars if Jade told everyone that the child she carried belonged to some boyfriend from school.

After the allegations were exposed to the public, various individuals delighted in telling Jade and her family how sinful they were to bring such outlandish charges against their pastor. Even though a DNA test could easily reveal the child's parentage, most members of the church preferred to think that Jade and her family made the entire thing up. Halfway into her pregnancy, the pastor's wife, Lady Sapphire, forced Jade into a bathroom stall and yanked up her blouse because the baby bump looked like nothing more than a little extra weight on an already heavyset teenager. It wasn't until Lady Sapphire felt Pastor Mitch's child kicking in Jade's womb that she even recognized the pregnancy was anything more than a lie and a ruse meant to tear down Morning Glory International and its ministry across the Mat-Su valley.

Ben's suspect list had grown to ten different names by the time Aisha sat down beside them. "We've got a few more volunteers on their way to relieve the ones who've been out the longest."

Jade couldn't believe she was hearing this. Couldn't believe there was actually a search team at this moment scouring the woods surrounding the church to look for her five-year-old daughter. As hard as it was to picture Dez wandering off into the cold without a coat or flashlight, the idea of an abduction was even more unfathomable.

If Dez had been taken, whoever had her was twisted. Demented. Who would want to harm a child? The thought made Jade even more terrified. Would the night ever end?

"I need more coffee," she told Aisha, who looked about as tired as Jade felt. But she wasn't going to sleep until her daughter was found. She finally understood what was going through her dad's mind when he found out what Pastor Mitch had done to her. Why he'd grabbed that baseball bat and waited to ambush his prey. It made sense now, that rage. That protective instinct. No parent could sit back and watch someone destroy their child's life, not without taking matters into their own hands.

Jade thought back to the vows people made back in the time of the Old Testament. *May the Lord deal with me, be it ever so severely* ... Right now, there didn't seem to exist human language that could describe what Jade would do to anyone who even threatened Dez's safety.

May God have mercy on their soul, she thought. But even God's mercy was too good for anyone who hurt her daughter.

CHAPTER 9

When midnight came, the temperature had dropped to thirty-two below, and there were now both helicopters and rescue dogs involved in the search. Nobody said so, but Jade knew everyone was thinking the same thing.

A five-year-old in this cold could never survive until morning. A soft blanket of snow fell, diffusing the search lights so it looked like Jade was looking at the world through an eerie haze.

Where was Dez?

Aisha was still outside, but most of the original volunteers had gone home, replaced by others ready to search through the night if necessary. Jade watched the snow falling with a forlorn resignation, knowing that in another hour or less, any tracks that might have led the rescue teams to her daughter would vanish forever. Then again, maybe the snow was actually a blessing. Maybe it would provide Dez with a blanket to keep her warm through the night.

No, she wouldn't think like that. Dez wasn't out in this cruel winter climate. And she hadn't been kidnapped or harmed by anyone from Morning Glory, either. She was still inside the church, warm and safe and sleeping peacefully. Jade would be so relieved to find her daughter perfectly unharmed that she wouldn't even dole out all the punishments she'd been daydreaming about earlier.

Was it really possible that this was the same night she'd stood in front of her church and shared her testimony? Just a few hours ago, being abused, pregnant, and shunned by everybody but her parents was the most traumatic experience Jade could imagine, the most challenging trial she'd ever have to endure.

Until now.

Dez was born out of despair, hurt, and humiliation, but Jade had loved her from the beginning. Throughout the pregnancy, even with those chaotic hormones and that relentless confusion, Jade had been protective of her baby. Her love for her child was no small miracle considering Jade had never been overly fond of children. She wasn't like other girls who dreamed of nothing but marriage and motherhood. Jade had goals too, but hers involved feats like winning the Nobel Peace Prize, working relentlessly to help the nation achieve racial equality, and earning her law degree before her twenty-fifth birthday.

At first, she convinced herself that her teenage pregnancy did nothing but put those plans on hold. The older Dez got, the more Jade had come to accept that her prior ambitions would have to go unrealized. As a single mother working for minimum wage at a daycare, Jade was lucky if she managed to pay her heating bill every winter. How was she supposed to put aside money for education, let alone find the time to take any classes?

Some days, Jade was depressed at the way life had derailed all her prior dreams, but now she hated herself for ever wanting anything more than to have her daughter by her side, safe and sound.

She longed for a kind word from her mother, a friendly hug from her father, but they were both gone. Her father met his end shortly after attacking Pastor Mitch with that baseball bat, and Mom's high blood pressure and failing heart couldn't hold up to the stress the family endured in the aftermath of the assault.

It wasn't fair. Because of Pastor Mitch, Jade had lost both of her parents.

"Here you are. I thought maybe you'd gone back inside the church to warm up."

Jade turned to see Mrs. Spencer, Dez's Sunday school teacher, and said, "I thought you went home hours ago."

"I did but just long enough to drop the twins off with their mom and grab warmer clothes." She looked down at her snow boots. "I'm so sorry about what happened. I was sure she was upstairs with you."

Jade didn't want to be angry with Mrs. Spencer. She wanted to accept her apology. But how different would this evening have looked if the old woman had just followed Dez upstairs instead of sending a five-year-old up to the sanctuary by herself? In a town as small and safe as Glennallen, with a church where everybody knew everybody else, Dez should have been fine. But the night was so dark, and the temperatures were still dropping.

Jade ignored Mrs. Spencer's apology, prayed that God would forgive her for her bitterness, and continued tramping through the snow in search of her daughter.

CHAPTER 10

"Ben's at the church looking for you. He said he found a warmer coat and some snow boots you can borrow."

Jade could barely process Aisha's words. "What time is it?" she asked.

"Almost two. I know you don't want to stop, but you need to come in and at least warm up."

Jade surprised herself by not protesting when her friend put her arm around her and started leading her in the direction of the church. Her legs ached, and everything below her knees was numb from cold and wet from the deep heaves of snow.

Aisha didn't try to talk while they walked, and Jade was grateful. She was too tired and emotionally drained to carry on any sort of conversation. It was good of Aisha to still be here. Most of the other volunteers had returned to their heated homes, leaving the search to the rescue dogs and professionals. If Dez had wandered outside, she would have been found by now, or at least someone would have stumbled over her tracks.

Which only left one conclusion.

The air inside the church was so hot compared to outside that Jade could hardly breathe. She had to find some way to escape from the feeling of intense heaviness that threatened to crush her under its impossible weight. She turned to head back out.

Ben hurried toward her. "Wait a minute. You need to warm up."

Jade braced herself against the sternness in his voice. "I need to find my daughter." The urge was primal, unshakeable. She couldn't reason it away or depend on common sense at the moment. She had to get Dez back, and she wasn't going to rest until her daughter was safe.

"We've checked on a few of the leads," Ben told her, holding up his list of suspects. "Don't worry, we'll find her."

Jade knew he was in no position to make any promises, but she clung to his words nonetheless.

He pointed toward the stairs. "One of the ladies from church brought you heavier clothes. And they've got basins of hot water in the kitchen for warming up your feet. Why don't you head down there now, and I'll be with you in a few minutes. I have some more questions for you about your old church."

Jade tried to read between the lines. If Ben was focusing all his attention on Morning Glory, did that mean he was convinced this was a case of kidnapping or intentional foul play?

It was a possibility Jade wasn't willing to accept. Not yet. Dez was a tiny little wisp, feisty as anything, but small enough she could roll herself into the size of a beach ball. Couple that with her stubbornness and her ability to fall asleep anywhere, and she might be perfectly safe in a cupboard or a drawer in this nice, heated church, somewhere nobody'd thought to look yet.

"Where are you going?" Ben called as Jade headed to the Sunday school rooms.

"I want to check everything one more time," she answered, thankful he didn't protest.

Dez was here. Jade knew it. Because if her daughter was outside in the cold or if she'd been abducted and was in danger, Jade would know. Her heart would cleave in two, making it impossible to think, to speak, to function. The fact that Jade was still standing on her own two legs was all the proof she needed that her daughter was alive and safe.

All she had to do now was find her.

CHAPTER 11

"I thought you were going to change into dry clothes," Ben said when he found Jade rummaging through the Christmas pageant costumes in the storage closet downstairs.

"I will. Soon." In a pile of shepherds' garb, Jade spotted a splash of color that might have been one of her daughter's barrettes. Tossing costumes haphazardly aside, she reached down to find it was only a fake jewel from a wiseman's crown.

Ben's voice was both firm and gentle. "You need to change your clothes and get warmed up. Then we can look around the church more."

"She is really good at hide-and-seek." Jade spoke the words as if she were trying to convince Ben of what they both knew was a lie. She couldn't stop herself. "At the daycare, she's always going around hiding in cabinets and drawers. Once she even crawled into the toy chest and fell asleep beneath all the dress-up clothes. She's here. I know that she's got to be here."

Ben touched her gently on the shoulder. "I've already searched this whole closet myself. Twice."

Something about Ben's touch shook her to her core. Or maybe it was the way her feet had finally started to thaw and were now screaming with pain. Her whole body began to tremble.

"She's got to be here," she repeated, her voice weak and almost as shaky as her core.

Ben rubbed her gently on the shoulder, and she turned to him as tears streamed hot down her face. "Do you promise that you're going to do everything you can to get my daughter back to me?" The inherent confession in her question, the admission that she knew her daughter was in danger, brought on another round of trembling and a sob that nearly worked its way out of her clenched throat.

Ben reached out and touched her chin, tilting her face up until she was staring straight at him. Wiping a tear away gently with his calloused thumb, he nodded. "I promise. Now let's go get you warmed up."

CHAPTER 12

While her feet soaked in a pan full of hot water, Jade sipped at some tea. Her legs ached as they continued to thaw. She would have preferred to be out in the cold, at least able to convince herself she was doing something useful.

Aisha sat with her and prayed, and Mrs. Spencer joined in for a little while too. Jade was thankful for their concern but couldn't help wondering if all that time and energy they put into their prayers would be better spent hunting for her daughter.

"Brought you something to eat." Ben stepped up and handed her a ham and cheese sandwich on a paper plate. Jade hated sandwiches and had since elementary school. Besides, how could she eat now when she didn't know if her daughter was kidnapped or lost in the woods or maybe already dead?

"You should have it," Aisha urged, and Jade nibbled at the whole grain crust with disinterest. Aisha stood up to get more tea.

"I've been going over the notes from the pre-trial," Ben said, crushing any hope Jade had that she might be able to stomach her food. He sat down across from her with a frown. "I read about your father."

Jade shrugged. She should have figured he'd find out the truth sooner or later.

Ben sighed. "I know it doesn't change what happened, but for what it's worth, I'm sorry."

She glared at him. "Why? It wasn't your fault." What right did he think he had, probing into her past and making her relive that awful pre-trial period? Did he seriously think that now was an appropriate time to bring it up?

Ben shuffled some pages he was carrying. "Well, we've managed to narrow down the suspect list."

She wished she could turn her ears off. She wasn't ready to face the reality that this missing child case was morphing into an abduction investigation. It was too much for her to handle. She buried her head in her hands.

"I'm so sorry you're going through this." He sounded sincere, but how could he understand even a fraction of what she was experiencing?

She met his gaze. "Do you have children, officer?"

He shook his head.

"I didn't think so," Jade mumbled. And yet here he was pretending to be sympathetic. What would he know about parenthood or the terror that comes from realizing you failed to protect your own child?

She didn't need more tea. She didn't need a stupid sandwich. She needed her daughter. How many times had she lost her temper or gotten angry at Dez, who was every bit as sassy as Jade had been at that age? She'd take it all back now if she could, the drawn-out lectures, the angry shouts, that infamous Mom stare she'd perfected when Dez was still in her terrible twos.

"It must be hard working with the police after what happened to your dad." Ben's voice was soft, so quiet Jade wondered if she should simply pretend not to have heard.

He didn't know anything. He couldn't.

Jade hated him. She hated his condescending pity, his flashy blue uniform and everything it represented in her past. She hated the fact that she was sitting here like a helpless victim instead of marching outside and leading the investigation to find her daughter.

Aisha returned, passing Jade a new cup of tea and taking her empty mug from her. "Maybe you should get some rest." Aisha had been Jade's best friends for years, but tonight was a clear and obvious reminder of their differences. If Aisha were a mother herself, she'd understand how insulting the suggestion was. Sleep? How could she expect Jade to sleep on a night like this?

"I think that's a good idea," Ben replied, as if his opinion settled the matter. "I can drop you off at your place if you want."

Jade crossed her arms. "I'm not going anywhere."

"I promise I'll call you with any updates."

She shook her head. "I'm staying here."

"Maybe you could rest on one of the couches," Aisha suggested softly. Jade rolled her eyes. Maybe Aisha was the kind of girl who could fall asleep on a whim, even with the investigation of her daughter's kidnapping ongoing in the next room, but Jade wasn't.

"I'm fine. I just need to get more coffee." She stood up.

"Are you sure?" Aisha asked with a pained expression on her face.

"Positive," Jade grumbled. She brushed past her friend and stormed over to the coffee pot, unable at the moment to look at her compassionate eyes without breaking.

She'd need all the energy she could get to make it through the night.

CHAPTER 13

"Jade? Excuse me. Are you awake?"

She jumped at the sound of the familiar voice, banging her head on some kind of shelf. "What in the ..."

"Shh." His tone was calming. Soothing. "It's all right. It's me, Ben. I just had a few questions for you."

She blinked. Why wasn't she in bed? How could she have fallen asleep?

"You're in the church closet." Ben reached down and picked up a wise man costume Jade had been holding.

Her brain wrenched in protest as every single horrible replay of last night crashed around her memory banks. "Did you find my daughter?" She stood again, this time knocking over a box of flannelgraph Bible characters before stepping out of the closet.

Glancing down the church hallway, she studied those around her, trying to figure out if Ben woke her up with good news or bad. Nearly all the faces were unfamiliar: police officers from Anchorage, troopers from the surrounding areas, search and rescue teams deployed from God alone knew where. They all looked tired and worried, not a good sign, but at least they looked busy, which meant the investigation was still ongoing.

Which meant there was still hope. Right?

She braced herself for whatever news Ben had for her.

"Do you need more coffee?" he asked. "A sandwich?"

She shook her head. Why couldn't he just get straight to the point?

"Let's take a seat."

As they passed through the church kitchen, she glanced at the time. Just after five in the morning, with at least another five hours to go before the sun even thought of rising. How much snow had fallen last night? How long could a child as small as Dez survive this long outside?

Jade clenched her fists and jutted up her chin. Whatever news Ben brought her, she was ready. Anything was better than this uncertainty, this waiting.

"What can you tell me about Keith Richardson?" he asked.

"Elder Keith?" It had been years since she stepped foot in Morning

Glory's ornate church building, but the title came to her out of habit.

Ben nodded.

"He was one of my dad's best friends." Jade wondered what kind of information Ben was looking for. What did he want her to say?

"He's the leader of Morning Glory now." From Ben's tone, Jade couldn't tell if he was asking her a question or stating a fact.

"Yeah, he took over after Pastor Mitch died."

"The church website still calls him Elder Keith, not pastor."

Jade shrugged. It was no surprise. The church would remain loyal to Pastor Mitch no matter how horrific his crimes had been in life.

"Was Keith Richardson upset when your family went to the police about your pastor?"

She nodded. At first, she was thankful to Ben for his discretion. Thankful he didn't use words like *rape* or *abuse*, labels that had been thrust on Jade's shoulders since she was a teenager. But the more she thought of it, the more his question smacked of condescension. Did he think she couldn't handle hearing the truth spoken out loud? Did he think she was that fragile? She sat, waiting for what he would say next.

"Have you been in contact with Keith Richardson since you left Morning Glory?" The question was direct. Abrupt. As if for a moment he'd forgotten that Jade was the victim's mother and not a suspect herself.

"We stopped having anything to do with him," she answered. "He was one of the most vocal opponents of us going to the police. He even offered to pay my family money to keep it quiet."

"But you haven't had any contact with him recently?" Ben was staring at her with an intensity that made her heart race. What was he suggesting?

She shook her head. "No. Why?"

Ben pulled out her cell phone. It was the first time Jade had realized it wasn't in her pocket like normal. "Where'd you get that?"

He didn't answer her question but just said, "Keith Richardson left you five different text messages in the past half hour."

Jade yanked the phone out of his hands. "What did he say?" Elder Keith had been like an uncle to her when she was younger. His daughter Trish had been her best friend, and they'd promised to go to college together and be roommates and study pre-law together. Jade knew for a fact

Trish had been one of the girls Pastor Mitch abused, but even if Elder Keith was aware of the crime, he was too loyal to Morning Glory to ever try to put a stop to it.

And now he was messaging her after Dez disappeared?

She scrolled through the texts, trying to will her hand steady.

It's Elder Keith. Are you there?

We need to talk. Can I call?

I know it's early, but this is important.

Are you getting any of my messages?

Jade's stomach flopped, and she physically recoiled from her phone when she read his last message.

I know what happened to your daughter.

CHAPTER 14

Aisha and Mrs. Spencer had both gone home, so it was Ben who was left to do what he could to soothe Jade's nerves.

"It's going to be all right," he assured her. "We've got someone in Palmer on their way to speak with Richardson right now. They're going to contact us as soon as they find anything out."

Ben sat patting her hand. It was a silly, fruitless gesture, but she couldn't find the words to ask him to stop.

"I'm so sorry you're going through this."

She'd lost track of how many times he'd said this or something similar. If he was so sorry, why wasn't he doing more to get her daughter back? She gritted her teeth, hating how out of control she felt.

"I went through something a little similar. I know it's not the same thing as missing a child." Whatever Ben was going to say next, Jade was certain it wouldn't be helpful, but he went on, and she stared at the wall blankly, too numb to speak.

"My dad was a cop down in LA during the race riots. He wasn't on duty that night, but he got called in anyway. My mom had taken me and my sister to my grandma's house in Redondo Beach to get away from the heat, and she kept us up late to pray for dad's safety. He didn't come home that morning, and by the next night we still hadn't heard anything. It wasn't until the following day his partner found out where my mom was to tell her that my dad had been killed."

Jade didn't speak.

"I know it's different when it's your parent and not your child, but I remember that day of waiting, how hard it was. If you were to look at my mom, you might have thought she aged a decade in twenty-four hours. I'm sorry for what you're going through."

Jade tried to swallow, but the lump in her throat made it impossible.

"I guess that's something we do have in common though," Ben said quietly. "Both of us losing our dads."

She didn't want to agree. Didn't want to acknowledge that what this trooper went through was anything like what she'd endured the night her dad died. Her father had known the police were coming for him. He had no regrets about what he did to Pastor Mitch. When it seemed clear that his daughter's abuser would go free, he'd taken justice into his own hands, and he was prepared for his arrest. He was ready. He'd even called some of his family members, people outside Morning Glory who were still speaking to him, and made some arrangements to make it easier for Jade and her mom while he was in jail.

What he wasn't prepared for was six white men barging into his home in the middle of dinner and making the entire family lie face down on the floor. Jade was eight months pregnant at the time, and when one of the officers shoved her roughly, her dad intervened.

The cop shot.

Her father was dead before he even hit the ground.

And now Jade was sitting here across from this white trooper whose white father had also been a cop. A white cop. The kind Jade had learned to fear. Had learned to hate.

And yet he'd been a victim of senseless violence as well. A victim of the racist disease that had plagued their country for centuries.

She felt sorry for Ben and what he and his family must have gone through. But she still wasn't sure she wanted his sympathy. Still wasn't sure he'd earned the right to presume that he could understand her situation.

She hung her head, listening to the drone of the church fridge and the muttered voices of those around her, trying to imagine what it would be like to live in a world where fathers always came home when they promised they would, where police — *all* police — could be trusted to protect the vulnerable.

Where five-year-old girls didn't disappear without a trace, leaving nothing behind but nameless fears and unbearable uncertainty.

CHAPTER 15

If Ben wanted help writing Keith Richardson's life story, he should have asked someone who'd actually managed to sleep last night. Jade filled in the details she could remember, but half an hour later, the sketch was still far from complete. She didn't even remember what Elder Keith had done for a living.

After Ben checked to make sure her phone was still set to record incoming and outgoing calls, Jade tried calling the number Elder Keith used to text her, but it went immediately to a generic message stating that his voice mailbox was full. She texted him back. Once. Twice. What did he know about Dez?

Then came more of Ben's questions. "Was Keith Richardson ever violent?"

Jade shook her head. "No. He was Pastor Mitch's right-hand guy, a yes man. He never wanted to rock the boat or do anything besides what Pastor Mitch specifically told him." Jade hated the way that even after she'd freed herself from Morning Glory's authoritative presence in her life she still referred to its leaders by their titles. It was as if she were still a little twelve-year-old girl being told that to disrespect her pastor, even in the privacy of her own thoughts, would be as sinful as spitting in the face of Jesus himself.

"You said Keith was angry with your dad about exposing the abuse."

Jade nodded. "Yeah. They got into quite a few fights. Just yelling though."

"Never violent?" Ben pressed.

"No. Not that I ever saw." In truth, it was her father who had the temper, her father who would raise his voice. Her father who had attacked Pastor Mitch with a baseball bat. Who had died trying to protect his daughter from being manhandled by a white cop.

What did Ben think? Did he side with the Palmer police captain? Just two days after her father's murder prompted an internal investigation, the cop who shot him was reinstated. As far as Jade knew, he was still serving on the police force. The policeman went on record claiming he'd been afraid for his life, and nobody thought to second-guess him. Nobody questioned why six armed men were entitled to use deadly force on a father trying to shield his child. The unspoken consensus was that her father deserved to die, shot point-blank in front of his wife and the pregnant daughter he was trying to defend.

"What can you tell me about Elder Keith's family?" Ben asked.

Jade was grateful for the chance to distract herself from memories of her father's murder. "He had a daughter in the same grade as me and a son who was already grown and out of the house."

"What about his wife?"

Jade shrugged. "She was the church receptionist. Pretty quiet and mousey." Just like all the women at Morning Glory were taught to be. "Mrs. Richardson was good friends with Pastor Mitch's wife. In fact, I think they were related, cousins or something like that." Jade hardly ever thought about her pastor's wife, but now a picture of Lady Sapphire popped into her head uninvited, the cold hardness in her eyes, the feel of her sharp fingernails pinching her skin. The sound of her hiss as she accosted Jade in the bathroom and whispered, "If you bring charges against my husband, I fear for your soul in the afterlife."

Jade could still remember the hint of wintergreen on Lady Sapphire's breath before she plastered on her fake smile and stepped out the bathroom like a queen presiding over her subjects. Which, in terms of the Morning Glory hierarchy, was exactly what she was. Pastor Mitch was the ruling dictator, and Lady Sapphire was his beloved confidante, the hauntingly beautiful reigning figurehead, whose words of exhortation were elevated to as high a level as her husband's.

Lady Sapphire was known for her vivid dreams, which all members of Morning Glory were taught to uphold as infallible as the Scriptures themselves. The story of Lady Sapphire's dream the night before she married Pastor Mitch took on the role of both legend and prophesy, the promise of a child who could carry on Pastor Mitch's apostolic ministry in the state of Alaska. Years later the medical community pronounced Lady Sapphire infertile, but she persisted in believing in that miracle offspring, the fulfillment of God's promise given decades earlier.

But Ben wasn't asking Jade about the pastor's wife. He was asking about

Elder Keith, and Jade took pains to answer each question methodically even though her brain was screaming from exhaustion. Elder Keith was, for the moment, the force's primary person of interest. Jade didn't understand why he would have bothered texting her if he was the guilty one, but Ben explained that the best possible outcome would be if Elder Keith claimed responsibility and made a demand for ransom.

If Elder Keith wanted money in exchange for Dez's return, he had incentive to keep her safe.

The teams were continuing to search outside, waiting for daybreak when a new round of local volunteers could be called in. Jade was grateful the troopers and police and everyone else involved in the search and rescue were being so thorough, but the more she thought about her past at Morning Glory, the more she had to admit that Dez's disappearance was almost certainly an abduction.

It made sense. The warning letter, the texts from Elder Keith.

Jade wondered when she'd hear back from the police sent to question him in Palmer.

She didn't think she had the energy to withstand even another five minutes of this torturous waiting.

CHAPTER 16

A little later in the morning, Mrs. Spencer showed up with four cartons of eggs and other supplies donated from Puck's Grocery store. Aisha came in just a few minutes later. While Mrs. Spencer set about making breakfast for the rescue workers, Aisha took Jade into Pastor Reggie's office to pray.

Over half a decade after leaving Pastor Mitch's church, it was still difficult for Jade to remember that she didn't need a pastor's permission or an elder's blessing to lift her requests up to God. She'd been trained so thoroughly by the Morning Glory leadership to rely on church hierarchy to grab heaven's attention that it took her years to learn to pray on her own. Even now, with the stress and anxiety so heavy on her, she found it nearly impossible. Having Aisha with her helped a little. Aisha was a newer Christian, having come from a Muslim background before she got saved and moved to Glennallen, but Aisha seemed to excel at the gift of prayer. As she raised her requests to God, Jade felt a fraction of the weight she'd been carrying lift from her shoulders. As soon as they said *amen*, the burden returned, but at least the short reprieve convinced her that God was listening.

He had to be. There was no one else now to watch out for her daughter. No one else to guarantee her protection. What was Dez thinking right at this moment? What fears or tortures was she enduring? It was too horrific to fathom. Jade had done everything in her power to shield Dez from the details of her past. Whenever her daughter asked who her daddy was, Jade told her that God was her Father and for now that's all she needed to know. The thought that the same people who had witnessed Jade's most humiliating abuse had now kidnapped her daughter was inconceivable.

Ben was still holding onto hope that Elder Keith was trying to contact her with a ransom demand, but Jade knew Morning Glory better than that. The church and its leadership had all the money they wanted thanks to a guilt-inducing tithing system. To remain in good standing, church members had to pledge up to thirty percent of their annual income and even provide tax statements to verify their faithfulness. It was more likely Dez's kidnapping was about power, the real currency Morning Glory's leaders cared about.

To continue to wield their power, Morning Glory enacted policies that could have been taken straight out of a dictator's rulebook. If a church member questioned the pastor, if they fell short in their financial giving, if rumors circulated regarding some petty offense, they were paraded in front of the congregation for public shaming. Once a young nurse was excommunicated simply because Lady Sapphire had a dream accusing her of a spirit of lust. When anybody was forced out of the congregation like this, their history was completely purged from the church records. Even their tithe statements — public record from Morning Glory's earliest days — were altered, their contributions listed anonymously. Jade was sure her own family had been erased as well, probably even more zealously given the way they had exposed Morning Glory's ugliest secrets to the world.

How many times had she been told to respect her leaders, not to question their authority? What she and her family had done was unforgivable. She wasn't sure what kind of changes had taken place after Pastor Mitch's recent death from cancer, but if things were anything like what they were before, it wasn't difficult to imagine the church finding a way to get back at her.

But why now? If Morning Glory was so angry with Jade and her family, if they were bent on retribution, why did they wait five years after Jade's pregnancy to act? What had changed? Was it because Jade had shared her testimony in public? Last night's audience couldn't have been larger than forty. Besides, her testimony was far more about God's grace delivering her from a life of church dictatorship and legalism than it was about besmearing Morning Glory's reputation.

It didn't make sense.

And how was Elder Keith involved? Even though he hadn't wanted Jade's family to get the police involved, he'd always been soft-spoken, docile, and in most cases completely unintimidating. Had his rise to leadership after Pastor Mitch's death corrupted him?

Jade hated to confront these questions alone. She longed for a word of wisdom or encouragement from her parents more than ever. It wasn't fair that God took both of them away. They never saw their granddaughter crawl or walk or eat solid foods or babble her first words. Why had God added sorrow upon sorrow in Jade's life like that?

In the book of John, Jesus promised his disciples not to leave them as orphans, but that's exactly what happened to Jade. She was an orphan, a single mom doing her best to provide for her daughter, working a menial job because it was the only thing she could find that would allow her to stay (mostly) on top of the bills and keep her daughter nearby. She'd tried so hard, working herself ragged, agonizing over every one of Dez's cuts and scrapes and ear infections and cold viruses. How many times had she begged God to give her strength to handle life as a single mother?

And now Dez was gone. Had God forsaken her? Was such a thing possible?

She thought of Jesus' words on the cross. If the Son of God could feel abandoned by his heavenly Father, why couldn't she? All Bible promises aside, Jade had never felt more betrayed. Here she was doing everything she could think of to live a godly Christian life. She brought her daughter to Sunday school, to Glennallen Bible's midweek services. They read stories from Scripture together each night before bed. Each night, that is, until last.

And if Jade felt so abandoned, how must Dez feel right this instant?

Mrs. Spencer handed Jade a paper plate with scrambled eggs, bacon, and toast. Jade had no appetite but picked at the food methodically, hoping it would get her mind off her troubles.

By the time she finished breakfast, she was still just as tormented as she'd been before, but now she had a stomachache on top of all her other worries.

CHAPTER 17

"I want to thank everyone for your continued support in this search and rescue," Ben told those gathered in the church kitchen. The smell of bacon grease made Jade queasy while people around her ate their hearty breakfasts.

The sun still hadn't come up yet, and when it did, they'd have less than five hours of functional daylight to keep searching for Dez outside. Jade wondered how long it would take until the teams gave up. How long was a child that little expected to survive in this cold? At least this morning the sky was overcast, giving Glennallen a cloud covering that warded off the most bitter of the cold. Temperatures hovered around zero, a vast improvement from yesterday.

"Even though we're continuing to follow up on leads in Palmer, we're going to keep on focusing locally," Ben stated. "We know Dezzirae is out there somewhere, and we're all committed to doing whatever it takes to see her safely reunited with her mother."

Jade tried to ignore the glances that passed her way and focused on Ben, wondering if he'd slept at all last night.

"We've got a lot of people this morning," he continued, "both local volunteers and workers from across the state. I'm not here to turn this into a big religious event, but for anyone who feels so inclined, I'd like to offer a prayer for Dezzirae's safe return. If you don't care to join us, there's no pressure or expectations. You can head on upstairs, and we'll meet you there in just a few minutes."

Nobody moved. A moment later, Ben was lifting up his voice to heaven. Aisha and Mrs. Spencer sat on either side of Jade, offering gentle back rubs and hand squeezes that only accentuated how numb she felt. If Ben wanted to pray and others felt like joining him, she wasn't going to argue. But as the morning hours passed without a single word from her daughter, Jade found herself trusting less and less in the power of prayer. If God wanted to bring her daughter home, wouldn't he have done so by now?

Would Dez even be the same child once they were together again? What if she'd been abused? Jade's first encounter with Pastor Mitch wasn't until she was fourteen. How could a child as little as Dez endure anything even remotely similar?

Mrs. Spencer squeezed her hand. Aisha cried softly, blowing her nose quietly every few minutes. All Jade could think about was that — Christian or not — she'd never forgive God if he let something so terrible happen to her daughter.

CHAPTER 18

Jade's phone rang as soon as Ben finished praying. She started, aware of dozens of eyes on her while she fidgeted clumsily to pull it out of her pocket. The number was blocked.

"Hello?"

Ben hurried beside her. His colleagues crowded around her until she wanted to scream. She wiped one sweaty palm on the leg of her pants and switched the phone to her other hand.

"Jade?"

She knew that voice. "Yeah. Elder Keith? Is that you?" She leaned forward in her seat like that could help her concentrate better on his words. As if she could give him any more of her focus and attention.

"I need to talk to you. I'm on my way to Glennallen now."

Out of the corner of her eye, she saw Ben signal to another one of the troopers. She wished they'd all give her some space. "Where is Dez?" she demanded. "What did you to do her?"

"I can't talk. They might have followed me."

"Who's following you?" It took all her self-control not to scream into the mouthpiece. "Where is my little girl?"

"I'm on the Glenn now. I've just passed Eureka. I can't talk. Reception's terrible."

A wave of static confirmed his words. Jade wasn't willing to lose him. "Keith, wait. Pull over and just talk to me. Tell me what's happened to Dez."

She could only hear every few words. The ones she caught were *Glennallen ... more ... soon.* Just when she thought the phone was about to disconnect, she heard Elder Keith utter a cry followed by the sound of clanging metal.

"Keith!" she shouted again, staring at the men around her. What was going on?

"Keith?" She gripped her cell, her voice pleading. "Keith, are you there?" The call disconnected. She turned to Ben. "What was that? What happened?"

"It sounded like a crash."

"What do you mean a crash? Is he all right?" All the blood drained from her face. "What if he had Dez with him?" The eggs and bacon she ate for breakfast sloshed around angrily in her stomach.

Ben's face was somber. "You know about as much as we do right now. Give me a few minutes to figure out our next step."

"What do you mean figure out your next step? He said he was just passing Eureka. We need to drive out there and find him."

"Just give us a minute." Ben retreated with some of the other officers, leaving Jade with Aisha and Mrs. Spencer and their smothering attempts at comfort. Jade didn't need soothing words or well-meant hand squeezes. She needed answers.

"You know God works everything out for good." As soon as the words left Mrs. Spencer's mouth, Jade wanted to throw up. She couldn't take it anymore. How could you say that to a mother whose daughter was missing? What if Dez had been in the back of Keith's car when he got into a wreck? There were no hospitals between here and Eureka. Aside from the small Glennallen clinic, the nearest hospital set up to handle emergencies was back in Palmer. She couldn't waste the day waiting, trying to guess what might have happened.

She stormed over to Ben. "I'm coming with you."

He looked surprised. "What's that?"

"You're going to Eureka to see if you can find Keith, right? And I'm coming with you."

He took her gently by the elbow and led her away from his little huddle of officers. "I don't think that's a good idea. We have no idea what to expect when we get there."

"This is my daughter." She clenched her fists. "You heard that phone call. You heard how it ended. Something happened on the road, and I'm not going to sit on my bum waiting to hear from you."

"Fine." Ben mumbled something to one of the other troopers before facing Jade once more. "You can ride with me. Come on. We're on our way now."

CHAPTER 19

"You really think it's a good idea to go with him?" Aisha asked as Jade pulled on her coat.

"I don't care if it's a good idea or not. I'm going to find my daughter." The sun was just starting to rise. The volunteer teams would continue their hunt for Dez here, but Jade was convinced they wouldn't find her. There wasn't any reason for Jade to stay in Glennallen. Elder Keith, if not the actual perpetrator, was involved in Dez's disappearance. She had to get to him. Had to find out what he knew.

Aisha reached out to give her a hug. "I'll be praying for you."

"Thanks." Jade ran her hand over the top of her hair, wishing she had her kerchief to cover up the mess. She hadn't looked in a mirror all morning, which was probably a good thing.

"You ready?" Ben asked, tucking his radio into his pocket.

She nodded, grateful that he'd agreed to take her with him. She still needed time to absorb the details he'd shared earlier about his father's death, but she knew she trusted him. He might be the only man in a uniform she did trust at the moment, but it was nice to feel like she had an ally.

"My car's right out here."

She followed him silently, trying to remember exactly how many miles it was to Eureka, whether that was before or after the part of the Glenn Highway with that steep drop-off. Last summer, one of the other daycare workers was run off the road and had suffered quite a few injuries. It would be even worse in the winter, where the dangerous temperatures and short daylight hours made rescue attempts all the more difficult.

Ben opened the passenger door for her, a strange gesture Jade hadn't been expecting. "Thank you," she mumbled.

"Mind if I put on some music?" Ben asked when he was seated beside her.

Jade could only guess what kind of music a white Alaskan state trooper would listen to and hoped it wasn't country. He pulled up a playlist on his phone, a contemporary gospel soundtrack. Jade had no complaints.

Soon they were on the road, following a caravan of officers.

"So you're new to Glennallen?" she asked after the first song ended.

Ben nodded. "I spent a few years as a public safety officer in Kobuk, then I was ready for a change from bush life and ended up here."

Jade figured the polite thing, the expected thing, would be to ask for more details. *What made you decide to go into law enforcement? What was it like working in the bush?* But she remained silent and stared at the spruce trees, spindly, sickly looking things that stretched out for miles on either side of the highway.

"What about you?" Ben finally asked. "How long have you been in Glennallen?"

"Four years now," Jade answered, and since it would be another hour or longer to Eureka, she told him more. About the heart attack that killed her mom shortly after her dad's murder. About needing to get away from Palmer, away from the memories.

"It sounds bizarre," she admitted, "but every Sunday after Dad died, I'd lay awake and wonder if I should go to Morning Glory. They were the only church I knew. We were family."

She glanced at Ben, wondering if he'd tell her how stupid she sounded. Who would ever be tempted to go back to a congregation like that?

"I can understand. In a way." His voice was slow. Thoughtful. "After my dad died, my mom started dating this real idiot. Lazy alcoholic, real piece of trash."

Jade tried to keep a neutral expression.

"He was abusive almost from the beginning. Not toward me or my sister," Ben added, "but he threatened my mom nearly every day. He'd push her around, but she always made it out like it wasn't that bad. Like since he never used his fists, it was totally justified. I hated that man, couldn't stand the sight of him, and I didn't get why my mom just wouldn't leave him. Well, she tried. Once. She found out he was cheating on her, and we moved out, but two weeks later he was knocking at our apartment door telling us how sorry he was and begging for a second chance. She gave it to him. And a third chance. Then a fourth.

"My sister Beth was out of the home by then, and I moved in with her my senior year of high school. Just couldn't stand seeing Mom put up with that jerk. For a while I thought if I stuck around, I could keep an eye on her. Protect her. Maybe try to talk her into leaving. Then I finally came to realize she was never going to walk out. He told her so many times she was fat or she was ugly or she was stupid, and he was always railing on and on about how lucky she was to have him because no other man in his right mind would ever love her, and I think after listening to those lies long enough she started to believe them."

Jade had never compared her relationship with Morning Glory to one with an abusive partner, but the metaphor fit.

"Interestingly," Ben went on, "my sister's also the victim of spiritual abuse." He used the term so freely that Jade didn't want to admit she'd never heard the phrase before.

Another perfect fit.

"She went to UCLA for their elementary ed program, and she got tied up in this Christian campus group. I went with her a couple times. Really dynamic group. Amazing worship music. I can see why she was drawn in. But the teaching got really skewed. First it was all about how God wants all his children to be rich and prosperous, and I know there are lots of churches who emphasize that, but these were nearly all college students living in studio apartments eating Ramen every night, and they were being fed these lies by this super sleazy pastor who drove a brand-new Jaguar and gave himself a full spa treatment every week. So he's making my sister and her friends feel guilty because they're not *praying in the blessings* like he put it. But then it got even worse.

"He got so focused on material riches that he told everyone they had to stop shopping at thrift stores. That God said he wanted them all to be *the head and not the tail*, so they couldn't wear secondhand clothes. I mean, who's ever heard a sermon about where college students can buy their hoodies from, right?

"The worst part was they had this whole discipleship program, which sounds all impressive, but it went way overboard. Everybody in the church was supposed to have a discipler. It's basically a mentor, which is a decent idea except these kids like my sister were relying on their mentors for things like telling them what major to declare or what internships to apply for. And it wasn't asking them for advice either. You needed your discipler's permission to do just about anything. And you don't even want to get me started on the whole dating part of it. First of all, if you were interested in someone, you had to confess that to your discipler right away. And it had to be someone from that same campus group or it was just a temptation straight from the devil to distract you. And then your discipler would pray, and if they thought God was telling them to, they'd approach that other person's discipler and basically make it into this whole matchmaking ordeal. Talk about creepy.

"I went to a meeting once with my sister where a college sophomore went up on stage and confessed that she and another boy from that same church group had gone on a date without getting their disciplers' blessing, and even though they got along really well, she knew God was telling her to call it off because she'd been unsubmissive."

Jade didn't reply. It sounded so similar to the schemes at Morning Glory, but she had a hard time picturing the same degree of control being exerted in other congregations as well.

"The really sad part," Ben went on, "was that this group had a lot of great things going for it. The preacher was really gifted in evangelism. He started the group my sister's freshman year, and by the end of that first semester, something like fifty or sixty students had gotten saved. Even for a big school like UCLA, that's amazing. It could have been great, but somewhere in there the gospel got confused with this bizarre discipleship mentality. It was a real shame."

"How did your sister get out of it?" Jade asked.

"Beth? She didn't. She's still living in LA, still going to that same church. They've expanded from just college ministry now, although that's still one of their primary focuses. They've got this huge lot set up in Hollywood, big gaudy church right in the middle of the projects down there, and they're still doing their thing."

"Is she happy?" Jade hoped her voice didn't sound too wistful.

"Happy?" Ben shrugged. "I assume so, although if she wasn't, I'm not sure how she'd manage to tell me. But she's doing well. She gave up on education and is now some executive type for this talent agency. She's making bank, just like her pastor told her she should be. She had a discipler at UCLA, and one morning this woman called her up and said she had a dream that Beth married this dude from their church, so now they're together and expecting their second kid. All that from one dream."

Jade hadn't prepared to spend the entire drive talking, but she found herself telling Ben about Lady Sapphire. "It was the same thing with our pastor's wife. If she had a dream, no matter what it was or how weird it sounded, people believed it."

"Sounds a lot like what my sister went through. What kind of dreams did this Lady ... what was her name again?"

"Lady Sapphire."

"Yeah. What kind of dreams did she have?"

Jade stretched back her memory. "All kinds. Once she had a dream that this girl who was a few years older than me was trying to seduce one of the elders. She made her come up to the front of the church and confess her sin, and then they all anointed her and laid hands on her to cast out the spirit of lust. Another time there was this guy at our church who was bidding on a construction job, and she told him she had a dream where a demon was sitting on the site of the new project, so he withdrew his bid, and then it came out that the business went bankrupt and they wouldn't have been able to pay him. So sometimes it actually seemed like it came true."

"Did she ever say anything or have a dream that turned out to be false?"

Jade told him about Lady Sapphire's dream of a child to carry on her husband's ministry. "Even into her forties, she had the elders anointing her and praying over her all the time so she could have this child. I don't know what she's said about it now that Pastor Mitch is dead."

Jade stopped as a sickening, sloshing feeling returned to her stomach.

Ben glanced over at her. "Something wrong?"

She couldn't respond.

"Did I upset you bringing up all the stuff about your church?"

"What? No, it's not that. I was just thinking." She let her voice trail off.

"What is it?" he asked. "Is it about your daughter?"

Her body shuddered as she let out a sigh. "I was just thinking. Lady Sapphire thought God promised Pastor Mitch a child to carry on the Morning Glory ministry, but he never managed to get her pregnant. What if she's decided Dez is the answer to that dream of hers? What if she thinks Dez is destined to fulfill that prophecy?"

Jade watched Ben's throat constrict as he considered her words, but he didn't have time to answer before a voice came over his radio. Jade heard the words, but the static and the pounding of her pulse in her ears made everything difficult to understand.

"What was that?" she asked when Ben put the radio down. "Is it Elder Keith?"

This time, it was Ben's turn to sigh loudly. "Yeah, they found his car down the side of the bluff. Major wreck."

Jade held her breath. "Was Dez in there with him?"

"No, and it's a good thing too. The car's completely destroyed. Nobody could have survived."

"Does that mean ..." Jade had a hard time finishing her thought.

Ben nodded. "Yeah. Keith Richardson is dead."

CHAPTER 20

They arrived at the site of the crash about fifteen minutes later. Jade could see the tire tracks in the snow where the car ran off the road, but the crash site itself was too far down. "You wait here," Ben told her. "I'm going to meet the team to see what they've found in the car."

"What are you looking for?"

"Anything that could give us a clue why he was on the road to meet you or what he knew about your daughter's disappearance. May as well tell you now that they've suspended the search back in Glennallen. The message just came through. This has turned into an official abduction case."

Jade blinked, hardly registering his words. All she knew was that Keith Richardson had answers, but now he was dead.

What had God been thinking?

"Are the roads really icy?" she asked. "Was it an accident?"

Ben sighed. "Your guess is as good as mine right now. That's another reason I want to get down. Just wait up here." He pulled the keys out of his pocket. "You can run the car if you get cold. I'll come up as soon as I know anything. Do you have phone reception here?"

She checked her cell. "No."

"Okay, I didn't think so. I'll come back to fill you in as soon as I can, all right?"

Jade nodded. She felt like she owed Ben a thank you or an apology or something. She was just too confused to figure out why.

Sitting in the passenger seat of his car, she thought through everything she knew. Elder Keith wanted to get in touch with her. He was trying to tell her something about the case. If he'd kidnapped Dez for revenge or ransom, wouldn't he have said so? Dez wasn't in the car with him, thank God, but he was speeding to Glennallen to tell Jade something. What?

And was he going so fast that he lost control on the wintery roads and crashed down the ravine? It was possible. Jade always hated driving this stretch of the Glenn Highway, with its steep embankment and sharp turns and no guardrail in sight.

But what if someone else — someone who didn't want Keith to tell

Jade what he knew — was responsible? What if they'd messed with his car or drove him off the road or ...

But who would do that? And if Keith hadn't kidnapped her daughter, who had?

Faces and nameless images clashed around chaotically in her mind, and she realized she was hungry. Apparently even a breakfast as hearty as Mrs. Spencer's didn't do a whole lot after a night spent tramping around outside in the snow looking for her missing five-year-old.

Jade squeezed her eyes shut, visualizing for a moment a nice peaceful morning at home with her daughter. No sore feet, no aching back. Just her and Dez eating breakfast, watching a few silly animal videos on YouTube ...

The passenger door flew open. She turned her head in time to see a figure dressed in black, pointing a gun at her through the window.

She didn't have time to scream.

Searing pain splintered through her skull.

Then there was nothing.

CHAPTER 21

"Come on, Jade. I know you're in there somewhere. Wake up." The sweet, melodic voice pulled Jade out of her pain-free slumber. The flickering lamp in the corner seemed as bright as Alaska's midnight sun on the summer solstice. Her head throbbed, and her eyes hurt.

She felt dizzy and almost threw up when she turned toward the figure beside her.

"Good."

Jade could hear the smile in the woman's voice even through the ski mask she wore.

"Do you know who I am?"

Did she? Did she know anything? Jade tried to remember where she was or what she was doing lying on the wooden floor in a strange room.

The woman raised her long, elegant fingers and removed the mask. "Now do you recognize me?"

Jade knew that her body was supposed to respond, that she was supposed to feel afraid.

"I hope Gabriel wasn't too rough with you. Was he?" A second figure, also in black, emerged from the shadowy corners, standing guard behind Lady Sapphire.

Her smile was like a snake's. "So sorry about your head. But I assure you that you'll be fine."

Jade reached up to rub her skull, but Sapphire grabbed her by the wrist. "Not right now, darling. You're lucky Gabriel didn't crack your skull open. He's stronger than he looks, my dear, which is saying quite a bit, isn't it?"

She let out a mirthless chuckle.

"Now, tell me, are you going to be a good girl, or are we going to have to deal with you just like we did with Elder Keith?"

Jade blinked, begging her mental processes to speed up. This wasn't the time to feel groggy or light-headed. She had to figure out where she was, and then she needed to escape.

"If you're looking for Gabriel's gun, I assure you we have no more intentions of shooting you now than we did back in that trooper's car. Let's

331

cooperate, shall we? For old time's sake."

Jade squeezed her eyes shut as if she could will away the pain on the top of her head.

Sapphire ran the back of her fingernails up and down Jade's arm as if she were trying to tickle her. Jade tensed her entire body.

"No need for that." Sapphire clucked her tongue disapprovingly. "The way I see it, you owe me an apology. After all those lies you spread about my husband, did you think I was just going to forget all about you?"

Jade forced herself to sit up, surprised when neither Sapphire nor her henchman made a move to stop her.

Instead, Sapphire smiled. "That's good. I knew you'd be feeling better soon. Once that goose egg dies down, you'll be as good as new."

"Where's Dez?"

"The child?" Sapphire widened her eyes in mock surprise. "Didn't I already tell you? She's in the next room."

Jade made a move to stand, but she was far too slow. Before she even got to a crouch, Gabriel had his arms wrapped around her waist and Sapphire held her finger to her lips. "Shh. The little one's sleeping. She had quite the eventful night, I can assure you."

Jade flung herself from once side to the other, but she couldn't break free. "Dez!" she tried to scream before Gabriel smothered her face with his beefy palm.

"We can't have any of that now," Sapphire scolded. "Didn't I just tell you she needed her sleep?"

"What did you do to her?" Jade kept her voice low to avoid getting suffocated again by Gabriel's massive hand.

"Told her the truth." Sapphire's smile widened. "All of it. Imagine how surprised I was to discover the child didn't even know who her father is."

"God's her father."

Sapphire nodded patiently as if Jade were the same age as Dez. "That's what she said. But don't worry. She was quite happy to learn that she had a real daddy who loved her very much."

"You won't lay a hand on her."

Sapphire shrugged. "Think what you will. It means nothing to me one way or the other."

"What do you want?" Whatever game this was, Jade was sick of it. If Sapphire was telling the truth, if Dez really was sleeping in the next room, Jade just had to bide her time and wait for the chance to make her escape. Gabriel had a gun, which meant that if he wanted her or her daughter dead, they would be by now. Jade simply had to wait. Try to win as much of their trust as she could, wait for them to grow complacent, and then she'd rescue Dez.

It took all her mental stamina to keep from calling out for her daughter, but if Dez really was asleep, it was a mercy that she didn't have to deal with this living nightmare. A nightmare that Jade would bring to an end, just as soon as she got her chance. She was bigger than Sapphire and outweighed her by at least sixty pounds. It was Gabriel she had to watch. Gabriel who had to be convinced she wasn't a threat.

No threat at all.

She glanced at him, trying to figure out where he kept that gun.

Sapphire was standing now, walking around Jade in a wide circle. She glanced at the small window, trying to guess how much longer until the sun went back down. How long had she been unconscious?

The view was blocked by spruce trees. How far into the wilderness had Sapphire taken her?

At least her daughter was nearby. Even though Jade had no proof, she chose to believe that it was true.

The hope of seeing Dez again, the promise of a safe reunion, was all she had to give her strength.

CHAPTER 22

"What's in the bottle?" Jade demanded, eying Sapphire suspiciously.

"Just some anointing oil," she answered. "It'll make your head feel better."

Jade gritted her teeth. "Don't come near me with that."

Sapphire's serpentine smile faded. "Have it your way." She looked over her shoulder and shrugged at Gabriel, handing him the vial then letting out a sigh. "Now, let's have a little chat about what's going to happen next."

Jade was resting on the hard floor with her back against the wall. Sapphire paced while she spoke, but Gabriel kept himself positioned beside Jade the entire time, stationed between her and a door. Was that Dez's room? Jade strained her ears. Could she hear her daughter on the other side? The slightest hint that Dez was nearby would be enough to give Jade the superhuman strength she'd need to take on both her assailants. She was sure of it. She just had to find the right time.

"I'm very sorry for what you went through as a teenager." Sapphire's apology came as a surprise, but she went on without letting Jade speak. "I always knew you had the spirit of seduction, and I'm sorry I didn't bring it before the church when I first suspected it. We would have prayed for you and anointed you and healed you from your sickness. But I had a certain fondness for you, and I'm afraid I let my personal affection for you cloud my discernment. I didn't want to embarrass you, and so I kept my observations to myself. For that I'm truly sorry, and I beg you to forgive me."

Her voice sounded sincere, but there was a haughtiness in her eyes when they met Jade's.

"My husband was a godly, righteous man, the most devout and anointed believer in Alaska, I'm convinced."

Jade wondered if they were talking about the same individual, but again Sapphire didn't give her time to speak.

"His biggest weakness was that he was so compassionate. It's what made him such a Spirit-filled preacher. He had the gift of empathy. He could look at a person and instantly understand what spiritual struggles they were going through. He told me everything about the day you came to him for counseling. Yes, I know all about it, about how that child of yours was conceived. He wanted to help you. He really did. I hadn't warned him about the spirit of seduction I sensed in you. Like I said, I didn't want to expose you to any embarrassment. As a result, my husband fell into temptation."

Jade didn't know what to say. Should she bring up the fact that Mitch's abuse persisted for years before her pregnancy? Should she mention the Bible verses Mitch used to coerce her into compliance, to scare her into silence?

The smile vanished from Sapphire's face, and she stared at Jade with a mix of both pity and contempt. "I want you to know that I forgive you. I know it wasn't you but the spirit of seduction living in you. My husband was a prime target for spiritual attack given his success in the ministry, so it's no wonder the devil decided to oppress him in this way. At first, I was heartbroken. Devastated that my husband would fall like this. But then one night, God gave me a dream. He showed me a picture of my husband, bent over and weighed down by his guilt and shame. He was chained to prison bars, him and many others, and then just like Paul and Silas in that dungeon, my husband began to sing. His praise released not only his own chains, but those of all the people around him as well. That's when I knew God was going to exalt my husband to an even higher place of leadership and authority, that he would use my husband's weakness to bring even more children into the kingdom. His prophesies always come true."

Something changed in Sapphire's countenance. "And speaking of prophesies," she went on, staring at Jade with the intensity and beady eyes of a cat, "let's talk for a minute about your daughter."

Jade glanced over at Gabriel, trying to figure out how many seconds she'd have to wrap both hands around Sapphire's pale throat before he intervened.

"You remember, I'm sure, that God gave me a dream in which he promised my husband a child to carry on the ministry at Morning Glory."

Jade didn't trust herself to respond. It was taking all her energy and focus to keep from killing Sapphire where she stood.

"For decades, I believed the prophesy meant that God would open my womb and give me a child, but I've since learned that his ways are so much higher than our ways, his wisdom so much greater than our own. God never promised that I would be the one to fulfill this promise, but that doesn't mean the prophesy itself could fail. God's calling and plans are irrevocable, and he promised Mitch a child. Your daughter."

Jade couldn't listen to this crazy woman anymore. She wouldn't. She pictured herself jumping up, charging Sapphire and barging into the closed room to grab Dez, but she remained immobile. What kind of strange mysticism was this? What was this woman doing to her?

Sapphire continued to pace, and Jade was acutely aware of the vibrations she sent through the floor with each step, as if the weight and force of Sapphire's stride had increased tenfold.

"I had a dream a few weeks ago," she began, and Jade clenched her hands into fists. It was the only control she had over her body at the moment.

"In my dream, Mitch had just returned home after a long trip serving God overseas. On his back was an empty sack symbolizing the burdens God had taken off his shoulders during his season of international ministry. His hair had turned white, but his eyes were younger and more joyful than I've ever seen, and as he came toward me, he knelt down on the ground and stretched out his hands, and then this beautiful brown baby girl ran toward him shouting, 'Daddy! Daddy! You're home!' and he hugged her and promised he was never going to leave her again.

"I woke up, and I could still feel the love and the joy that surrounded my spirit in that reunion, and I knew what the Lord was telling me. I wasn't the one he chose to bear Mitch a child to complete his life's work and calling, but I could see the prophesy fulfilled nonetheless. It was a glorious picture. The next night, I had the same dream, except after that little brown girl ran into Mitch's arms, she turned to me and smiled and said, 'I love you, Mommy.' And that's when I knew what God was calling me to do."

Jade felt heavy. Heavy and tired and subdued, as if each word she heard was a chain tying her down. She needed to think, needed all her mental acuity, but she found herself inexplicably drawn to the rhythmic cadence of Sapphire's words.

"I'm sure you're worried about your daughter. That's why I've included you in my plan. That and the fact that Elder Keith wasn't strong enough to do what had to be done. He was with us at first but then changed his mind. He'll receive his reward, I'm sure. Now the biggest question is up to you. Will you be reunited to our fold? Will you come back under the congregational headship God has called you to? Think of what a glorious testimony that would be when you and your daughter come to live with me under one roof, held fast together by the cords of Christian love. I've talked to your daughter, and I sense a great destiny's been placed over her. What do you say?"

Sapphire stopped her pacing, releasing Jade from her state of transfixed confusion. She leveled her gaze. "I say you're a monster and a freak. You deserve to rot in jail just like your husband should have."

Sapphire frowned, lifted her hands toward heaven, and started mumbling under her breath.

"And stop praying for me," Jade snapped. "I don't want to hear any more about your dreams or your deluded fantasies. I don't want you anywhere near me or my child."

Sapphire's incoherent mutterings grew louder and more intense. The mental fog returned, but Jade strove to break free from its hold.

"You're not a real church," she shouted. "Your husband was a disgusting fraud, and the only power either of you ever had was only because people were terrified of both of you. You pretend to know God's will for others' lives, but you're so crazy you actually think you can get away with kidnapping and murder."

Sapphire chuckled. "Murder? I'm sorry, aren't you the one whose father tried to kill my husband?"

"He didn't want to kill him," Jade replied, even though she wasn't sure if that was the case.

Sapphire raised an eyebrow. "No? Your father was afflicted with the most oppressive spirit of anger and violence I've ever witnessed. That's why I wasn't surprised to hear what that policeman had to do to him."

Jade jumped to her feet. Sapphire wanted to talk about a spirit of anger and violence? Jade could show her a spirit of anger and violence. She threw her weight into Sapphire, knocking her to the ground as easily as she could have blown out a candle. Straddling her, Jade tried to shrug Gabriel off long enough to land at least one good punch.

Sapphire screamed. "Get behind me, demon."

Jade managed to pry one arm away from Gabriel's grasp and elbowed Sapphire in the gut before slamming her fist into that perfectly upturned nose that always made her pastor's wife appear both haughty and regal.

She couldn't get in any more shots before Gabriel overpowered her, grappling until he had both her arms pinned behind her. She threw her head back but only hit his chest and may as well have been a newborn cub wrestling a lion.

"I wash my hands of you." Sapphire stood clumsily and smoothed down her clothes. "I gave you a chance at restitution." She spat down at Jade on the floor. "And you were a fool to disregard my gracious offer. I wipe the dust off my feet. Everything that happens from here on is your own fault. Your blood is on your own head now."

CHAPTER 23

Jade struggled helplessly in Gabriel's arms while Sapphire took a key from her pocket and opened the door on the far side of the cabin.

"Mama?"

The tiny voice made Jade's pulse surge, and she strained against her confines. Unfortunately, Gabriel didn't seem to be exerting any extra effort keeping her immobilized.

"Dez!" Jade shouted. "Dez! Mama's here!"

Breath and warmth and relief coursed through Jade's entire body when her daughter ran toward her, throwing her arms around her neck. Laughing, Dez ignored the man who kept Jade's arms pinned behind her back.

"Mama, Auntie Sapphire says she knows where my daddy is and that I really do have a daddy besides God."

"Sweetie, we'll talk about it all later." Jade nestled her head against her daughter's cheeks, soaking in her presence, praising the Lord for allowing her to be with her daughter again. "What have you been doing, honey? Did you get hurt?"

Dez shook her head. "No, I'm okay. Auntie Sapphire told me you were coming, but I didn't think it'd take so long. Why did it take so long, Mama?"

"Mama had a few things to take care of first." She tried hard not to choke on her words. Her heart swelled with love for her daughter, with gratitude for her safety and a simultaneous primal instinct to do everything in her power to keep her safe.

Even kill.

Gabriel was so close behind her she could feel the gun in his pocket. If she could only find the right opportunity ...

But that was all secondary. Dez was safe. Keeping her that way was the only thing mattered. She breathed out a silent prayer of thanks, drinking in the sight of her precious child.

Dez put her hands on her hips and jutted out her lip. "Hey, what happened to the top of your head? It's all bumpy."

"Mama got a little owie. It's all right."

"Let me give it a kiss." Dez leaned in and got close enough to Jade's ear to whisper, "I know she's not my real auntie."

Jade's whole body swelled with relief. Of course Dez was smart enough not to be fooled, but she was putting on the perfect act. Jade didn't trust herself to reply to her daughter's words and hoped Gabriel hadn't heard.

"Well, have you been good for Auntie Sapphire?" Jade figured that if her daughter could put on a show, so could she.

Dez's eyes widened in apparent understanding. "Oh, yeah. I had a bit of a hard time falling asleep last night, but then Auntie Sapphire gave me a little pill, and I'm just now waking up."

Jade held back the choke that threatened to well up in her throat. "Well, I'm really proud of you. You've been a big, brave girl, haven't you? Come here and give me one more kiss."

Dez leaned in and whispered, "Don't be scared. I prayed, and Jesus is going to help us."

Jade didn't know what she'd ever done to raise such a perfect, precious, intelligent child. She found herself making God every promise imaginable, all the ways she'd be a better mom if he would only get them both out of this situation. She knew where Gabriel's gun was, but she had to wait for the right time. After her father's murder, Jade had taken several handgun classes, vowing to never let herself meet the same kind of fate as her father had. Other women in her class wondered if they'd have the fortitude to actually take a life if necessary, but with her daughter's freedom and safety at stake, Jade had no qualms.

"I love you so much, baby," she told her daughter. "And Mama's so, so proud of you."

CHAPTER 24

"Hey, what's that for?" Dez asked when Sapphire came in from the back room carrying a long rope.

Sapphire smiled sweetly. "Well, darling, do you remember that talk we had last night? About how some people have those big, mean demons who want to make them do bad things?"

Dez widened her eyes and nodded.

Sapphire handed the rope to Gabriel and continued to talk as if she were a Sunday school teacher telling her students about Jonah and the storm. "Well, sometimes those big, mean demons have to get prayed out of people, and sometimes when that happens they make them do mean things, like try to fight off the ones who want to help them. So the rope's to make sure your mommy doesn't hurt herself when we pray the demons out of her."

Dez crossed her arms and pouted. "What makes you think Mama's got demons?"

Jade tensed. Wished she could find some way to communicate with her body. Dez was doing such a good job playing the role of the obedient, compliant child. She had to keep it up if they wanted to get out of this alive.

Sapphire's voice was patient and melodic. "Well, your mom's angry. She's got a lot of hurts about a lot of things, and we want to pray to make her all better. But sometimes this kind of praying we're going to do makes people get angry first, so we're just going to use this rope to make sure she doesn't hurt herself or anyone else."

Jade's mind was working five times as fast as normal. As long as it was a human constraining her, she had a chance of escape. If Gabriel got complacent or distracted, she could make her move. A rope didn't have those kinds of weaknesses she could exploit.

Get closer to the door, she tried to tell her daughter. Why couldn't telepathy work? *Move closer to the door, baby.*

At this point, Jade knew that hoping for her safety as well her daughter's was too much to expect. She just needed to give Dez a chance to run. Jade had no idea where they were, if they were still near Eureka or not, but it wasn't dark out yet, and if they were surrounded by woods, Dez could get away.

That was the goal.

Get closer to the door, baby.

Dez was still staring at the rope and ignoring her mom.

Sapphire took a step closer, her face hardening as she addressed Jade. "Remember now, I gave you the chance to do this the gracious way, and you turned it down." She draped the rope around Jade's shoulders like a scarf.

"What are you doing to Mama?" Dez demanded. With her eyes, Jade tried to calm her daughter's fears. Tried to communicate what she needed to do. *Get by the door, baby.*

Dez took a step backwards. One step closer to the exit. To freedom.

Good job, baby.

Jade tried to give her daughter an encouraging nod, and while a Sapphire tied knot in the rope, Jade kept her eyes on her daughter, praying she could understand.

By the door, baby. Keep going. I love you. You're going to be okay.

The knot was complete. Jade couldn't wait much longer.

Sapphire leaned down to tighten the noose. "Don't make this any harder on your daughter than it has to be," she whispered.

Now.

Jade kicked Sapphire in the groin, splaying her backwards. "Baby, run!" she shouted. She turned around as Gabriel pulled out his gun. She tackled him onto the floor, grabbing his wrist with all her strength.

He wrapped one leg around her, trying to knock her off balance. Jade held fast. She couldn't see if Dez had fled or not, but there wasn't time to check. If she lost her grip, she was dead.

Letting out an animalistic grunt, Jade held onto Gabriel's wrist, trying to slam his hand on the ground to make him lose his grip. The flickering lamplight glinted off his eyes, and she knew what she had to do. It was her only hope. She gouged one of his eyes with her free hand, turning her brain off so she didn't have to register the feel of it.

He screamed. The distraction had worked.

Jade grabbed the gun.

There wasn't time to think. If she stopped to think, she might change her mind. Might not have the courage.

She aimed. Braced herself for the deafening burst, the powerful kickback. Gritted her teeth in determination.

Jade pulled the trigger.

CHAPTER 25

There wasn't time to look back. Jade had to find her daughter.

She stumbled out the cabin door, praying to reach Dez before anybody else did. Sapphire had fled the cabin while Jade was fighting Gabriel, which meant she could be anywhere. Jade had to be ready.

And she had to protect her daughter.

She screamed Dez's name, uncertain if she was making noise or not because she couldn't hear anything, not the crunching of snow beneath her feet or the sound of her panting or frantic yells.

"Dez!"

Previously, during the fighting, her vision had blurred. Narrowed. Now, her periphery slowly returned to focus. "Dez!"

She scoured the snow for tracks. Where had her daughter gone?

Jade still had the gun. Gabriel would never come after her again, but Sapphire might. She had to hurry. Had to get to her daughter before that woman did.

"Dez!"

There inside some ATV tracks were footprints small enough to be her daughter's. Racing ahead, she stumbled through the snow heaves until she caught sight of a tiny bundle making her way down the trail. "Dez!"

Her daughter turned around, running toward her. As she came near, Dez's tear-streaked eyes danced with joy. Jade bent down to embrace her.

"I'm sorry, Mama," Dez was sobbing. "I knew I shouldn't go with that lady last night, but she said she knew my daddy, and she seemed awful nice at first. But I was really bad to go with her. Please don't be mad at me."

Jade's tears mingled with her daughter's while they hugged in the snow. "Shh. It's over now. Everything's going to be okay."

"So we're safe?" Dez asked.

Jade wiped the tears off her daughter's cheeks. The last thing Dez needed was for them to freeze to her face.

"We're going to be."

"I didn't know which way to go." Dez was still crying softly. "I didn't want to get lost, but you told me to run, and I didn't want to disobey you again, so I just went."

Jade looked down. Dez's pants were covered in snow and ice. She had to get them someplace dry.

"Do you know which way we should go?" Dez sniffed.

Jade's first instinct was to get them both as far away from that cabin as possible, but she had to be more logical than that. She had no idea what time it was, but the sunlight wouldn't last much longer. Neither of them had coats, and Dez was already shivering. Jade took off her oversized sweatshirt and wrapped her daughter up.

"What about you, Mama? What are you gonna wear?"

"Don't worry about me. It's my job to worry about you."

She took her daughter's hand and looked around, trying to gauge by the position of the mountains which direction they needed to walk.

"Are you mad at me, Mama? For going with a stranger last night?"

Jade shook her head. "Don't be silly. Of course I'm not mad. I'm so happy to find you safe and sound I could give you about a million kisses right now."

Dez grinned. "Oh, yeah? Prove it?"

Jade didn't waste her time arguing.

CHAPTER 26

"Mama, how long do you think we've been walking?"

"Shush, baby, and let me think."

"But my legs are sore, and I'm freezing."

"Stop whining, and hush for a second." Jade paused to study the mountains. She'd been certain that as long as she kept them to her back, she'd end up at the Glenn, but it was twilight now, and there was still no highway in sight.

"Listen, baby, when those bad people brought you to their cabin, how'd they get you there?"

"What do you mean?"

"I mean, did you walk or take a snow machine or a car or what?"

"It wasn't a car. It was a truck."

"Okay. And when you were driving in the truck, before you turned to get to the cabin, where were the mountains? Were they on this side of you or were they somewhere else?"

Dez pouted. "Which mountains do you mean?"

"The big ones, baby." Jade noted the irritation in her voice and tried to soften it. "The big mountains," she repeated more gently. "I want you to think. Were the mountains over here like this?"

Dez shrugged. "I don't know."

Jade let out her breath. It wasn't her daughter's fault. None of this was her daughter's fault. In fact, if Jade had been more open in talking to Dez about her biological father to begin with, none of this would have happened.

"Mama, are you mad at me?"

"What? No, baby." Jade leaned over to give her daughter a comforting hug. "Mama's just trying to figure out which way we need to get to. That's all."

Dez scrunched up her nose. "Are we lost?"

Jade mulled over her next words. "No, baby. I just need to get us to the highway. That's where we'll find some help."

"Well, how long until we get to the highway? I'm hungry."

346

"I know, baby. This is all gonna be over real soon. And then we'll stop for something to eat. I think there's a lodge in Eureka. We'll get nice big bowls of hot soup. Doesn't that sound good?"

"I want a burger," Dez announced with a pout.

"Fine. You can get a burger and a bowl of hot soup."

"Will they have ice cream?"

"Too cold for ice cream, baby."

"Yeah, but last night you said you'd get me ice cream."

Jade had forgotten all about that. "Fine. Tell you what. Once we get to that lodge, we'll ask if they have ice cream and if they do, you can have as many bowls as you can finish off."

"Promise?"

"Promise."

Dez revived a little at the prospect of food and sweets, and she walked for a while without complaining.

"Hey, Mama?" Dez finally said as the sun made its last faint glimmer on the horizon.

"What, baby?"

"Is anything that lady said true? Was my daddy really a pastor in Palmer?"

Jade could think of a thousand other topics she'd rather be discussing. "Well, baby, he called himself a pastor, but he wasn't."

"Then what was he?"

How was Jade supposed to answer that? Was she supposed to tell her child that her own father was a criminal? A serial rapist and child molester? "He's someone God loves, but he did a lot of bad things and hurt a lot of people, so I don't want you to worry about him none, you got that?"

Dez seemed to consider her words. "Did you love him?"

The question surprised her. Where did her child come up with these crazy notions? "No. I didn't love him. I trusted him, but it turned out I shouldn't have. He was dangerous."

"Kind of like Auntie Sapphire?"

"Right. Like Auntie Sapphire."

"She isn't my real auntie, right?"

"No, baby. She's nothing to you. Nothing at all."

"I didn't think so."

They kept on walking, and Jade let out a silent prayer for help. She was doing everything in her power to stay calm and composed for her daughter's sake, but she had no idea what she'd do if the sky went black while they still were out here lost in the woods.

"Hey, Mama?" Dez finally asked.

Jade sighed. "What, baby?"

"Was my daddy handsome?"

Jade tried hard not to laugh. Pastor Mitch handsome? "I suppose some people thought he was."

"Did you?"

"No. No, I didn't. But I think his daughter's the most beautiful out of all of God's creations."

Dez wasn't deterred by the flattery. "Was he black like you or white like Auntie Sapphire?"

"He was white, baby, but it doesn't matter, okay? God made you just the way he wanted you to be."

"Is that how come you didn't like him? Because he was white?"

Jade needed God's help to get her daughter of the cold woods alive, but she also needed his help to keep her patience. "There's lots of white men I like. Color of their skin has nothing to do with it. Your father did some bad things, things that you don't need to know about. But God loved him, and that's all that matters, okay?"

"Will I ever meet him, do you think?"

"I don't think so, baby," Jade answered. "I don't think so."

CHAPTER 27

"Why are we stopping, Mama?" Dez's voice was muffled by the heavy mounds of snow surrounding them on all sides. "Don't we have to keep walking to get to the highway?"

Jade had spent the past few hours doing what she could to protect her daughter from worrying, but she couldn't keep up her pretense anymore. "Baby, we've got to stop. I don't think we're going to find the highway tonight, and it's already dark."

"So what are we gonna do?"

"I think we're gonna have to snuggle up real close to stay warm and try to rest here."

"You mean outside?" Dez sounded as incredulous as if Jade had told her that her real daddy was Santa Claus.

Jade tried to keep her inflection positive. "Come on. It'll be fun. Remember last summer when you were begging me to take you camping?"

Dez pouted. "But it's not summer."

"No, but we'll think of it as an adventure, all right? And then when you're a little old woman you can tell your babies and grandbabies and great-grandbabies all about the night you slept outside with your mom in the winter, and they'll think you're making it up."

Dez continued to pout. "Well, what's the point of telling them a story like that if nobody's going to believe me?"

"I guess you'll just have to tell them it's true whether they believe you or not."

Jade squatted down with her back against a spruce tree. Its branches were wide enough that they'd kept most of the snow off the ground. She wondered if covering Dez with the spruce needles would help her stay warm.

"It's pokey down here," Dez whined.

"Shh. Let me think for a minute."

Jade situated her daughter between her legs and wrapped both arms around her. "I think you better give me that sweatshirt back," she finally said. "We'll tuck it around us both. Is that okay with you?"

Dez shrugged. "Fine."

"You're a good girl, baby. Did you know that?"

Dez didn't respond. Jade put the sweatshirt back on, thankful that it was large enough she could zip it up with her daughter snuggled against her chest.

"It's a good thing you're my little skinny britches, or else you wouldn't fit. Now you're like a baby kangaroo in its mama's pouch."

She waited for Dez to laugh, but she was silent.

"You okay, baby?"

Dez let out a melodramatic sigh. "Yeah. But next time I say I want to go camping, can we please do it in the summer?"

"Yeah, baby. We can do it in the summer."

Dez fell quiet again, and Jade wondered how she'd ever manage to fall asleep.

"Mama?"

"Yeah, baby?"

"I'm hungry."

Jade squeezed her eyes shut. So many times in her life as a single mom, she'd felt ill-prepared, unequipped to care for a child on her own. So many times she'd had to make sacrifices. Coffee in the morning or money to pay the heating bill. New winter boots for Dez or gas to drive to Anchorage where groceries were cheaper. There was that time she got behind in her rent because Dez caught strep throat so they were out of the daycare for a week. Jade had gone whole days eating nothing but a can of beans. But that whole time, no matter how bad things got, her daughter had never missed a meal.

Help me, God. I can't do this.

Jade still wasn't sure if resting here was the best idea or not. What if Dez drifted off to sleep and never woke up? But Jade was exhausted, and the longer she walked around in the woods in the dark, the more likely she was to get them even more lost. No, the best thing was to stay put. Was anyone out here looking for them? She hadn't thought about Ben all night, but he must be searching for her. She prayed God would lead him to this part of the woods. Wherever this part of the woods was.

She held her daughter close.

"Mama?"

"Yeah, baby?"

"That guy who was holding you, he was a bad guy, right?"

"Yeah, baby. He was a real bad guy."

"Is that why you had to shoot him?"

Jade tried not to show her surprise. "What makes you think I shot anybody, baby?"

"Because I heard the bang when I was outside running away. And I can feel the gun you've got in your pocket."

Jade squeezed her daughter more tightly. "You're a smart girl. Has anyone ever told you that before?"

"You had to do it, right, Mama? Because he was such a bad guy?"

Jade decided she couldn't avoid her daughter's questions anymore. "Yeah, baby. Mama had to do it."

They sat in silence, a silence that reminded Jade of everything she'd done at that cabin. Everything she'd risked to save this precious little girl, a little girl who might freeze to death overnight zipped up in this oversized sweatshirt.

"Hey, Mama?"

"What, baby?"

"Is God gonna be mad at you?"

"For what? For shooting that bad guy?"

"No. I mean about the demons."

At first Jade didn't know what her daughter was talking about, then she let out her breath. "Oh, baby, that was just a whole bunch of nonsense. That woman was crazy. I don't want you to think about a single word she said, okay?"

"Yeah, but did you really have demons making you do bad things?"

"No, silly. Of course not."

"Are demons real then?"

Jade would have loved to talk about nearly anything else, but she knew Dez was stubborn enough she would just keep on asking until she got her answer.

"Yeah, baby. There's demons. But the Bible says God's stronger than all of them, so it's not something you need to spend a lot of time worrying about."

"Do you think demons make me do any of the bad things I do?"

Jade was surprised. "What kind of bad things are you talking about?"

Dez lowered her voice and leaned into her mom. "Well, once at daycare I told one of the Cole twins she was stupid. I know it's a bad word, Mama, and I felt really sorry for it afterward and even gave her my Twinkie at snack time. I don't even know why I said it. We were just playing together is all, and I wasn't even mad, but I looked at her and said that. Think it was a demon in me making me say such a bad word?"

"No, baby. Demons can't live in people that way, not people who belong to the Lord."

"Do we belong to the Lord?"

"Of course we do. Remember when you were down in Sunday school with Mrs. Spencer and you asked Jesus to forgive all your sins and teach you how to live a good life?"

"Uh-huh."

"Well, that means you're a Christian, baby, and demons can't live in Christians. So I want you get all that nonsense out of your mind. It was just crazy talk from a crazy woman."

"Do you think Auntie Sapphire has demons, Mama? Is that why she did all those bad things to us?"

"I don't know, baby. I don't know. Now I want you to try to get a little rest okay? Give Mama a chance to think and figure out what we're gonna do next."

Dez turned and nestled against Jade's chest. Her body relaxed, and her breathing slowed down.

"Hey, Mama?" she said sleepily.

"What, baby?"

"Do you think God really talks to people in dreams like Auntie Sapphire said?"

"I'm sure he does, but I want you to stop thinking about that woman now, you got that?"

"Okay, but I was just wondering, what if we pray and ask God to give us a dream to tell us how to get out of the woods?"

"You go ahead and pray that, baby. Mama's too tired."

"But if I pray it, do you think he'll answer?"

"You go ahead and pray, and I'll listen in, okay?"

Jade shut her eyes and listened to her daughter's confident prayers. Her five-year-old trusted God to give her a dream to lead them out of the woods. But all Jade hoped was to stay warm enough that they'd both be alive when morning rolled around.

CHAPTER 28

"Mama! Mama! It worked!"

Jade forced her eyes open. Had she been asleep? "What worked, baby?"

"My prayer. When I asked Jesus to give me a dream."

Jade waited for her brain to snap to alertness. "What are you talking about?"

"Remember when I prayed that God would tell me which way we'd have to go to get out of the woods? Well, he did. I was just falling asleep, and I remembered. I remembered looking out the window when I was in the car with Auntie ... with that mean lady. When we got to the place where the road turned real bumpy, the mountains were behind us. I could see them behind us in the little mirror on the side of my door. I just thought it all of a sudden while I was starting to feel sleepy."

Jade glanced around to see if there was enough moonlight to make out the mountains from here. If Dez was right, then Jade had been walking the wrong way. The Glenn would be in the opposite direction.

"How long have we been resting here?" she asked, still slightly disoriented.

"Just a minute. I stopped praying, and then I shut my eyes and felt tired. Then all of a sudden, I pictured myself sitting in that car and looking at the mountains behind me."

Jade still wasn't sure if they should try to rest a little more. Without any coats or proper shelter, it was probably safest for them to keep moving, and Dez seemed energized from her answered prayer. Jade, on the other hand, wasn't sure she had the strength.

"I may just need to rest a little more," she muttered.

Dez squirmed in their shared sweatshirt. "But, Mama, I think if God answered my prayers like that to let us know which way we've got to go, then we should follow him and go that way, right?"

Jade sighed. "Yeah, baby. You're right. Let's go." She hated to think about how far they'd headed in the wrong direction and prayed that it wouldn't take them nearly as long to get back to the highway.

"Wait a minute." Dez tugged at Jade's sleeve. "We can't go yet."

"Why not, baby?"

"Because God answered my prayer. Don't you think we better thank him?"

"Yeah, you're right. You go ahead. You pray, and I'll listen, and then we'll start walking."

A familiar voice from the woods answered, "I'm not sure that's the best idea."

Jade jumped up, spilling Dez out of her sweatshirt. She pushed her daughter behind the trunk of the spruce. "How'd you find us?"

Sapphire shrugged. "Your tracks are all over. It only took me this long because you've walked yourselves in circles. But I knew my persistence would pay off. God honors the patient, right?" She took a step forward. "Now, about my husband's daughter."

"You're not going to lay a hand on her." Jade pulled Gabriel's gun out of her pocket.

Sapphire let out an undignified snort. "You think that will frighten me? You may have turned your back on my husband's church, but you're still a child of Morning Glory whether you acknowledge it or not. And you'd never go against me. I'm your pastor's wife, the first lady of ..."

Jade pulled the trigger. The snow muffled the worst of the echo.

From behind the tree, Dez screamed.

"Stay there, baby," Jade shouted back at her. "Stay right where you are and keep your eyes shut or you're grounded off the TV for three whole months. You understand me?"

"Yes, Mama."

Jade's body was trembling. She ran behind the tree, scooped up her daughter, and ran. She kept Dez's face covered with her hand until they were far away from Sapphire's body. When she got too tired, she set Dez down and they raced together toward the mountains.

CHAPTER 29

"Over here! We're here!" When Jade saw the search lights in the distance, she scooped up her daughter and started running. Dez had gotten lethargic, and Jade tried to pass on her enthusiasm.

"That's the search team. They're looking for us. Come on."

She followed the light, nearly choking over her joyful laughter. A few minutes later, her daughter was wrapped in a heated blanket, carried in the arms of a search and rescue paramedic. They were a little less than a mile from the highway, and Jade was positive it'd be the easiest hike of her life. Adrenaline propelled her forward. Adrenaline and the need to get her daughter to safety. She begged the man carrying Dez to run on ahead instead of waiting for her. She nearly collapsed into the arms of the other paramedic when she stepped over a major snow heave and the Glenn Highway came into view.

"The ambulance is right down there, ma'am. We'll get you checked out and warmed up."

"I'm not worried about that. I just want to make sure my little girl's all right."

A man in a trooper's uniform stepped up toward her, wearing a familiar smile. "Well, look who finally decided to pop out of the woods."

She tried to match Ben's grin even though she felt ready to die from exhaustion. He wrapped an arm around her, and they walked together to the ambulance where paramedics were already getting Dez warmed up.

"I'm glad you're all right," he said.

Jade didn't know what else to say, and so she lifted up her silent prayers of thanks to God who had delivered her and her daughter once again.

CHAPTER 30

Jade sat in the back of the ambulance next to her daughter's gurney. The paramedics had covered Dez in blankets, and everyone seemed excited that her body had finally picked up its cues to start shivering.

"She's going to be fine," one of the men assured Jade.

The road to the hospital was paved with ice and frost heaves. Jade figured it was probably a good thing that the driver wasn't rushing. He hadn't even turned on his sirens.

"Mama?"

"Yeah, baby?"

"What time is it?"

Jade looked to Ben who was sitting across from her.

"Time to get some sleep." He gave Jade a soft smile.

"Mama?"

"Yeah, baby?"

"We didn't miss Christmas, did we?"

"No, we didn't miss Christmas."

"Good. Because I'm ready to do my lines for the play at church."

"You are?"

"Uh-huh. *And the angels said, 'Glory to God in the highest, and on earth peace to men on whom his favor rests.'*"

Ben burst into applause. "Very good job. Are you sure you're only five? I know some teenagers who couldn't learn their lines that well."

Dez beamed.

"Thanks again for all the time you spent looking for us." Jade didn't know what else to say. Ben wanted to ride with them in the ambulance so he could talk with Jade about the case, but so far the entire conversation had been focused on Dez and keeping her warm and happy.

Jade couldn't believe their trouble was over, couldn't believe the extent Sapphire had gone to in order to steal her daughter.

"Mama?"

"Yeah, baby?"

"How long we gonna be at the hospital?"

357

"Not long. We just want to get you all warmed up and make sure you're all right."

Ben leaned forward. "You, too. You're getting checked out just like she is."

Jade shrugged. "I'm fine. The doctor's probably going to tell me all that exercise was good for me."

She caught Ben's eye. When she met him last night, she would have never expected to feel so thankful to have him looking out for her safety. Thankful to have him by her side.

You really do have a sense of humor, don't you, God?

Ben continued to stare at her then cleared his throat. "Well, I guess we should make the best use of the time we've got and compare notes. Let me tell you what I know first."

Jade was happy to let him take the conversational lead.

"We checked out Keith Richardson's car. Someone cut through the brake lines, not all the way but enough to get him to that icy pass and let gravity take care of the rest."

Jade was thankful he spared her any further details.

"We found a letter in his pocket where he talked about how he feared the pastor's wife was the one behind the kidnapping. Said something about her having a dream about her husband's kid ... real woo-woo stuff, just like you said. But we compared the handwriting with the note you got earlier. Seems he was trying to help you. Give you some kind of warning. I can show you if you want."

Jade shook her head. "Not now." In fact, she wasn't sure a letter like that was something she'd ever want to see. "How'd you know where to look for us in the woods?"

"Well, I got back to the car after checking things out at the crash site. Saw a blood splatter on the head rest. Pretty amateur move. We figured Sapphire had you, and we also figured she had someone to help, so we looked into it. Guess there was this Elder Gabriel, some guy who recently moved to Palmer to help run the church. Keith mentioned him in his letter. We looked into it, and it turns out he's got a little cabin near the Sheep Mountain area. We went to check it out, found Gabriel shot and a few kiddie toys in the back room. That's when we brought in the search and rescue team."

He glanced at Dez resting on the gurney. "I'd really like to hear your side of it now, but maybe we should wait."

Jade nodded. There was no need to make her daughter relive every horror and trauma she'd endured.

Dez blinked her eyes open. "You should tell him about the dreams, Mama."

Ben glanced at Jade. "What dreams?"

Dez grew animated. "All kinds of dreams. You should have heard them. Like one about how that lady was supposed to turn herself into my new mom because my dad was the pastor at this church, only Mom says it's not a *church* church, just some weird fake thing. Have you ever been to a fake church?"

Ben shook his head. "Can't say that I have."

"Me either, but if it's got people like this lady, I wouldn't want to go either. I think Mama had the right idea shooting her."

Ben raised his eyebrows, and Jade nodded. So much for trying to protect her daughter from frightening memories.

"Where was that?" Ben asked.

"I couldn't say. Somewhere in the woods. We got turned around."

Dez nodded her head enthusiastically. "Yeah. It was scary. Mom thought we were going to have to spend the night outside even though I've never been camping before because Mom refused to take me last summer when I really wanted to go, and all we had was one sweatshirt for both of us to share, and it was really dark, and Mama got us lost in the woods. It was kind of my fault because I was awake when that bad lady drove me out to the cabin place, only I couldn't tell Mama if the mountains were behind me or to the side or what, so she didn't know how to get us back to the road. And she was getting kind of tired and even a little grumpy." Dez stole a glance at Jade who sat there wondering where her daughter's sudden burst of energy came from.

"Well," Dez went on, "Mama said it was time for us to get to sleep, only I didn't want to spend the night in the cold, and I was hungry too, so I asked Mama if maybe we should pray and ask Jesus to send us a dream to tell us which way to go. Because I figured if that weird church lady had dreams and God talked to her except she didn't even go to a real church, God would definitely talk to us if we asked him nicely, so we did. And then Mama was already starting to snore a little bit, but I wasn't asleep quite yet, only I was about to fall asleep, and I remembered where I saw the mountains in the car, and I knew they were behind me when we were driving. So I told it to Mama, and she said that meant we'd been walking the wrong way, but there was enough moonlight we could see the mountains by then, and if we went toward them we'd find the highway. Which we did but not until we found you guys first."

Ben reached out and ruffled her hair. "You're a good story-teller. Did you know that?"

Dez pouted. "It's not a story. That's how it happened. Tell him, Mama."

"I know it happened," Ben said. "I meant you tell the story in a really exciting way."

"It was a compliment," Jade explained.

Dez glanced at the trooper. "Oh. Well, thank you, officer."

"You're welcome. And on top of being very smart and a good storyteller, you've got excellent manners."

"Oh, that's because Mama says that when I meet a police officer, especially if he's white like you, I've got to be extra polite and make sure ..."

"Okay now," Jade interrupted. "I think maybe you should let the grown-ups talk a bit."

"Why? Are you gonna tell him how you shot that big scary guy when that church lady was tying a rope around your neck?"

"Is she making this up?" Ben asked.

"I wish." Jade rolled her eyes. "No, it happened pretty much like she said." Jade started from the point when Sapphire tied her up and explained how they escaped the cabin and ended up in the woods, where eventually Sapphire caught up with them.

"Mama was really brave," Dez inserted. "I don't know if I would have known what to do with a gun because Mama's always telling me I can't go near them or touch them or if I see one lying around I'm never allowed to pick it up and I have to tell someone right away."

"Those are very good rules," Ben said approvingly.

Dez shrugged. "Nah. It's just good sense. Guns are tools, not weapons."

Ben chuckled, which forced Dez into an exaggerated pout. "I wasn't making a joke."

"I know you weren't. I just wish every kid in the state of Alaska were as smart as you are."

She shrugged again. "It's not smart. It's just common sense."

"That's probably because you have a very good mom." Ben glanced over at Jade again, and this time the approval in his eyes was directed at her.

CHAPTER 31

"See you later, kiddo." Ben gave one of Dez's cornrows a playful tug. "Don't you be giving that doctor a hard time, you hear me?"

"Okay, officer."

He leaned down and smiled at her. "Hey, you know what? After all we've been through together, you don't have to call me officer. You can just call me Ben."

"That's *Mister* Ben," Jade added more sternly than she needed to. She turned to him and softened her voice. "Thanks again for all you've done."

"Hey, no problem. That's what I'm here for." He dusted off the front of his perfectly pressed uniform in a gesture that was surprisingly endearing.

Jade tried to figure out what else she could tell the man who helped save her and her daughter's life. "How are you getting back to Glennallen?" It wasn't quite what she meant to say, but at least it was something.

"Pastor Reggie and his family are flying in from their vacation this afternoon. I'll hitch a ride back with them."

Jade set her hand on her daughter's gurney. "Well, I guess I better go. We've got to get this little girl warmed up."

"Don't forget to let the doctors take care of you too," Ben added, scratching at his cheek.

Jade nodded. "Okay."

"Okay."

She turned to follow the paramedics then stopped. "Oh, Ben?"

"Yeah?"

"Since you're gonna be around town for a little bit, come on by once we get settled in. I can text you what room we're in."

A smile broke across his face, and Jade realized how tired he looked.

"That'd be great."

"I think they have reclining chairs in there too. You know. If you needed a place to crash for a few hours."

"I may take you up on that."

The paramedics had already started to wheel the stretcher down a brightly lit hallway.

"You better go." Ben raised his hand to signal goodbye.

Jade tilted up her chin. A wave with her head. "See you around." She hurried to catch up with the paramedics.

It was time to focus on her daughter.

CHAPTER 32

After a thorough exam in the ER, a nurse finally led Jade and Dez to the children's wing of the hospital. Jade was fine, just like she'd told every single trooper and paramedic who wanted her to get checked out, but the doctor thought Dez could benefit from warm saline through an IV.

"We could do it here in the ER," he said, "but frankly the pediatric nurses are better equipped at handling such little veins, and I think you'd both be more comfortable."

It wasn't difficult for Jade to agree. The transfer to the children's area was time-consuming, but the nurses on the children's floor were fabulous, and they kept Dez distracted enough while putting in the IV that she hardly fussed at all.

"How long do I got to keep this in?" Dez asked.

Jade yanked Dez's free hand to keep her from scratching the site. "It'll probably just be a few hours. They want to make sure your temperature goes up, and they think you need your rest. Which you do."

"But I'm not tired."

"That's because you like being the center of attention."

Dez pouted. "No, I don't."

"Yes, you do. I saw the way you were hamming it up for Officer Ben."

"He told me to call him *Mister* Ben."

"Well, as long as you're under my roof, you're calling him Officer."

"I'm not under your roof right now."

"Stop being smart with me."

"I thought it was a good thing to be smart."

Jade reached her hand under Dez's pile of blankets to tickle her daughter's ribs. "Too smart for your own good, that's what you are."

Dez giggled, then her face grew more serious. "Mama?"

"Yeah, baby?"

"That church lady, do you think she would have killed you?"

"What makes you say that?"

Dez's whole body heaved as she let out a sigh. "I was just thinking. That's all. I guess it's good you shot them both, huh?"

"No, baby. It's not good. I just did what I had to do."

"Are you gonna get in trouble for it? Is Officer Ben gonna have to arrest you?"

"What? No. They know I did what I had to do to protect my little girl. That's not against the law."

Dez's face twisted.

"What are you thinking, baby? Tell me."

"Did you want to kill them, Mama? Were you mad at them for what they did to us, and that's why you killed them?"

Jade reached toward her daughter and held her while she started to cry. "No, baby. It wasn't like that at all."

"So it wasn't the demons that made you do it?"

"What?" Jade pulled back just long enough to look her daughter in the eyes. "No, of course not. You listen to me. Demons are real, but they don't have any power besides what God gives them. And nobody can make you do anything that goes against God's rules."

"Not even the devil?"

"Not even the devil. I know what happened to us was scary. I'm glad it's over, but it's still really bad that those two people ended up getting shot. God tells mommies and daddies to take care of their kids, just like he tells people like Officer Ben to take care of regular folks like you and me."

"Do you like Officer Ben, Mama?"

Jade shrugged but didn't meet her daughter's eyes. "Sure, I like him. He's a very nice man and good at what he does."

"Would you ever want him to be your boyfriend?"

Jade couldn't keep in her laugh. It felt good to have her daughter talking to her about something as innocent as dating and crushes. "What? Of course not. Why? Do you want him to be your boyfriend?"

Dez giggled.

"Tell you what." Jade picked up the blankets the hospital staff had given her. "Why don't you scoot over in that bed, because these nurses must think you're the size of a baby elephant giving you all this extra room."

"What are you doing, Mama?"

"I'm getting up here and cuddling my baby. That's what I'm doing."

Dez's eyes widened. "Are you allowed to do that?"

"Am I allowed? What do you mean? Are you my child? Did I give birth to you? Do I hug you and feed you and tell you I love you every single day of your life?"

"Yeah."

"Well then, I guess that makes you my baby, and I just happen to think that it's time to snuggle with my baby. Is that all right with you?"

Dez scooted over in the bed. "I suppose."

"Well, thank you very much, Your Highness." Jade gave Dez one last round of tickles and then got busy adjusting the two of them under the blankets. "We'll stay warmer like this, you know."

Dez let out a snort. "Want to hear what I think?"

"What do you think, baby?"

"I think it's just that you don't want to sleep in that chair all by yourself. I think you're too scared."

"You know what, baby?"

"No, what?"

"You're a very smart girl. Have I ever told you that?"

Jade propped herself up on her elbow long enough to watch Dez roll her eyes. "Only, like, every day."

Jade kissed her daughter on the forehead one more time, snuggled up a little closer, and soon was fast asleep.

CHAPTER 33

"Good morning, sunshine!"

Jade groaned at the chipper, perky voice that interrupted her perfectly sound nap. "What time is it?" She blinked at a young woman wearing smiley face scrubs. Nurse Happy pushed a few buttons on the few different monitors and pulled out a thermometer.

"Time for a temperature reading," she announced in a singsong voice.

Jade untangled herself from the blankets and landed back in the reclining chair. She certainly wouldn't win any points for being graceful, but she was far more concerned about the numbers on the thermometer than she was about anything else. "How's she doing?"

The nurse frowned. "96.8. Still not quite as high as we'd like." She reached over Dez and massaged the IV bag. "It's probably time to get this warmed up again. How are you feeling, sunshine?"

Dez blinked up at her. "What are you doing?"

Jade was about to remind her daughter to mind her manners, but the nurse was apparently running on multiple shots from Starbucks and was more talkative than Dez at her most energetic. "We're just checking your temperature. Want to make sure you're strong and healthy so you can go home today. Did you sleep well?"

Dez shrugged. "Mom was snoring in my ear."

"What? I was not."

"Yes, you were. You snore all the time."

"I heard that."

Jade started at the voice and looked over to see Ben standing in the doorway. It was the first time she'd seen him out of his trooper uniform. He looked casual and ... nice. Jade wondered where he got the change in clothes. "Can I come in?" he asked.

The nurse slipped past him with a cheerful, "Just holler if you need anything," and bustled out of the room.

Ben walked up to Dez's bedside and set down a shopping bag by her pillow. "How'd you sleep, kiddo?"

"What's this?" she asked. "Is it for me?"

"Dezzirae Rose Jackson," Jade snapped. "Your mama taught you better than that. Where are your manners?"

Dez looked at Jade sheepishly. "Sorry." She turned back to Ben. "What's in the bag, officer?"

He laughed. "Open it and see."

Dez reached over with her arm and pulled out some word searches and animal fact books.

"I figured a smart girl like you would want something to read while you were stuck in bed," Ben said with a smile.

Dez frowned. "I don't know how to read."

Jade crossed her arms. "Did that nurse put rude juice in your IV or something?" she demanded. "When someone gives you a gift," she said sternly, "you tell them thank you."

"Thank you," Dez muttered.

"What'd you say?" Jade pressed.

"Thank you, officer."

Jade let out her breath. "That's better."

Ben leaned toward Jade. "So, how's the patient doing?"

Jade met his gaze with a smile. "Still as stubborn and ornery as ever."

"I think you mean bright and charming, don't you?" he asked, winking at Dez.

"Right," Jade agreed with a slight rolling of her eyes. "That's what I meant."

Ben sat down in one of the stools and stretched out his legs. "Well, I'm glad to know you're both safe. Any word on how long they're keeping her here?"

"We just woke up," Jade admitted, "but from what everyone was saying, we should be released by the afternoon, I'd imagine."

"Need a ride back to Glennallen?"

"Do you have room?"

Ben nodded. "I already texted Reggie. He said they've got enough seats for us all."

"If you're sure it's no trouble."

"Not at all."

Jade licked her lips, suddenly uncertain what she should be doing with her hands.

"Would you like a coffee?" Ben asked after a torturous silence.

"That would be wonderful."

He stood back up. "Got it. Any special way you like it?"

"Strong and black," Dez answered for her, and Jade grimaced when she suspected what her daughter was going to say next. "Just like she likes her men."

"Dezzirae Rose Jackson," Jade hissed.

Dez shrugged her shoulders. "What? That's what you always say when you make yourself coffee at the daycare because the coffee maker we've got at home's broke."

"It's a joke and something that's not fit to be repeated, especially not in front of ..." She glanced at Ben, who was standing in the doorway trying not to laugh. "Never mind. But you best start remembering your manners, or I swear with this policeman as my witness I'll tan your hide."

Dez rolled her eyes. "No, you won't. You're just saying that."

"Well, I mean it this time," Jade grumbled, her face still hot with embarrassment.

Ben cleared his throat. "All right. I'll be back in a few minutes with some coffee." He met Jade's eyes and gave her a grin that only deepened her flush. "No cream. No sugar. Just the way God made it."

"I'm sorry," Jade sighed.

He laughed. "Don't worry about it. I like a girl who speaks her mind." He tousled Dez's hair again. "Watch out for your mom while I'm gone. Don't let her get into any trouble."

"I won't." Dez grinned widely.

Ben gave Jade a small wave. "See you soon."

"Take your time." She watched him leave, staring at the empty doorframe until her daughter interrupted with, "Mama?"

"What, baby?"

"Why do you got that goofy grin on your face? Is it because Ben's getting you a coffee? Does that mean the hot policeman likes you?"

Jade snapped her head around. "What'd you call him?"

"Oops, I forgot. I mean Officer Ben. You were staring at him like this." Dez tilted her head to the side, clasped her hands beneath her chin, and batted her eyelashes.

"What?" Jade tried to sound upset but couldn't hide her laughter. "I was not."

"Yes, you were. Is it because you think he's hot?"

"Five-year-old girls don't say *hot*," Jade told her. "You can say he's handsome, and I guess he is if you like that strong, athletic type."

"He's not handsome, mama. He's hot."

"Dezzirae Rose Jackson!" Jade snapped.

Her daughter shrugged. "Well, it's true."

Jade didn't respond.

"You're doing it again." Dez tilted her head and batted her eyes.

"No, I'm not."

"Yes, you are."

"Read your new book, baby. Mama's tired."

CHAPTER 34

Jade didn't realize how badly she needed a caffeine infusion until Ben mentioned coffee. She hoped he wouldn't be too long and tried to convince herself that her impatience was only because she needed help waking up, not because she was anxious to see him again.

Dez was too perceptive for her own good. The truth was Jade did find Ben attractive, and the more she'd gotten to know him, the more she found herself wanting to spend time with him. Yesterday, she would have told herself that was just the crisis talking. Her world was in shambles, her daughter missing, and Ben could help her find her daughter. But even now that she and Dez were reunited, Jade found herself wondering if she'd see more of Ben in the future. Hoping their paths would cross more often.

It was silly, really. What did she know about him? They went to the same church, and he was a Christian. He'd told her little bit about his past, and in some ways they shared common life experiences. Both had lost their fathers. But in other ways they were the exact opposite of each other and always would be.

It would never work.

She shook her head. She should just be thankful that God had protected her and her daughter and focus on making the time leading up to Christmas as joyful and happy for Dez as possible. She wasn't planning on going all out on gifts this year, but she was going to find money somewhere. Even if all of Dez's toys came from the secondhand store, Jade was going to make sure this was a Christmas she wouldn't forget.

The phone by Dez's hospital bed rang. Jade didn't know if she was supposed to pick it up or not and gave a tentative, "Hello?"

"Hey, it's me."

"Aisha? How'd you find out where we were?"

"I called Ben, and he gave me the hospital room number. Is now a good time?"

"I have a few minutes." Jade eyed the doorway, wondering when Ben would return with those coffees.

"I was so happy to hear you found Dez. Is she all right?"

371

"Oh, yeah. She's fine. Getting some hot saline in an IV, but her temperature's coming up, and they'll probably send us home today."

"That's great. Will you need a ride or anything?"

"No, we'll be riding back with Pastor Reggie's family and Ben."

There was an awkward pause. "Oh. So is he with you now?"

"He just stepped out to grab some coffee."

Another somewhat stifled, "Oh." Aisha cleared her throat. "Well, we've all been praying for you. Last night, Mrs. Spencer organized a prayer vigil at the church. It was really special. I'm just so sorry you guys went through what you did. Ben said it ended up being your old pastor's wife?"

Jade wasn't sure how much Ben and Aisha had been in touch and resented the small, unwelcome rush of jealousy. Who cared how often two adults decided to talk with one another? He was probably just filling Aisha in so she could pass along any prayer requests to the church. You couldn't blame him for that.

"Tell everyone back in Glennallen thanks for the prayers," she said.

"I will. And hey, I wanted to ask you something about Ben if it's not too awkward."

A nurse stepped into the room and started fidgeting with Dez's IV bag. "Listen, someone just came in. I've got to go. We'll talk soon though, okay?" Jade didn't know what Aisha had to say to her about the trooper and wasn't sure she wanted to. She hung up the phone and watched the nurse inject a syringe into Dez's IV port.

"What's that you're putting in there?

He cleared his throat. "Just some antibiotics to help with the infection."

Jade frowned. "Nobody said anything to me about any infection."

He kept his face turned slightly, but there was something familiar about his profile.

"That's all here. Got to check on another patient." He gave a weak wave and turned to go.

Jade wanted to stop him. Where had she seen him before? He didn't look like one of the paramedics who transported Dez here.

"Hey."

She watched as he turned around, keeping his gaze focused on the floor.

"Where's our regular nurse?"

He glanced over his shoulder. "She'll be here soon."

Something wasn't right. "I want to talk to the doctor."

He looked relieved. "Sure. I'll go get him."

"Mama?"

Jade turned toward her daughter. "Not now, baby."

"I feel funny."

Jade jumped to her feet and rushed toward the nurse. "Hey, get over here. What did you put in there?"

The stranger started sprinting down the hall. Jade hollered for help. She hated to let him get away, but she wasn't about to leave her little girl. She grabbed the IV, trying to figure out what button would turn it off or how she could stop the flow.

"Help!" she screamed again.

Dez's former nurse ran in. Jade was breathless as she tried to explain, "He put something in the tube then ran away."

The nurse bent down over Dez's hand and disconnected the port. Jade heard a commotion outside but was too busy praying for her daughter, watching as Dez's eyelids fluttered and her head rolled lifelessly to the side.

CHAPTER 35

Jade had never prayed more intensely in her life. Several workers had been called into Dez's hospital room, and Jade was forced to wait outside. Nobody knew what drug the man had injected into her daughter's IV, but it was making her heart rate drop dangerously low.

Jade turned her back to Dez's window. The curtains were drawn, and it was too painful to try to strain her eyes in hopes of making out what was going on.

Please, Lord. You didn't deliver her out of those woods just to let her die here. I'm not ready to lose her.

Jade's whole body was trembling. How much suffering was one little girl supposed to endure before God decided it was enough?

She thought back over every sin, every time she'd lost her temper or yelled at her daughter. Was God punishing her for those things? Had he decided that Jade was an unfit mother, so now he was going to take Dez away?

You know I can't live without her, she prayed. *Maybe that means she's become an idol to me, but I can't help that. If you want her with you in heaven, you may as well take me too, because that child is my only reason for living and breathing.*

She thought back over all her former plans — college, law school, advancing social justice. Remembering how upset she'd been that her pregnancy derailed each and every one of her goals, she was ashamed now to think she would ever have preferred her education or career over being the mother of this precious, precocious baby girl.

If you want to take her home, Lord, you're going to have to fight me for her.

Even as she prayed the words, Jade knew how stupid they sounded, but she couldn't help herself. If God's only plan was to take Dez away from her, he should have let Sapphire kill them both back at the cabin.

She became aware by degrees of a figure standing next to her. "Is this seat taken?" Ben held out a cup of coffee.

She shook her head.

"I heard about what happened. Do you know what's going on in there?"

She shook her head once more, not trusting her voice to hold.

"The good news is security apprehended the suspect."

She didn't respond. What did it matter, unless the man was willing to tell the doctors what he put in her daughter's IV?

"Want your coffee?" Ben asked.

No.

He sat beside her quietly, and it wasn't until Jade let out a heavy sigh she realized she'd been holding in her breath.

"Should we pray?" Ben finally asked.

Pray? Right now? Did he actually think she'd been doing anything else?

She turned to face him and croaked, "Okay."

CHAPTER 36

"We've got your daughter's heart rate back to a safe range." The doctor poked his head out of the room and held the door open. "Do you want to come in?"

Jade jumped to her feet.

"I'll wait out here," Ben said. "I've got some calls to make anyway."

Jade rushed past the doctor as he explained, "She'll be groggy for a while, but she's going to be fine."

Jade hurried to the bedside and grasped Dez's hand. "You hear me, baby? Mama's here."

Dez's eyes fluttered open. "Mama?"

"Yeah. It's me."

"Mama, I want to tell you something."

"What's that, baby?"

Dez took in a breath that sounded far too labored for a healthy child her age. Jade glanced at the nurses to see if any of them looked concerned. Who would have done this to her baby? Who would have dared?

She squeezed her daughter's hand, praising God for the warmth and life she felt. "You're hurting me," Dez complained.

Jade forced herself to loosen her hold. Dez was lucky there were still so many other people around. Even with the crowd, Jade was half tempted to crawl into bed and smother her daughter in kisses. "What did you want to tell me, baby? I'm right here. The doctors have given you really good medicine, and your heart's going to be just fine and healthy, and everything is under control. You're safe now. So you can tell me anything. What did you want to say?"

Dez opened her eyes wide enough for Jade to see her rolling them dramatically. "I wanted to say that I think you should ask Officer Ben on a date. That's all."

CHAPTER 37

"Well, here it is." Ben stepped into the room, balancing a cafeteria tray in his hands. "A can of soda for the patient, a bowl of soup for Mom, and a fresh cup of black coffee since that first one didn't really go as planned."

Jade took the tray from him. "Thanks so much. Did you get something for yourself?"

"I ate earlier."

Jade didn't want to admit that she was disappointed.

"Sorry it took me so long to get here," he said. "I've been going back and forth with hospital security and the Anchorage police, trying to fill in all the gaps so everyone knows what's going on."

"What is going on?" Jade asked. "I'd like to know myself."

Ben sat on the stool, stretching his legs out from under him. "Well, the guy you saw really is a nurse here, but he's also a member of Morning Glory International. Does the name Caleb Houghton mean anything to you?"

"Houghton?" Jade repeated. "Yeah. Their family was one of the really vocal ones when we went to the police." She didn't say any more.

Ben sighed. "We're still trying to decide if he acted on his own or not."

Jade didn't respond. All that really mattered was that Dez was feeling better. She was safe.

Ben stared at Jade eating a spoonful of soup then leaned down toward the hospital bed. "Hey, kiddo," he whispered, "mind if your mom and I step outside for just a minute?"

Dez drank a sip of Coke from her straw and grinned. "Why? Do you want to kiss her?"

"Dezzirae Rose Jackson," Jade snapped, nearly choking on her food.

Dez shrugged. "It was only a question."

Jade didn't have the courage to meet Ben's eyes. She set her bowl of soup down and followed him out into the hallway. "What's going on?"

He turned to her, his eyes full of seriousness. "I heard from the search and rescue team. They found the spot where you shot Sapphire."

Jade had been waiting for this. Even though it was clearly a case of self-defense, Jade had shot an unarmed woman. She'd also killed Gabriel

377

back in the cabin. That wasn't the kind of thing you could simply walk away from.

"How much trouble am I in?" she asked. "Do I need to find a lawyer?"

He looked confused. "What? Oh, no. That's not it."

"Then what is it?" Her stomach churned at the worried expression on his face.

"It's Sapphire. The rescue team discovered the spot where she fell. They saw the blood, but they didn't find a body. In fact, they were able to follow the blood drops for almost a quarter of a mile."

"What's that mean, exactly?"

"It means Sapphire survived. She's still alive."

CHAPTER 38

Jade wasn't going to believe it. This was some sort of social experiment, where independent film directors with far too much time on their hands set up elaborate hoaxes just to see how people would respond. Somewhere behind her were cameras, a film crew ready to catch her reaction. She wasn't going to give them the luxury of laughing at her for being the world's most gullible person.

"That's ridiculous," she argued. "I shot her myself."

"Did you actually check the body once she fell?"

"I was a little too busy to feel for a pulse if that's what you're asking."

Ben took a step back. "I'm not blaming you. I'm sure there was a lot of stress. It's something anyone could miss."

"I shot her." Jade spoke the words definitively. She could still hear the sound of the gunfire, could see the way Sapphire fell.

"I know you did. And from the looks of it, she lost a lot of blood. But then the trail vanished, and no body has turned up, so we have to assume she survived. We have to be very careful."

"She wouldn't be stupid enough to come after us a second time." How desperate could one woman get?

"I'm afraid she already might have. So far, the nurse in custody isn't talking, but I'm willing to bet she put him up to it. I don't see how else he would have known to tamper with your daughter's IV. Your story hasn't hit the news yet, and he doesn't work on this floor."

What kind of security system did this hospital have if strange men could just walk into a patient's room and inject a child with God only knows what? Jade clenched her jaw. Anything to channel her anger and her fear. Anything to get her mind off Sapphire.

"She can't be alive." Even as she said the words, Jade realized there was no other explanation. "So what do we do now?"

"We tell our guys to keep their eyes open for her. And we give you and your daughter tightened security."

"What's that mean?"

"Well, if it won't make you feel too cramped or uncomfortable, it probably means that you and I will be spending quite a bit more time together."

CHAPTER 39

"Well, we've watched *How the Grinch Stole Christmas, A Charlie Brown Christmas,* and *Mickey's Christmas Carol.*" Is there anything we're missing?" Ben asked.

"I wanna watch *Frozen*!" Dez piped up.

Jade laughed. "I don't really think that's a Christmas movie, baby."

Dez stuck out her lower lip. "But it's got snow in it."

Ben gave a playful shrug. "She's got a point there."

Dez turned to her mom with pleading eyes. "Please?"

Jade stood up. "Fine. I'll go see if they have it at the front."

"Let me go." Ben stood up. "I need to return a few calls anyway. I'll be back soon." He smiled down at her, and his hand brushed her shoulder as he walked past and out the door.

"You're doing it again."

Jade turned to her daughter. "Doing what? What are you talking about?" she asked, even though she had a feeling she already knew the answer.

"You were staring at him again."

"No, I wasn't."

"Yes, you were. And you looked just like this." Dez puckered up her lips into a kissing face. Jade couldn't keep from laughing.

"You better be careful, or he'll come in here and see you doing that."

"Come in here and see you doing what?" Ben's voice at the door made Jade jump. He flashed a grin. "Sorry. I left my phone. Did I miss anything important?"

"Just the part where Mommy said she wanted to kiss you."

Jade felt the heat rush to her face. "No, I most certainly did not say that."

"Yes, you did." Dez smacked her lips together noisily.

"That's enough." Jade could hardly force herself to meet Ben's eyes to see his response.

He kept his focus on Dez. "Well, tell your mom that kissing is something very special. You should only do it with someone you care about

381

very much." He grinned. "See you in a few minutes."

After he left, Jade leaned closer to her daughter. "What do you think you're doing, talking like that?" She didn't know if she was more angry or mortified.

Dez shrugged. "I was only trying to help."

Jade searched her daughter's face for the tell-tale signs of sassiness, but they were missing. "Well, don't do it again. You'll make me die of embarrassment."

"I didn't know adults got embarrassed."

"Well, they do. Especially when you're talking about your mother kissing someone she hardly knows."

"You know him well enough. And you do want to kiss him, don't you, Mama?"

"Just lie down and get some rest. Aren't you supposed to be sick or something?"

Dez grinned. "I still think that you should ask Ben on a date."

Jade pointed her finger in her daughter's face. "There you go again. What have I told you about talking like that?"

Dez sighed loudly. "Sorry. I mean you should ask *Officer* Ben on a date."

CHAPTER 40

Lab reports came in that afternoon. The drug in Dez's IV could have been fatal, but she'd received antidotes soon enough that nobody expected serious complications.

"I wouldn't be too surprised if she was a little drowsier than normal," the doctor explained.

"I should be so lucky." Jade grinned at her daughter.

"Hey." Dez gave a playful pout.

Right before dinnertime, the nurse came in with all the discharge paperwork and instructions. The timing couldn't have been more perfect, since Pastor Reggie and his family were due to land at the airport any minute. Thankfully the pastor's van would have enough space to fit Jade, Dez, and Ben. It would be midnight or maybe even later by the time they reached Glennallen, but at least they could spend the night at their home.

Two different police officers stopped by to hear Jade's story about shooting Gabriel at the cabin. Ben assured her it was standard procedure and that she didn't have anything to worry about. She wanted to trust him, but she still had a hard time believing the justice system would be completely fair and unbiased toward her. Hopefully, the fact that Gabriel had held Jade at gunpoint, that the gun she'd shot him with was his own, and that he was one of the men who'd abducted her daughter would free her of any murder charges. Ben knew a lawyer in Anchorage he promised to get her in touch with, even suggesting he might help her out *pro bono* if she ended up needing legal advice.

Jade was thankful for his help. Thankful that in this sea of cops in their imposing uniforms, she had someone she could count on as a friend. An ally. Ben spent nearly the entire day at the hospital, laughing when a therapy dog came in to cheer Dez up with some tricks, keeping Jade supplied with as much coffee as she could ever want.

"You sure you're not getting too bored with plain old black?" he asked, his teasing eyes twinkling.

She grinned back. "Are you saying a little cream might do me some good?"

"Never know unless you try."

It was nice to have a friend.

After all the discharge paperwork was filled out, Dez hopped into a wheelchair to head downstairs. While she kicked her light-up tennis shoes on the foot rests, Ben insisted on taking a few selfies with her. "It's not every kid who gets to ride their own chariot. I don't think even Elsa had one of these in *Frozen,* did she?"

"Elsa could have made one out of ice."

Ben smiled. "But I bet she wouldn't have looked as smart as you do, though."

Halfway down the hallway, he asked the nurse if he could be the one behind the wheelchair. "Now I can say I've pushed a real princess around."

Jade worried he was spoiling her daughter. Most days, it took all of Jade's energy to get them to the daycare on time and come home and crash on the couch for a few minutes before it was time to heat up something for dinner. She was thankful for all of Ben's attention, but she hoped Dez wouldn't be disappointed when they got back to Glennallen and life returned to normal.

At least the daycare was closed for Christmas break. Jade would try to find the energy to do some arts and crafts with Dez. Maybe bake some cookies. The downside was that no work meant such a meager paycheck at the end of the month. She still wasn't sure what she was going to do about presents. How sad was it that just a few hours after promising God to be better mom if he only brought her daughter back to her, Jade was reverting right back to her old tired, worried self, stressed out about money, easily annoyed if Dez asked too many questions or demanded too much out of her.

Ben wheeled Dez into the hospital gift shop, insisting that she pick out anything she wanted. Jade watched them, despising the familiar feeling of guilt that seemed to permeate her entire life as a mother. Guilt she wasn't doing enough, buying enough, being enough for her daughter. Ben was nice, but Jade couldn't shake the feeling that he was showing off.

See? Being a parent is easy. Look how good at it I already am, and she's not even mine.

Ben would never know what it felt like to be Dez's mom. To be so terrified for her daughter's safety you nearly threw up. To experience those heart palpitations and that cold sweat every time you thought about what might have happened. What had already happened.

Kids are resilient. It was something Jade had been telling herself for years, ever since Dez was a baby and managed to roll herself off the bed and land on the hard, wooden floor.

"Kids are resilient," the phone nurse said, calming Jade's fears, assuaging her guilt.

Maybe the nurse was right. Jade watched her daughter in the gift store checkout line, holding two new books plus a giant Elsa balloon she'd conned Ben into buying for her. There was no visible indication that her daughter had just survived a kidnapping, a night in the woods, and a poisoning attempt. Dez was smiling, playful, and as lively as always.

Kids are resilient. Maybe Dez had already bounced back from all the fear and trauma she'd endured. But what if she was carrying it beneath the surface? What if the trauma wouldn't come out for months or even years? Would Jade wake up when her daughter was a high-schooler only to learn that Dez's eating disorders and propensity to self-harm all stemmed back from the past twenty-four hours?

Someone like Ben didn't have to worry about that. All he had to do was crack jokes and hand over his credit card to the cashier behind the counter. Jade had no idea how much money Alaska state troopers made, but it was certainly more than a thirty-hour-a-week daycare employee.

"You're doing it again, Mom," were the first words out of Dez's mouth when Ben wheeled her out of the store. Jade wasn't about to argue and risk Ben's overhearing. She pried her eyes away from him and smiled at her daughter. "Ready to go home, baby?"

Dez nodded. "Yeah. But can we make a quick stop first? Officer Ben's gonna buy me a big old hamburger with lots of French fries. And ice cream, too."

CHAPTER 41

Jade had never been happier to find herself on the Glenn Highway, headed for home.

Dez knew Pastor Reggie's kids from Sunday school, and she was happy to sit in the back of the van with them. With Reggie and his wife up front, that left enough space for Jade and Ben to sit side by side on the long drive back to Glennallen.

Reggie had a cough and was losing his voice. His wife was exhausted after a week in the Lower 48 with two little kids and was asleep about ten minutes into the drive.

Jade took advantage of the relative silence to think. At some point, it would probably hit her that she'd killed a man. She should also be more concerned that Sapphire was still alive. But right now, she was fixating on Christmas, wondering how she could move things around to find money for Dez's gifts. The heating bill wouldn't be due until after the New Year, but with such a small paycheck coming in at the end of the month, she couldn't afford to waste a penny. She had no idea if the oil company would actually turn off heat to a home with a single mom and five-year-old girl, but she didn't feel like testing her luck.

"Sounds like they're having fun," Ben observed after a round of giggles erupted from the back seat.

"Yeah, they're pretty good friends."

"I'm glad you two are on your way home."

"So am I." She glanced over at him. There were so many things it felt like they should be talking about. Like the fact that Jade would have to answer for her role in Gabriel's death. That she'd seen people of color denied justice too many times, and she was scared.

That the woman who tried to abduct her daughter was still alive.

One thing among many that Jade still didn't understand was the drugs in the IV. So far, Ben didn't have any updates about what the police had learned from the nurse they caught. Had Sapphire put him up to it? Why would she kidnap Dez only to try to kill her the next day?

Sapphire was nothing like the villains Jade had learned to fear. She was capricious, led by dreams and whims and *words of God* that could come from anywhere. It made her unpredictable.

And terrifying.

Ben let out a sigh. "Long day, huh?"

Jade only had the energy left to nod.

"Why don't you try to get some sleep?" he suggested, then cracked a grin. "I promise not to tease you if you snore."

CHAPTER 42

It was after midnight when Reggie pulled up in front of Jade's house. Ben insisted on double and triple checking every room, nook, and cranny before Jade locked herself in for the night. Some of her friends in Glennallen kept their doors unlocked, but even with its relatively low crime rate compared to places like Anchorage, Jade had always been careful and protective of her home, her belongings, and most of all her daughter.

Ben wasn't working tonight, but he said another trooper he knew would park outside her house and keep watch.

Dez had fallen asleep in the back of the van, and Jade was relieved that tonight she could tuck her daughter into her own bed. She just wished she could find that kind of rest herself. Even with a squad car in her driveway, Jade jumped at every noise, convinced that Sapphire had returned to finish what she'd started. Jade wouldn't admit it, but she was thankful when Ben called to check up on her. At one point, she even thought of erecting a barricade against the front door. When she wasn't freaking out over every single stray sound, she was terrified that Dez was sick, that her core temperature had dropped, or that the medicine dumped into her IV had caused her heart to fail.

Between investigating every noise and running into Dez's room to make sure she was still alive, Jade didn't get any more than three or four hours of sleep total. Eventually she gave up on her own bed, and she crawled on the mattress beside her daughter, snuggling her tight while she stared at Dez and worried. Worried that Sapphire was going to try to kidnap her again. Maybe even kill her. Worried that the events of the past two days would scar her, change her, transform the bright, fun, sassy little girl into a timid, frightened creature.

Worried that she still didn't have Christmas presents or money to buy any.

Years earlier, Jade had memorized verses about casting her cares on the Lord, trusting him to provide for all her needs, relying on him, and no longer living as a slave to fear. But as the endless midnight wore on, as her body kept reacting in terror to every single sound, every perceived change in her daughter's breathing, nothing she remembered helped.

A picture of Ben floated through her mind, an image of him smiling and joking with her daughter. For a moment she experienced the peace and happiness she'd felt earlier when she was with him. Then the feelings vanished, and she was alone again in a dark, eerie room, with only her fears and her trauma there to comfort her.

CHAPTER 43

"Mama! Mama! Wake up!"

Jade opened her eyes. It was already light out. How long had she slept in?

"Mama! Look. Santa's here."

"It's not Christmas yet. Go to sleep, baby."

"No, Santa really is here. He just knocked on the door."

"What are you talking about?"

"Go see for yourself."

Jade glanced at the time. She threw on her slippers, tossed a dirty sweatshirt over her flannel pajamas, and peeked out the window.

Dez crossed her arms and jutted out her hip. "See? Told you it was Santa."

"That's not Santa, baby. I don't know who it is." Jade stared at the dressed-up man on her porch, wondering if she should call the troopers. The squad car that had been parked outside all night was gone. The man on the porch turned and caught her staring at him from the window. Smiling, he waved as he set down a huge black trash bag.

"Look, Mama!" Dez exclaimed. "He's brung presents."

Jade hurried to the door, wishing she'd actually gotten dressed. "Ben, what are you doing here?"

"Ho, ho, ho," he declared, stepping into their home and lowering his very fake looking white beard. "I'm bringing you your gifts."

Jade stared at the bag he dumped on the floor. "What's this?"

"Presents for you and your little girl. Ho, ho, ho."

"You can talk normally, Ben." Dez ran to the trash bag. "We all know it's really you."

"That's *Officer* Ben," Jade corrected.

He took off his bright red hat and smiled.

She glared at her daughter. "Don't go opening that bag without permission," she told Dez. "Who taught you your manners, young lady? A moose?"

Dez giggled and pulled out a wrapped gift. "Look! I bet this is one of those huge coloring books." She pulled a package out and shook it. "And these must be the colored pencils. I hope there's a pencil sharpener in here too because mine's broke."

"Dezzirea Rose Jackson," Jade huffed.

"It's okay with me if she opens them now," Ben said quietly. "These are from everyone around town. People brought them to the church yesterday. The sled and new mittens and snow boots are from the trooper's station. So are the ice skates."

Dez's eyes widened. "Ice skates?" She turned the whole bag upside down, spilling at least two dozen packages onto the floor.

"That package with the blue snowflake paper is for your mom," Ben said, "so don't open it." He glanced at Jade. "I heard that someone around here might need a new coffee maker." He pulled a plastic grocery bag out of the mix. "And I brought you creamer. I hear it's an acquired taste."

Jade didn't meet his eyes. "You really shouldn't have gone to all this trouble." Jade stared at the booty, wondering how much of it would be broken or lost by January first.

Ben scratched beneath his Santa beard then finally took it off. "The only trouble was getting into this suit. I had no idea it'd be so itchy. We rented it for the troopers Christmas party tonight. Which is actually one more reason why I wanted to stop by." He dusted a piece of white cotton fuzz off his suit's belly, lowering his gaze. "I know it's short notice, but I was wondering if you'd be my plus one."

"Tonight?"

He nodded. "We're having prime rib. And I hear the captain's wife makes a mean pumpkin pie."

Jade glanced at her daughter, who fortunately seemed more interested in unwrapping her gifts than in eavesdropping.

"I've got to take Dez to church for her Christmas rehearsal tonight. Otherwise it sounds like a great time." She licked her lips, hoping he wouldn't be too upset.

He moved his Santa hat from one hand to the other. "What if I told you that Aisha already agreed to take Dez home after rehearsal?"

"You talked to Aisha?"

He smiled. "Guilty."

She stared at the buckle of his Santa suit. "I don't know. With all she's gone through ..."

Dez glanced up. "Come on, Mama. You should go to the party with Officer Ben. You'll have a great time."

"I don't want to leave you alone, baby. Besides, this is a grown-up conversation, and I don't remember asking your opinion."

"Yeah, but he's invited you, and it would be mean to say no."

Ben grinned. "That smart girl of yours has got a point there."

He really wasn't making it easy for her to turn him down. And when he gave her one last, hopeful smile, Jade realized she didn't want to.

"Okay. What time do I need to be ready?"

CHAPTER 44

"No, Mama. It's a Christmas party, so you have to wear red."

"But I think this black dress makes me look skinnier."

Dez scrunched up her face. "Why would you want to look skinnier?"

"It's just what people do when they get to be old like ... oh, never mind. So you really think the red one's nicer?" She held up the dress on the hanger.

Dez nodded. "Uh-huh. It's more like a party. The black one would just make you look like ..." She cocked her head to the side and considered. "Like a lump of coal."

"Well, thank you very much, Miss Fashionista."

She shrugged. "It's what I'm here for."

"Well, you go scram now so I can get dressed. And you better have all those new toys off the floor by the time I come out or I'm taking them away for two whole weeks. Got that?"

"Okay." Dez jumped off the bed and scrambled down the hall. Jade shut the door and eyed both dresses one more time. She didn't want to wear the red one. She hadn't even asked Ben how fancy tonight was supposed to be. The black dress was simple and elegant. If she wore the red, everyone would think she was trying to stand out. Like Rudolph's nose or a giant pimple.

Well, maybe after all she'd gone through there was nothing wrong with standing out. At least not a little. And she did have a pair of heels that would go great with it.

Jade squeezed into the red dress, the one she'd bought herself two years ago as an incentive to lose weight. She'd never lost the pounds, but she managed to zip it up with a little help from her daughter. Jade had just finished applying her makeup when someone knocked on the door.

"I'll get it!" Dez called from the other room. Jade sprinted to intercept her. For all the danger she'd been in, Dez didn't seem to have a single scared bone in her body. Her carefree recklessness made Jade nervous.

She glanced out the window, saw Ben in his trooper uniform looking crisp and clean, and opened the door. "Hello."

He stepped in, and a blush settled on his pale cheeks. For a minute, it looked like he didn't know if he was supposed to give her a hug, kiss her cheek, or stretch out his hand for a hearty shake.

Jade took a step back, hoping to save him his dignity.

"You look nice," he finally said.

"You're supposed to tell her she looks *beautiful*," Dez announced.

Jade gave her daughter a warning look.

"You ladies ready?" Ben asked, holding the door open.

"Yup," Jade answered. "Just let me close up, and we'll be right out."

Jade checked the lock twice, glanced at herself one last time in the small mirror, and followed Ben out the door toward his car.

CHAPTER 45

It was stupid for Jade to leave home with nothing but her shawl to keep her warm. Even in the community hall, she shivered each time someone new came in, bringing icy gusts of freezing air with them.

When she agreed to attend Ben's Christmas party with him, she'd failed to consider that most of the people he worked with had been actively involved in her daughter's search. Between congratulations, well-wishes, and questions about Dez, Jade hardly got a chance to talk with Ben before dinner was served.

The meal was delicious, a no-expense-spared ordeal that Ben and the others dug into with gusto. Jade took small bites, wishing she had stayed home tonight. Even when she walked Dez into the church to drop her off at her Christmas play rehearsal, Jade tried changing plans, tempting her daughter with promises of ice cream and hot chocolate both.

Dez would hear nothing of it.

Jade didn't feel right being separated. After all both of them had gone through, they needed each other.

At least Jade needed her daughter.

"You okay?" Ben asked as couples started to get up from the table to enjoy some music. "I was going to ask if you'd like to dance, but I'm a little scared of those heels you're wearing."

Jade tried to match his smile. It wasn't his fault that tonight had been a bust. He'd certainly tried to make everything perfect, from the small bottle of somewhat generic perfume he gave her in the car to arranging for Aisha to babysit after Dez's play practice was done.

"Did you eat too much dinner?" Ben asked. "I know I did."

Jade sighed. She'd gotten herself all made up, hoping to make a good impression on Ben and his coworkers. All that to realize she couldn't pretend to be anything other than what she was. And right now, she was a worried mom who was anxious about her daughter.

And her feet were killing her.

"I'm sorry." She searched Ben's eyes. Did he understand? "Everything's been great, and dinner was really nice, but I can't stop worrying about Dez.

I really shouldn't have agreed to leave her tonight. It's too soon."

She watched his expression for signs of disappointment. He smiled gently then nodded. "That makes sense. I'm sorry."

She reached out and touched the sleeve of his shirt. It was a small gesture but felt somehow intimate. "Don't be. I'm glad you invited me. And maybe if things hadn't just happened like they did ..."

"I understand. Should we call it a night?"

"If you want to stay here, I can call Aisha. I'm sure she wouldn't mind picking me up."

"Don't be silly. We'll go pick up Dez, and then I'll take you both back to your place."

"Thank you, Ben." She held his gaze for a quiet moment.

His sad, almost tired expression softened into a smile. "Don't mention it. That's what friends are for."

CHAPTER 46

"So, where are we going?" Ben asked as they rolled out of the parking lot. Behind them, Jade could still hear the sound of the Christmas music blaring out the community hall windows.

"I don't know if Dez is still at the church or not. Let me give Aisha a text."

She opened her purse. "Uh-oh."

"What's the matter?"

"I left my phone at home."

"Well, there's the church up ahead. I don't see any lights on. Do you?"

"No, they must be finished. Do you mind swinging by Aisha's house?"

"Of course not."

"It's about two miles up the Glenn. You turn at the first stop after the clinic."

"I can do that."

Jade tried to think of something else to say. She'd already apologized for ending the night so early, but even though he'd been gracious about it, she still didn't think she'd told Ben everything.

Like how she hoped he'd give her another chance soon.

Was this going to be life from now on? Was she always going to be this nervous, unable to spend ten or twenty minutes away from her daughter without breaking into a cold sweat and heart palpitations?

How did you just pick up after something like this and make life go back to normal?

Ben turned onto Aisha's road, and Jade directed him toward her friend's driveway. He pulled in, and Jade unbuckled her seatbelt. "I'll be back in just a minute."

"I'll be here waiting."

Something in his tone caught her off guard. She turned to look, fully expecting to see something different, but there was that same kind and open expression. The gentle smile he probably gave to everyone.

"Be right back," she repeated and shut the car door behind her.

If it hadn't been for her ridiculous heels and the fear that Ben might be watching her, she would have run. Even though she'd tried to stay composed, she'd been trembling on the ride over here, and now that she was so close to her daughter, she wanted nothing but to find Dez and crush her in a strong bear hug.

She knocked on Aisha's door and stood shivering in the cold.

"Jade?"

"Yeah, I'm sorry I didn't text. I left my phone at home. We decided to call it an early night. How's Dez been?"

Jade had been so relieved at the thought of having her daughter back with her, it took a few seconds to recognize the confused expression on Aisha's face. When it sunk in, her racing pulse stopped, crashed to a halt. "What's wrong?"

Aisha shook her head. "Nothing. Did Ben drive you over?"

"Yeah. Why?"

Aisha twisted the bracelet she was wearing and kept her voice low. "I wanted to talk to you about something while you're here. I can drive you home in a little bit if that's okay with you."

Jade studied her friend. "Sure. Did Dez get into trouble?"

Aisha winced. "No, nothing like that. Could you just let Ben know I'll take you home in a bit?"

"Sure." Jade paused before turning around, trying to guess what Aisha wanted to say.

Ben rolled down his window as she approached his side of the car.

"I'm going to hang out here for a while and grab a ride home later with Aisha," she told him.

"Everything okay?"

She nodded, trying to believe it was true. "Yeah. We just haven't had a chance to talk through everything yet. She's a pretty good friend. Just wanted to have a little girl time." At least that's what Jade hoped was going on.

Ben nodded. "All right. Tell Dez good night for me."

"I will. And thanks for everything. The dinner, the party, the perfume. I ..." She stopped herself. She couldn't really say *I had a great time*. He'd know that wasn't true. "I hope we get to do something like this again soon."

Ben smiled. "Me, too."

She figured he'd say something like that just to be polite. Tonight might have been the worst date he'd ever been on, but at least he wasn't making this any harder on her. She paused in the driveway, wondering if there was anything more to say. "Well, goodnight," she finally offered.

"Goodnight."

She walked slowly back up to Aisha's front door, listening to the sound of his tires rolling back down the driveway. Jade stepped up to the porch and let herself in. The first thing she saw was her friend lying on the floor.

The next thing she saw was Sapphire holding a knife up to her daughter's throat.

CHAPTER 47

"Don't move a muscle." Sapphire was shorter than Jade, but she kept her eyes level with hers.

"What are you doing?" Jade didn't move forward but studied her daughter from head to toe to see if she'd been hurt.

"Just obeying God's word." A smile spread across Sapphire's face. "Why don't you come in. Nice place your friend has here, isn't it?"

Jade looked down at Aisha. "What'd you do to her?"

"She'll be fine. I just needed her to get that trooper to go home, and now she's served her purpose. Come on. I hate standing in doorways. Feels so rude."

Sapphire backed up slowly until she was in Aisha's living room. "Take a seat."

Jade shook her head. "I'll stand, thanks."

Sapphire paused for a moment before shrugging. "Suit yourself."

More than anything, Jade wanted to talk to her daughter. To tell Dez that everything would be okay. She tried to read her daughter's expression. What was going on?

Sapphire sat down in Aisha's white plush reclining chair, positioning Dez on her lap, careful to keep the knife just a centimeter from her throat. Jade balled her hands into fists. Her senses drowned out everything but Sapphire, her cruel and striking face, the melodic cadence of her speech.

"My husband often preached that discipleship is costly. If we want to experience the full riches of God's destiny in our lives, we must be prepared to make sacrifices. He still tests his children today, just like he did when he told Abraham to take his son up on Mount Moriah and sacrifice him as a burnt offering."

Jade kept her eyes on Sapphire but took in her surroundings, hunting for anything that might serve as a weapon. A metal bar, a vase, anything she could throw. But what could she do without risking her daughter's life?

She searched Dez's face, but her daughter's expression was unreadable.

Jade's soul recoiled when Sapphire resumed her speech.

"Last night, God told me that he was going to heal my shoulder where you shot me. He also told me that he was going to test my faith. I didn't know what he meant until I heard that your daughter was in the hospital, and I knew what I had to do. Isaac was the child of promise, but God still commanded Abraham to carry him up to that mountain, to tie him on that altar and sacrifice him there.

"I didn't want to do it." If Sapphire had been any other human being talking about anything other than Dez's attempted murder, Jade would have thought those were actual tears born from true emotion. "I told God I love this little girl as if she were my own. She's my child of promise." She held Dez closer. Jade didn't know which worried her more, the knife so close to her daughter's throat, or Dez's expressionless face. Jade wasn't even certain if her daughter knew she was there in the room with her.

Was this some kind of psychological protective mechanism? Was God allowing Dez's brain to shut down momentarily so she wouldn't experience the fear and the horror of what she was going through? Or had Sapphire already done something to her?

Jade's stomach churned to see the way Sapphire wrapped her free arm around her daughter's body. "Thankfully, like Abraham, God saw that I was faithful. He saw that I'd rather see this child of promise dead than disobey his word. I set out to do what he told me last night it was my duty to fulfill, and now he's blessed me with this sweet child to call my own."

"She'll never be yours," Jade hissed.

Sapphire waved her hand as if she were swatting away a fly. "God's already shown me our future together. Mother and daughter leading others to their glorious destinies in Christ." She leaned in and kissed Dez on the cheek.

It was too much to endure. "Dez," Jade snapped. "Dezzirae Rose Jackson."

Sapphire shook her head. "I've prayed over her. Prayed that God would protect her from the lies you'd try to use to woo her back to you. Her destiny and her future are already sealed. The only thing you have to worry about now is making this transition as easy for her as possible."

"You're insane."

Sapphire smirked. "Christ's followers have been called worse things throughout history. As for me, I count it a joy and an honor to suffer slander for the sake of my Savior and King."

Jade would do anything to make Sapphire shut up. She'd already shot her once. She'd do it again if she had the right weapon, only this time she'd be sure to check the body afterwards to make sure she did as thorough a job as possible.

"I know you're angry and confused," Sapphire went on, "but this doesn't have to hurt at all. In fact, I'd like to pray for you, to ask God to make your passing as peaceful as a baby falling to sleep at its mother's breast."

Jade knew there was only one way out of her situation. She started to laugh.

"What's so funny?" Sapphire demanded.

"You are." Jade tried to hold it in, but soon her sides ached from the chuckles that shook her whole body. "You're nothing but an old, pathetic, dried up nobody who thinks you're important because your husband called himself a pastor. You're both nobodies. In fact, you're worse than nobodies. You think you're righteous and holy and doing God's work, but I wouldn't trade spots with you on the day of judgment in a million years."

Sapphire pointed the knife blade toward Jade. "What does the Bible say about speaking badly against the leaders of your people?"

"You're not my leader. You're nothing to me. Your husband was a dirty, manipulative old man who died lonely and pathetic. The only future he deserved to see was the inside of a jail cell, and that's where you're going to rot away like the miserable piece of trash you are."

The plan was working. Pushing Dez aside, Sapphire rose from the seat, lurching toward her.

Jade was ready. She lifted her knee, ramming it into Sapphire's gut. The knife clattered to the floor. Sapphire reached down, but Jade got to it first. While Sapphire pummeled her from above, Jade grabbed the handle with one hand and Sapphire's long hair with the other. Wincing in disgust, Jade stabbed once. Twice. A third time until she was certain Sapphire had given up her attack.

Then she ran to her daughter.

CHAPTER 48

"Baby? Baby? Can you hear me? It's Mama."

Jade knelt beside her daughter, her fingers shaking while she tried to dial 911 on Aisha's cell phone. She waved her hand and snapped her fingers in front of her daughter's face while she waited for the call to go through.

"Baby, look at me. It's over now. We're going to be okay."

Ben was the first to arrive on the scene. The ambulance crew was only a minute behind.

"Is she dead?" Jade asked as Ben leaned over Sapphire's body.

"No."

A clash of emotions raced through Jade's body. Relief. Disappointment. Confusion.

Ben walked over to Dez. "Can you hear me, sweetheart? Are you hurt at all?"

"She's been like that since I got here," Jade explained, holding her daughter tight.

"Probably the shock. But we should take her to the clinic to make sure."

"What about Aisha?"

"Hit to the head," he explained. "She'll have a nasty headache, maybe a concussion, but the paramedics don't think it's anything to get too worried about."

Jade took her daughter's hand. "Baby, you want to come with me to talk to the nurse at the clinic? Make sure you're doing okay?" There was nothing in the world Jade wouldn't give up in order to hear some kind of sassy reply. Tears leaked down Jade's cheeks. "I don't know what's wrong with her."

"She's all right," Ben answered. "Probably just scared." He reached out his hand and rested it on Dez's shoulder. "You know what, princess? All the bad guys who wanted to hurt you are gone now. You don't have anything to be afraid of anymore."

Jade waited for some sign of life to light up her daughter's expression.

Nothing.

She squeezed her eyes shut. She couldn't stand to see her daughter like this.

"Hey, Dez?" Ben asked. "Want to go for a ride to the clinic with me? Want to take a trip with your good pal Ben?"

Dez blinked, and a small, quivering smile spread across her lips. "I think you mean *Officer* Ben, don't you?"

CHAPTER 49

Christmas Eve

Ben knelt down and adjusted the halo of Dez's angel costume. "That was the best Bible verse reading I've ever heard, young lady."

She beamed at him. "I memorized it myself."

"Yeah, well, I bet your mom helped a lot, too."

She shook her head. "Nope. Only a little." She slipped her hand into Ben's. "Come on. Didn't you hear Pastor Reggie say there's cake downstairs?"

Ben hesitated for just a moment, glancing at Jade. "You coming?"

Jade adjusted her earrings and nodded at him. He slipped his hand behind her back then leaned in. "Mmm. What's that beautiful smell?"

"That's Mama's perfume you gave her," Dez announced. "She wears it all the time because she says it reminds her of you and how you kissed her that night the crazy lady got arrested."

Ben raised his eyebrows. "I thought you were asleep in the backseat when that happened."

Dez shook her head proudly. "Nope. I'm just a really good actor."

He chuckled. "Yes, you are. Your performance tonight was bar none."

Dez pouted. "What's that mean?"

"It means you were fabulous, baby," Jade answered. "Now leave Mr. Ben alone."

"Don't you mean *Officer* Ben?"

They made their way downstairs, and Dez rushed toward the dessert table.

Ben turned and faced Jade, taking both her hands in his. "So she's doing well?"

Jade nodded. "Yeah. She's talking with a social worker at the clinic about what happened, and we'll drive in to see a play therapist in Palmer next week. From everything I can tell, she's doing fine. I'm the one who still feels like a wreck around here."

He leaned in and rested his forehead against hers. "I think you're doing a wonderful job."

Jade squeezed his hands. "So, you're still coming over for Christmas dinner at Aisha's tomorrow, right?"

"Yeah, what time should I be there?"

"Around three, but don't expect to eat until five or later."

"How's Aisha after getting knocked out, by the way? I haven't talked to her since that night in the clinic."

"She's fine. They ended up sending her to Valdez for an MRI just to be safe, but the swelling was already way down, and she's back to her normal self."

"That's good."

Upstairs, a Christmas carol soundtrack played loudly enough to be heard over the laughter and conversations in the fellowship hall. Jade looked around at her friends from Glennallen Bible Church, men and women had braved the cold to search for her daughter, families who had donated some of their own presents to make sure Dez had plenty of new toys, far more than she would ever need.

It was a hodgepodge collection of young and old and far from a perfect assembly. Pastor Reggie was still suffering from laryngitis and could barely croak out tonight's closing prayer. His small son had fallen asleep backstage, leaving the bottom half of the donkey to complete his role without a head. While folks mingled around the dessert table, a mother scolded her teenage daughter, and a husband who was known to only come to church when his wife dragged him in on holidays was sulking in the corner.

If you were to poll everyone here, each one would probably have a handful of suggestions on how to make Glennallen Bible a better church. Some were vocal in their complaints about the music, the children's ministry, or the way the pastor's kids fidgeted in their seats. But tonight, there was no other group of people Jade wanted to spend the holidays with.

Tonight, she truly felt at home.

CPSIA information can be obtained
at www.ICGtesting.com
Printed in the USA
BVHW082350141221
624011BV00003B/47

9 781393 349 7